The Road Into Chaos

Book Three: Chaos Reigns Saga

Carol Hightshoe

WolfSinger Publications ❧ Security, Colorado

Chapter One

Kyrianna watched as the others left. She didn't remember much from the time she had been pulled through the portal until she awakened in this room. There had been the demoness who questioned her about Myrith and Andrinor. She claimed to be working against Thynitic but still threatened to turn Kyrianna over to the Lady of Chaos if Kyrianna didn't answer her questions. Despite not wanting to, she found herself answering those questions. Then Myrith and the others arrived and the demoness told her Thynitic was having an amulet made for her and the goddess already had everything she required to bind Kyrianna to it once it was completed.

Her mind retreated into itself at those words. She could still feel the pain Brular suffered constantly from being tortured. She did not want to imagine herself as a plaything for the Lady of Chaos for all eternity—without even the hope of death releasing her. Brular had said when he died, his soul would again be trapped by the amulet. Now, even if she escaped Thynitic's influence, she knew when she died, her soul would not go to Frayrith but would instead end up trapped by Thynitic. She didn't know what Thynitic needed to bind her soul to the amulet, but the image of the goddess standing before her as she cut her cheek and caught the blood that flowed from the wound came to her and she knew the demoness had spoken truthfully.

As she had lain there, unable even to whimper, Tristan Duvall's face had flashed in her mind forcing the image of Thynitic away. The same fear that he was in danger grabbed at her heart just as it had at Tyril's cabin. After that, everything had faded into a swirling gray fog. She had felt someone helping her up, but had been unable to focus on anything through the fog. Then had come a sensation of something powerful studying her. Something that tried to block the chaos and give her a thread of order to grasp onto, then it was gone. Gone too had been the fear she had felt for Tristan.

She had emerged from the fog and chaos to find herself being held by Myrith and Andrinor in this small room. The older woman held a vial and urged her to drink. As the warm liquid flowed down her throat, she felt something blocking the memories of what had happened. The sharp edges of the pain were dulled and she found she could ignore them to focus on what had to be done—find a way to rescue Brular from Thynitic.

She considered the Cleric of Hellavar a friend and he had given her something she could never repay—she was not going to let Thynitic have him without a fight. Myrith had said they would talk tomorrow about going after Brular, but she needed to talk to her now. Kyrianna had no doubt Myrith would be willing to attempt the rescue, but she needed to know about the demoness' interest in both her and Andrinor.

Kyrianna waited until the noise in the hallway died down then got out of the bed. Shadow Seeker whined softly as she approached the door to the room.

"Don't worry Shadow, I'm not running off." She opened the door to see Andrinor looking at her.

"Myrith told you to rest."

Kyrianna shook her head at the frown on the young man's face; a frown not reflected in his pale blue eyes.

"I'm sure she told all of us to rest. What are you doing here?"

"Guarding you—per her instructions."

Kyrianna sighed. *Still trying to protect me. I thank you for it, Myrith, but there are some things even you cannot protect others from.*

She placed a hand on Andrinor's arm. "Do me a favor and tell Myrith I need to talk to her. Now, without the others. I will remain here and Shadow can alert you if anything happens."

The wolf moved past them to sit in front of the door.

Andrinor nodded. "We'll be back shortly."

Kyrianna left the door cracked open as she sat on the edge of the small bed. Perhaps now, before she lost the chance, she should also tell Myrith about her past as well as the demoness and the amulet.

She looked up as Myrith entered the room. "What's worng?" the older woman asked. Her concern was evident in her disheveled clothes and her sword in her hand.

Kyrianna caught Andrinor's gaze from where he stood next to the door. The young man just shrugged then turned to leave.

"Please stay," she said.

"You need to know the demoness seemed extremely interested

in both of you. I don't know why, but she kept asking me questions about you. Andrinor, she was interested in where your power came from. Myrith, she seemed more interested in where you came from and who your father might have been."

"While we did not know she had questioned you about us, she did not hide her interest when we arrived. She made a comment that indicated she had a son by my father. We will deal with her if we have to." Myrith paused and looked at Kyrianna. "Was there anything else?"

"The demoness told me Thynitic is having one of those vile amulets made for me." The words came out in a rush and Kyrianna sat there not saying anything as she waited for Myrith to react.

"Then that is one more thing we will take care of when we face her. I have no intention of letting her have you again," Myrith said. "Her power was weakened by the events of the last day. If we hurry, we may yet be able to rescue Brular and destroy both amulets." She turned toward the door then stopped and turned back. "Drink the potion, Kyri. Allow it to help you sleep. We'll talk again in the morning." With that she turned and left the room, followed by Andrinor.

Kyrianna glanced at the vial of pale blue liquid sitting on the table as Shadow Seeker came back into the room and jumped on the bed next to her and pushed his head under her hand. She closed her eyes for a moment as she scratched the wolf's ears, letting her mind still enough to hear the murmuring in his mind telling her to rest; he was there to protect her.

"Thank you," she whispered. Kyrianna turned to blow out the candle on the small table next to the bed. The flames puffed brightly and smoke filled her eyes. She coughed, then found herself staring at a familiar clearing. It was the place she had seen in her link with Brular. The clearing where he found Torliana as she prepared to perform the dance to welcome the coming of spring. The place where she asked him to stay with her and he failed to see what she was truly offering. An offer that, if it had been accepted, could have changed many things.

She picked up the vial and threw it against the wall. She had had enough of magic being worked on her. Shadow Seeker whined and stuck his nose in her face. "Ugh, dog breath," she said as she pushed him away.

The wolf barked playfully then pounced at her, his tail waving. Kyrianna reached out and grabbed him around the neck and hugged him tightly. The wolf relaxed and she rested her head against him and started to drift off to sleep.

Kyrianna froze as she heard a voice; no it was two voices woven together as one, whispering in the silence. *No*, she thought. *No.*

:*Peace, Kyrianna*, the voices said.

"Frayrith?" She whispered the name into the darkness; her breath held as she waited.

:*Yes, Daughter of Arielle.* There was a pause. :*You have won back your soul. You witnessed what could have unleashed Chaos and have turned it back toward the Balance. You have done well—see the change you have brought about.*

An image formed in her mind of Thynitic's throne room. Brular lay on the ground with Torliana sitting beside him their hands clasped together.

:*Order and Chaos joined. Balance can yet be restored. Rest, Kyrianna, you have braved the darkness; tomorrow wake in the light.*

~ * ~

When Kyrianna woke the next morning, she found herself more rested than she had felt in many months. Yes, there was a fog in her mind blocking the pain and dulling the edges of the memories she knew she still had to face, but at least she would have the chance to do so without the sharp ache and guilt buried behind the fog. This had to be an effect of some magic cast on her, but she was willing to accept it.

"Where are we?"

:*The Coliseum, Jerietlan called it*, Shadow Seeker's voice said. :*A temple to Mykaylene.*

"Then I shouldn't need these." She placed her swords on the bed. "However, I do need something better to wear. She rummaged through her pack until she found a clean tunic and riding skirt. It was the closest to appropriate attire she had, other than the one gown she had brought, but that just didn't feel right. She started looking around for her boots, when she heard something moving outside the door. She glanced at Shadow Seeker, who put his head back down on the pillow on the bed.

She shook her head when she opened the door to see Myrith standing there. "You can't guard me every hour of every day," she said, smiling.

"I can most certainly try." Myrith didn't return the smile.

Kyrianna sighed. "I'm up and will call if there are any problems."

Myrith nodded and started to walk away, then stopped. "Did you have a vision in smoke or fire last night?"

Kyrianna took a deep breath then nodded. "Yes, I saw the glade where Torliana invited Brular to watch her dance. Something tells me I should visit that place."

"Hmph." Myrith shook her head. "I was given a vision of this very temple. I guess you go without me."

"Don't worry. I'll be fine. I will have both Cewyr and Shadow Seeker to protect me."

Myrith nodded once then turned and headed down the hall, barely avoiding Hendandra as she stepped out of her room.

"Come on, Myrith. Do I have to watch out, even when we are in the safety of a temple?"

Kyrianna laughed as the older woman didn't break her stride. "Every minute of every day," Myrith said.

Hendandra shook her head as Myrith entered her own room. "She needs to lighten up."

"She feels responsible for us and we will be traveling into even greater danger this time," Kyrianna said.

"Stop reminding me. I don't want to go, but he did help us and I can't let you go alone and get skewered by some trap."

Kyrianna placed a hand on Hendandra's shoulder. "Scared?"

Hendandra stared down the hall and nodded her head. "Myrith told me she would prefer that I stay behind." She turned and looked up at Kyrianna. "I think she is afraid for me. I think that demoness Drezmona said something to her. Kyri, what could she have said that Myrith, who really doesn't like me anyway, is concerned for me?"

Kyrianna knelt down in front of her friend and placed a hand on her cheek to still the fear she saw in her eyes. "Don't worry, Hendandra; we will all be there to face the dangers—together. She is just being—Myrith."

"Come on, Kyri, let's see if we can find something to eat. A temple this large must have a dining hall."

Kyrianna smiled. "Let me get my boots on. I'm sure Shadow Seeker can locate the kitchens if not the dining hall for us."

Chapter Two
Jerietlan

Jerietlan paused and looked around at the others as the door to Kyrianna's room closed. He understood what she would be going through. He too had come close to losing his faith when he had stepped through the portal to limbo on the word of a demon who served Thynitic.

He glanced down at the bracelet he wore. The one that showed all who saw it how close he had come to falling. The band was seamless, with no way to remove it without damaging it. Still, he had earned it, because of his lack of faith and he would wear it until Mykaylene decided it should be removed.

He glanced back at the closed door and frowned. He thought Kyrianna's goddess would forgive her, but wasn't sure she would forgive herself. The passion in Kyrianna's soul was strong, despite her denials, and he knew her guilt over what had happened would eat at her for a long time.

"We all need to get some rest," Myrith said. "Tomorrow, we prepare to rescue Brular from the Lady of Chaos herself."

Jerietlan nodded then followed one of the novices down the hallway to one of the small rooms normally assigned to visiting clerics.

He carefully folded his robes and laid them across the chest at the end of the bed as he looked around the almost bare room. He shook his head and sighed as he placed his left hand on the bracelet and knelt in the center of the room. Here, in the Coliseum, there was no shrine to Mykaylene in this room. *No matter,* he thought as he focused his mind. *The most important shrine is the one in the heart.*

When he finished his prayers, Jerietlan rose and stretched. He was both looking forward to and dreading their attempt to rescue Brular from Thynitic's citadel. It would be exceptionally dangerous, but the potential good that could be achieved outweighed the risk. Besides, he doubted there was anyone short of Frayrith herself who could stop Kyrianna from going after the Cleric of Hellavar, and he wasn't even sure Frayrith would be able to stop her.

He picked up the candle and stared at the dancing flame. *Brular called Torliana a Flame Dancer and his Kindling,* he thought. *She renounced Thynitic at the end, but will that be enough to save her as well?*

He blew across the candle and the flame went out, creating a billowing cloud of smoke. He looked closer at the smoke and saw something in the twisting shadows. A large forge and a hammer; the hammer he had seen before. It was the Hammer of Forging carried by Ferdinand Vernas. He remembered the cleric from their first encounter at the Duvall Estate and later when the man had rescued him and the others from the plane of limbo. A large man, whose appearance would be considered disheveled at best. He had almost lost control of himself to one of the souls who inhabited the hammer. Jerietlan had no doubt that if Zanif had not arrived when he did, Ferdinand would have forced Kyrianna to call on Thynitic before she was ready or killed her in the attempt.

There is much assistance to be acquired in a short time, Hellavar said to us. I guess I have a visit to make before we can leave for the Abyss.

"Mykaylene guide me always," he whispered in the darkness as he stretched out on the bed. The first one he had lain on in a long time.

:Jerietlan. The goddess' voice spoke in his mind as he drifted off to sleep. *:You have held to the proper course, though you are erratic and do not always consider the full consequences of your actions. Despite this, I have forgiven you and restored your clerical powers. However, you will continue to wear the bracelet as a reminder of your previous faithlessness until such time as I chose to remove it. I also charge you with mentoring Myrith. She has the heart but not the training or education that those called to serve should receive.*

The goddess' voice faded as sleep claimed him.

~ * ~

Jerietlan paused as he entered the dining hall. It had been over four months since the last time he had had a meal here. He hadn't even been given time to finish it before Sir Balthas had called him aside and informed him he was to join a group seeking to cleanse the Duvall Estate of the evil that had destroyed Rhinehart Duvall and his family thirty years ago. He had also instructed Jerietlan to have Sarasnar return to be confirmed as the Shield for the temple.

The conversation had bothered him then and remembering it now was even more unsettling. He had questioned why he, a recently ordained priest, was being sent to replace one of the senior priests in a place where a powerful evil had been growing for thirty years after destroying a respected paladin, one honored by the goddess herself, and his family. Balthas felt Jerietlan's powers were sufficient to aid the group the way they deserved.

At the time, he had thought Sir Balthas was complimenting him, however, he had heard the brief exchange Kyrianna and Myrith had had at the estate regarding Sarasnar. He hadn't wanted to believe their suspicions then, but the reception Sarasnar had given them when they arrived had not been what he was expecting. He understood the Shield not wanting to admit the half-dragon—they were an omen of evil that only appeared before times of great crisis. But his reluctance to help Kyrianna—that didn't fit with what Jerietlan thought he understood of Mykaylene.

"Good morning to you, Jerietlan," Sarasnar called as he entered the dining hall.

Jerietlan looked up at the Shield then bowed his head slightly. "Good morning to you this day as well, Shield Sarasnar," he said.

The Shield sat across from him, his eyes on the bracelet Jerietlan was wearing. "What happened?" Sarasnar finally asked.

Jerietlan took a deep breath as he told the Shield how the group had finally defeated Mikyl Duvall on the estate and then agreed to act as escorts for Tristan back to Raspa.

"And why did you agree to this course? The task you were set was completed; you should have returned here immediately," Sarasnar said. "Instead you let yourself be drawn in with this group and look what it cost you." He flicked a finger against the bracelet.

"Mykaylene has forgiven me for the actions that earned me this," Jerietlan said, jerking his head up to stare at the Shield.

Sarasnar nodded. "Indeed she has. What else happened to you during the time you have been away?"

Jerietlan paused for a moment, then slowly told the Shield what had happened in the place created by Torliana. He was surprised when Sarasnar didn't comment on the reasons why he had been given the bracelet, but didn't elaborate any further.

"A most dangerous task you have been asked to go on," Sarasnar said when he finished. "While I do not know this Thynitic you have named, it will not be an easy matter to walk into the citadel of a deity, particularly one who makes her primary home in the Abyss. I am not certain this is something you should be a part of."

"They are my friends; Brular is a Cleric of Hellavar. It was

Hellavar himself who also asked us to make the journey."

"Your friends? I hear nothing of friendship in your tale, only chaos and suspicion. By your own account, this Thynitic is primarily interested in the girl, Kyrianna. A person who is not from our world and one who willingly called on the power of this dark goddess. I find it interesting Myrith did not tell me of this when she was asking us to help Kyrianna." Sarasnar started to stand.

Jerietlan reached out and placed a hand on the Shield's arm. "Shield Sarasnar, Kyrianna fought an internal battle against Thynitic for many days before she was taken by Torliana. She was helpless as she watched us fight the demons Thynitic sent against us. Kyrianna did not give in to the goddess' seductions out of a desire to serve her, but to save us. She used that power to banish the demons, then to open a portal back to Shokar. She begged us to leave before Thynitic forced her to hurt us. It was Myrith who helped Kyrianna force the goddess out of her mind. Though her path may be chaotic at times, Kyrianna does not willingly serve the darkness or walk the darker paths of chaos."

"Very well. I see you are determined to help them in rescuing the Cleric of Hellavar. Perhaps there is some good that can come of this task. Because of something that happened years ago, King Dracenhalts acts as if he owes some debt to the Temple of Hellavar and gives them a greater voice in the council than we who serve Mykaylene. Returning this cleric, I suspect, will cause a disruption in the current leadership of the Fire Lord's Temple. A disruption that should lead to more equality among the temples who sit on the council. Yes, you should aid them." He pulled his arm away from Jerietlan and sat back down. "What aid do you require from the Coliseum?"

"Last night I had a vision; one which I believe is guiding me to seek out the cleric Ferdinand Vernas."

"Ferdinand Vernas? He is not one to be disturbed except at the direction of Mykaylene herself. He has been given guardianship of an ancient relic, one that has almost driven him insane. I suggest you reconsider this course."

"I cannot. Lord Hellavar told us there was much aid to be gained, though time was short and as my vision came in smoke and fire, I believe he is telling me to seek out Ferdinand's assistance."

The Shield stared at him for a moment then nodded slowly. "Very well. Know this, Jerietlan, the place where Ferdinand lives is guarded by powerful magics and is not an area to enter uninvited. I will provide you with the means to reach the entrance, but from that point, you will be on your own." He stood and shook his head. "I believe you are undertaking a fool's errand, but we will provide what aid we can." He turned and left.

Jerietlan finished his breakfast then returned to the small room he had been given to prepare his equipment.

~ * ~

Jerietlan looked up as the door to his room opened slightly and one of the novices stood there. "Shield Sarasnar sent me to give you these," the boy said, holding out several glass rods.

He took the rods and nodded.

"He said those are for your companions, so they may return here after their own individual quests are completed. This one," he held out a blue-tinted rod, "this one is so you can reach Ferdinand."

"Inform the Shield you have delivered the rods and give him my thanks," Jerietlan said.

The novice bowed slightly then turned and left. Jerietlan placed the blue rod and one of the others into a pocket of his pack then picked up his equipment and headed for the training hall where Myrith had left a message they were to meet.

The woman was already in the hall and she nodded when he entered.

"Mykaylene's blessings on you this day," Jerietlan said.

"And you. Have you seen any of the others?"

"No, but I'm sure they will be here soon. Sarasnar sent these." He held out the glass rods. "Their magic will allow the user to be transported back here." He paused for a moment. "I take it several of the others had visions which will lead them somewhere before we leave for the Abyss."

"Yes."

"If I may ask."

Myrith looked at him and shook her head. "I will wait for the others; I don't want to have to explain it several times. Besides, I do not know what all of them saw and some may not care to share their information at this time."

"Very well. However, the last thing we need at this time is people keeping information to themselves—again."

"I agree, but I cannot force them to tell us where they are going."

"As long as someone knows where Kyri is going, we should be okay," Andrinor said as he walked into the hall.

"I would be happier if she and Hendandra were staying here," Myrith said. "However, they have both been given visions as well."

"You can't personally protect each of us all the time," Andrinor said.

"I will take whatever steps I can to ensure they stay safe," she said. Jerietlan frowned as Myrith turned away from him and Andrinor. "Even if it isn't enough, I can try," he heard her mutter.

He shook his head as Andrinor started to place a hand on Myrith's shoulder. The young man nodded and took a step back.

"Okay I be here; now what be this meeting about?" Nirev entered the room and dropped his pack on the floor as he looked up at Myrith.

"We need to discuss a few matters and make plans," Myrith said. "We wait for the others."

Falden entered the hall and nodded a greeting to each of them as he moved to stand against the far wall.

~ * ~

"Damn it, where are those two?" Myrith said. "They should have been here long before now."

"Did you tell Kyri about the meeting?" Jerietlan asked. "I saw her and Hendandra entering the dining hall as I was leaving."

"No, I didn't tell her, but I did tell Hendandra—so one of them knows they're supposed to be here."

"Hey, I'm here, so don't blame me," Hendandra said from the bench near the sparring ring.

"And where is Kyri?"

"Here." Kyrianna came into the room followed by Shadow Seeker.

"Nice of you to finally join us," Myrith said.

"My apologies. I was stopped by a messenger then got lost."

Jerietlan followed Kyrianna's gaze to where Hendandra sat giggling then turned his attention back to Myrith.

"So each of us were visited by Hellavar?" Myrith paused for a few moments and Jerietlan noticed the nods each of them gave.

"Then it appears he has given us paths we are each meant to

take; unfortunately it appears these paths will lead us in different directions. I have spoken to Shield Sarasnar and he has provided the means for your return to this temple when you finish the tasks you have been set."

"Why here?" Andrinor said. "I can think of better places. Ones that don't insult or turn away our friends."

Myrith nodded and Jerietlan knew she was unhappy about what had happened, but she wasn't going to argue the point.

"I am to remain here," Myrith said. "Because of this, the magic of this temple will be a benefit to you in your travels." She held out the crystal rods Jerietlan had given her. "These have been enchanted for your return to the temple."

"I neither want nor require such assistance," Falden said. "Keep it."

"I already have one." Jerietlan held up his hand.

"Very well." Myrith looked around at the others. "You four do not have a choice in the matter. You do not possess the power to transport yourselves back."

Jerietlan dropped his head to hide a smile as Nirev spat on the floor.

"It is best we all know where each of us is going. As I said, I will be remaining here." Myrith held out the rods.

"I travel to the Dragonspire Mountains." Andrinor took one of the rods.

"I be traveling to Domar." Nirev stared at the rod for several heartbeats before he took it. The dwarf held the glass by only two fingers, letting it dangle from his hand.

"I will be seeking Ferdinand," Jerietlan said.

"Be careful," Falden said. "That one has been driven insane by the artifact he guards. I question the wisdom in seeking him out."

"Have you found a way to contact him?" Myrith asked.

"I have been given the means to reach him. However, the place where he dwells is guarded as if it were a dragon's hoard and he is almost as dangerous as a dragon himself. I am beginning to question the wisdom in seeking him out as well." He looked at Falden and grinned.

"Go. Hellavar directed you there; there must be a reason." Jerietlan nodded.

"I will be seeking an audience with the Council of Mages in Gormanghast," Falden said. "I hope they will lend their power to this task." He held up a hand and waved away the rod.

Jerietlan glanced toward Kyrianna, who had stood up and reached for one of the rods. Myrith seemed to hesitate for a moment then allowed the girl to take one of them. "I will be traveling to Mount Veri," Kyrianna said.

"I am going to Justula," Hendandra said.

"Very well."

"I wasn't finished," Hendandra said, standing up and grabbing the rod. "I go to Raspa first."

"Why?"

Hendandra's voice dropped almost to a whisper. "I want to go home. I want to spend at least one night away from this." She gestured to the bloodstains on her clothes.

Jerietlan moved closer to the small woman as Myrith took a deep breath.

Her face was red as she glared at the thief. "We have no time for this."

"I. Don't. Care." Hendandra put her hands on her hips and glared up at the older woman. "One night is all I ask. I will find my own way to Justula."

Myrith threw her arms in the air, turned and walked away several paces before turning back around. "If you are not here at the appointed time, I *will* leave you behind."

Hendandra drew herself up straighter then nodded once.

"Falden, can you get everyone where they need to go?" Myrith asked.

He looked around then closed his eyes for several minutes. "There are several good transfer sites that have been noted and accepted by the Wayfinders Guild which I can use. I can take Nirev to Domar and Hendandra to Raspa first as they are the most assessable. I will then return for the others. Kyrianna, Jerietlan and Andrinor go to places without such points. More care will be needed to get them to their destinations."

"Actually, I can get there without Falden's assistance," Kyrianna said. "Part of the message I received this morning. However, I do want the rod to return to the temple."

"As I mentioned, I already have the means to reach Ferdinand," Jerietlan said. "I do not doubt your abilities, my friend, but I am not sure your power would be sufficient to get us to him—at least not with us alive."

Myrith glanced at Andrinor. "Have you been given anything to help you reach your location that we are unaware of at this time?"

"No. I would appreciate Falden's assistance," he said.

"Four days. That is all I give you to return to this place. I know each of you stood before Hellavar and pledged to go after Brular. However, I hold none of you to this task. The danger will be great as we will be going to the very heart of the Abyss to challenge a goddess in her own citadel."

Jerietlan saw a shudder go through Kyrianna, but she only nodded as she wrapped her hand around the hilt of her sword.

~ * ~

Jerietlan took a breath before he entered the cave the blue rod had brought him to. It was too late at this point to refuse and he would not turn coward and go back without attempting to talk to the cleric. Numerous glyphs lined the entrance to the cave and he paused at the threshold. "Ferdinand, it is Jerietlan, the cleric you rescued from limbo some weeks past. May I enter?"

There was a long pause, then Ferdinand's voice came from the cave.

"Wait there, Jerietlan. Zanif will be there shortly to guide you to me."

Despite the nearness to High Summer, Jerietlan found himself shivering as he waited.

"Jerietlan?"

He looked up to see Zanif standing in the entrance to the cave and nodded.

"Follow me." The mage turned and entered the cave, not waiting for him to follow.

Jerietlan hurried to catch up to Zanif. He walked carefully, taking care to place his feet in the same place the mage had placed his. The magical auras interwoven on the path made it impossible to discern where it was safe to step and where it was not. By the time they had passed through the outer room and a narrow tunnel into a large open area, Jerietlan was soaked with sweat. He took a deep breath as most of the magical auras faded and he could now read the lines of protective magic woven into the area.

Jerietlan paused for a moment as the magic in the room increased and he had to dismiss the spell allowing him to see the glowing auras in order to clear his eyes. This room was filled with armor and weapons of every type imaginable.

In one corner of the cavern stood a forge, long cold and covered in a thick layer of dust. *Cleric of the Battle Maiden and Wielder of the Hammer of Forging*, Jerietlan thought as he looked around.

"This way," Zanif said, motioning to a small alcove.

Jerietlan's breath caught in his throat when he saw Ferdinand lying on a pallet. The man he remembered from the Duvall Estate, the man who had rescued him and the others from limbo, had been a large, boisterous man. One no one would doubt he could wield any of the weapons in the room behind him. Now, all that was left was only a remnant of the man he had once been. He did not look fragile, but there was a frailness that seemed to surround him. An etherealness to the body, as if the spirit of the man was being pulled away.

He turned to Zanif and frowned at the anger mixed with sorrow he saw in the mage's eyes.

"Jerietlan, we have much to talk about," Ferdinand said, his voice only a harsh whisper. "But I do not have the strength today. Tomorrow."

"When you are ready, I will be here."

Jerietlan bowed his head as he stepped out of the alcove, Zanif following him.

"He doesn't appear to be the same man who destroyed that dragonlike creature on the Duvall Estate," he whispered.

"He is not." Zanif led Jerietlan to another room, one filled with books and maps, and motioned for him to take a seat.

Zanif opened a cabinet and removed a platter of cheeses, breads and meats as well as a decanter of wine. He waited as Jerietlan selected a couple of items then poured two glasses of a shimmering gold-colored wine.

"Is this Starfall?" Jerietlan held the glass Zanif handed him carefully.

"It is." Zanif raised the glass slightly.

Jerietlan returned the gesture then took a slow sip of the wine. Starfall was an elven wine, one that was rare even within the elven communities. It was almost never seen outside the Forest of Johran, and for it to be in the hands of humans was unheard of.

"I was not happy to hear you would be coming here, Jerietlan," Zanif said after a few minutes. "His strength is waning—not from physical work, but the constant battle he fights to hold his sanity.

The last thing he needs at this time is to be distracted from that. That little trip into limbo to rescue you and your friends cost him dearly. The power you faced at the Duvall Estate as well as in that other place was birthed from Chaos. Being exposed to that much chaos awakened more of the power of the Hammer than any one person could be expected to hold back. The demon-spawn Bisbul and the elf Arcantanog had both been quiet for nearly a decade. Now, both are awake and striving to take control—both of the Hammer and of Ferdinand's mind. It is a battle he will eventually lose."

"Perhaps, I can give him some respite from this battle." Jerietlan started to stand.

"Do you not think if that were possible, I would have taken him to the Coliseum myself, despite the order banishing him from Irrmar? Zanif shook his head. "No, the Hammer's hold is far greater than the magic channeled by mortals."

"Then we will seek even greater magic." He paused as Zanif again shook his head. "Surely Mykaylene will help her servant."

"That servant is paying the price of having lost his faith once before," Zanif said.

Jerietlan felt himself drop back into the chair. The bracelet he wore on his wrist was burning, but he refused to reach for it. "Explain," he finally said.

"Decades ago the Malavar Dominion threatened to attack Dh'Mark. Ferdinand led his temple's clergy and soldiers against them. In a moment of betrayal, the noble Houses of Rotstahl and Wailing left the field and the army at the mercy of their enemies. The battle was lost and those of his temple were decimated.

"Ferdinand lost his faith in others. He lost confidence that what he protected was worth protecting. After that he sought only one thing: to win the war Mykaylene had chosen to have him lose. To do this, he sought the Hammer of Forging, an artifact created by Mykaylene and Tharlin to forge the weapons to protect the ancient land of Ryssia. They believed the skill of the users should be preserved and so the hammer holds the souls of all those who have wielded it." He paused and closed his eyes. "But, even gods make mistakes," he whispered.

Jerietlan waited as Zanif took a long swallow of the wine before continuing. "Neither the Battle Maiden nor the Artificer considered what would happen if the Hammer fell into the hands of those who served only darkness and chaos."

"And it did," Jerietlan said.

"Yes, it did. The Hammer eventually found its way to the lower planes where the demon-spawn Bisbul discovered it. With it he created the great weapons and armor of the chaos demons. As horrible as his creations were, they came from the mind of a demon-spawned man. He lacked vision; something that elf Arcantanog had." Zanif shuddered then poured himself another glass of the wine and downed it in one gulp. "Pity those who must face his handiwork—those golems still walk today. It is said they seek the Hammer to bring Arcantanog back. There have been others, but they were weak compared to the power of those two."

"Did he know all this when he decided to seek the Hammer?"

"I do not believe so. However, if he did, it is not beyond reason that he would have chosen to ignore it—believing he was strong enough to control the weapon and the souls within it. In his search for the Hammer, he ventured to Styr." Zanif paused.

"Styr?" Jerietlan leaned back in his chair as he stared at the mage. "Styr no longer exists. It was destroyed by the mage wars. There is nothing there."

"Actually, it is there and not there at the same time. The war left the city in a state of planar flux. It is accessible only a few times a year. Ferdinand tells me the demons summoned by both the Faithless and the mages still battled among the buildings when he was there."

"Faithless?" Jerietlan set his glass down and leaned forward. "I have not heard that term before. The war was fought between two mage factions. Was it not?"

"I do not have time to undo all the historians have done—and with reason. I will tell you of the Hammer; the rest must wait."

"Very well."

"The city of Styr was the Gorman Empire's last stand against the invaders. All of their magic and power was gathered there. In order to help them fight, they located the Hammer and had a great sword forged. The sword was Stormrender and it was given to the warrior Strumgurd Iron Fist of Domar. The stories say Strumgurd and his companions ventured to lands north of Dh'Mark and destroyed a fortress of the Faithless. It was this act which ended the war, but not before Styr was besieged and eventually driven into the planes.

"Ferdinand found the Hammer under the protection of one of the Faithless.

The way he tells the tale," Zanif glanced in the direction of Ferdinand's alcove, "they fought for hours. In the end, he was the only one standing. He claimed the Hammer and left before he became trapped within the city.

"With the Hammer's power, he forged himself a great suit of armor and took the battle, alone, to the Dominion Army. He fought not in Mykaylene's name, but in his own. He left his place as leader of his army to rage among his enemies. They fell by the score and he continued on without rest. What he did not know at that time, was that those within the Hammer fed on the carnage and gave him strength. There were even those who channeled some of their vile magic through the Hammer into him to kill even more."

Zanif lowered his head and shook it. "He was not Mykaylene's crusading servant; instead he had become a rampager. A ravager whose slaughter rivaled that which Gladius reaped on the Jafia Plains. He killed hundreds, thousands. However, he did it not to protect others, but so he would have his victory. It was a victory without meaning."

"And this exile is the price of that victory?"

"Yes, it is. He became an exile from his own people who feared they would be next. His brother, who was King of Irrmar at the time, could not allow him within the city. Even his nephew, who sits on the throne now, will not let me take him there."

"I'm sorry." It sounded weak as he said it, but it was all Jerietlan could think to say.

Zanif nodded. "He is dying. Maybe not today or tomorrow, but he will not see the next winter, I am sure of that. When that happens, his soul will be lost to the Hammer. He will never find peace while it exists."

Jerietlan closed his eyes. Another soul lost. It wasn't right. Brular had lost himself to his need for vengeance, Ferdinand to glory. They had almost lost Kyrianna to the Lady of Chaos because of… He wasn't actually sure in that case. There was no self-serving desire he was aware of—only her desire to protect her friends. Kyrianna had been brought back because they refused to abandon her. Brular had been called back from the darkness he had been walking in to renounce his need for vengeance. He had even forgiven Torliana for her crimes against his church. They would rescue him and he would walk Hellavar's path once more. Ferdinand however, would be trapped. Trapped in the Hammer not able to seek Mykaylene's forgiveness even after his death.

His eyes snapped open and he smiled. "How can the Hammer be destroyed?"

Zanif shook his head. "It is an impossible task as the only way to destroy the Hammer is in the volcanic heart of the plane of fire. Despite the books of planar lore I have researched, I can find nothing about that location."

Jerietlan nodded. "That will not be a problem. My friends and I know a man who might be able to get us there."

"Where is this man?" Zanif leaned forward in his chair; his gaze searching Jerietlan's face.

"On the sixty-third level of the Abyss." Jerietlan stood and moved to look out at the weapons and armor scattered in the other room. "We will be going to retrieve him." He turned back to face Zanif. "I am in need of proper equipment."

Zanif stood and moved to stand next to him, his hand on Jerietlan's shoulder. "He has told me that he wishes for the weapons and armor to be given to the church upon his last days."

"Then let us see if this poor servant of his patron can find what he needs to take up the battle for not one friend, but two."

~ * ~

Zanif had left him in the arms room and Jerietlan stared at the enormity of the task he had set himself. Everywhere the gleam of a weapon or of a set of armor met his eyes. When he had cast his spell to separate the magical from the mundane, he had been stunned by the intensity of the aura in the room. Nowhere did it seem was there anything that did not have some sort of magic woven into it.

"Where to start?" he asked the empty room. Nothing answered him, which was a relief, though he doubted he would have been surprised if something had. He glanced down at the leather armor he had left the Coliseum in. It was what was given to all the novices when they graduated to ordained priests. It was simple and while it had served him so far, he knew Ferdinand would have something better. Something which would be of better use where he would be going next.

His first priority then would be the armor and he began sorting the various pieces into groups by weight and metal type. Working to make sure matching pieces were placed together, he had over forty complete sets of armor arranged along one wall when he was done. He took a moment to gulp down some water and used the sleeve of his robe to wipe his face.

Looking at the armor, he immediately discounted the lighter chain. While he had seen speed was an asset to Andrinor and therefore the lighter armor he wore an advantage, it would not be so for Jerietlan. Still, he did not want to be weighed down in such a way he would be unable to move quickly when he needed to. He concentrated on the middle groupings and was rewarded by several auras that were stronger than those around them.

A single breastplate caught his eye and he picked it up to examine it closer. While the magical aura was not as strong as several others, it was similar to the enchantment that had been on Brular's shield. The same shield he had given in payment for calling the avatar of Mykaylene. He had given up the shield so he could ask the Battle Maiden to forgive Jerietlan and to also bless Myrith. "This is a good omen, I think," he said, setting the breastplate aside for a moment to remove his leathers.

He again picked up the breastplate, surprised at the lightness of the material, loosened the straps a bit and put it on. The metal shifted as the item resized itself so it properly covered his upper body. With a little work, he was able to reach the straps and buckles on the sides and tighten them. He picked up a spear and walked through a couple of patterns with it, bending and moving as if he faced an unseen attacker. "Strong, sturdy and mobile. A good choice I think. Now a shield."

He set the spear aside, removed the breastplate and sat for a moment to rest as he scanned the remaining items in the room, trying to decide the best place to start sorting the shields from the weapons. They were jumbled together and he realized it would take several hours more to just find and sort the shields. It was getting late, but this task was not even close to half done and he did not want to risk Myrith's anger by being late in getting back. He thought for a moment, cleared his mind and cast a spell to remove the fatigue he was feeling, then moved to the task of retrieving the shields.

Jerietlan found the task becoming more difficult and not easier as he pulled each shield from the pile, exposing more and more of the weapons jumbled together. A spiked chain dangling from one of the shields slammed into his knee and he fell into the pile of weapons. He was rewarded for his clumsiness with several small cuts on his legs and arms. He quickly surveyed the injuries as he stood and frowned as the blood continued to flow from one of the smallest nicks. "A sword of wounding," he said. He chanted the words of a minor healing spell then shook his head as he looked around at the clutter. "What if it had been even greater magic or worse?" He glanced up at what he assumed was a trophy wall with several weapons displayed. One of the swords had a ragged edge to it—much like the sword the demon had used to take Brular's head. *What if that had not been on the wall?* he thought. *What if I had fallen against it? And, if that is on the wall, there is no limit to what lies within this jumble.*

He knew the sun had risen and been up for several hours now, as Zanif had greeted him on his way to a tutoring session with the children of Lord and Lady Dragonhorn of Windemere. The mage had been adamant he should not awaken or disturb Ferdinand. Saying if the cleric was able to converse with him, Ferdinand would find him. While he worried about possible delays, Jerietlan was glad he had his search through the equipment to keep him occupied. He would wait until Ferdinand was ready to speak to him or until he was no longer able to wait.

Jerietlan finally found the last of the shields and arranged them by size and type, separating out the spiked shields first. Spiked shields were designed to be used as an additional weapon—something he found to be very awkward. Still, he served the Battle Maiden and would not intentionally stay out of a direct fight and could use the protection a shield would offer. He looked over the various pieces reading the magic on them and was surprised by an aura stronger than any of the others.

The shield sat by itself; the single tower shield in the room. He had been going to dismiss it as well; tower shields were too big and clumsy to even consider. Jerietlan knew fighters who used them received specific training to do so effectively. The tower shield was also notoriously heavy and could cause a person's swing to be unbalanced. Still the enchantment on this shield was so strong, it was worth the time to investigate it.

He lifted the shield and found it easy to maneuver. He raised it so its full weight rested on his arm, but it felt no heavier than any of the other shields he had picked up in his sorting, if anything, it felt lighter. The shield also moved as if it were an extension of his arm as he shifted it in front of his body. "Enchanted to allow anyone to use it properly," he said. "Ferdinand, your home is absolutely amazing."

"Is it?"

Jerietlan spun around, the tower shield moving with him without problem. "My apologies if my sorting through the equipment disturbed you," he said with a slight bow.

"It did not," Ferdinand said. "You like the Shield of the Great Keep?" He gestured to the tower shield.

"That is an interesting name for a shield."

"Hold it in the air and speak the words: I seek safe rest, my Lady, so I can carry my battle further in your name."

Jerietlan shifted the shield off his arm and raised it slightly as he repeated the words. The shield glowed then floated before him and elongated to form not one but two large doors that stood ten feet tall. He stepped back—his gaze bouncing between the doors and Ferdinand who was grinning broadly.

"Open them," Ferdinand said as he moved to stand next to Jerietlan.

The doors swung open at his touch, and Jerietlan felt his eyes open even wider at a sight he doubted he would ever get used to seeing.

"It is yours," Ferdinand said. "Use it to give secure rest to you and your friends as you travel. Shall I show you around?"

Jerietlan could only nod as he stepped into a place he knew shouldn't be able to exist.

"Each of the stalls has a watering and feeding trough that fill with the proper food for the particular mount," Ferdinand said as they stepped into a stable. "The tack chests will produce the appropriate grooming tools for the mount in the stall. The stalls themselves are also enchanted so that they are cleaned and fresh bedding is spread each day." He gestured to the double doors at the end. As they passed the tack rooms, he opened one of the doors. There were several different sets of tack in the room.

"If a set is removed, another is created each day to replace it. Anything that is removed will only last as long as the mount lives and is wearing it."

"So this room will provide for ten mounts, including additional tack as required," Jerietlan said.

"Correct." Ferdinand opened the doors to a grand room on whose walls hung numerous different weapons. There were stands with sets of armor set all around the room.

"This room provides additional arms and armor that may be needed. Like the stable, it renews itself if something is removed. Anything taken from here that is dropped in the outside world must be retrieved quickly or it vanishes." Ferdinand waved his hand indicating the size of the room. "The room is open so it can be used for sparring and training purposes.

"This way." Ferdinand turned to the right to an archway in the corner. He motioned down a small hallway. Ferdinand opened the first door on their right. "Here is possibly the most important area of the keep," he said as he led Jerietlan into a smithy. "That box there is enchanted to repair any item that is broken if at least eighty percent of the pieces are recovered and placed inside. The sharpening stone is enchanted to improve the quality of any weapon so it can be magically enhanced. The small barrel of oil will do the same for armor as the stone does for weapons. The smithy is fully serviceable so a skilled individual can make armor and weapons. Raw ore is provided daily."

"Impressive." It was all Jerietlan could say as he looked around the room.

Ferdinand grinned as he gestured to the hallway then moved to the next door. "Chronicler's office. There are empty books for notes and records, but they are required to remain in the keep. The box there can generate scrolls and ink. If the raw materials are removed before they are used, they disappear." He shut the door and moved to the next door.

"The alchemy lab." He opened the door to a room filled with shelves and stocked with numerous glass containers. "Clean water is provided in the barrel. The box in this room can produce several different types of raw materials to be used here. As in the chronicler's office—if they are removed before being used, they vanish."

Ferdinand stepped across the hall. "Shower, water closet and laundry," he said, opening the door. The entry hallway opened into an area with five barrels suspended from the roof. "Water is warm. There are an additional five stalls for private showers. This area can be used for mounts or to quickly remove acids or other substances. The wash basin here holds cold water."

Jerietlan laughed as he looked around the room. "Hendandra

will be pleased with this set-up, she has a tendency to be the one who gets covered by the most blood and gore. Usually from some-one else."

"I find spider to be most distasteful myself," Ferdinand said. "This way to the main living quarters." He led the way back into the hallway and to the next door.

"The beds are cleaned and remade daily. Unfortunately, they seem to be somewhat hard."

"I imagine they're better than the ground," Jerietlan said as he looked at the room. There were a total of ten beds, each with a wooden chest at the foot.

"True. The chests have keyed locks. If a key is misplaced it is returned to the chest each day." He walked through the room and left through a second door.

Jerietlan stopped and stared at the food and drink that ap-peared on the table in the room. There were several loafs of baked bread, fruits, cooked vegetables as well as meats and fish. He picked up one of the pitchers and sniffed—mead.

"There is also wine, ale and water," Ferdinand said.

Jerietlan nodded. On a separate table were several cakes, pies and other sweets.

"The food renews itself daily and is triggered by the opening of this door. If you stay within the hall for more than one night, I advise eating the cooked foods first and saving the bread and fruit for breakfast."

"We will have to find a way to hold Andrinor and Nirev back from eating everything before morning," Jerietlan said.

"Not my problem. Come, there is still more." He left through an archway back into the hallway. "Coming in from the hallway will not trigger the food. So if you wish to use the table for meetings, I would suggest you enter from this direction." He continued up the hallway.

The last set of doors led into a partitioned room. "This room is separated so multiple shrines to different gods can be conse-crated. Be careful which gods you place next to each other as some of them are easily offended."

"This keep will be able to sustain my friends very well for a long journey," Jerietlan said as they left the shrine and returned to the large hall.

"There is one last thing." Ferdinand approached an area of the north wall that did not have weapons or armor placed on it. He touched the center of the area and an archway appeared. "This room stores things. Anything you place here will stay with the hall. Anything in the other rooms that is not a work in progress will appear at your feet as you close the door on the outside. The only other exceptions are items stored in the chests and anything that has been consecrated as part of a shrine."

"This place is beyond my expectations and even my dreams. Thank you," Jerietlan said as they left the storage room.

"It is a sanctuary, is it not?" Ferdinand asked as they exited the keep. Jerietlan placed a hand on the older cleric's shoulder. "That it is."

~ * ~

With Ferdinand returning to his alcove to rest, Jerietlan found himself returning to his task of sorting the weapons. He paused only to share a silent meal with Zanif when he returned and then again when the mage appeared in the morning on his way to Windemere.

"So you are still trying to catalog this mess," Zanif said as he looked around at the amount of organization that had already been accomplished.

"Not so much catalog as organize it just enough to get a general idea of what is here. I have already chosen a breastplate and Ferdinand told me to take the tower shield. I am looking for a weapon, but am concerned about exceeding his generosity."

"You go the Abyss. Yes, the Shield of the Great Keep will be invaluable to you there. Do not worry you might exceed his generosity. I have never seen one who did, when he was willing to give them what they required."

"Thank you. I will remember my promise and I will do everything I can to destroy the Hammer before it is able to claim him."

Zanif only nodded as he stood and left the room.

Jerietlan returned to sorting the weapons. He had originally thought to find weapons to bring back for the others, but realized that was something he probably would not need to do. What he needed to do was prepare himself for this journey. He had found armor to replace the leathers he had been wearing; the tower shield to replace the one Mykaylene had left to replace the one she had taken from Brular. There had been no enchantments on it that anyone could detect and when Brular had gone to face Torliana, Myrith had allowed Jerietlan to have the shield. He almost felt guilty about leaving it considering it had been given to them by Mykaylene, but he knew the tower shield would serve all of them much better.

The long spear was Mykaylene's favored weapon and the one he had trained with. Normally, it was adequate in two hands, but worthless in one. Still, he had found two such weapons with the others. The first felt overly heavy as he picked it up, so he set it aside. The second he lifted easily and it balanced well in just one hand. He lifted the tower shield and found the spear handled just as easily with only one hand as his previous one had with two. He would have to practice working the shield and spear together as the large shield was still apt to get in the way, but he knew that would improve. He practiced a lunge and the spear shot out from his hand. He dropped both the spear and the shield. "What?"

"Got a surprise, did you?" Ferdinand said from the archway of his alcove.

"This spear?" Jerietlan tried to steady the weapon as he picked it up in a hand still shaking.

"I forgot I had that here. I originally made it as a gift for my brother, but he died before I was able to give it to him. It is a fine weapon and as you have seen, it has an enchantment that allows it to reach further than a normal spear and can be handled easily in one hand. It is yours."

Jerietlan bowed his head. "I am in your debt."

Ferdinand only grunted then turned to the wall of shields. "I have not seen this before," he said as he lifted the shield Jerietlan had brought with him.

"Yes, I brought that. I would leave it, my spear and leathers for you in trade; though I know they come nowhere close to the value of what you have allowed me to have."

"Hah, the spear and the shield, yes. I don't do cow. Remove it. Take it to Irrmar."

"Very well." Jerietlan paused as he looked at the shield still being held in Ferdinand's hands. There was a magical aura surrounding it. "Odd, the shield is radiating magic when you hold it. It has never done that before."

"Hmm. Catch." Ferdinand tossed the shield to him and he dropped the spear to catch it. The shield continued to glow to his eyes as he held it. He placed it on the ground and the aura faded. He picked it up and it returned. "Odder still, it only radiates when one of us holds it. As I said, it never did that before when Brular held it. However, it was provided by Mykaylene herself." He raised an eyebrow as he looked at Ferdinand.

"Maybe you should ask her," Ferdinand said.

"Perhaps I should."

Jerietlan left the cave and found a spot where he could meditate and call on the goddess. He cleaned the shield and laid it across his lap as he prayed.

His mind cleared as he called out to Mykaylene and touched the shield. It was only a heartbeat before he heard her voice in his head. *:The shield was a prize for the finding. It activates only in the hands of my servants. It will allow them to channel their faith into the shield to further enhance their defense. Let my champions use it well.*

:We will endeavor to do so, he thought.

After the goddess' presence faded, he glanced up at the sun. It was well past noon and he had been here at least two, maybe three days. It was time to return to Irrmar.

"Well?" Ferdinand said after he returned to the cave.

"She says it was a prize for us to find."

"Then it is yours. I will not claim what she meant for you to have." He picked up the set of leather armor and tossed it at Jerietlan. "Get this out of here before it stinks up the place," he said.

He smiled as he gathered up the armor then removed the glass rod from his pack. He glanced again at Ferdinand and saw his brows knit together in a look of puzzlement. "What?"

"You carry a rod in your belt and I can sense power about it. How did you intend to hold the spear, a rod and a shield? Use your teeth perhaps?"

"I hadn't considered it," Jerietlan said, as he felt his cheeks grow warm.

Ferdinand stepped forward, took the spear and placed a band around it. He also did the same to the rod. He held out two rings then placed them on the middle and third fingers of Jerietlan's weapon hand.

"Make a fist and think of the first ring."

Jerietlan did that. There was a flash and the spear appeared in his hand.

"Drop the spear and do the same, but this time the second ring."

This time the rod appeared. "I need not worry about being armed or where the rod is," Jerietlan said.

"Yes and no. If the item you are summoning is tightly held by another, the magic fails."

"Even so, thank you." He placed the rod in his belt and summoned the spear back to his hand. Although it was difficult, he managed to snap the glass rod against the spear, breaking it.

Chapter Three
Falden

This was only the second time in his life Falden had walked these halls. Gormanghast was a magnificent city and the Academy was the grandest place in it. He had seen the great work of the architects of Raspa. Even with all their skill with stone, it did not compare to the spires of Gormanghast. For it was not stone and mortar that held the structures of this city together, it was the power of arcane magic.

Magic was everywhere in the city of mages. Most of the populace were at least novices and many were adepts in power. The city thrived on its use and the prestige those powers granted to it. None of the other city-states were held in the awe Gormanghast was. Even greater still was its long-standing pact with Tormasus—City of the Myrmidons. The cities of sword and spell, when united in common cause, made the others tremble.

It was said all of Shokar was ruled from the Circle's chambers prior to the mage war. Now, the city only controlled the peninsula. That same war had seen Gormanghast fall from the height of its power and the creation of the Jafia Wastes. Once a beautifully lush and alive savannah, the Jafia Plains were now a gray wasteland of few plants and animals. Those that could be found there were poisonous and twisted into abominations of what they once were.

What had happened in that war? No one spoke of the battles. No one sang the praises of the mighty warriors. It was as if the world had forgotten that time. Why?

"I seek an audience with the Circle of Mages," Falden told the administrator sitting at the small desk in the main office.

"Unless you are here by the sanction of one of the city-states, you will have to file a request and wait for it to be reviewed. Do you have a letter of introduction?"

Falden thought about the letter Brular had written him and shook his head.

He did not want every minor official in the city to know his business.

"The forms are over there," the administrator said, gesturing to a small table with his quill. He then turned his attention back to his ledger in dismissal.

"This is madness," Falden said. "I cannot wait for your bureaucracy to finally grind its wheels forward. I leave for the Abyss in only four days."

The clerk glanced back up. "I cannot help your questionable intent. Only a fool would dare to go there."

"Is there any way outside of these blasted rules to be granted an audience?"

"One of the Circle can call a special session, but that is outside of the norm."

"One of the Circle." Falden turned toward the twelve busts of the current members of the Circle. "Hmmm."

He walked around the busts, his right hand rubbing his beard. He studied their features then smiled.

"How old are these sculptures?" he asked.

"Only a few months," the clerk said. "New ones are commissioned yearly."

"Very good." Twelve members of the Circle, odds were with him that at least one of them had known Brular. He continued to study the faces. Four of them he dismissed immediately as they were human and nowhere close to the end of their years. Another, an old elf, he discounted as being much too old. He searched his mind and decided the other elven member was also improper, as their rulers would have only appointed one with centuries of experience here. The dwarf as well wore more wrinkles than he would expect from a younger individual. That left three older humans and two half elves. "What are the ages of Thadidius, Galania and Lortain?"

The administrator looked at him closely, shaking his head. "Thadidius is some seventy years; Galania is sixty-five and Lortain has seen his seventy-eighth year."

Falden rubbed his beard again. "Lortain may be an option. What of Bellatran and Parvania?"

"Bellatran is one hundred ten years and the Lady Parvania is one hundred fifty. Why the interest?"

"A friend studied here a long time ago. Is it not true that all members of the Circle have studied in these halls?"

"It is. Was your friend from one of the longer lived races?"

"No. However, he is old indeed. When did Bellatran study in

the Academy?"

"I would have to check, but that would have been some eighty years ago."

"Please confirm the year and I will draft a letter to the archmage concerning the issue at hand." Falden smiled as the administrator nodded and left the room.

~ * ~

Falden waited in the small room he had rented at a nearby inn. He had wanted to visit the grand library, but had been refused. He could have tried using his letter from Brular to gain entry, but something told him he would still be refused. Kyrianna had told them arcane magic was distrusted on her world and magic users almost nonexistent. In some ways, to be in a place like that would be better than the prejudice he faced here.

Here magic was divided into two groups: wizards who gained their powers through years of study and learning and those like him, sorcerers, whose magic was more limited, but who were able to call on the power of the arcane around them. It was from some innate force they manipulated their magic. Here in this great city of arcane power, he was looked at as a second-class citizen, even those who did not wield magic were accorded greater respect than sorcerers.

He still held bitter memories of when he had come here years ago to apply for entrance into the Academy. He had heard of Brular, even then. A cleric who had gained admittance and had learned much of arcane spellcraft and ways to wield the arcane and the divine together. He had hoped with that precedent, there might be a way for him to gain entrance as well. But that hope had faded when he had first stepped inside the doors and the clerk had determined his power lay in sorcery, not wizardry.

He had not even been allowed to fill out an application to be tested as anyone was supposed to be able to do. Denied the right to visit the library, he had left dejected, but determined that one day he would return and see things were changed. He had found an elf who also claimed to be a sorcerer and traveled with him for a number of years, before he finally decided he needed to travel on his own for a time. It had been only a few months after that when he had met up with Bukon and Etewyn and they had told him about the relics Ballan's priestesses had stolen from a temple to Rhyra. From there he had joined up with Myrith and the others. Now he was back trying to gain an audience with the Circle. Though he was not in a position to change anything at this time, he felt there was a chance that day would come.

He was confident in his power and had seen powerful magics of late. Torliana had a great deal of power. The clerics he traveled with also wielded power. Thynitic's power had invoked awe—but she was a goddess; therefore she should have access to that kind of power. Falden shuddered as he pushed that memory away. *I have agreed to go after Brular, and we will face that one again.* He smiled. *Let her come.* He trusted his and the cleric's powers to get them to the gates. He trusted the steel of Myrith, Andrinor and Kyrianna to cut through the opposition. He laughed to himself and realized he trusted Hendandra to steal her treasures, without ever telling him or the others.

A knock at his door interrupted his thoughts and Falden waved his hand opening the door. He sat up on the bed as the administrator walked into his room.

"I take it by your arrival Bellatran wishes to speak with me." He tried to mimic the easy arrogance of the wizards who ruled here.

"Yes, but he wishes to speak with you with all members present." The administrator bowed slightly. "He has called a special session of the Circle. I have been sent to escort you."

Falden felt his eyes go wide in surprise. "I was expecting him to speak with me alone first. When is this session?"

"Now. Please bring anything you may require." The administrator bowed again.

What is going on? Falden thought. The ruling body of Gormanghast was taking his letter to Bellatran to far greater lengths than he would have expected. Without at least first having one member speak to him. *There has to be something else going on here. There has to be.*

~ * ~

The chamber of the Circle of Mages was large and austere. The ruling Circle sat behind great granite slabs surrounding the speaking chamber. Falden didn't like it. The room was designed so anyone speaking would feel like they were subject to an inquisition without any way of escaping. It was obvious the Circle enjoyed their power and used it to control others.

As he slowly scanned the room, he recognized each of the faces from the busts in the main office. The artist had been very accurate in his portrayals.

Bellatran was the first to speak. His voice, while strong despite his years, did not have the melodic nuances Falden remembered hearing whenever Kyrianna spoke. "What do you know of Brular Eglis, Cleric of Lord Hellavar and Keeper of the Flame of Mount Veri?"

Falden cleared his throat and silently wished he had borrowed the circlet or ring Vesir had given to Hendandra to help reinforce his case. "The story is long and complicated. I will only mention what is important," he said. "First the deity involved was Thynitic. The true incarnation of not only Ballan, but also Laraeng and Coressa."

Falden paused as there was no reaction from any of the Circle, only looks of boredom. He pushed any consideration of the reason for their nonreaction from his mind and continued. "Brular was imprisoned some sixty years ago, through the actions of Torliana, his student and pawn of Thynitic. The foul goddess tied his soul to an accursed amulet that allows it to be brought back time and time again. He was rescued almost twenty years after his imprisonment by a group of celestials who took him to their realm. They did not recover the amulet though, and it remained in the Abyss.

"His body recovered from its injuries, and he used the celestial's great library to research Thynitic. His mind was twisted by the time he had spent in the Abyss so all he could think of was revenge against Torliana. He eventually made his way to the pocket plane she created where he joined my companions and I. While there, he realized Torliana had been deceived by Thynitic and surrendered himself to the Abyss in a bid to prevent Torliana's soul from being destroyed by Thynitic."

"Did he succeed?" Lortain asked. "Is Torliana still alive?"

Falden stared at the elder of the humans. The question wasn't pertinent given the circumstances and seemed very odd. "She renounced Thynitic, but she was imprisoned by the goddess. May I ask the reason for the interest, Sage Lortain?"

"No, you may not. We ask the questions here."

Falden frowned.

It continued for what seemed hours as the Circle asked questions concerning not only Torliana and Brular, but also about his companions. He provided the details they asked for as he felt his answers were being weighed by magic. However, he gave them nothing more than what they asked. He did not volunteer any information regarding Andrinor's power, Kyrianna's possession of the magical figurine that allowed her to call Cewyr. He told them nothing of Myrith's heritage. Nor did he tell them anything of Bukon or Etewyn, who had traveled with them when they had first met, or of Vyroris.

~ * ~

He was exhausted after the long interrogation, and he wished Jerietlan was there with his magic to remove the fatigue he was feeling, but his friend was not; he had his own task to complete.

He had just stretched out on the bed when a knock came at his door. He opened the door with a wave of his hand. "More questions already?"

"More questions. However, my Lady also promises answers as well, Falden," a deep voice said.

Falden turned his head to see a warrior standing in the doorway. He was over six feet in stature and had a two-handed sword across his back. His armor was jet-black plate. Falden sat up. Jet-black and emblazoned with the insignia of Tormasus.

"Who has sent you, Myrmidon?"

"Lady Cassandra Shindar of the Circle. You will follow me." Falden nodded. A private audience was more to his liking.

He found himself almost having to run to keep up with the long stride of the myrmidon. "Do you have a name?" he asked after several blocks of following the man.

"Lord Orlundru Shindar. Fifth Sword of Tormasus."

Fifth Sword! Falden almost stopped in his tracks as the title rang in his mind. He hastened to catch back up to the man. "You are the commander of the Fifth Legion of Tormasus."

"Yes." It was a simple statement of fact, not an acknowledgment of rank.

"Why then do you serve as a messenger for one of the Circle?" Falden almost choked on his words as Orlundru stopped and looked at him.

"My wife, Cassandra Shindar, asked me to escort you. She did not say in what state you had to arrive. You would do well to hold your tongue, lest my hand drag it from your head."

Falden swallowed hard as Orlundru turned back and continued

walking. Could his magic take the myrmidon? Maybe, maybe not. He was not about to incur the anger of the warrior's wife as well. A member of the Circle married to one of the legion commander's of Tormasus—that was an ominous revelation. The cities had ties closer than he thought. The power of both combined was tremendous and he was about to meet the other of a pair who held power in both. He wished now he had taken the crystal rod Myrith had offered, maybe having a ready escape would have been wise.

The residence Orlundru led him to was a large walled compound with Tormasians guarding the gate. "Lord Orlundru, is the legion stationed within Gormanghast?" Falden asked as they entered the gates.

"Yes."

The city of mages allows a legion to be housed within its walls. He felt his heart race and his throat tighten. Gormanghast enjoyed its reputation of being able to deal with any threat through its command of the arcane. The Fifth Sword had just told him the Circle feared something—something that could resist their power.

Falden paused as they passed some strange-colored tigers. His eyes grew wider still—they had wings. He had never heard of such creatures. A halfling hung on one tiger's back as he seemed to be trying to train the beast. "Where did they come from?"

Orlundru laughed. "You will need to ask Cassandra that question," he said. "She awaits you. I must see to my troops." He pointed toward a large tower at the southwest corner of the fortress.

A member of the Circle living within a Tormasian Legion; this bodes ill for Shokar, Falden thought.

"I can scout the area," he heard his hawk say. To anyone nearby, it would have only sounded like normal bird squawks—it was part of their bond that they understood each other.

"Absolutely not." He looked at the guards armed with crossbows. "Don't tempt them to take target practice. You will find them quite able I believe and do not think for a moment the arrows and crossbows are not enchanted. Keep close, my friend. Let us see what Cassandra Shindar will tell us."

He walked up the outside staircase about thirty feet before coming to a door.

"Falden, what do you think is in the sealed lower levels?"

The door opened. "I do not believe I wish to think about it," he said.

A construct of iron held the ten-foot door open as it peered down at Falden. It turned its head and Falden followed its gaze to a woman sitting in a cushioned chair watching him.

"Falden, come in," she said. Her voice was light, but resonated with power.

He immediately moved to put distance between him and the golem still holding the door. He wished Andrinor or Myrith were here, he felt too vulnerable with that monstrosity at his back.

"Falden, sit," the woman said, a slight smile on her face betraying her amusement at his discomfort. "If I had wanted you dead, Orlundru would have brought me your head."

"Maybe I am stronger than you think."

"Or maybe I know my husband well enough to know he would have brought you to an area where you would be unable to teleport away and would have been forced to face him."

Falden frowned. She understood him and was making it quite plain she was his superior. He knew her kind. She wanted him to be humbled, and then she wanted something from him.

"I acknowledge the power of a member of the Circle, but be aware, dragon blood flows in my veins," he said with pride.

"Ah, that little myth again. We have allowed that story to continue for centuries because it does acknowledge the tiny bit of truth that started it and prevents unwanted attention where we do not want it." She paused and smiled again. "There is no dragon blood in your veins." Her tone was absolute.

Falden stared at her. "All who wield innate arcane power praise the dragons who gave them the lineage to channel their magic."

Cassandra laughed. "There is always a bit of truth to the myths. Would you like to know the truth?"

"There is a price I take it."

"Oh, yes."

"What is the price?" He would know if it was worth it before going any further with this conversation.

"The Circle wants you to ensure the return of Brular Eglis."

"I have already sworn to do that."

"But," she paused and leaned forward a bit, "in addition to that, you are not to kill Torliana."

"Why not! She is powerful and dangerous. She is too much of a threat. I fear she could match any of the Circle in raw power. Her control of that power seems to be a bit lacking, but I assure you what she lacks in finesse, she more than makes up for in tenacity. Even if I were not going after Brular, my companions would surely wish to end her threat to us and especially to Kyrianna."

"It was not a request, Falden. The Chosen are needed."

"The Circle needs Torliana? That is absurd."

She shook her head. "There are many things occurring you do not know about," she said. "We need all of the Chosen. The gods create the Chosen, just as the Circle created you."

Falden stared at her. Her eyes were as hard and uncaring as the steel of Myrith's blade.

"Falden, you have no idea what you and your friends have gotten involved in. We are all pawns on this board we call Shokar and our opponent is ready to take the field. Temples burn and one of the last dragons is dying as we speak. A war is coming, one that will either finish what was started nearly five hundred years ago or our resolve will finally end it."

Falden could only stare at her. He didn't understand what she was talking about, but was sure she would make him do just that. There was one thing he was certain of, she believed every word she was saying and there was more than just a twinge of fear in her voice. If something made a member of the Circle, one who sat among a legion of Tormasians afraid, he had better listen, because his life and the lives of the others could well depend on it.

"What do you know of the First Mage War?" She looked at him now without blinking or smiling.

"First? There has been only one."

"That part is true; at least for a few more years it will be true." She still watched him through half-closed eyes.

Falden leaned back in his seat. "The war was fought between two factions of the Gorman Empire. They fought themselves almost to extinction at the city of Styr, which was obliterated in the process. The empire fell apart shortly after."

"That is all you know?" Her tone was condescending.

"I am sorry if I disappoint you. I do not have the benefit of the Academy to assist my knowledge. The Circle sees to it that I and those of my ilk don't have that chance." He didn't bother to hide his irritation.

"You would change that if you could?" This time there was the slight hint of a smile at the corners of her mouth.

"Of course."

"Interesting." She paused as if considering the possibility and dismissing it.

"However, we must return to the matter at hand. So you have never heard of the Faithless?"

"That name means nothing to me. Are they of the war?"

"Oh yes. The historians have done their job well; most have never heard of them."

Falden sank back into his seat as Cassandra continued speaking.

"They were the enemy. Cyral is the name they were once known by. The Faithless, as we call them, have powerful magic but there is one difference. They have no gods. It is said they once followed a god who abandoned them. After centuries of trying to find him again, they went mad and are now determined to prove all of the gods are false. They worship only their own magic. It is everything to them. It is believed to be what sustains them.

"The war was ugly. The Faithless had carefully positioned people within the hierarchy of the empire. Even some members of the Circle were in fact of the Faithless. They caused great confusion during the first years of the conflict and the empire fought hard to regain the trust of allies and fill the ranks of the fallen. I am told their power was immense. My feeble golem, which you stumbled at seeing, is nothing compared to their constructs and armor. I have seen these monstrosities. They resist our magic quite effectively and can unleash their own with impunity.

"It is no wonder the empire made a deal with the dragons to share power if they would take the field with them."

Falden's mouth dropped. "The dragons took the field en masse against the Faithless? Alongside the empire?"

"Oh yes. The accounts were of a glorious victory near Mysita Keep, but the aftermath of the battle led to something insidious. The empire did not imagine the Faithless could create a weapon to fight the dragons. A weapon horrible and complete. They called it Dracoblight—a disease that went for the old and young first. It killed the great wyrms first to weaken their ranks, as well as the young to break their spirit. Even the elves wept as the draconic young were wiped from Shokar. The others were left sterile. There are only six left now."

Her gaze went past him and he turned to see a painting on the wall where a patch of green faded away. "Now, only five," she said.

"There are but five dragons left?" Falden spoke softly.

"Yes. Do you want to hear about them or what you came here to learn?" She paused and smiled as she waited for him to answer.

"My apologies," Falden said. "Continue."

Cassandra nodded. "The empire was running out of options, so a bold plan was initiated. All of the remaining strength of the empire was gathered at Styr. However, it was only a ruse. A great sword had been forged and given to a dwarven warrior and his companions. He took this sword to the Faithless stronghold and buried it in the source of their power. It disrupted their magic and the Faithless retreated. As they left Shokar, the ties between their world and others were sealed by the power of the dragons and the expended life force of many great wizards. They gave their lives to buy us time. Those wards were to hold for five hundred years. Breaches have already begun appearing, as is evident by some of your friends' stories. Soon the wards will fail completely and the Faithless will be among us again." She paused and took a long drink from her glass.

Falden waited for her continue, not saying anything this time.

"The dragons knew their race was dead on Shokar," she finally said. "A deal was struck for them to have their revenge. They made a pact with the Circle. As they would die, we would harvest their blood."

Falden felt his eyes narrow. "All of it?" He didn't want to think about Andrinor's reaction to this.

"Every last drop," she said. "Both young and old. This blood has been treated and poured into the major sources of drinking water throughout the cities of the, at that time empire, and the current Confederation for over four hundred years."

Falden felt himself shaking as she spoke.

"You were not born of dragon blood, but instead your mother consumed it. As so many others have. At first there were…" she looked down at the glass in her hand, "failures. But, I am told only a few hundred incidents were reported. The alchemists eventually perfected their art and the deformities lessened. Now, almost all sorcerers appear as you do."

Falden stood up. "The Circle consists of monsters. You are the coldest person I have ever met. Even Torliana showed more emotion than you."

Cassandra raised a hand. "No, Falden, you are the monster. A creation of the Circle, born of a concoction your mother drank."

He started to turn to the door then stopped. "You should have been Thynitic's Chosen. You pervert nature on a whim. You destroy and alter lives because it suits your purposes. The Circle is an abomination that begets pain and misery. All of that is in keeping with the Lady of Chaos' nature."

"You think you could do better?" She looked up at him, her eyes unwavering and unconcerned.

"Could I do worse?"

"Everyone needs a goal to strive for. I will give you yours. If you return with Brular intact *and* Torliana still among the living, I will give you a chance to best me in the arcane. If you succeed, you may have my position on the Circle."

"You're serious?" He felt his jaw drop and fought to regain his composure.

"Absolutely. The rules of this city hold me back too much. I need a successor. If you have the power, use it. Take my position and then make the changes you desire."

"Very well, Cassandra. I look forward to showing you and the Circle the error of treating us from the blood and people as a whole as your tools." He turned toward the door.

She laughed. "You think the Circle has wronged you? That we have used you? What of the gods? They prepare also, Falden. They have been playing with their followers' lives all this time to find the ones who will serve them in this fight."

He stopped and spun around to face her. "Torliana," he said.

"Yes, but just as she was twisted by Thynitic to be her Chosen, another was forged and tempered by years of misery to test his faith. Why would his god have allowed him to suffer as he did for no reason?" Falden took a step back.

"And there is another who is being tested, one whose goddess may claim her or who may allow another to have her. That is part of her testing. If she fails, it is doubtful she will survive."

Falden turned and strode to the door. The golem stepped in front of him and with a wave of his hand he teleported behind him and left. The open sky was a blessing and the lack of attention from the Tormasians a relief.

"Falden, do you know what she meant?" his familiar asked.

"Yes, my friend. I know what she meant."

"Brular is one of the Chosen and Kyrianna is the one being

tested?" The hawk clenched his talons slightly then relaxed them.

"No, they are both damned, just like the rest of us. Damned to play the hand dealt us by others." Falden looked back at the tower. "Our fate has been written by others."

"What will we do?"

"Rewrite it, my friend. We will rewrite it."

Chapter Four
Andrinor

Andrinor picked his way over the rocks. He had come to the Dragonspire Mountains—specifically to the Dragon's Mouth in the northeastern edge of the range. He glanced around at the snow-covered trees, and smiled. He was of the silver—the cold would not touch him.

Falden had bought him to the mountains yesterday and still he had not reached the place he felt he was meant to be. The terrain was difficult even for him, who had been raised in the Dragon Flame Mountains of Rhysia. Still, he would find the cave he had seen in his vision; he would not admit the task was beyond him, and return to the Coliseum.

He paused at the edge of a shallow valley—there an area of darkness among the rocks—the opening to a cave. This must be the place, he thought as he began to work his way down the non-existent trail.

His foot found a loose rock under the snow and he slipped. He shook his head at his own clumsiness and paused at the sight of the tracks in front of the cave. There was no mistaking the claw marks. They were immense. He thought back on the training he had received in the temple of He Who Watches as he studied the tracks. There was a slight hook to the middle claw print—this was a green dragon; one who was approaching the twilight.

He held his double-bladed sword in a defensive position as he entered the cavern. He would not attack the dragon, but he would defend himself if it became necessary. The cloying stench of death and decay was heavy in the air and he choked and coughed as he moved through the cavern. He twisted his body, using his blade to help balance himself as the layer of bones under his feet shifted.

Andrinor froze at what lay before him: the cavern was filled with bones and whole skeletons. This was not the lair of an ancient dragon; this was the place where the dragon had come to die. "Spread your wings over them and welcome them to your endless skies," he said as he continued to stare at the bones. He felt tears burning his eyes as he caught sight of a group of smaller bones. Four or five sitting together; all small enough to still be wyrmlings.

He turned slowly as a soft hiss came from his right. The sound was unmistakable; not all was dead here. He bowed his head as a large, green, scaled head rounded the corner. It sniffed the air, then a tongue snaked out to touch his cheek. He looked up to see the dark green eyes watching him; the dragon's ears were perked forward as she cocked her head to the side.

"Has She sent you?" The dragon's voice cracked, betraying her age as even greater than he had suspected.

Andrinor blinked. He had met many dragons in his years, but never had he seen one who appeared this impassive to what was around it. He started to answer her, but froze as a familiar voice whispered in his mind.

:Decroma.

It was the name Ghainaess had given him, when she called him as one of her initiates. However, this was not the gentle voice of the Great Mother. This voice was demanding, summoning him.

He felt cold surround him. A sensation he had not felt in a long time. However, it was not his body that felt the chill—it was his soul. Something was forcing him to his knees and he dropped his weapon as he tried to fight the unseen force. The dragon's roar of anger shook the cavern as he was surrounded by a cloak of darkness and the cavern faded from sight.

His vision cleared and he found himself kneeling on a white marble floor.

"The mighty Andrinor. Ghainaess' Warrior Initiate. I welcome you to my citadel."

That cold voice was the same one which had spoken to him once before.

"Drezmona," he whispered as he slowly stood and looked around.

He was in a small room of no more than twenty feet. The circle of runes that surrounded him, though not made by Brular, had a particular pattern that reminded him of the fire cleric's wards. The inscription was in Draconic.

"I am speaking to you, Andrinor."

He had no sword, but the claws on the gauntlets made from the scales of a blue dragon would suffice. He lunged at the demoness only to find himself thrown back by an invisible wall of force.

He looked at her and let his blood freeze as he called on the silver.

She raised her hand and waved a finger in warning. "Take care. That circle is only big enough for a human. If you use your draconic form, you will quite possibly crush yourself in there." She stepped forward and smiled. "I assure you, my magic will hold against yours."

He glanced around quickly; she was right. The runes were carefully positioned. The barrier he stood in would only be a few feet wide. He calmed his emotions and dismissed the magic. "There will be a time, demoness," he said. "There will be a time."

"Good. I don't want you to strain yourself, quite yet," she said. "You and I have unfinished business. Or perhaps it will be pleasure." She smiled as she walked slowly around the circle. "You are strong. Your offspring would have a piece of that heritage. Combined with the proper lines, your child could be a god among men and dragons."

Andrinor took a step back from the demoness, but was stopped by the barrier. The idea of her as a mate was repugnant. The idea of her as the mother of his child was a sin against everything his tribe had taught him. To give his power into her hands would be an abomination.

"I will give you a few minutes alone to think about my offer. I could always give you to Thynitic to keep the fire cleric and his wench company." She laughed as she left the room.

He looked again at the runes, but they made no sense to him. "Ghainaess, help me. I know she has the power to force this. Help me to stop it." There was a hiss in his mind. "Ghainaess?" He felt hope in his heart.

:*No, wyrmling.*

Andrinor almost fell into the wards again. It was the voice of the green.

"How?"

:*Shut up, hatchling, and let me observe. Show me the floor.*

He found himself looking at the floor. :*Nice, practiced and perfect. Show me more.*

He turned slowly.

:*Decroma? Is that your name, human scaled one?* The green's voice was calm as she spoke in his mind.

He paused but saw no reason not to answer. "Yes, the Great Mother calls me that."

:She has your true name—that is bad. You will need to kill her. There was a brief pause. *:I see by her work here she is determined and proficient. Having your true name gives her great power over you. Too much power. Keep turning.*

There was another pause—longer this time as he continued to turn and the presence in his mind studied the inscription. *:Ah, there it is,* she finally said.

"What?" Andrinor looked at the spot in the floor, but saw nothing different.

:The crack. She missed the tiniest of spots. Release your mind to me.

"What are you going to do?" He tried to force himself to relax. He trusted the dragon; she was one of Ghainaess' children and had done nothing to harm him when she had had the chance. However, it was difficult to allow another to control him willingly.

:My name is Clorhydruis, wyrmling. I did not send my mind to the sixty-third level of the Abyss just to have you act the fool. You saw the bones. You have not the understanding yet as to the truth. She paused and waited for several heartbeats. *:My time is short. Do you wish her to have you and then your child?*

"No!" he whispered. "I am sorry, but what you ask is difficult for me to do." He took a calming breath and relaxed as he felt the presence of the dragon grow stronger.

:I am the last of the greens and I am dying even as you waste my time with chatter.

Andrinor felt his mind forced back by both her words and her power. He felt almost like a ghost within himself as he heard his voice began to chant.

"So, Andrinor," the demoness said as she walked back into the chamber. "Have you decided…?" her voice trailed off. "Impossible. You have no such power."

His voice bellowed like an angry dragon. "No, he does not. However, he must leave."

There was a sudden flash as the circle exploded and Andrinor felt himself fall into a pile of bones. He took several minutes to stand as he heard her again.

This time her voice was not in his mind, but to his right.

"My sight is failing, wyrmling. What do you see?"

"Bones. Many bones. I see clutches of wyrmlings and young dragons huddled together to die. I see great wyrms defeated and broken." He felt his voice break. "What could have done this?"

"The Faithless. They have power, great power."

"I can see that, but how!" His sorrow was turning to anger as he continued to stare at the bones of what had to be all of Shokar's dragons. All of them here; all of them dead.

"A disease that killed the old and wise as well as the young and future. A disease that left the others feeble, broken and sterile."

"I have never heard of such a disease, where did they find it?"

"They made it."

Andrinor stumble back a few steps. "Made it? What magic is this?" He retrieved his sword and sheathed the blades.

"The magic of the Faithless."

Andrinor stepped forward and placed his right hand on the dragon's head. He bowed his head as he felt life leave the green. After a moment, he dropped to his right knee. "Ghainaess, please guide the spirit of Clorhydruis to your endless skies. Spread your wings over her and protect her from the corruption that has come to this place. Give me your strength and guide me so I can find a way to stop the evil destroying your children in this world."

He continued to kneel there, not fighting the tears as they flowed. He knew he would have to learn more about these Faithless as Clorhydruis had named them. He had given his word he would go after Brular. He had pledged his life, his blade and his soul to Kyrianna as a friend. He was bound to follow her into the Abyss and anywhere else she might call on him to go. There was only one who could sever the oath he had sworn—Ghainaess. He had also made a pledge to Brular to seek the amulet and destroy it. He would not be foresworn of these oaths. He would go to the Abyss, then when they returned, he would seek to find a way to save Ghainaess' Children. If they survived, something told him Kyrianna and Myrith would insist on helping him.

A sudden flash of light and the sound of two voices, one male and the other female, interrupted Andrinor's prayers. He moved to a protected outcropping where he could see the pair as they approached the body of Clorhydruis. The male was dressed in full plate and carried a two-handed sword.

The woman was dressed in robes and only carried a staff.

"Let us be done with this task," the woman said. "I grow weary of being the Circle's servant in this matter."

Andrinor moved cautiously. He placed his feet with care to not disturb any of the bones as he moved closer to watch and listen to the pair. There was something in the woman's tone he disliked and distrusted.

His grip on his sword tightened as he watched the woman's staff elongate into a thin, sharp spear. He gasped as she thrust it into Clorhydruis' side. The spear's lower shaft slowly turned red and the color began creeping up the wood. He stared at the scene. The staff was drinking the blood from the dragon. There were no prayers, no respect, just desecration. He could not allow this to continue.

"Desecrators!" He stood up. "Who are you who would tempt my sword by this sacrilege?"

Both of them looked up at him in surprise. It was the woman who spoke first. "Cassandra Shindar of the Circle of Gormanghast. This is not your concern."

"Yes, it is." He leapt down, his sword cutting the air with a powerful stroke meant to take the woman out of the fight. His blade hit, but the wound it left was not as deep as it should have been. *Magical protections*, he thought.

"Pyremar's Fires," he cursed as he realized his momentary distraction had left him open to an attack from the man.

He was fortunate, the swordsman's swing went wide hitting a rock outcropping next to him. Andrinor took a hasty step back as the sword severed the top half of the rock. He felt a twinge of fear when he saw the man was still ten feet away and yet, his blade did not appear to be that long. *What kind of magic will allow his weapon to do that even though he is nowhere near the target?*

"I am Orlundru Shindar, Fifth Sword of Tormasus. Who are you that you would dare to attack my wife? One who is prepared to enter the afterlife, I believe."

"I am Andrinor, Warrior Initiate of the Great Mother."

Andrinor charged in, his weapon swinging back and forth. The armor of the Fifth Sword proved to be resilient to his blows. There was blood on the man, but not nearly what he had expected.

"No discipline," Orlundru said as he swung.

The Fifth Sword's first strike connected with Andrinor's weapon, and cut a deep notch in the haft. Before he could react, the blade swung down again and shattered his sword. He could only stare at the remains of his weapon as the man took a step back.

"Pathetic."

"Then let us see how you handle the power of the Great

Mother." His body convulsed as it grew, his armor growing with it. He roared as he stretched out his neck to release his icy breath, but he felt something strange. He was transforming back. "No!" He turned to see the woman with her hands outstretched. An aura of power reached from her to him.

He turned his attention back to the warrior.

"Are you done with your little display? I am still waiting for you to show me some skill. So far, I am not impressed."

Andrinor knew he was losing. He had challenged both a mage and a skilled warrior. Two who were confident in both their own and each other's abilities. He was committed though; the sacrilege they had committed could not be left unchallenged. He charged again, the claws on his dragon scale gauntlets leading.

"You do not even carry a proper secondary weapon," the warrior said.

"No!" Andrinor jerked his arm back as the Fifth's sword cut deeply into the dragon scale buckler he had been given when Ghainaess chose him as one of her Initiates. The sword shifted quickly and he gasped as it left two deep wounds against his abdomen.

He is only playing with me, Andrinor thought. *The battle is lost.* He looked at the bones. *Who will avenge them if I die?* His left knee hit the ground. "I yield."

"Finally, some sense," Orlundru said.

"Take him to my chambers; I wish to study him," Cassandra said.

Andrinor looked at her, his soul as cold as when Drezmona had summoned him to her.

"No." The word seemed a command as Orlundru said it.

Andrinor fought to hide the smile he felt on his lips at the rage he saw on the woman's face as she turned to face her husband.

"No? He has the power of the dragon. He must be studied by the Circle."

"He yielded to me. By Tormasian code, he is mine to do with as I please."

Despite his fear of being turned over to the mage, Andrinor did not find Orlundru's statement very comforting.

Cassandra walked over to Orlundru and looked up into his visor. "Very well, husband. But he is to be returned to me if he disappoints you."

"Accepted." He sheathed his sword and turned to Andrinor.

"Get up, we are leaving."

"Wait," Cassandra said. "Did she speak to you?" Andrinor looked at her and remained silent.

"You will answer her, or I will take your head," Orlundru said.

He glanced at Orlundru and nodded. "She spoke to me here and when she took my mind in the Abyss."

Cassandra leaned back her eyes wide for a moment. "How did you come to be in the Abyss?"

"I was trapped by a demoness called Drezmona. I would add that she is almost as cold as you."

Orlundru's sword was at his neck. "Do not taunt her, lest I give you to her. You could wind up being something you never dreamed of."

"Show me," Cassandra said.

Andrinor felt her power touch his mind. The intrusion was painful as she picked her way, without his consent, through his memories. He was left gasping as she withdrew.

"Very interesting. Orlundru, remove the dragon's head. I need it to come to Gormanghast with me."

"No!" Andrinor dropped to both knees. "That is sacrilege. The Great Mother would never allow this. I beg you do not do this."

Cassandra turned. "You would be amazed at what the gods have allowed," she whispered. "You have not been to the back chamber, have you?" she asked. "Go." She pointed south. "See what is there and then tell me what she would or would not allow."

He started to stand, but stopped himself and looked to Orlundru for permission.

"Good. You are capable of learning." He turned toward the dragon. "Go and return quickly." He paused. "Lest I come for you."

Andrinor left the two of them to their task. He tried to close out the sound of Orlundru's blade striking Clorhydruis' neck as he walked through the bones of the dead and entered the chamber he had been sent to. At the sight of the large skeleton at the back of the chamber his knees gave way and he fell to the floor.

The remains were larger than any known dragon. The skull looked down on the room—filled with the remains of hundreds of hatchlings. Its empty eye sockets still filled with sorrow.

His voice was only a harsh whisper. "I beg your forgiveness for what I must do." He reached up and grabbed one of the floating ribs and pulled with all of his strength until it snapped free. He held it out in his hands, the same as he would his sword when offering it in service to another. "Ghainaess, Great Mother, I vow this bone will be forged into a blade to defeat the demons I must face. Then I will see to restoring Your Children to their place. I will face the demons called the Faithless and they will pay for what they have done."

He returned to Orlundru as he had been directed. Cassandra's spear was once again buried in Clorhydruis' side. "Why do you take the blood?" he asked.

"Ask no questions," Orlundru snapped.

"No, husband, it is fine. He should know and I am sure he will soon anyway. The blood is needed to be put into the various city water supplies."

"This is madness," Andrinor said. "You seek to give a city the blood of a dragon. Even the demons know no such foulness."

"You know not what foulness is. When the Faithless return, you will know and you will thank me and the Circle for our preparedness. Rescue the fire cleric from the Abyss, if you can, but make sure you also talk to your friend, Falden. Yes, you should definitely talk to him."

"How do you know Falden? Did you go into other memories as well?"

"I spoke to him not an hour ago, fool. He spoke little of you to the Circle. That was a mistake! I assure you he will be punished for it. However, he will still join you on your journey." She turned toward her husband. "That is if you can show you are worthy in the arena and then be released from my husband's service."

"Cassandra, you do not need me here any longer. I am returning to Tormasus." He pulled a crystal rod from his belt.

Andrinor recognized the device as being similar to the one he received at the Coliseum. He thought of reaching for it, but knew it was not a matter of escape as these two would find him and his friends. He needed to free himself from Orlundru. "Let us go. I do not fear your test." Orlundru nodded and broke the rod.

~ * ~

"Why did you bring that bone?" Orlundru asked as he led Andrinor through several corridors.

"I need a new weapon. This bone is from the avatar of the

Great Mother. I believe it holds power; power I may need in my journey into the Abyss."

"You are thinking. There is hope for you yet."

They passed through a set of steel doors into an open-air arena. Andrinor paused at the cheers and clang of steel he heard.

"You have been brought here to prove to me you are worthy to stay among the living," Orlundru said.

"How long will that take?"

"It should only take a few weeks. And I will be referred to as Commander while in Tormasus."

"Yes, Commander," Andrinor said. "I don't have weeks. My group leaves in three days."

Orlundru looked at him. "Then what are you waiting for?"

Andrinor placed the bone on a nearby table then looked up at the weapons that adorned the walls at this entrance to the arena. He jumped up and grabbed a two-handed sword and gauged its weight. He looked at Orlundru who just nodded.

Andrinor returned the nod with a grin, then jumped the twenty feet to the arena floor and charged the creature. The sword dulled against the strokes and hits they traded, but Andrinor stood while the creature fell. He was covered in blood as he looked up at Orlundru. The commander held the bone he had brought, nodded and pointed to the east.

Another door opened and Andrinor turned to face the roaring beast that charged him.

~ * ~

"I am not a horse; I will not be branded," Andrinor said as another Tormasian fell to his fist. "I am not someone's property."

The click of a crossbow caught his attention and he flung a helmet toward the sound. He was rewarded with a thud and a curse. About fifteen Tormasians littered the room. As he was still standing and they were not, he believed they had been told he was not to be killed if he resisted. A noise to his left caught his attention. He whirled to strike again, but this time held the blow back. He stared at Orlundru who held the brand.

"You do not yield to another. You have earned the right to show me your resolve." He held the brand out.

Andrinor looked at the brand then at Orlundru. He took the metal shaft by its shortest end. He was of the silver, the heat would hurt him, more so than others, but he would not let go. He was determined he would earn his life back from this man and go with his friends to the Abyss. If this was what it took, then so be it. He pressed the red-hot end into his right shoulder until the pain melted into agony and beyond, but he did not take his eyes away from those of the commander. When Orlundru nodded, he released the brand and let it fall to the floor.

"The arena awaits," Orlundru said.

Andrinor took several deep breaths, then nodded and left the room.

~ * ~

Another foe fell as Andrinor collapsed to his knees. He had been fighting almost nonstop for two days. Only allowed brief breaks to eat and be healed by the priests. Each time the priests removed his need for sleep, the fatigue came back faster and faster. "How much more?"

"You have done well, but your skill is still lacking. It is time to fix that.

Follow me."

Andrinor followed Orlundru through a door leading out of arena.

"I know of your quest," Orlundru said. "Did you know Brular himself graced these halls?"

"Yes," Andrinor replied. "He trained here and then later returned to win the right to mediate over a dispute between your city and Irrmar."

"Knowledge is also a weapon. Did you know that because of Brular's service, the then High Lord General was willing to send a legion anywhere the priest wished for a month? A thousand warriors at his call, but that call never came. The High Lord General hoped Brular would pass judgment on Rejki and give cause to its obliteration, but the priest refused. He simply stated justice should be just, not swift. He held the High Lord General back from not one war, but two. Much is owed to him. Today, I start the repayment." He slammed opened the two steel doors to the branding room Andrinor had been in before, but this time a huge cage had been positioned in the room and several robed figures stood by.

Andrinor turned to stare at the commander.

"Get in." The voice was that of the Fifth Sword.

Andrinor knew he dared not refuse this command. He entered the cage and the manacles closed on his limbs of their own accord.

The robed figures began chanting and a large brand in front of him began glowing. Heat on his back told him there was a second brand behind him. Orlundru stepped in front of him. "With pain, there comes power. Know that."

Andrinor nodded and Orlundru moved out of the way as the brands moved against him. He was unable to keep from screaming at the pain he felt. His whole body was burning and he fought to keep the power of the silver from rushing forward to burst his bonds. When the iron was pulled away, he felt blackness reaching for him as he dropped against the manacles.

"Good," Orlundru said. "Get him cleaned up, then back to the arena."

~ * ~

Andrinor nodded to the squire as the boy held out a double-bladed sword to him. *Finally*, he thought. This was his preferred weapon and it was the first time he had been allowed to use one. The boy was grinning as he turned and lifted another item from the pile of equipment at this entrance.

"Commander Shindar had this delivered specifically for you this morning." The boy held up the dragon scale buckler which had been cut into two pieces by Orlundru's sword.

Andrinor took the buckler and felt a tingle of magic as he placed it on his arm. The commander had had the item repaired and restored. Perhaps there was hope he would soon be released from this place.

He patted the boy on the head, then stepped into the arena to face his next opponent. The door in the floor of the arena opened and a hydra rose up to face him. The first of the creature's heads came at him and his reflexes took over. The blades of his weapon flashed left then right to quickly take five of the heads from their necks. He froze for a second as he stepped back to assess the situation. As the remaining heads came at him, his left arm reacted, almost on its own to block one. His next flurry of swings ended the contest. He looked up at the grand box to see Orlundru looking down at him. The commander raised a glass in salute.

Andrinor raised his sword in the air and the crowd cheered its approval.

~ * ~

Andrinor leaned against his blade as another day of almost continuous fighting continued. They were to have been back today; would he be left behind?

The crowd fell silent and Andrinor looked up to see Orlundru entering the arena. "Come, show me what you have learned."

Andrinor moved his sword back and forth as he slowly approached the Fifth Sword.

"What, no charge?"

"And give you the advantage? Not today." Andrinor stopped and waited. "Good." Orlundru slowly stepped toward him.

Andrinor continued to wait even after the Fifth Sword was within five feet of him.

"Do I scare you?" Orlundru asked.

"No," Andrinor said. "However, your skill is nothing to be trifled with."

Orlundru nodded. "Maybe you will live through the Abyss."

Orlundru's sword came in at his abdomen and cut a slight gash. Then the sword flashed three more times, as it cut him twice. He didn't back away. He needed to win this battle or be forced to bury the memory of his friends, as they would go without him and he would be forsworn and dishonored for violating his oaths to Brular and Kyrianna. His weapon became a blur as he attacked the commander. He managed to draw blood, but not enough. Orlundru came at him again and he wondered if his stay in the arena would indeed be over. Still, he did not move.

He knew he was losing again; he needed to change this battle in his favor.

He closed with the commander and took a serious blow as he drove the Fifth Sword down. The commander's sword was now useless. The fight would be his dragon-clawed gauntlets against the commander's own gauntleted fists. He knew the claws were superior as they rolled around in the dirt trading blows.

Andrinor however, began to grow weaker as everything began turning gray and he felt faint. He was slowing and fell back as Orlundru struck a solid blow against his chest. He almost hit the dirt, but found himself being held by something. He let his mind clear as his ears filled with cheers. Orlundru held his hand in the air; the mark of a draw.

"Well fought, Andrinor, Dragon Warrior of the Great Mother," Orlundru said. "You have earned the right to try and get yourself killed in the Abyss. Clerics!"

Orlundru stood as Andrinor continued to kneel on the ground. "See to him at once. He leaves for the Abyss within the hour," he told the clerics.

Another man came up carrying a steel bucket with a piece of iron in it. Orlundru took the brand and moved toward Andrinor. Andrinor forced himself to his feet and held out his hand. Orlundru smiled and placed the hot iron in his hand.

Andrinor raised the brand high as the crowd cheered and placed it against his right arm. His time in the arena was at an end. He held the brand out to Orlundru, however blackness claimed him before the commander took it from him.

~ * ~

Andrinor woke in Orlundru's private quarters. A cleric stood over him. "He is well enough to travel now."

"Leave us," Orlundru said.

The priest bowed then left the room.

After the door closed, Orlundru nodded and held his hand out to Andrinor to help him up. "Nice display, warrior, but it would have been better if you hadn't fainted at the end." He chuckled.

Andrinor nodded. "I am free to go?"

"Yes, but first see to your things on the table."

He approached the table and recognized his gear, but some of the items were not his. He picked up the hilt of a double-bladed sword that had no blades.

"I don't understand," he said.

"Hold it out from your body. Now, think of a blade made of silver and another of cold iron."

Two blades appeared, one of each kind of metal. "It made the blades?"

"No," Orlundru said. "Look in the case."

Andrinor opened the ornate metal case. Inside were two more blades: one of bone and one of adamantine, along with places for the two he had just summoned.

"They are summoned to the hilt by your will," Orlundru said. "The pommel is enchanted to reform the blades if they are de-

stroyed, while it is made of a substance that will allow it to be re-
formed if the pieces are brought back together. So the pommel can
be remade without magic and once it is whole, it will reform the
blades that were destroyed. The box and the pommel are linked.
Don't lose the box. Oh, one other thing; the pommel can charge
the weapon with energy. Fire, cold, acid, damaging sound as well as
the power of lightning can be bestowed on the blades. A far superior weapon to the one you had."

Andrinor reached for a green dragon scale helmet sitting on
the table. The horns of a green dragon still rested on the scales. His
hand shook as he felt a hand on his shoulder.

"Calm yourself. My wife said Clorhydruis wanted this. She saw
a message the green had left in your mind. The helmet will allow
you to use her acid breath instead of your own, as you choose."

Andrinor relaxed as he let what Orlundru was saying sink in.
The dragon had helped him again, even in her death. Another debt
the Faithless would have to pay.

"The boots?"

"The journey will be hard and long; the boots will keep your
speed and endurance equal to that of a horse."

"Thank you, Commander. These will help a great deal in my
task to rescue Brular." He placed the rest of his gear in the pack and
shouldered it as he pulled out the rod.

"Why did you not use the rod before?"

"You would have followed me. I needed to end this properly
so you and your wife would not interfere with my friends."

"You have more wisdom than many would credit you with,
good. Farewell, Dragon Warrior, remember to tell those of the Coliseum that you hail from the Arena of Tormasus. Let them wonder
at your strength."

Andrinor smiled as he broke the rod.

Chapter Five
Falden

"Greetings, Falden, we need to talk."

Falden sat up and dove for the side of the bed. He wasn't quick enough as a large metal hand grabbed him and forced him back onto the bed. He moved his hand slightly, but he could not touch the arcane power needed to teleport away.

"Silly novice," Cassandra said. "Do you think I would not have prepared for that? When you entered the Circle's chamber, all the magic you carried both within and without was laid bare before us. That little ability Leikor gave you which should let you wiggle free is suppressed as well. My servant wears an amulet that suppresses all magic. I believe you are familiar with such a spell."

He turned his head to look at her. The golem tightened his grip and he found it harder to breathe as the pressure increased against his chest. "What have I done to deserve this?" He forced the words out.

"You held back information about the dragon warrior in the Circle's chamber and my own. Andrinor has the power of the Great Mother. You did not deem that important."

"It is his power. Not mine or yours!"

"That lack of information led me to not anticipate." She pulled back her robe to show a long scar. "From your friend."

Falden smiled despite the danger of his situation. "Good for him. I will have to tell him that he needs to aim higher next time."

"I should kill you now, but I need that priest back," she said. "Hold him!"

The hand pressed down even more on his chest and Falden coughed as he fought to breathe.

Cassandra approached and held out a vial of a dark red liquid. "You have fared well so far, Falden. For too long, you have gone unnoticed among the pure humans. That ends now." She grabbed his face, pushed her fingers against the place where his jaws came together and forced his mouth open. She held his head still as she poured the potion into his mouth then held his mouth closed. He coughed as the warm liquid flowed down his throat.

His skin burned as if on fire and his eyes felt as if they were melting from their very sockets. The golem released him and he screamed from the pain. He fell to his knees on the floor. The last time he had felt such pain was when he had been struck by Thynitic's torture spell. He hadn't said anything to Kyrianna about what had happened and he knew she hadn't forgiven herself. Andrinor had approached her and forgiven her, but he wasn't sure he was ready to do the same yet. He wouldn't condemn her, but he wasn't ready to forgive. He coughed a few more times, then slowly forced himself to his feet.

"Finished?" Cassandra asked.

His head snapped around.

"Very nice. I like the color. It matches your skin." She started laughing as she continued to watch him.

Falden turned to face the polished mirror. His skin now had a thick layer of green scales and his eyes were slitted like those of a dragon with a greenish tinge. "What have you done?"

"I have awakened more of the power you garnered from the blood. Normally I would not have been able to, but the recent death of the last of the greens gave me what I needed to accomplish this." She smiled. "I believe it is an improvement."

"Why do this?"

"Because I can." Her voice was harsh and cold.

He looked again at the mirror. His vision was different, sharper and the lack of light in the room was no longer as much of a hindrance. "What now, Cassandra Shindar of the Circle of Mages?"

"I am through here. There will be a man visiting you in the morning. He will bring a few gifts. Accept them." She reached for the door.

"This is not over between you and I. There will be a reckoning." Even as he said it, he wondered if he would ever have the power to challenge her.

"I hope as much, but you need to be aware my station doesn't come cheaply. If you fail to take it, I will leave you as a dark smear on the floor of the Circle's Chamber. The Circle requires the priest's return." She turned to leave then stopped. "Remember my words about Torliana. Leave her among the living. Thynitic needs a vessel for the coming battle. She will have it." She turned back to face him, her face impassive. "If not Torliana, then your friend—Kyrianna."

Falden felt his mouth go dry and he swallowed.

"I have the Circle's sanction in this. I will leave as many of you dead as necessary to take her back to the Lady of Chaos. My husband and I didn't come to our positions by politics, but by broken corpses." A flash of light and she was gone.

The golem moved through the door and the echo of its footsteps faded slowly.

He sat on the bed trying to comprehend what had just happened. "Falden, undo the knots—please," he heard his hawk say.

"Not a very good alarm, are you?" he said as he untied the rope holding the hawk.

"She came with a globe of silence then animated the rope to bind me, while within the globe of silence."

"She cast a spell while within an area of complete silence. She is correct; I am a novice." He dropped his head into his hands. What should have been a time to celebrate their victory over Torliana even while preparing to go into the Abyss had turned into a time of deep misery.

~ * ~

Falden rose as a knock came on the door. He reached for the door then paused.

"Falden, I was sent by Cassandra," a male voice said.

He opened the door. "That is supposed to be a comforting thing? I think not."

The man recoiled as the door opened and Falden frowned as he realized he would see that reaction on a regular basis now. "Your mistress' handiwork. Be quick, I want to leave this foul city." He walked away from the door and glanced out the window, though he did not move to close to it. "She has made me an outcast in what was once my home."

The man closed the door and went to the table. His pack came off his shoulder quickly as he opened it. He removed several smaller items then drew a staff out. He looked at Falden as if he had expected him to be surprised. Falden only yawned. Hendandra had a similar pack.

"The staff was fashioned by a great wizard. It can take you to the planes as well as summon others from them. It has been crafted to perform the enchantments to do the calling. It is also enspelled to be an effective weapon against those it has summoned." He held the staff out.

Falden took it and felt the power residing in it. The man had spoken truthfully.

"I was told you have two rings of wizardry." His hand was stretched out.

Falden rolled his eyes, though he removed the rings and held them in his hand. "Why should I give them to you?"

"They are inferior to this." He opened his other hand.

Falden read the aura on the ring and took it as he handed the man the two he had worn.

"Take this as well." He handed Falden another ring. "It will focus your power to break through the resistance of your enemy."

He lifted an amulet made of amethyst. "This is the last item."

"And what is that?"

"This will allow you to transmute your spells to generate damaging levels of sound instead of the other energies." The man smiled. "Demons have many resistances. You do know lightning is almost useless, correct?"

Falden shrugged as he took the amulet. "Be gone."

The man turned to leave. "I almost forgot—one more thing. This is a teleportation beacon. It will let those of the city you travel to know who you are. This will permit you to teleport to city streets and common areas without incident or provoking an armed response. Fare well on your journey."

Falden picked up the amulet and held it carefully. "By its very nature, a device for scrying." He looked at Talon. "But we hardly have a choice, do we?" Falden looked around the room and grabbed his pack. "Let us leave this misbegotten city." He turned to the door. Before he could open it, he heard a different voice on the other side.

"He of the blood, who speaks to the Circle, I would speak with you." Falden opened the door and found no one standing there.

"Not here," he said, choosing his words with care. "Not like this. The Circle watches."

"To the streets. My friends will guide you." The voice was gone.

Falden held up his arm for his hawk. "It appears we are not done here," he said when Talon landed.

~ * ~

He had seen the man's reaction earlier and knew he had to be prepared for it from others, but he found he wasn't. He remembered the way Kyrianna had tried to hide her ears and then stood in the middle of their group as they walked through the town of Nanitial. Now, he wished he could do the same. "I am the hideousness of their own doing," Falden whispered. "How many in this city know and never speak?"

"They all know in their hearts. They just refuse to let their ears find the words spoken in the alleyways."

Falden looked around for the source of the answer but saw no one. "You have me at a disadvantage."

"I am a friend; more so than she of the Circle. Cassandra Shindar did not start this, but she continues it, as do they all. To the right and then left. I will direct you as you go." The voice faded as it moved in front of him.

The trail became convoluted and Falden paused as he sensed magic following him. He took the teleportation beacon and placed it around Talon's neck. "Go, I will be fine, but I want that thing away from me for now."

"Tomorrow, by the fountain," Talon said.

"Yes, go," Falden said before the bird could add anything else.

"Good, I was waiting for you to get rid of that," the voice he was following said.

"A test then?"

"Yes, now we can go."

Falden felt someone grab his sleeve and relaxed as the world began to spin. Once the initial disorientation of the teleportation spell wore off, he found himself in a dark chamber. Again, he noticed he had little trouble seeing in less than ideal light. There was a figure standing in the darkness.

"I am here as you requested," Falden said.

"Falden, I am Morgorth. I lead the Blooded. We are the children of Gormanghast's heresy against the people." He stepped forward.

Falden felt himself flinch, then silently berated himself for it. Morgorth's face was only half formed, with the left side in a state of melting.

"My body has been affected by the blood of a black," Morgorth said. "Unfortunately, it attempted to grant me the acid breath of the dragon. But as you can see, my flesh cannot fully resist its own making of the fluid."

Falden nodded. Cassandra was correct, he had been lucky. Even now with his scales and eyes, he could hide much of his appearance under a hooded cloak or with magics that would alter his outward appearance. But even with alteration magic, Morgorth would not be able to hide the putrefying stench. Falden watched Morgorth as he took another couple of steps. He was only a few inches above five feet and despite the pain he had to be enduring, his step was strong and sure.

"Why have you brought me here?" Falden asked. "What is it you want?" He didn't like the way things had gone with the Circle, then Cassandra's punishment for his withholding information from her and the others. He knew if they found out he had been speaking with Morgorth and the Blooded, it would cause even more problems.

"She offered you a chance to assume her position within the Circle?"

"Yes, but I have other business first."

"I understand, but you must know that you..." He paused. "We cannot miss this opportunity." Morgorth took another step forward. "The Children of the Blood have been a secret of this city for centuries. They still use the blood; look at what they did to you. But they never tell us why."

Falden's head jerked up. *They do not know of the Faithless.* "I understand your confusion, but I must go."

"No!" It started out as a command, but turned into a plea. "Please—wait. We can help you in your task. We only seek an ally in the Circle. We have no voice."

"And what do you offer for this alliance?" Falden looked around. They were living in a ruin. There was no sign of anything of value.

"We are like you. We understand the blood, maybe as well as the Circle." He lifted a large object from a nearby table. "This is our masterwork. We give it to you." He handed the object to Falden.

Falden concentrated for a moment then a light appeared over his head. The book was bound in thick black leather. He placed it back on the table and let his hands examine the edges of the pages before opening it. They were thicker than normal paper and the last few held a golden shine to them. He lifted the cover and gasped. Arcane symbols were etched into golden dragon scales. He turned the pages to find more and more spells written on the pages. The last pages of the book were sheets of pressed gold. He looked up at Morgorth.

"One of the Blooded can inscribe the pages with his own blood. The book provides runic symbols for every one of the regularly taught spells of the Academy. It is yours."

"An impressive gift, but why? Only for the hope of having a voice in the Circle?"

"We have waited for decades hoping one of us would be granted an opportunity to advance to the Circle, but we are not permitted; only graduates of the Academy may seek such. We have never been allowed within. When I heard of your audience, I sent my watchers. When she talked to you this morning, she said you could challenge her for her position. Has she promised this?"

"Yes, but you knew that," Falden said. "Or you would never have offered this."

"Yes, but it is nothing compared to that which we ask of you if you can take the seat," Morgorth said. "You would be the only Blooded. You will be challenged from below many times. You will not sit for long as the wizards seek to oust you. We ask that you bring the existence of the Blooded to the surface. We ask that the Circle face justice for what they have done."

"To have justice, you need only find the proper authority," Falden whispered.

"True, but they control who can become a judge and who can rule in their courts. None will hear us."

Falden looked at him for a moment and frowned. "Does not Tormasus and Gormanghast have a treaty that makes them the sole cities of the New Gorman Empire?"

"Yes, the Circle has kept the Tormasians from riting any judges for decades and the existing ones will not hear our case," Morgorth said.

Falden smiled. "I will bring you your judge; a judge from the Tormasian Arena itself. A judge who would dare pass judgment on a god. He will face the Circle. Let them explain to him how this serves the Order."

Morgorth stared at him, his eyes wide with hope. "You know such a man?"

"Oh yes," Falden said with a nod. "I must go." He picked up the book to leave.

"Please stay. I did not realize you offered more than we could have hoped for." He removed his cloak and handed it to Falden. "It enhances my powers. It is yours."

Falden held up his hand to refuse the cloak, but Morgorth draped it over his arm and took a step back. He decided to not insult Morgorth and nodded his thanks. "I must go," he said again. "There is still much I need to do to prepare for this journey."

"You need allies?" Morgorth asked. "We know many."

Falden tilted his head to the side as he waited for him to continue.

"For decades we have scoured the planes for aid. We have a library full of information on the infernal, celestial and elemental. Let us help you."

Falden nodded. This was the type of help he had wanted to gain from the Academy. The type of aid he had been refused, even with the Circle sanctioning his task. "Lead on," he said. He still had some time before he had to be back in Irrmar; he would use it wisely.

Chapter Six
Nirev

Nirev walked the stone streets of Domar, the Dwarven city that stood guard at the great pass through the Dragonspire Mountains. They were all that stood between the Malavian Dominion and the Dh'Mark Realms. The smoke the previous evening had clearly shown him the gates of the city. It was said the gates could stand against even dragons. He smiled at that thought. He had seen more dragons in the last few weeks than the populace of Shokar had spotted in many years. What would his brothers think if they heard he traveled with not one but two dragon warriors? And would continue to travel with one of those when they entered the Abyss.

He was unsure of where to go within the city; the vision had not been specific—the gates had been discernable, but nothing else. He was near the center of the city now as he wandered the streets, hoping something would give him a sign he was where he needed to be. The human district was to the south and the gnomes and halflings were to the east. *Who or what be I looking for?*

"Mulog has called him," he heard a voice say. He turned to look for the speaker and saw a large crowd gathered to the west in front of a building carved into the mountain itself. He studied the carvings and statuary in front of the building. Tools and weapons etched into the stone created a frame around the large stone doors. To one side was a statue of Mulog and to the other was Tharlin. This was the Master Guild House, the true seat of power in Domar. He worked his way through the crowd close enough to see a body laid in state at the entrance to the House. The burial shroud fluttered in the breeze and he felt the whisper of a storm in the air. *I be here*, he thought.

He turned to the person on his right. "I have been away from the city for too long, what great person is honored here?"

"Sturm Giantbreaker, High Priest and First Hammer of Mulog. Some even say he was Mulog's blessed servant. May lightning show him the way and thunder announce his arrival to Mulog."

"His blessed servant," Nirev whispered. "How did he fall?"

The other dwarf seemed to study him for a moment. "In combat of course." He turned back to his contemplation of the body. "However, it be not a giant, dragon or even an ogre that took his life." He paused and spit on the ground. "It be said he be killed by an elf."

"An elf?" Nirev took a step back. It was rare one of that race could stand in combat against a dwarf; they were not fierce fighters, preferring to attack from shadows with their arrows. Yes, he had seen Kyrianna stand with her dual blades to face their enemies, but that was with others at her back. He did not believe she would last long in direct combat by herself. It would have been bad enough if the First Hammer had fallen to a human, but to have fallen before an elf. A dwarf preferred to die at the hands of a towering enemy; a testament to the tenacity and strength needed to drag one of them from the realm of the living. To die at the hands of an elf brought no glorious titles or songs in the taverns. "Does this great enemy of Mulog and dwarves have a name?" Nirev's hand tightened on the haft of his maul.

"I would rather not say," he said.

"Why?" Nirev stared at the other dwarf.

"The priests have said it be an ill omen and should not be repeated."

"I need to speak to the priests. Where be the temple to Mulog?"

Nirev frowned as the other dwarf turned to face him, his face lined with fear and sadness. "The temple be gone."

Nirev took a step back jostling several others as he regained his balance.

"Gone? The temple of strength and battle gone? How?"

One of the others nodded toward the body of the First Hammer. "It took us a day to clear the rubble. They fought to a standstill in the temple's main hall. The First Hammer would not let himself be dishonored by fleeing and allowing the temple to crumple. He fought hard and well, but to no avail."

Nirev straightened his shoulders. "I will see the temple for myself." The second dwarf pointed to the west. "There be no mistaking it."

~ * ~

Nirev stopped and stared at the remains of temple. What had

once been a grand building dedicated to strength, was now only a loose pile of rocks and debris. He had hoped to find guidance in making this trip as he had been directed; instead he only found devastation. There were several dwarves working to remove the rocks and debris. "Have all of the priests and worshippers been found?" he called.

Several of the workers looked up in shock. "Yes, though almost all were killed in the collapse," one said. "Ye are a priest." He knelt in front of Nirev. "I am ashamed I did not perish by his side."

Nirev looked down at the brand on the dwarf's arm. He was a novice of the church. Unlike the Church of Hellavar, no titles were given when one first entered into Mulog's service. A title was considered too high of an honor for one who had yet to prove himself.

"I would speak to yer elder," Nirev said. "Take me to him."

"My apologies," the novice said as he stood, his head still bowed. "When I present ye to the elder, what should I tell him be yer name and title?"

Nirev paused. He had taken the mantle of Mulog during his time at the Duvall Estate and had yet to visit a temple to be formally ordained. His title should be Anvil, a tried and proven devotee to the Lord of Storms, but how could he hold that title without the approval of a priest? "I am Nirev. He who has faced Ballan's Chosen and seen her dragged back to the Abyss. He who goes to that vile goddess' realm to rescue a cleric of Hellavar. Tell him that."

"I be honored to serve ye, Nirev," the novice said. "Though I have yet to earn a title, I be called Velrek." He turned and led Nirev through the streets to a large house.

Nirev ignored the family in the great room as he and Velrek entered the house. He had never been one to care about courtesy and today he was here on business. A temple of Mulog had been attacked and destroyed. If they were offended, so be it.

Elder was a good description of the priest Velrek presented him to. The one before him was easily older than some of the buildings in the city. "Corinor, a priest of Mulog has come from outside the city," Velrek said bowing deeply before the elder dwarf. "His name be Nirev, and he says he faced Ballan's Chosen in battle and goes soon to the Abyss to free the Cleric of Hellavar."

Corinor motioned for Velrek to leave. "Nirev, speak and speak quickly," he said. "Tharlin's priests have done what they can, but my body fails me regardless of any magical cures. Resare calls this aged body to its final rest."

"Who did this sacrilege?"

"Seal the doorway from prying eyes and ears," Corinor said.

Nirev paused for a moment, then glanced at the door and back at Corinor.

"Be ye a priest or be ye not?" Corinor stared at him, a challenge burned in his dark eyes. "Silence the doorway and cover it in darkness."

"My apologies, Elder. I found Mulog not by proper training in the church, but instead by faith in his strength as I called on him in my many recent battles." Nirev bowed his head as he chanted the respective spells and laid them on the door. He cursed his lack of comfort with the power Mulog had given him. Brular had wielded his power with skill and guile while he barely knew how to control it and knew even less about the guiding of another's faith, even his own.

"So ye found yer power outside the church," Corinor said. "That be good, Nirev. The church has grown weak, but maybe ye are the one. Maybe ye are his next Hammer."

Nirev stared at the Elder. "Weak? Ye speak blasphemy. If ye had the strength to wield a weapon, I would force ye to defend yer heresy."

"Say what ye will. Look at the strength of the church and all ye will see be its weaknesses. The Anvils and Hammers seek adoration and respect from the masses. That be a job for the likes of Thedrin, Mykaylene, Jocal and the other weaklings of Thedrin's court. Mulog be about deeds and competition. Even our temple's greatest champion be unable to defend his temple. What a statement on the atrophy of our worshippers and priests."

"I will avenge this wrong!" Nirev pulled his maul from his belt and slapped it against his hand. "I will find this elf and pound him into the rock itself." His grip on his maul tightened and he heard the wood creak in protest.

"Good. Anger be strength and rage be prayer, but that be not enough. Go to the temple. There be a room below the ground level you must see."

"I will, Elder. However, first I will have a name for this killer of the First Hammer."

Corinor lay back and took several deep breaths before he spoke. "Godfeller."

~ * ~

Nirev paused as he approached the ruins of the temple. This time he looked at it as Corinor had suggested—looking for its strengths. All he saw were weakness. Only weakness in the structure would have resulted in this kind of devastation. Other than the altar, no area of the temple had been left intact. He began searching for the most likely place for the stairs to be and began working his way through the rubble. In the corner, behind and to the left of the altar he saw a depression in the scattered pieces of wall, which could mean there was nothing solid supporting it. He grabbed the largest of the rocks and tossed it aside as he tried to clear the stairs. Even as he worked, he could see the cracks in the floor that went down to the very foundations of the church. *Weak.*

He looked at the stone that blocked his path. He was not weak. He raised his maul. "By your strength," he cried. He felt a slight vibration in the handle of his weapon as he slammed it against the rock. A cloud of dust rose from the shattered rock and Nirev again slammed his maul down. This time, thunder echoed as the rock gave way and a path down the stairs was cleared.

Nirev knelt to peer down the darkened stairs and reached for his coin pouch. He pulled a bit of copper from the pouch as he chanted the words of a light spell. Lightning crashed around him and he dropped the coin before the spell was completed. What was he doing? He was here to see if he had indeed been chosen to be the next First Hammer. Careful planning was the province of those who, like Myrith followed Mykaylene. "Let my enemies face me in the dark, and then Mulog in the sky." He jumped into the darkness with his maul held close against his chest. He landed on his feet and his weapon came up, but no one challenged him. He looked around and saw the outline of a hallway. "A good place to start," he said.

He moved through the hallway and passed several doors. He did not bother to open or try them. He needed to find the starting point to the hall. True, he worshipped Mulog and he relished combat, but Mulog preferred his combats with progression to their challenges. Just swinging madly in a hallway as the doors opened had its thrill, but how would that sound in the mead halls? He smiled as he wondered if Hendandra would write an epic of their journey against Thynitic. That would be glorious. Not only a story, but a prayer to Mulog and the other gods involved. However, she would most likely leave out the Lady of the Mists. That one had a streak almost as mean as Thynitic. *Perhaps the Lord of Storms has some influence with the mists. I will have to ask if the opportunity presents itself.*

He found the beginning of the hallway and nodded. "There you be. Now where did the Elder say to go? To the right and two doors down." He proceeded as he had been instructed, but found only one door.

"The Elder be old; however he be not likely to forget his way." He studied the wall carefully. "Ah," he muttered. "A test be it?" He let his gaze trace the darkness. "Well hidden, but in time." He worked his hands along the wall. "There you be." A loud creak resonated in the hall as a section of the wall pulled out.

He entered the room and approached a large block of granite. "Sturm Giantbreaker, the Ninth Scion of Mulog," he read the inscription aloud. He turned to look at a second block that sat next to the crypt. "The Tenth Scion."

"This be strange." He walked around the block. It appeared to be set into the floor. He tapped it with his maul and was flung across the room. He frowned and placed his hands on the block. "By your strength," he called as he pushed on the granite. It moved less than a thumbs breath, but it did move. "A test of strength be it, my Lord?"

He bent low and wrapped his arms as far around the block as he could and strained against the weight. The block moved only a fraction from its seat then resettled. "Of course it would not be that easy." He placed his legs wide and summoned images of Kyrianna as she had hung in the chains in Torliana's chamber. Images of Andrinor and Falden writhing in agony after Kyrianna had called on Thynitic to prove her power. And finally an image of the demoness who had held Kyrianna as hostage while she threatened the group. That one had said something to Myrith that had disturbed the knight he was sworn to follow. "It has to stop!" He felt his rage take him and he embraced the block again. "By Mulog's will and my hand." The block scraped against the stone as he pulled it up and free. He hurled it to the side.

He looked inside the shallow depression he had uncovered and nodded.

He had been given his sign. A war hammer had been sealed and left for the tenth Scion. He cast the spell that would let him see any enchantments placed on the weapon and felt his stomach lurch when he did not see any. "No," he muttered as exhaustion hit him and he sat on the floor.

A heavy rumble brought his focus back. Mulog was speaking. He was speaking not only to him, but to all of Domar. Another clap of thunder echoed in the ruins of the temple. Nirev looked at the crypt. "He has come to see you off and to usher me in," he said.

He glanced again at the hammer. Brular, who had summoned efreeti and even the avatar of a god not his own, had said power was always there—just not the will to use it.

"Not today, Brular. Today and for long as I need it, there be the will." He reached down and grabbed the hammer. It was made of adamantine. "As hard as Mulog's muscles," he said with a smile.

He returned the way he came and found Velrek by the temple's entrance. "Bring the First Hammer."

"Nirev, it be the custom he be buried on the fourth day."

Nirev pointed to the sky, which crackled with lightning. "Do ye not hear the call? Mulog beckons him to his side and me to his service. Bring Sturm Giantbreaker. Bring him now!"

Velrek charged off, yelling for assistance. *Leave that task to him*, Nirev thought. He looked at the altar. "No, this will not do. Mulog's servant of the sky, come to me." His command was answered by a small whirlwind. "Remove the dust from the altar..." He stopped and looked around. "However, leave everything else untouched." It was appropriate the temple be shown as decayed and battered, but the altar would show reverence.

Soon a procession arrived at the temple gates. There were several angry faces. "What be this madness? Ye have not the right." They were all speaking at once.

"It be not my summoning, but his." He pointed the war hammer to the sky and thunder erupted. Many of the group gasped, but still more looked at him with loathing. *Good*, he thought. *It be not me they really loathe, but their weak faith.*

"Simple tricks," a voice called from the crowd. "Many priests are able to call lightning."

"I did not call it." He pitched his voice low like the coming storm. "It calls me."

A hand went up from one of the Elders in the crowd. "Great words, but they are only that."

Nirev turned back to the ruined temple. "Those of ye who have no fear of his wrath enter and bear the First Hammer. We will give ye yer proof."

"We?"

Nirev walked into the ruins and simply raised his hammer to the sky.

Only a third of the group followed him into the church, but they stayed near the back. He could see Velrek behind the group. "Mulog, we have much work to do," he whispered. "But it appears they need a sign." The thunder boomed and he looked skyward. "Yes, my Lord. Not a sign; a beacon."

Nirev took a deep breath and projected his voice so even those who had remained outside could hear him clearly. "Ye think ye understand the Lord of Storms. Ye be wrong! This church was not destroyed these days past. It has been crumbling from within for centuries. The First Hammers have failed ye. Even more importantly, they have failed Him!"

"This be blasphemy," one of the Elders called out. "You should be struck dead where you stand."

Nirev turned his head to the sky and raised his hammer. Brular's words again echoed in his mind: *There is always power, just not the will.*

He nodded. *Today there be the will,* he thought. He raised his voice. "Mulog, he be correct. I have challenged the church and therefore I have challenged ye." Another deep breath as his voice projected even louder than the thunder shaking the city. "I call upon yer wrath, Lord of Storms."

He gave his body and soul over to Mulog as the lightning came. The bolt struck him as he stood next to the altar. He could feel the tingling and burning as the energy surged through him. The brightness almost took his sight from him, but he could still see the sky. Several smaller bolts had joined together as they streaked through the clouds to form a web of crackling energy. A web that took shape above the ruins of the church—a hammer: Mulog's hammer.

He heard the crowd gasp as he stood and looked at the altar. It had not been he who had cracked against Mulog's power, but the altar. He glanced back out over the group; all were kneeling in prayer; some to Mulog's might, others in fear.

"Enough!" Nirev shouted. "Yer faith be as weak and decayed as this church. It be time the First Hammer be laid in his tomb and buried in and with this temple."

Velrek stepped forward. "But what of the church?"

Nirev frowned at the novice. "The church be nothing more than a building, which be built upon faith. If there be no faith, how can a church stand?

"First ye must rebuild yer faith, then I will rebuild this church. Move quickly." Thunder shook what was left of the walls. "Mulog grows impatient." It was Velrek who led the others out of the temple and returned carrying the body of the First Hammer. Nirev only pointed with his war hammer toward the stairs when the group paused and looked at him.

"It be done," Velrek said when the group returned.

"By the strength Mulog has given me, I claim the title of First Hammer." He looked over the group and saw their nods of acknowledgement. "Now, leave, lest Mulog smite ye as well as this temple."

He waited until all, except Velrek, had left. "I must send ye into the world to find yer strength. Ye will go alone, without even a church to call upon." Nirev handed him his maul. "However, I give ye a stout weapon and the knowledge Mulog be strong in this world and not just the next. Go, Velrek, and find yer strength."

Velrek knelt. "No!" He looked up at the sky. "I will not leave my First Hammer." His head dropped. "Not again," he whispered.

Nirev placed a hand on Velrek's shoulder. "Ye have taken yer first step, Anvil." He turned his head to the sky. "Anvil Velrek shall stand as yer witness." Thunder answered his call.

Nirev walked to the center of the room and looked down at a set of footprints that had been burned into the stone; longer and narrower than a dwarf's. He had not seen Kyrianna leave any footprints in the places they had walked together, but knew hers would be similar to these. *I will finish what Godfeller started*, he thought. *However, it be not a sacrilege, it be the start of a reformation.*

He raised his hammer. "Come, Mulog. This church's stone and I challenge ye. Smite us both and see which will fail and which be the true servant of yer will."

Lightning crackled and struck. He embraced the pain brought to him by Mulog and felt his knee hit the stone; again it was the stone that cracked. What felt like hours as the tingling and burning sensation crawled over and through him, was only a few heartbeats of time. His hands burned against the metal handle of his war hammer. He looked up as lightning continued to dance around the walls of the temple.

"I can help ye," Velrek said as he placed a hand on Nirev's arm. "I can shield ye in part from the lightning."

"No!"

Velrek took a step back. "Ye don't want my help, First Hammer?"

"No." He held his head high as he raised his hammer toward the sky. "Does one shield himself from his god? No, he embraces." He stood and looked at Velrek.

Velrek moved away.

"Mulog, I still be here, as be this temple. I grow weary, not from yer assault, but from boredom. Lord of Storms, show me yer power and show me I either be worthy of yer blessing or yer final judgment—but show me now."

Lightning danced in a crisscross pattern across the sky gathering strength.

Nirev glanced at Velrek who approached and knelt at his side. "Mulog, yer Hammer and Anvil await."

~ * ~

There was only one stone left intact when the lightning faded. The stone where the First Hammer stood. While his own clothes were scorched with the power of the lightning, not a mark was to be seen on Velrek.

"The stories they will tell in the taverns of this day," Velrek said as he stood. He pointed to where the only prints left in the stone were those of the First Hammer; the marks left by Godfeller were gone.

Nirev could only nod. Tomorrow he would return to the Coliseum in Irrmar. Tonight he would rest, here in the place that had been resanctified by the strength and power of Mulog.

Chapter Seven
Hendandra

Hendandra arrived with Falden at the Wayfinder port in Raspa. She shook her head as he immediately teleported back to the Coliseum. The clerk sitting at the desk waited patiently as she fought the wave of nausea and dizziness that hit her again. This was worse than the portal that had dumped her back in Shokar from that planar temple where she had met Myrith and Kyrianna.

The clerk held up a small vial. "To clear the remaining effects," he said.

"Thank you." She took the vial and gulped the contents, before her trembling hand could drop it. She waited a few more seconds to be sure the potion had taken effect then set the vial on the clerk's desk. "What is the fee?" she asked.

"The port fee is one hundred gold—that includes the potion," he said. She dropped several gems on the clerk's desk. "That should cover it."

"It is about twice the fee." He held up a small ruby.

Hendandra smiled. "Thank you." She took the gem and dropped it back in her pouch. She couldn't believe she had made that large of a mistake. She had intended to give the clerk a little extra for being polite and waiting until she was coherent before asking for the port fee, but not that much.

She smiled again, then hurried out of the port station and to her house.

~ * ~

It took her almost three hours to make her way to the modest house she had purchased just two weeks prior. Her previous house having been seized for failure to pay taxes. *A nice soft bed will do me good*, she thought.

"Leikor's cursed luck. What happened?" She stopped and stared at the huge hole in the north side of the building. The kitchen was clearly visible through the opening.

She shook her head as she walked around the house, looking for additional damage. "Gods of Shokar!" She stopped again. The back of the house was burned, the wall charred and crumbling. In the middle of the wall was the outline of a tall creature with four arms.

"Hendandra?" a voice called from around the corner.

"Vela?"

The woman stepped around the corner, her arms wrapped around her chest. "It was awful. First the city guard came and went through your house and asked all kinds of questions. They wanted to know if you knew any spellcasters or had ever used any powerful magics. Then they showed up." Her body shook as she nodded toward the outline on the wall.

Hendandra felt her eyes go wide. "You mean there was more than one?"

"There were only two." Her trembling was growing worse. "It was horrible. They moved about as if the soldiers were just annoying insects. When a mage showed up to assist, they…" She started to cry.

"I need to know."

"The guards' weapons were absolutely useless against them, and the arrival of the mage only seemed to provoke them. They killed them all! Even the mage couldn't escape."

"Surely the guard sent reinforcements."

Vela stared at her. "They died in moments. The thing's size hides great speed." Her voice broke and she looked away. "I'm sorry; I have never seen that type of carnage. One shattered the body of one of the guards by squeezing him between his four hands."

"I will go speak to the guard and find out more," Hendandra said.

"No! They believe you are in league with the creatures." She paused and took a breath. "You're wanted. You cannot stay here." Another pause. "Besides that, what if they return?"

Now, I am outcast when all I ever wanted was a home.

"Wait here," she said. "I need to get something." Hendandra entered what was left of the house to find the chimney still intact. She hadn't had time to commission a proper craftsman to make changes to her house, but she had found a decent hiding place under the chimney's slates. She slid the slate away to see the bags she had left there before Ferdinand had returned her to the group. *Good,* she thought.

She picked up the smaller bag of coins the group had collected. The heavy weight was reassuring in her hand. *I have to leave, but maybe a coin or two for Vela is in order. It won't hurt me and it should help her to forget I was here.* She opened the bag and removed a couple of coins. With care she retied the knot in her normal complex pattern.

She set the coins aside and reached for the second bag, the one that had been filled with gems and jewelry. Her hand froze about three inches from the bag. *That isn't my knot.* Her hand shook as she pulled the bag up and untied the strings. "Leikor's cursed luck!" She crushed the cheap paste copies she pulled out of the bag.

She dumped several more stones out of the bag. "All paste? How?" She glanced at a small wooden coin that lay on the floor. Carved on the surface was the shifting veil of Rhyra. She threw the coin across the room and took a deep breath.

It wasn't all gone. The house and her reputation were gone, but she still had a fraction of the wealth she had secured. She felt her fists clench tightly. Compared to the value of the gems Rhyra had taken from her, the coins she had left were barely equal to a finder's fee. Rhyra wasn't being nice leaving them either; the Lady of the Mists was mocking her.

"I hate you, Rhyra," Hendandra said. "More than I hate Thynitic. At least she does not pretend to be a willing and kind friend."

"Hendandra," Vela called. "Guards come. This is not part of their normal rounds. They may know you're here."

Hendandra stood as tears flowed from her eyes and threw the bag of fakery against the stones of the chimney. The sound of the paste shattering gave her little satisfaction, but it was something.

"This is for you." She pressed three of the gold coins into Vela's hand as she left the ruins of her house.

"You were never here," Vela said.

Hendandra nodded then darted into the shadows as she headed back to the Wayfinder's port. *The isle of Justula can't be any worse than here*, she thought.

~ * ~

The chamber swirled and changed into a carpet of green. Hendandra dropped to her knees as her stomach rebelled against the second teleport within the same day. She leaned forward and gagged several times as she fought to keep her breakfast down—she lost.

No one had told her they would be leaving today and she had indulged herself at breakfast that morning. She grinned as she realized Kyrianna was probably suffering the same problem.

What an absolutely pathetic day, she thought. *Gods, I am glad neither Myrith nor Andrinor can see me like this. They would never allow me to come with them if they did.* She didn't understand what was going on with Myrith. The woman had been very clear she didn't like or trust Hendandra, but had become very protective after they brought Kyrianna back from the Abyss, almost insisting Hendandra not go with them. Hendandra had surprised herself by demanding to be allowed to go and Myrith had relented by saying she could not stop someone from risking their life to protect another.

The trip home had cost her time and then after losing so much of her wealth, she had to pay a fee of one thousand gold to get the Wayfinders to send her here. Brular had helped the halflings here over sixty years ago, and she believed the vision meant they would help her. *Help? I find I need it more and more as this trip continues.* She checked her pack for the rod Myrith had given her to get back to the Coliseum. It was still secure.

She coughed to clear her throat then took a drink of water from her canteen to rinse the taste from her mouth. She started to spit, stopped and swallowed hard instead.

The thick jungle, definitely not a forest, hid its predators well, but her eyes were sharper than most. A long, narrow, reptilian head was looking at her from only twenty feet away. She had to look up from her kneeling position as it stepped forward. The creature was almost eight feet tall—taller than Vyroris. Its skin was a blend of several muted greens, giving it excellent camouflage. It opened its mouth to hiss and she shuddered at the long pointed teeth in the creature's mouth. Even as the reptile held her attention, she caught movement to her right and left; it was not alone. Her hand went slowly to her rapier and she suppressed a laugh. A rapier against this thing? These things? It was not a pleasant thought. She tried to study the creature, hoping to find a weak spot where she might be able to attack it. Her gaze only shifted between its teeth and the hooklike inner claw on its legs.

Maybe this was a bad idea.

The creature jerked its head up and was now looking past her. She heard the trees behind her rustle and the ground tremble. Even though she didn't want to take her gaze off the threat in front of her, she found herself turning to look behind her.

Gods of Shokar, where have I taken myself! The creature coming out of the jungle reminded her of a bear. A bear with much longer legs and a more rectangular head.

There was another hiss and she turned back to see the reptiles disappearing into the jungle. *They fear this thing so much they leave their dinner without a fight.* She swallowed hard. "I don't need to ask Kyri what that means," she whispered.

The thing moved closer, though it did not seem to be threatening her. *Maybe it has poor vision. Just don't move.* Its long arms could easily reach her now. It paused and sniffed the air then lowered its head and growled at her.

Time to go! She moved to get up, but the thing was on top of her, literally. Its claws caught her and knocked her to the ground. She was surprised they didn't pierce her skin. The thing placed one of its paws on top of her, again not driving its claws through her skin, only pinning her to the ground. It raised its head and roared.

She was confused by the creature's actions, but knew staying where she was wouldn't be a good thing. She slipped from between its claws and rolled a few feet away. "Leikor's cursed luck," she muttered as the thing slapped her back to the ground. This time, it pressed harder as it held her down. *Please break the rod,* she thought. *Please break the rod.*

A male voice said something in a halfling dialect she didn't understand. The paw relaxed a little. The voice came again, this time in the human tongue. "Human, why do you dare to come to Justula?"

Hendandra turned her head to speak, but could not see anyone from where she lay on the ground. "I have come to speak to the chiefs of the island."

"Then you have come a long way to die." The voice while soft was harsh and confident in its statement. "You even use foul magics to come to the island. I have seen no ship or boat and your tracks begin only feet from where you lay."

"I care not what you think; I will speak to the chiefs." Hendandra tried to muster all of the confidence she could as she spoke, but knew it fell short.

"No, human, race that enslaves, vile beings who steal our children, you can speak to the elder spirits once you enter their world." The voice lapsed back into the halfling dialect.

Hendandra didn't understand the single phrase that was spoken, but its meaning became clear as the thing holding her applied pressure to her back and lowered its head to sniff her.

"Please." Her voice was small in her ears. "I am a friend of Brular Eglis, the one who stopped those ships decades ago. Please let me speak." The nose of the creature was cold against her skin as it opened its mouth. It stopped, its teeth grazing her neck as it raised its head slightly. Its breath was still hot on her skin.

"Speak, human. That one is long dead and your voice is young, too young to know the Lawgiver."

"He is not dead! He needs help as he is trapped in a most foul place. I came here to seek aid in rescuing him."

The weight lifted and she slipped from beneath the paw and stood. Her rapier came to her hand with the tip aimed at the source of the voice. He was only a few inches taller than three feet and she actually looked down on him. She hadn't had to look down at a person in what felt like ages.

Her sword was only inches from the skin of his neck, but he didn't flinch. His brown eyes seemed to study her for a moment as they grew wide. "You are human?"

She smiled. "I get that a lot. I am human, but far shorter than most. I have pretended to be a halfling once or twice." She glanced at the creature that had been holding her and nodded as it watched, but maintained its distance. "Throw down your weapons," she said.

The small man smirked at her. "I carry none." His gaze went to her blade. "It is your kind who settle things with your accursed steel."

Her gaze took in the man and she saw he was wearing only a leather jerkin and short pants. He did not even carry a walking stick.

"How can you not be armed with those big reptiles about?"

"You consider them large? You are in for a surprise, little human."

"Enough of this," Hendandra twitched the rapier as she pressed it forward against his neck. "Tell your large friend to leave."

His eyes were impassive as he stared at her. She was about to tell him again when the large beast moved back into the jungle.

"It is done, master," he said with another smirk. "Do you enjoy your power?"

Hendandra paused at the mocking tone in the halfling's voice. He had no weapons, his pet was gone and she held his life at the tip of her rapier. She looked at his face as the breeze ruffled his dirty brown hair. She didn't understand it, but she felt fear growing inside her. She wasn't really a coward as the others teased her about being; she was just smart enough to know when she was seriously in danger of dying. After all it was better to live to fight another day than to die in a pointless show of bravery that meant nothing after she was gone.

She saw his gaze move to the jungle and she followed it to see the large reptiles had returned. Their heads moved as they looked at her then at the halfling before they focused their attention on her and took a step forward.

She didn't take her gaze off the reptiles. "Command them to stop," she said.

"I cannot," he said. "I never commanded them to come." He paused as the reptiles took another step. "They are hungry and they sense a kill. They smell your scent," he paused and took a deep breath, "and your fear."

"They don't come toward you," she said. "Why?" She was surprised to not see her rapier shaking as she raised it toward the lead reptile. "Never mind, they obviously fear your pet." She watched as the reptiles took another step. "What do I need to do?"

She turned away from the reptiles and toward the halfling.

"Maybe it's not fear they smell," he said. He looked at her rapier. "Drop your weapon." His right hand came up toward her. "And take my hand."

She stared at him for a moment. She had known many liars in her life, and even considered herself proficient at the art; however he did not seem to have that in him. Her gaze went back to the reptiles and she realized she had no other choice. She dropped the sword and grabbed his hand as they sprinted toward her. She felt a spark of power as their hands touched and she gave her life into his control. He yanked her behind him as he stepped past her and put himself between her and the charging reptiles.

Her mouth dropped open as they stopped only a few feet from the halfling. They hissed, but she didn't see him react in any way. She found it hard to move as he pulled her forward and took a step toward the reptiles. However the surprise she felt at seeing the creatures stop was minor compared to what she experienced at seeing them jump back nearly ten feet as he took another step.

They hissed again then melted back into the jungle.

It made no sense. He was only a halfling and he carried no weapons; why would a predator run from him?

"Hey." She reached for her rapier as he picked it up and threw it into the jungle. "I need that." She pulled her hand away from his.

"Why? Has it served you well so far—here?"

Hendandra opened her mouth, but stopped as the ground shook. She turned toward the crunching underbrush and saw a creature that dwarfed the earlier reptiles. Its mouth had teeth the size of large daggers. "Dragon?" she whispered.

"Not dragon, a thunder lizard," he said. "The others that were here are called sickle claws." His voice was calm as if there were no danger.

Hendandra glanced toward the area where her sword had vanished and pulled her hand away from his.

"Go get your weapon of steel if you believe it will help you."

She slipped her hand back in his and took a step closer to him as his fingers closed around hers. She didn't understand it, but he had a sense about him she had seen in few people. Myrith had it, Andrinor basked in it and Brular radiated it. It was the confidence that no matter the enemy, they would prevail. She found that thought comforting as the thunder lizard sniffed the air then turned away from them.

"Come, my village is this way." He started to move away, but stopped as she refused to move.

"My sword first," she said.

"I will wait here." He relaxed his grip on her hand.

Hendandra looked toward the jungle then took a small step toward him.

His hand closed on hers again and he started toward the east.

She was surprised he maintained a comfortable walking pace and even walked beside her instead of dragging her along.

"Tell me about the Lawgiver," he said after several minutes of silence.

"It would take far longer than a few minutes to explain. Much of it I would not believe myself."

"The walk is long. I would hear this tale. I find it interesting a human, such as you, shows courage in front of the thunder lizard and the sickle claws."

"Courage? That is something my friends would never attribute to me. Not that I think what I did was courageous either. Besides, you gave me no choice. There are many who would say dropping my weapon was a sure sign of cowardice."

"You put your trust in another—that is courage. Your actions saved your life—that shows wisdom. You will be the first human to visit my village in the time I have been alive." He paused and smiled at her. "That shows your power."

Hendandra took a deep breath then told him what she could about what had happened at Mount Veri and how Torliana had damned Brular to an eternity of torture. From there she told him how Brular and her companions had ventured through the pocket plane Torliana had created.

"He forgave her for what she did to the temple of Hellavar?"

"Yes. He saw through his blind hatred and need for retribution to see the truth he had been blinded to earlier. She was in love with him and it was her perception that he had rejected her which gave Thynitic the power to turn her on him and the temple."

"And Hellavar allowed this? Surely he would have wanted Torliana punished for her crimes as well. The Lawgiver failed to follow his wishes."

Hendandra shook her head. "That I cannot answer. When Brular confronted Torliana and forgave her, he was dragged away to the Abyss by Thynitic's demons." She went on to tell him about the group's fight and the journey to the Abyss to rescue Kyrianna from Thynitic.

"A terrible tragedy," he said. "Your plea for assistance must start with my father. If you can convince him, the others will assist as well."

"Then I need to talk to him immediately."

"No! You carry too much of the outside world with you. My father lost his mother to those slavers. It is taboo to have, let alone wear metal of any kind here. The make of your clothing will not sit well with him either."

"This is absurd." She stopped and put her hands on her hips as she glared at the halfling.

"It matters not what you think." He stopped at a small hut. "Rega," he called.

A halfling woman appeared at the doorway.

"Please see that…" He stopped and turned toward her. "What is your name?"

"Hendandra." Her gaze went from her escort to the woman

and back.

He smiled. "Have her washed and dressed properly to see the chief."

"She is human. She should be put to the sea."

Hendandra could see this was not going to be an easy task for her, but then she doubted the others would have done any better.

"She will see the chief," he said. "Do not allow anyone to interfere."

"As you wish, Feric."

Hendandra followed Rega to a secluded pool where she was told to remove her clothes and jewelry. She started to protest then stopped as she realized it would be useless to argue and she did not want to risk returning to the Coliseum and telling Myrith she had failed completely.

As she finished bathing, Rega brought her a dress. It was simple in its design, similar to the dress Rega herself was wearing. The back was open except for where straps tied it at the neck and across the shoulders. She slipped it on and frowned as it was a little short on her, stopping just above her knees, instead of just below them. She smoothed the fabric; it was soft and comfortable in the humid heat of the island. Rega had also removed her boots and replaced them with sandals.

Now, I definitely could pass for a halfling, she thought. Gone was everything that tied her to her former life as a thief. Well, almost. She slipped the pouch with what was left of her gold inside the dress.

"Follow me," Rega said after she was dressed.

The woman didn't wait for Hendandra to acknowledge her before she turned and headed into the village. Rega led her to a large house with fabric draped across the sides to keep the sun out while still allowing the breeze to blow through. An older halfling sat on a raised set of planks and looked up as she entered.

Hendandra bowed slightly. "I have come to ask your assistance in my mission to rescue the one you named Lawgiver from the pits of the Abyss." She forced herself to remain polite and respectful despite feeling this trip would be in vain.

"Speak," he said.

She again told the story of what she and the others had been through as well as what they had learned from Brular. She watched as sadness etched itself on his face and his eyes brightened slightly.

She was sure she saw a tear at the corner of one eye.

"Your tale is a sad one. The Lawgiver helped us much and his story is sure to touch the hearts of many," the chief said.

Hendandra felt a surge of hope as she looked up, only to have it dashed at his next words.

"However, you must leave here with nothing."

"Nothing!" She couldn't believe what she had just heard. "He worked to end the slave trade all those years ago. Nothing! What a heartless excuse for a leader you are. What of the debt you owe the Lawgiver for what he did?"

"The law given by the Lawgiver himself was clear. Justula shall not be a part of this world's foulness. We do not associate. We do not trade. It has been written. The Lawgiver would understand. You may rest here this night, but you must be gone with the coming day."

She just stood there and stared, not really seeing him. Her efforts had been wasted. She had failed. She closed her eyes to hold back the tears as she felt her lower lip start to quiver.

"You will not reconsider?" She heard Feric ask.

She opened her eyes to see the chief shake his head.

Hendandra turned and stormed out of the hut. She pushed the cloth aside wishing it had been an actual door she could slam. *All for nothing*, she thought. *Was this simply another joke by the gods at my expense?*

She sat on the sand of the beach and stared at the waves as she finally let the tears flow.

"What are you thinking about?" Feric's voice was soft and close behind her.

Leikor's cursed luck. How could I not hear him walking on the sand? She wiped her eyes, "Go away! You told him not to help me, didn't you?"

"I tried to help your cause. However, I know what the law is. He is a good man, though he will not budge from the law."

"A good man is trapped in the infernal pits. A man who would give part of his own life force to save another. That is my measure of a good man and your father is not one if he will not help Brular."

Feric was quiet for a long time. "You will be leaving soon," he finally said.

"Yes, I am just trying to figure out what I should tell my companions of your sorry chief and tribe."

"Before you pass judgment, I can show you more."

She sighed at the pleading tone she heard in his voice. *Wonderful. This little man has taken an interest. Wait, he is the chief's son; maybe I can use his interest to convince him to fight his father a little harder. At least returning with something, however small, would be better than nothing at all.* She stood up and brushed the sand off her legs. "Where would you suggest?"

He pointed to the west toward one of the mountains. "You can see a good part of the island from there."

She smiled. "Lead on then."

~ * ~

The jungle was thick and without a trail. Feric moved as easily as if he were walking on a street in Raspa. "Is there an easier way?" she called as she picked herself up for the second time.

He turned and whispered something in a language she had never heard before as he extended his hand toward hers. She let her fingers brush his and felt a tingle as they touched. He turned and darted into the underbrush.

"Hey, don't leave me alone." Her reflexes took hold and she took off only steps behind him. She dove into the foliage in pursuit. The thickness of the jungle had her following more by sound than sight, but she was not going to let him get away with leaving her behind.

The footfalls stopped and she froze where she was. Her ears told her nothing. *Is this a game? Or a trap?* She studied the foliage. The thinnest of outlines was visible and she had almost missed it. *He is good.*

She melted into the brush as well. As soon as she was comfortable with her concealment, she threw a high arcing rock at his position.

The rock bounced off Feric and she saw him look around before moving. She frowned as she lost sight of him. Several minutes later, she heard the slightest rustle of leaves behind her.

She tossed a handful of dirt behind her as she turned. "If you are done, can we go now? I am still waiting for the easier path."

He wiped his face as he stepped out from his cover and the entire area around him shimmered as he moved. "You need no path." He glanced back in the direction they had come from.

She looked as well and saw the branches and vines were a dense weave, but she had run through them. She smiled. "So your magic allows me to pass through the brush without hindrance."

She looked up toward the mountain. "You started this race." She turned on her heels with the agility of one who lived on the streets. "Can you keep up?" She sprinted into the dense foliage of the jungle.

She laughed as she heard Feric fall further and further behind her. Her footsteps slowed when she realized she had lost any sound of him behind her.

Losing him is probably not a good idea.

"I grant you the footrace."

She spun around to see Feric leaning against a tree. "How? There is no way you could have beaten me through the jungle. How did you get here?"

"There is more than one way to travel a path. Can you climb?" He pointed to the mountain.

She stared at him. "Climb? There is no path."

"Do humans need to change things everywhere they go? Our children climb the rocks for sport." He looked at her, tilted his head to the side and grinned. "You cannot?"

He hates humans, so he is pushing me to find a weakness. She turned toward him and kicked off her sandals. "Is there rope or am I expected to die if I fall?"

"The climb is easy this low. No one fears falling. Do you?"

She scanned the mountain; the climb was easily five hundred feet. Her anger at his pushing and taunting her was growing, but she forced it aside. To allow herself to be distracted by anger would be dangerous. Even a drop from half that distance could be deadly. She knew he wanted her to be afraid and she was, but even more, she hated him for taunting her.

She moved to the rock and found her handholds. "Fine. You coming?" She moved up to her next handhold and looked down at Feric who hadn't moved, but was smiling as he looked up at her.

Hendandra jumped down and stormed over to him. "You think you are climbing behind me." She smoothed her skirt.

He smiled and she knew she had guessed correctly. She kept her tone harsh to cover the amusement she felt. "Not today, little man. You want to climb, then you first."

He nodded then jumped up to grab his first handhold and began to climb.

Hendandra found his pace slow enough she was able to stay with him. She had a few missteps, but her longer stride aided her in moving to the surer crevices and outcroppings. She reached the ledge just seconds before Feric. Hendandra laughed. "Still too slow," she said.

Feric lifted himself from the edge and looked beyond her.

Hendandra turned to look down over the ocean and the sun sitting low on the horizon. She yawned then turned and sat down. "Is this what you wanted to show me?"

"Part of it. Look to your left."

She let her gaze travel to the valley where she saw several large reptiles moving in a swamp. As the sun moved lower, the colors radiating through the sky basked the valley in brilliant hues. "Quite beautiful," she whispered.

"All of my people find it to be so."

"Even with the sickle claws and thunder lizards?"

"Yes. The predators, we understand." He paused. "Not like your people."

"Feric, they were not my people."

"They were human. And they came to take us away to serve them." His tone was harsh, but she could hear a note of sadness under the anger.

She had helped to put to rest spirits trapped by another's evil actions and fought alongside a priest whose need for vengeance had led him down the darkest of paths, but in the end, he left that path in an effort to save the soul of his last student. The world was a confusing place, and she knew it could not be judged in simple terms of good and evil. "Feric," she finally said. "You should not judge someone by another's actions. I understand why you think all humans are evil, but it is not true."

He looked down at her for a moment. "So, when I leave this island tonight to follow my goddess' instructions, I will not find the vileness I have spoken of?"

She stared at him. "You're going to the mainland? Why and for how long?"

"All I know is I have been directed to go. What will I find?"

She looked out over the valley. "Honestly, you will find lands full of predators who will pick you clean. There are some who may help you, but many more will choose to deceive and use you."

"Are you one of those people, Hendandra?"

She turned back toward him and then dropped her head to hide her face.

"Yes."

"How will I fare in your world?"

"They will eat you alive."

"That would be interesting."

She turned to look down the cliff to the water almost a thousand feet below.

"Shall we continue higher?" Feric asked.

She looked up. The rock looked daunting. "Is it really that much more beautiful?"

"It rivals even Hendandra."

She smiled as she looked at him. "Can we at least use rope?"

"Of course. He lifted his jerkin and revealed a length of rope wound about his body.

She smiled as she watched him unwind himself from the rope and place it on the ground.

Feric took the rope and brought one end around her waist as he tightened and knotted it. He took his time checking his work and she felt his hand against her bare lower back.

At least he found a somewhat unique excuse to touch me. When she looked at the knots, she smiled and giggled.

"What is it?" Feric seemed concerned as he checked the knots again.

"I was just thinking about a friend of mine who likes ropes." The confused look on his face made her laugh harder.

He stopped and smiled. "This is the first time I have heard you laugh." He started to make a large loop with the rope.

"There has been little to laugh at of late."

He stepped in front of her and grabbed the rope at her waist. "Are you ready?"

"To best you again?" She looked down at Feric, who had the rope looped diagonally around his neck and dangling down his right side. "Not a problem."

She took a step closer to him and found herself being pushed as he dove into her. Her surprise turned to fear as she realized they were falling off the cliff. Her scream filled her ears and she felt her life slip from the mountain.

The fall was a jumble as she grabbed for a passing rock or

branch, but Feric had pushed them both too hard. She felt something soft even as she registered the ground coming toward her. There was now a large, dark shape next to her. "Gods of Shokar, what now?" she whispered. "Isn't it enough that Leikor cursed halfling threw me off a cliff?" She felt the shape press against her body pushing her further away from the mountainside. She was slipping down the shape but felt a rough surface over her face. Her hands grabbed the rope as the thing raced away from the mountain and out over the ocean.

She looked at the rope and saw she was tied to the creature. "Feric?" There was a loud squawk from the creature.

She let her gaze move to the bird's head. He had taken the shape of one of the great eagles. She felt the wind over her back as her hair fluttered wildly.

The eagle kept a smooth, straight course as they appeared to chase the sunset.

She slowly leaned back on her knees and held the length of rope between them. The wind and salt air were intoxicating. She placed her left foot on his feathers as she forced herself to stand. The rope was tight between them as she rose to her full height.

"You promised to show me the island from higher up. Well?" she yelled, hoping he could hear her over the noise of the wind.

The eagle banked and she smiled as she shifted her balance with the turn and kept her footing. She stamped her right foot on the feathers. "Is that the best you can do?" She felt the bird turn sharply one way and then the other as Feric accepted her challenge. There were moments when she thought she would be flung off despite the rope and her own agility, but she kept her place.

The eagle finally leveled off. "I guess I win, again," she said, before she laughed. "Now show me."

The great wings began to beat as she held the rope. Feric took her to the edge of the clouds and she looked down at the island.

The colors were magnificent as she watched the shadows in the valley creep and change. *He was right; it is beautiful.* Her thoughts returned to his words. "It rivals Hendandra," he had said.

She smiled then found herself shivering violently. The wind and cold air were blowing right through her dress; a dress that had no back and nothing below the knee. It felt like it was going right through her. "Feric, I am cold…so cold… Take me back to the island... Please...please...make it quick," she said through chattering teeth. She lowered herself to his feathers hoping to at least warm her chest and legs.

The eagle did not move to dive. "Feric, please."

He squawked several times and she felt him shake. Her teeth stopped chattering and her body warmed. "You are full of surprises," she whispered.

His feathers were soft and she stretched out on them. It felt like the fine material only the nobility could afford. It was like a warm comfortable bed as the sun set on the horizon. Just for a moment, she thought before she faded off into sleep.

~ * ~

When her eyes opened she saw the moon closer than she had ever seen it. Her hand went to the eagle's back. He would have had to remain gliding to let her sleep and the moon would have taken hours to rise to where it hung in the night sky. She smiled. "Thank you. I have not slept so soundly in weeks." She stroked the feathers. "We need to return."

The eagle turned as he dove. They were almost in a freefall, but Hendandra only laughed. For once she did not worry about anyone or anything. All she cared about was the wonderful freedom of flight.

It took them an hour to return to the island. He brought her to a rocky beach north of his village. He landed easily and let her slide off. She watched in wonder as the feathers and wings collapsed into the small halfling.

He smiled at her as his hands went to work on the knot at her waist. "Feric, thank you. It was truly wonderful." She felt the knot come off and the rope slip to the ground. He looked up at her. "It was wonderful," she said again. She leaned down and he looked up into her eyes. Her left hand came up with the first finger extended. "But..." She paused and stared at him.

He looked at her questioningly as he doubled over from where her right fist struck him hard in the abdomen. "You threw me off a cliff! I cannot believe you threw me off a cliff! I cannot believe I am saying this: Don't. You. Ever. Throw. Me. Off. A. Cliff. Again!" She turned and started to walk away.

After only a few steps she turned and was surprised to see him already standing straight and smiling at her.

"I wanted to see you," he said. "Not the falsehoods you try and shroud yourself in." His voice was calm and soothing as he spoke. "I wanted to see you—without your guilt and without the pain you carry. I saw those dashed on the rocks when I took you from the cliff."

She put her hands on her hips. "But a cliff? You could have gotten me killed."

"You were never in danger."

There it was—that aura of confidence she had seen in him. He wasn't just saying it to make her feel better; he was saying it because he honestly believed it.

She glanced up at the moon and sighed. "It was wonderful up there." She paused and looked at him closely. "Why did you bring me here? Why did you take me up there?"

"I believe you are a good woman, in spite of what you say about my people and even about yourself. I wanted to see your soul and in many respects, I think I did see it tonight." Feric moved forward as she tried to keep her attention focused on the ground.

"What do you think you know of me?" she asked.

"You want to be safe. You want to enjoy life. You want to be accepted."

Hendandra let her head tilt up a little to see Feric's eyes. "You want a home," he said.

She smiled and turned away. His words echoed those she had spoken to Brular not so long ago. It warmed her soul to hear Feric speaking them for her.

"I was wondering..." his voice trailed off.

"Wondering what?" She looked up and smiled at the desire she saw in his eyes. This was what she had been waiting for.

"I want to remember this time we had as I travel through your world."

She smiled as she remembered the many sailors and their lovers she had watced as they parted at the docks. "Really," she said cocking her head slightly. She closed her eyes and thought of the long kisses she had seen given to those who went to sea as she felt him lean in and up. The words of her friend Tinaniel came to her: *The key to a man's help is his hunger—his hunger for more.* Feric's lips just barely brushed hers then were gone. She waited a moment but he did not return. She opened her eyes to see him smiling.

"That was it? What in the name of all the gods of Shokar was that?"

Feric took a step back from her. "I just kissed you."

"I have seen numerous ships leave port with men and women saying goodbye. I can tell you that was the sorriest excuse for a goodbye I have ever seen."

Feric continued to stare at her, a stunned look on his face and Hendandra congratulated herself. She had found a way to take him off-guard. She pressed forward with the game. "I feel insulted. Do you find me ugly or something?"

"No," he said with a stutter.

"That almost kiss is supposed to make me remember this night? It is supposed to make you remember me?"

He only stared at her. Perfect. She stepped in and placed her arms around his neck and her lips softly touched his. She did not press though. Tinaniel's words were in her head. *Let them caress and glide.* She slowly moved her lips along his. She could feel him press against hers, but she kept hers from him—just a bit. *Build the hunger. Don't feed it. Tease it. Let the hunger have him.*

She let her fingers glide across his back as she felt his arms slip around her waist and his hands rest on her back. *Slowly, not quick. Never quick.* She let her lips slip higher off his, but she returned immediately. She opened her mouth as she teased his upper lip open. *Let him taste, then take it away. Then you have him.* She let Tinaniel's words trail off in her mind and her thoughts dissolved.

The next minute brought nothing but confusion. She forgot what she was doing. She slowly released Feric and looked into his eyes. She smiled at the hunger she could see in them. She turned her gaze to the ground when she realized she could feel it in herself as well. She trembled as she stood there with Feric. When he reached up to her cheek, she almost pulled away, but she didn't. She felt his closeness and then the world started to dissolve away. She wasn't sure how long they kissed and she didn't care. She looked into his eyes and she saw the longing, but he stepped back.

She leaned back against a large rock and silently cursed Tinaniel for her advice. *This was not supposed to happen. I don't need this now. I need him to talk to his father. I don't need...* Her thoughts trailed off and she looked at Feric staring at the moon. She bit her lower lip. *I really don't need this.* She cursed herself again as she realized she had cut her lower lip in her own absentmindedness.

"Hendandra, I must go soon."

"You mean tonight?" Her mind raced. The kiss and these infernal feelings inside her were for nothing. She needed him to talk to his father. "When?"

"I must leave within the hour."

She felt her heart sink. "I'm sorry."

"Sorry for what?"

Oh, Vesir, how does someone explain that you played with their emotions just to gain their aid? A lie came instead. "That you have to go into my world." She reached into her dress and pulled the coin pouch out. She spilled a handful of the coins into her hand. "Here take these."

"What is it?"

"Gold. You will need it to buy proper clothing. I would also suggest armor and a sword."

He looked at the coins in her hand. "It is of value in your world?"

"Yes."

He held up his hand. "I cannot take it."

"Why not?"

"I have no need for such things."

"Feric, you are a fool."

He placed his hand over hers and guided it back to the pouch. The coins clinked together as they dropped back with the rest.

She inhaled deeply as he stood close to her.

"I do not need or want such things."

She smiled and let her head tilt to the side. "What do you want?"

Her eyes closed again as their lips met. All those times at the docks she had seen girls saying farewell to their lovers, and she had wondered what they felt. Now, she understood. Her body tingled and her eyes seemed to fail for a moment, but when they returned the moon was shining twice as bright. Their lips parted slowly.

"Stay awhile, Hendandra; they are good people." His voice was like the warm air, soothing.

She turned away from him. "They hate me. Rega suggested I be put to the sea." She turned back. "I'd stay here with you at least for a few days, but there is nothing for me after tonight."

Feric placed his hand on her cheek. "See my father tomorrow. I promise you, things will be different. Just see my father. Please."

"Very well," she whispered. Their lips barely touched this time, but it was like touching fire. She let the sensation warm her.

"Feric, what of the predators?" She grabbed his arm as he started to turn away.

He stopped and unknotted a piece of fabric wrapped around his left arm. He pulled her to him, pressed her hand against his chest and tied the fabric to her arm. When he was finished, he stepped closer and she slid her hand up to his cheek.

"And this is to protect me from the predators?" She looked from the knotted fabric to Feric.

He nodded. "None will dare harm you." Again he spoke with that aura of confidence. He turned his head and kissed the palm of her hand before he stepped back and melted into the jungle.

~ * ~

Hendandra was still struggling with her thoughts as the first rays of dawn started to stream over the horizon. She had tried to sleep but found too much had happened and her mind wouldn't let any of it go. Just when it seemed things couldn't get any worse, she managed to actually make them do just that.

"Time to go," she said as she got up and dusted the sand off. She took a step, but stopped when she heard a loud crashing coming toward her. She turned to see trees bending as something large moved through them. She froze as her gaze moved up and up and up. The thunder lizard was not the largest of the lizards here. This matched nothing she had ever seen or heard of before. It stood nearly thirty feet tall and its snout was longer and thinner than the thunder lizard's. A fin, almost a sail, rose from its back and ran from its head to the tip of its tail. Its head dropped as it looked at her, and Hendandra felt herself stiffen. *Feric, why did you leave me here?* The thing took a step toward her and she could see scars covering its face and chest. She swallowed hard and looked toward the jungle. She could make it, but could she keep away from it? She was unarmed and in a garment that provided little protection from the night chill, let alone teeth. The finback, as she was thinking of it, closed at a walking pace.

She touched her arm and felt the fabric Feric had tied there and remembered his words. "None will dare harm you." She looked up at the approaching reptile and waited. "Please be right," she whispered.

The finback stood over her and lowered its head with its mouth open. It sniffed then backed away. Hendandra looked at it; it seemed confused. She smiled and stepped forward. It took another step back. "What? Am I not juicy enough?" She touched the fabric again. "Or is it my smell?" The finback roared and moved off.

She smiled as she touched the fabric again. "Maybe this day will be better. Seeing that thing run from me was definitely a good way to start."

The sand was difficult to walk in, but she preferred being where she could see any other predators before they approached. Fortunately, the rest of the stroll was uneventful. She paused as she approached the village. She spotted Rega's hut; even though her previous time with the woman hadn't gone that well, she felt more comfortable approaching someone she had at least met.

She found the hut occupied by several young girls, though Rega was nowhere in sight. "Are you Hendandra?" they asked.

"Yes."

"Mother said to tell you she left another dress for you." The eldest of the girls pointed to one of the smaller rooms off of the main one. "Were you out there all night?"

"Yes," she said as she went into the other room. There on the unused bed was another dress similar to the one she currently wore. Her equipment was piled on the bed as well, including her rapier. She smiled. Only Feric knew where it had been lost. He hated it and what it represented, but he had still returned it to her. She picked up the dress, closed the door and changed.

He had told her to see his father, the chief, once more. She owed him that at least for returning the weapon she had threatened him with. She glanced at her equipment as she turned to leave, then took off the pouch of coins and placed it under her armor. *Maybe, just maybe, when I carried it last time, the chief sensed it.*

She stepped out of the room to see the two girls smiling at her. "What are you two up to?"

"Were you out there with Feric?" The two of them spoke together almost as if they had rehearsed the question.

"Did your mother say something?"

"No," the eldest said.

"The only one who stays in the jungle at night is Feric," the younger one said. "Everyone else fears the sickle claws, the thunder lizard and the great spine."

She grinned. "Great spine? Tall one, about thirty feet, long snout and a sail on his back?"

"Yes, that's him."

"Oh, he ran from me this morning." She winked at the girls then left the hut and headed toward the chief's.

As she approached the chief's hut, she saw Rega walking toward her. The woman was frowning and her eyes were dull, as if she were very tired.

"Hendandra, Feric wanted me to give you this." She thrust her hand out.

She looked at the object Rega was holding; it was similar to a cameo, but larger. She took the pendant and gasped as she realized her own face was looking back at her. A second figure was there also, a great eagle whose head was just to the left of her face so her hair flowed into its feathers. The work was flawless, no chisel marks, no imperfections. The stone itself was not valuable, but she had never seen such perfect work. It could easily go for several thousand gold to the right customer. The piece was extraordinary.

"It is beautiful. You made it?" She felt her eyes go wide at the woman's nod. "You made this in one night?"

"Yes. Several of our people have been blessed with the ability to mold the stones."

Hendandra felt her mind race. She knew clerics and druids could shape stone with their magics, but she had never heard of them using it to create this kind of exquisite art. Her gaze dropped to the thin band on Rega's finger. "May I?"

Rega raised her hand. "Impossible," Hendandra said. "That looks like pearl, but in the shape of a ring."

"From my husband," Rega said with a smile.

Hendandra shook her head. These people were walking around with precious stones, which had been molded into art and jewelry that was even more precious—as if they were trinkets. She looked at Rega who was now twisting the ring on her finger.

"Rega, if I may ask, where is your husband?"

"Dead. He was killed by the last human raiding party." Her eyes were filled with tears. "The Lawgiver did much, but they still come every few years. He died saving our children." She inhaled deeply. "He died at the end of a blade not much different than the one Feric brought last night."

Hendandra had seen companions die during the last few months and understood Rega's pain. "Did they…?" She hesitated. "Did the humans take anyone?"

"No, they are all dead."

"The villagers defeated them."

"No. The villagers were no match for them. They brought magic and wore their accursed steel. We have few weapons able to be used against them." She stopped for a moment then looked directly into Hendandra's eyes. "Feric killed them—all of them."

She stood there as she let those words sink in. Feric had killed an entire crew of slavers, supposedly by himself. He carried no weapon and wore no armor to speak of. The giant eagle was impressive but hardly capable of that task. He could speak to the animals. His bearlike friend was definitely capable of doing serious harm. "How?"

"We do not speak of such things. He is our protector. To speak of his power is taboo. It is believed to do so weakens him."

Well this isn't going to get me anywhere, she thought.

"Rega, could I get anything else, a ring or something else? They are so pretty."

"It is not my place or anyone else's to give such things to an outsider. It is forbidden." She pointed to the pendant. "Feric has given you that. He has the right. I do not." She turned and walked away.

Hendandra stood there holding the pendant. Feric was their protector and the chief's son. Obviously, that gave him some privileges under their law. That meant the chief had some as well. *So he lied. The law is not all binding. I just need to convince him.*

"Thank you, Feric," she whispered as she slipped the pendant over her head. *Something to remember the last evening by while I journey through the Abyss and a weapon to open the laws of your tribe to help me. Just a few of those pearl rings would go a long way toward buying equipment.*

She approached the hut and saw the chief coming out toward her. "I told you to be gone with the coming day," he said.

"I came because your son told me to see you this last time."

"The law is binding."

She looked her gaze with his as she lifted the pendant. "It doesn't seem to bind everything," she said.

"Where did you get that?" He reached for the pendant.

Leikor's cursed luck. What if he really didn't have the right? What if his father takes it from me? Her hand closed over the pendant to protect it. "Feric had Rega make it for me," she said.

He looked over her shoulder. "Is this true?" She turned to see

Rega nod.

The old chief smiled. "Call the runners; there is news to carry." He turned back to Hendandra. "You look tired. Why don't you rest in one of the rooms, daughter?"

"You told me to leave. Now, you tell me to stay in your home. I don't understand." She watched as Rega ran to a group of young men working on a set of nets.

He smiled as he spoke. "Where else would a father have his only daughter stay?"

The word daughter stuck in her mind. Her hand was still wrapped around the pendant and her mouth was dry as her mind screamed, *I'm married?*

She stood clutching the pendant.

"Daughter, are you okay?"

She heard the chief's words, but didn't answer.

"I..." she stuttered. "We...This pendant means we are married?"

The chief cocked his head to the side. "You did not know?"

"How could I? I just came here. I thought it was a simple gift."

He reached out, took her hand and led her to the hut's steps and sat there with her. "No gifts are given between an unwed man and woman. A man gives his wife-to-be a gift that she is to keep— a heart token. It symbolizes his love for her and when she accepts it, her love for him. The giving of a heart token is not a small matter. I believe Rega can better explain."

Her feelings were still in knots but her voice was calm and detached. "Since I did not know this, am I bound by it?"

"I am sorry," he said softly. "The custom is specific. You accepted his gift and even sought to protect it from me. You are his wife. For him to have not explained is not like Feric."

"What if I don't want hi—?" She shut her eyes. "What if I don't want to be married?"

The chief placed his hand on hers. "It would be a simple matter, if he were here. You would only need to appear before me with Feric, and hand him the heart token back. You would not even need his consent in the matter. But he has left, so it appears I have a daughter who did not want to be such." He looked at her and waited.

"I...I...I need to sleep," she finally said. "You said I could rest here."

He stood and held out his hand. "Come with me."

"What should I call you?" Hendandra forced herself to her feet.

"Father will do. I was never blessed with a daughter and have waited a long time for a woman to call me that."

"Thank you…Father," she said. The words were so simple, but the emotions they brought were as heavy as lead.

He led her to a room open toward the sea with only one wall. She sat on a mat made of straw then laid down. She watched as he lowered the fabric from the roof so the light was shielded but the breeze could still flow through the room. Her dreams were a reflection of the turmoil she was feeling. She had seen people marry for love. She had seen people marry for convenience and even power. Both had their problems. She herself had never even considered marriage and now she was married, without even consenting to it. *Why did he do this? Does he think he loves me? Did I do this last night?* She remembered the kisses they shared, the embrace. *Did I trick him into marrying me, by doing that?* She felt her eyes fill with tears. *Please don't let it be that. Please, don't let this be because of a lie.*

Her mind moved to darker interpretations. *I am an outsider. He hates humans. Are women property here? Does he own me? Has he conquered the humans in a different way? Am I a trophy? No, I am not a trophy!* She woke with her hand holding the pendant and went to drive it into the floorboards, but a strong hand grabbed hers.

Rega glared at her. "Don't ever do that or I and every woman on this island will make your existence here a torment."

Hendandra's eyes were full of tears. "What am I to think? Am I his prize against my people?"

"For you to even consider that tells me how shallow your people really are." She removed her hand from Hendandra's. "I told him this was wrong. One should not play with another's emotions." Her face hardened. "But I believe two played that game this past day."

Rega's words cut her deeply and she nodded.

"Hendandra, a heart token is never given lightly. A Justulan man would never give one to a woman he did not care about. It is too precious to us. It is said men gain their strength from their women. In many ways that is true; we give them something to return to. There are more than a few stories of villagers who strove on to return home when others would have given up. We hold this belief quite strongly and so does Feric."

"Why would he do this?"

"The laws that bind us, bind us only to dealings with outsiders. When you accepted his heart token, you joined our tribe. The laws no longer constrain anyone from helping you."

Hendandra cradled the pendant. "So I belong to the tribe now. If he would have told me, I would have accepted that."

Rega looked at her. "I told him I suspected as much, but he insisted you not be told. I believe he feared you would agree and more importantly, he was adamant you not come into the tribe on a lie." She paused and locked her gaze with Hendandra's. "He said you needed to be free of the lies so the tribe could see you. He wanted your heart to be free and not heavy with that burden. He took that from you, even though he realized it might make your heart heavy against him."

Hendandra turned the pendant over in her hand. "So much meaning wrapped up in this single object."

"He has looked for a long time to find a wife." Rega's eyes were now heavy with tears threatening to fall.

"Do you love him?"

"Part of me does, but in truth—no. He is our protector. He is the saver of our children. He has brought peace and safety to the beaches. More than there has been in years."

"Why did he not find a wife among your people, Rega? With his position and the way you and others view him, I don't understand."

"He is our savior and also our nightmare at the same time. We have grown up in fear for so long, it is second nature to us. He is those nightmares. May Isdela protect him and the tribe. No woman here will stay with him. We fear he will succumb to the nature he venerates."

"I did not see that. I did not…" her voice trailed off. "I did not feel that."

"Enough, you have slept a long time and the feast will begin shortly."

"Feast? There is a feast?" She stopped and looked at the smile on Rega's face. "For me? Is that what…" she hesitate, "Father was sending the runners for?"

"Of course. The great chief's son has found a wife. His wife goes to rescue the Lawgiver. They come to bring you gifts for your journey."

"Great chief?"

Rega smiled. "Yes. When the Lawgiver came, one chief was given power to speak for the island as a whole. That is the great chief. Feric's grandfather was the first. His father is the second. He will be the third."

Hendandra's jaw dropped open. I...I...I'm a princess!

"Hendandra, are you okay?"

"Yes. They, the other tribes, bring gifts. You mean weapons?"

"Yes and armor. The finest on the island."

"Unfortunately, I don't think that will help. Where are the weapons brought by the raiders?"

"Destroyed. You don't think we can help you, just because we hate your steel. You have a great deal to learn about us."

She walked to the wall and stuck her hand inside and drew out a sheathed sword. She knelt down and unsheathed the blade. Where Hendandra had expected to see steel was only a shining brilliance. Rega smiled as she swung the blade in front of her.

Hendandra felt the prick of a blade against her abdomen and looked down to check for a wound. She could not see it through the fabric of her dress, but a bead of blood spread over it. She looked up at Rega as she placed her hand under the dress to touch the area. Her fingers only found a small scratch. Rega buried the sword, to the hilt, in the floorboards then turned the blade up so it came through the wood without so much as a jerk. The floor was unscarred.

"It is a spirit blade. Fashioned to slice through your steel and into a human without effort," Rega said. "What do you think now?"

"I believe I need a new dress." She held out her hand. "And a good weapon."

Rega placed the sword in her hand. "Your father was to give you that tonight, but he will not mind. He would much rather have his daughter."

Hendandra smiled as she looked at the weapon after Rega left. *Thank you, Feric*, she thought.

Rega returned with a new dress and an older woman. "Let Brena check the wound."

She turned and untied the straps at the neck and shoulders of the dress then turned back with her arms crossed over her chest. The scratch was small across her belly, just above her navel.

"This is hardly a concern," Brena said as she cleaned the cut and applied a salve. "Turn around if you would."

Hendandra tilted her head to the side, but did as the woman requested.

"Beautiful skin you have, wife of Feric. I can do much with it."

"What?" Hendandra spun around.

"She isn't going to skin you," Rega said with a smile. "Brena is an artist of the skin; she produces very powerful images." She opened her own dress to reveal an ocean scene on her belly.

"It is beautiful." She stared at the way the colors flowed on Rega's skin.

"You said they were powerful. What do you mean?"

"Rega's provides her with the speed of a fish in water and she can stay underwater longer than twice most men. It depends on the image or the image depends on the power sought."

"I once offered to provide my best work to his skin, but he refused. He always refused." She paused as she looked at Hendandra. "Would you accept my gift for Feric?"

Hendandra glanced at Rega, knowing she would understand her confusion at the question.

"Feric has never cared about such things though he has marveled at Brena's skill. It would be fine to accept a gift on his behalf and it would give Brena pleasure to give it."

"What should it be?" Hendandra asked as she turned away to retie her dress.

"What is it you desire?" Brena asked.

Her mind went to Feric for a moment, but she forced that image from her mind. "Stealth, silence and speed."

Brena looked at her. Rega leaned over and whispered in the older woman's ear. They both laughed as they looked at her.

"What is it?"

"I will prepare the dyes," Brena said. "I would like to start tonight, as it will take many hours."

Hendandra looked at Rega. "It ends at moonrise," she said.

"I guess a few hours will be okay."

Rega nodded and Brena left them alone. "Good, the feast will have a demonstration of her work," Rega said.

"What? When does this feast end?"

"Moonrise," she said with a laugh. "Tomorrow."

"Tomorrow? The feast lasts an entire day? And I am going to

be tattooed during it!" She glared at Rega who was still laughing. "It seems I got an annoying sister as well when I got a husband and father." She didn't fight the giggle she felt bubbling up.

Hendandra had traveled with the others and while she got along with them, she hadn't thought of any of them as family. She had seen the friendship which existed between Myrith and Kyrianna and had felt a bit jealous of the two. She was pretty sure Kyrianna thought of her as a friend, but during those last days or weeks in that place of Torliana's creation, the half-elf had withdrawn so much from everyone, she wasn't sure. They had spent a short amount of time together before they split up for their individual tasks and Kyrianna had even joked with her about Myrith's serious attitude. Perhaps there was a chance for a real friendship there. She hoped so, because she would miss having someone to talk to and joke with, as she was now able to do with Rega, once she left the island.

Rega looked at her. "Don't worry; you will be on your stomach for yours. I was on my back at my own wedding feast. My husband kept teasing me that he was going to pull my towel off."

The image of Rega, flat on her back and clinging to a towel being pulled by her husband made her laugh. Yes, she was going to miss this.

Rega reached over and touched Hendandra's hand, which still held the pendant. "The wearing of a heart token is very symbolic of the marriage. If it is not worn, there is deep trouble within the relationship. The more prominently it is displayed, the greater the strength of the union. Where will you wear it tonight, Hendandra?"

She looked at it and placed it about her neck. It dangled near her navel. Hendandra looked at it and frowned. She pulled the cords up and knotted them together so the pendant rested in the middle of her chest, near her heart.

"I thought you were not sure," Rega said.

Hendandra thought of the previous night. "He loved me enough to not ask me to lie to his people. He gave me a father, a home and the assistance I asked for. He asked for nothing in return and never tried to take more than I offered. How can a woman ask for more than that?" She smiled. "His actions alone speak for the strength of the union."

Rega nodded as she opened the door to the sound of chanting. The feast had already begun.

~ * ~

"I cannot believe this!" Hendandra stood behind the partially closed door.

"It isn't funny!" She could hear Rega laughing uncontrollably on the other side.

"Maybe not to you."

"Here you are, Mother," she heard one of Rega's daughters say.

"Did you get it?"

"Yes," Rega said, between giggles.

"Stop it." She stuck her hand out. "Give it here."

"I can't believe you didn't warn me before the druid cast the spell to make the ivy grow around me." She slipped the new dress on.

"I told you, no woman has worn moon ivy armor for nearly fifty years. I wasn't even born then. How was I to know it would be so…so…" She started to laugh again. "…uncomfortable?"

"This dress is just like the one I was wearing. This isn't going to help with those accursed vines."

"Give it here." Rega stuck her hand behind the door.

Hendandra didn't hand the woman the dress, instead throwing it at her through the door crack.

She peeked through the opening to see Rega examining the skirt and then locating a set of buttons and holes and fastening the material so it formed a set of shorts.

"Thank you," Hendandra said as she stepped into the dress.

Hendandra opened the door then placed a necklace of ivy around her neck.

Rega grabbed her hand. "We need to ask the druid to regrow the armor before returning to the feast."

Hendandra froze and refused to move. "Do we have to?"

"The chief from the western village will be insulted if you are not wearing the full suit. The skirt is closed up, so you won't have the same problem."

"But it itched so bad."

"Yes, I noticed and I am sure others did as well. Let us go. Brena cannot start the tattoo until the chiefs are done. And you will have to remove the armor for her to be able to work on your skin. So…"

"So, the sooner we get this done, the sooner I can get it off me." She started for the door, but stopped as Rega started laughing again. "Now what?"

"Itch," she said before she doubled over, laughing.

"Huh?"

Rega stood and slowly walked to the door. "My new name for you," she said as darted past Hendandra and bolted from the room.

"Don't you dare tell anyone else that!" she shouted as she chased after the woman.

~ * ~

Hendandra stood beside the post of her new father's home in the night breeze. The party had finally ended. Her back still ached from the needles, but Brena had done a wonderful job.

Rega handed her a drink. "So you like the tattoo?" she asked.

"It is quite eye-catching," Hendandra said. "She is truly an artist."

"The placement of the head and eyes were my idea. It looks as though the ties blindfold it as they cross your shoulder blades. The colors are so real; it is a shame it will be covered by the armor." Rega sipped her drink. "Does it still hurt?"

"Just a little. Brena's compresses and magic stopped the sting and much of the soreness has gone away." She thought back to being lifted above the pool of reflecting water and twisting her head so she could see her back. The image of a tiger staring out from the jungle had greeted her. Yes, the ties of her dress had indeed created a blindfold across its eyes.

But the beautiful tattoo and the magics it contained were not the only gifts she had been given. In addition to the problematic armor, she had been given a set of quilled bracers. She plucked at the one on her left arm and realized she would have to be careful with them. The quills were exceptionally sharp.

Her hand went to her neck to the strip of cloth she wore tight around her throat. The chief of the southern village had said the choker was prized among fishermen as it would allow them to continue breathing for some time—even underwater.

In addition to the armor, the chief of the western tribe had given her a set of moccasins. Much more comfortable than the sandals she had been wearing, he had told her they would make her step so light others would be unable to track her.

Opposite the spirit blade her father had given her, she wore a dagger made from the claw of a great celestial bear that had defended the northern village years ago.

She wondered what the others would think of the things she had been given. Kyrianna and Andrinor would probably find the items interesting as they both had ties to nature. The others wouldn't care. She wouldn't be surprised if Nirev found them inadequate.

The feast had been fun. She enjoyed how the halflings celebrated with music, dance and laughter. She had even played the violin several times during the day. Such an instrument had never been seen on the island and many of those there had found its sound enchanting.

Hendandra glanced up at the moon and found her thoughts turning to Feric. *Where are you now?*

"You're thinking of him again?" Rega's voice interrupted her thoughts.

"How did you know?"

"You're looking up at the moon with a small smile on your face," Rega said. "I would like to hear another answer, Itch."

Hendandra snapped her head toward Rega.

"What will you do? When he returns, I mean?"

Hendandra dropped her gaze to the ground. "You mean if. My world will be difficult on him."

"You do not know your own husband that well. He will be difficult on them."

They stood in silence for several minutes. Hendandra looked out toward the ocean; there had been the sound of something moving in the water.

"What did you do with him that night?"

Hendandra felt herself jump as Rega's question broke through her concentration. She spun around. "Not that," she said. "We only kissed."

"Kissed? When he came to my hut, I would have thought him drunk. Just how did you kiss him?"

Hendandra turned away, grateful for the darkness as she felt heat rising in her face. "Purposefully," she finally said.

"Purposefully? Hmm. That can be taken a lot of ways."

Hendandra raised her hand to silence anything further Rega might say. There was something moving in the water—something large. She handed Rega her drink and headed out across the dark beach as she tried to penetrate the darkness for the source of the sound.

As she listened, she heard another sound from the rocks; the whispered voices of a man and woman. Several of the men had passed heart tokens to lovers from different tribes at the feast. No doubt this couple had stolen away for some time alone. The smile she felt vanished as she again heard something moving through the water. She turned toward the sound and saw a long, slender form moving toward the beach.

"Rega," she called. "Get the villagers. There's something in the water."

"What?"

"Just go get help."

Rega turned and sprinted for the village.

The thing rose up and Hendandra knew she didn't have time to wait for the others to arrive. The thing's neck was easily ten feet long and its mouth gleamed with teeth. It moved toward the rocks and Hendandra broke into a run.

She was determined it was not going to find its dinner there.

She yelled as the creature snapped at something in the rocks and she heard the woman scream. She drew the spirit blade as she sprinted across the sand and buried it to hilt in the creature's side.

The creature ignored the presence of the blade as it snapped its head down again. "No!" Hendandra cried as she pulled the blade out and dropped it. The creature held a young man in its teeth. The woman was still screaming.

Hendandra brought both arms up and slammed the quills of her bracers into the creature's side. "Let him go!"

The creature howled as the quills found their mark and stuck. The young man was dropped roughly to the sand and the creature turned to look at Hendandra.

It moved quickly and she found herself suspended in the air as the creature held her leg in its mouth. She screamed as she lashed out. She felt something warm and sticky across her body. She twisted her foot and pulled free of the creature's mouth and rolled away from it as it fell to the ground. As she wiped at the blood covering her, she saw she held the dagger she had been given. She didn't even remember drawing the weapon; however the evidence of it having been used was clear in the cut across the creature's throat. It was the creature's blood that covered her, not her own.

She walked around the creature to be greeted by the entire village. They were cheering and praising her bravery. She smiled as she wondered if the others would even believe she had faced this thing by herself. She doubted they would. After all, she hadn't demonstrated any overt courage before. She frowned as she looked back at the thing lying on the beach. Why hadn't she run away? Because she had found something worth standing her ground for. Something she had always wanted and needed.

~ * ~

Hendandra stood and looked out over the village. She had only been here three days, but it was her home. *Home,* she thought. Yes, she finally had a place she would willingly call home. A place where she was safe and where she truly belonged. She knew it was going to be difficult to leave. The halflings had welcomed her into the village after her marriage to Feric, more so than she would ever have suspected they would.

She looked down at the heart token and grasped it lightly in her hand. Her heart was still torn.

"Good morning, daughter," Feric's father said as he and Rega approached.

She only nodded as she continued to stare at the token.

"Hendandra?" Rega placed a hand over hers.

"If I decide to return his token, what becomes of me and the village?"

"I do not know."

Feric's father placed his hand over theirs. "The custom of the tribes is that those who marry into one are always part of it, regardless of what happens later."

He smiled at her. "You will always have a home here, daughter."

Hendandra threw her arms around the older halfling and hugged him tightly.

"Hello, Hendandra. Enjoying the island?"

Hendandra pulled away from the chief and froze as she turned to see Rhyra standing behind her.

"What, you don't say hello to an old friend?" Rhyra said.

Hendandra glared at the goddess. She had plenty she wanted to say to her, but not here; not in front of Rega and Feric's father—

her father. Instead she turned and stalked off toward the trees.

"I guess I could turn this one into a hermit crab then."

Hendandra turned to see Rhyra's hand only a hair away from Rega.

"Leave them be! You have no right!" She turned and sprinted for the trees.

As she ran, she could hear several of the halflings following her. "You're going to take this too," she whispered.

She stopped in a small clearing, tears flowing as she looked back at Feric's father, Rega and the others.

"Hendandra, what is wrong?" He turned to one of the others. "Get a healer—quickly."

She dropped to the ground and just sat there as Rhyra's voice came from beside her. "How easy it is to trick and manipulate, but you know all about that. That is how you got what you are now so worried about losing. I applaud you, little thief." She laughed. "Little, what an absurd statement that is, in this place, is it not?"

"I didn't." Hendandra's voice broke. "He did it. He made that decision. I didn't ask." She looked up at Feric's father. "This is not a lie."

Rega dropped down next to her and grabbed her hand. "What is wrong?"

Her mind reeled. How could she tell them she was a toy of the Goddess of Illusion?

"So what should I whisper in their ears?" Rhyra was almost cooing as she looked from Hendandra to the villagers standing there.

"Absolutely nothing!"

Hendandra looked up as she felt a strong hand on her shoulder; a halfling woman dressed the same as she was stood there. "Stand up, my wayward child; she cannot hurt you here," she said.

"Is that so, Isdela?" Rhyra asked. "I am everywhere and nowhere."

"You are here." Isdela's hand rose and the group of villagers gasped. "And now they know you."

Feric's father and Rega helped Hendandra to her feet. She didn't acknowledge the looks of hatred they turned toward Rhyra.

"This changes nothing. She can protect these people here, but not out there, Hendandra. What should I tell Feric?" Rhyra was surrounded by mist and when it cleared, a duplicate of Hendandra stood there.

Hendandra gasped. "No," she whispered.

"What should I have him call you?"

Her knees felt weak. *What is the use of fighting? She will not stop.*

"Liar?" Rhyra held the duplicate of the heart token in her hand. "Cheat?"

She can make him believe anything she wants him to.

"Trollop?"

Hendandra felt the tears burning her eyes again and she closed them tight.

"Tramp?"

She knew the goddess could turn Feric against her with her games. "How about my favorite..." Rhyra paused.

Feric had given her everything without being asked and now a petty goddess whose feelings had been hurt would take it away.

"Filthy who—"

Hendandra opened her eyes at a surprised yelp from the goddess and as something warm and sticky hit her face. Another woman was standing there. Blood flowed from several scratches on Rhyra's face even as the injuries were healing. The other woman reached out and placed her hand on Hendandra's cheek. It came back covered in blood—Rhyra's blood. She smiled as she placed her fingers in her mouth and licked the blood off them.

Rhyra's face was almost healed. "So these are your new patrons? Have you already abandoned Vesir?"

Hendandra shook her head.

Isdela stepped forward and looked up at Rhyra. "He has no business here. The court of Thedrin was established by civilized folk who destroy their very world at every turn. He is certainly not needed here."

The other woman snarled. "Since when do we women need men to interfere in our business? You come to a place where you have not even one worshipper. She need not worship us to be worthy of our protection. She served this tribe as a protector last night. She is therefore one of these people." She turned to Hendandra. "She is my favorite pet's mate and you just threatened to come between them. I have been told you are wily prey, Rhyra. I wonder if that is true?" Her hands extended to show claws. "Shall we see?" Rhyra faded into the mists, then vanished.

Hendandra stood there staring at the place the goddess had

been. She expected Rhyra to reappear at any moment.

"Please leave us," Isdela said.

Hendandra stood there alone as the rest of the villagers left the clearing.

"Please sit," Isdela said as she took a spot on the ground and the other woman did the same. "I am sorry this had to happen, child. Rhyra needs a proper lesson." She grinned at the clawed woman. "And, Shyada, filleting her face will not solve matters."

Hendandra sighed softly. *Isdela, goddess of the halflings and Shyada, goddess of cats and pleasure seekers. I see more gods than most priests.* "Why did you do that?" she asked.

"She has no place here," Isdela said.

Hendandra looked up. "Do I?"

"If you wish. They have accepted you and more importantly, you have accepted them."

Hendandra nodded.

"Have you never wondered about your height? There is a little of me, I mean halfling, in your blood. I awaken that blood now." She reached out and touched Hendandra on the forehead. "I grant you the agility and hearing of that long-past ancestor."

Hendandra did not smile.

"What is wrong?" Isdela asked.

"What's the catch? I am tired of the games of the gods." She didn't care she was questioning a goddess; she was tired of being treated as she had been.

"The gift is yours as long as you strive to protect these people, my dear. I require nothing else. However, I offer you a deal if that is what you want. The outside world has done horrid things with metal. The Justulans once had that material, now they refuse to use it because of the evil it has come to represent. If you can keep yourself pure of it, I will grant you the luck all halflings have."

Hendandra cocked her head as she looked at the smiling goddess. "You can't be serious. How will I pay for things? I need weapons and armor."

"You have those. There are other ways. Think about it some." Isdela stood and walked away.

Hendandra turned to Shyada. "Are you offering gifts today?" she asked with a laugh.

Shyada smiled. "No, you took a gift the other night."

"I don't understand," Hendandra said.

Shyada laid a hand on hers. "My gifts have nothing to do with me, but with Feric. He has searched for a wife, but found none. He is my favorite pet, but he has had no companion or mate. I wish him only happiness. If you are that, the blessings are yours."

"How do I get these blessings?"

Shyada smiled. "I leave that to you to find out. However, the first was activated when you kissed Feric. You have noticed a certain sharpness to your vision?"

Hendandra nodded. "But what if I don't love him?"

"Then give him back the token. My gifts are hardly something to weigh against a man and woman's happiness. Choose your own heart; I will not choose it for you." The goddess smiled again then melted back into the foliage.

Hendandra continued to sit there as her mind raced. *Feric serves Shyada, not Isdela, and they are both willing to help me if I stay among the halflings or remain with Feric. The nice thing is—Rhyra didn't want any part of these two.*

She finally stood and returned to her room in the chief's hut. Her circlet and rings had been transformed. The circlet was now made of polished ebony and the rings were quartz and pearl. She slipped the rings and circlet on then threw her coins and other metal items into her pack.

She started to close the pack up then stopped and opened the pouch that held her lock picks and other tools. They had been transformed into wood. "These will never work properly," she muttered as her fingers moved over the surface. The picks were strong and as well crafted as they had been before they had been transformed. "Maybe, just maybe, they'll work."

Hendandra picked up her pack and looked around the room. She had a home, a place to return to when this mess was finished. She remembered how sad Kyrianna had been at being taken from her home. Now, even though she was leaving voluntarily, she could understand what her friend had been going through. Even though she had complained and joked about wanting to go home, she had never been that tied to one place. She had had a place where she lived, but it wasn't truly a home—not like Justula had become in these few days.

"You are leaving soon?"

She turned to see Feric's father—her father—standing in the doorway.

"Yes, I have to return to my companions or they will leave without me."

"I understand. Go with the blessings of Isdela and my prayers for your success and safe return."

"Thank you." She wrapped her arms around him and hugged him tightly. "I look forward to returning here when this is done."

"I welcome that day."

Hendandra pulled the glass rod out of her pack and held it up. "With your permission?"

"It is magic?"

"It is."

The chief took a few steps back and nodded. "Fare well in your journey, daughter."

Hendandra smiled as she broke the rod.

Chapter Eight
Kyrianna

Kyrianna paused at the entrance to the Great Grove. This was where the messenger had told to her to come before she left for Mount Veri. How the girl had known she would be traveling to that distant place when she had told no one other than Myrith, she didn't know. The girl had also told her Cewyr would need to be present so she could transport Kyrianna to her destination. While she thought the distance too far, even for the unicorn to travel in the time Myrith had given them, there was something about the girl who had approached Kyrianna in the corridor that led her to trust what the child had said.

She placed the figurine Brular had given her on the ground. "Cewyr," she said softly.

A golden glow surrounded the figure and when it cleared the unicorn was standing there.

"Dwycia sends her greetings and blessings to you both," a voice said nearby.

Kyrianna spun around to see Mylena, the same woman who had been at the chapel on the Duvall Estate, standing there holding a silver chain in her hand. :*I thank the Lady for her greeting and blessing*, Cewyr's voice said in Kyrianna's mind.

Mylena smiled and nodded indicating she had also heard the unicorn. "It is an unfortunate limitation of the magic used to allow you to visit this plane that it only permits you to remain for one hour. Where you are going, your group will need to travel quickly and for much longer than one hour each day. Dwycia offers this gift to two who serve the Balance." She held out the silver chain. "It will allow you to remain on the material plane indefinitely. It is recommended you return to the astral plane when possible though so you can properly heal and rest."

Kyrianna's hand shook as she took the chain. "My thanks. I only hope Dywcia's trust has not been misplaced."

Mylena bowed slightly. "You still wear the pendant and the marks of those who would ask you to serve the Balance. Her trust is not misplaced."

Kyrianna dropped her head as Cewyr rubbed her head against Kyrianna's cheek.

"There are a couple of other things you need to know." Mylena placed her hand against Cewyr's forehead. After a few minutes she stepped back. "You have the knowledge you need to travel within the forests of Shokar. Know also there is a link between Shokar and Rhysia—one which will allow you to travel between them. You can already see a path through forests, now you have the ability to open a portal between Shokar and Rhysia. But only from a place dedicated to Dwycia or Frayrith."

She turned her attention back to Kyrianna. "Do not shun the gifts your patrons have given you. Fare well on your journey." She turned and disappeared into the grove.

"I guess we had better get going." She hooked the chain around Cewyr's neck. "No objections to wearing this?"

:*No,* Cewyr's voice said in her head. :*As Dywcia's messenger said, we should not shun their gifts.*

Kyrianna pulled herself onto the mare's back.

:*We should make our way around the city to the eastern gate. Across the river I will be able to open the path to the clearing. Shadow Seeker will be able to walk the path as long as he stays close to me.*

:*And travel home and back?* Kyrianna fought back tears.

:*You will need to hold him on my back.* Cewyr dropped her head to look at the wolf.

:*I understand,* Shadow Seeker's voice said.

"Let's go."

"Cewry," Kyrianna said. "When I called you previously you were able to speak to me. Now you are speaking in my mind.

:*The magic that bonds us together, allows us to speak mind to mind— just as you and Shadow Seeker speak. It is a minor magic that allows my thoughts to be vocalized as if I were speaking.*

Kyrianna was uncomfortable with some of the looks they were receiving as they rode through Irrmar.

"Are you willing to sell the unicorn?" a voice called from the side.

Kyrianna saw an older man standing there, wearing the robes of a mage.

"No!"

"I can offer more than just gold for her."

"No!" Kyrianna drew her sword and laid it across her lap. "Another time perhaps." The mage stepped back and vanished from her sight.

:*Why was that mage interested in Cewyr?* Shadow Seeker asked.

:*I don't know. But there are others watching us with the same greed on their faces.*

:*You have little experience with magic, Kyri,* Cewyr said. :*There are many spells that can be enhanced by using unicorn hair and powder ground from a horn in the casting.*

"What?"

Kyrianna's yell caused several other people to stop and stare at her. She shook her head and ignored the looks. :*He wanted you for spell components?*

:*Most likely.*

:*Let's get out of here.*

~ * ~

Kyrianna looked around the clearing. It was more overgrown than she remembered from the vision she had received, but she could still see the tree formations Brular had walked through that night. "She stood here as he turned away. I wonder if that was the only time he missed her signals?"

Cewyr raised her head and looked at her from across the open grass. :*Maybe you should save those questions for when we have Brular.* The silver chain around her neck gleamed in the moonlight.

Kyrianna dropped her gaze to the ground. "Easier said than done." She kicked at what remained of a ring of stones in the center of the clearing. "We came here looking for help. This place has given us nothing." A small rock flew into the trees. "I don't believe there is nothing here. The smoke showed me this place. Why would Hellavar send one of those trying to help his servant here, if there was nothing to find?"

A sharp bark from the north part of the clearing got her attention. She looked up to see Shadow Seeker staring at a hill a short distance away. A single fire flickered at its top.

Kyrianna searched the area. *There has to be a path to the temple.* She felt a moment of disorientation and her vision changed to the shades of gray Shadow Seeker saw. However, his eyes were better suited to the fading light. There, almost hidden were the signs of a decaying trail. She shook her head to clear the wolf's thoughts from her own. Her own eyes were now able to pick out the trail.

"Mount Veri," she whispered.

She felt Cewyr bump her back with her muzzle. :*I can see it also; we should go*, the unicorn said.

It wasn't the clearing, but something we could see from it, Kyrianna thought. She felt Cewyr's silent agreement in her mind.

Kyrianna swung herself up onto Cewyr's back even as the unicorn leapt forward onto the trail. The unicorn and wolf matched strides as they covered the distance to the ruined temple. "Hellavar light the way," she called as they plunged into the woods.

"Wait here," Kyrianna said as she slid off the unicorn in a small stand of trees near the summit. Kyrianna shivered in the cool night air and glanced up at the stars. It was only a few days before High Summer; she doubted the cold was normal for this time of year. Perhaps there was some lingering presence of the chaos and evil that had been called to this place that night.

:*Perhaps you should return to your home*, Kyrianna thought as she placed a hand on the silver chain.

:*And if you need my help?*

Kyrianna pulled her hand back. She knew Cewyr could appear quickly if called, but she didn't want to risk revealing the unicorn's true nature. If Kyrianna needed her, Cewyr could cover the distance in only a few heartbeats.

"Point taken," Kyrianna whispered. She patted the unicorn on the neck then turned and headed toward the ruins of the temple.

Kyrianna peered around a crumbling wall and blinked several times in surprise when she spotted a young woman in the robes of a Kindling standing near the huge fire. Even though the fire was large enough for a whole encampment, the girl was continuing to feed it as it grew higher.

:*Go get Cewyr.*

The only answer was the wolf bumping her leg before he vanished into the shadows. Kyrianna pressed her thumb against the ring she had claimed at the Duvall Estate and concentrated on appearing as a true human. She felt a tingle of magic go through her body and she hoped it had worked properly.

She looked back at the fire; the girl was nowhere to be seen. She drew the silver sword as she scanned the area.

:*Where did she go?* Melissa's voice whispered in her mind.

:*I don't know, but it will do me no good if she thinks me an enemy. She returned the sword to its sheath.*

:Be careful, Melissa said.

Kyrianna took twenty paces toward the fire through the rubble, but did not see the girl.

"You brought an unsheathed weapon within the temple walls."

Kyrianna spun around at the voice. *Chaos!* She cursed herself for making two stupid mistakes. The first for not considering the possible sacrilege of carrying a weapon on the temple grounds and the second for not seeing the infinite hiding places in the rubble. She bowed her head slightly. "My apologies. I did not realize the temple had been reclaimed. I beg your forgiveness."

"Forgiveness cannot be begged for; it must be earned." The girl moved toward her.

Kyrianna's mind raced. Hellavar was a god of Order, though those who followed him could be either benevolent or malevolent. The girl's words did not remind of Brular, instead they seemed more appropriate to Ashe as did the aura of confidence she held about her.

"I am Kyrianna, a ranger of the goddess Frayrith who is kin to Dwycia." She paused as she named the goddesses. It was the first time she had spoken their names in some time and her tongue felt heavy in her mouth. She had forsaken them and even though they had spoken to her since that time, she did not feel she had the right to call on them. Even so, she would still honor them. She glanced down as she felt a slight tingling in her wrists and winced at the scars that still showed where she had tried to remove the marks she had seen as being nothing more than branding her as a pawn. She took a deep breath and looked up at the girl, trying to ignore the uncertainty that fluttered in her heart.

"What is the law concerning this transgression?"

The girl stopped, confusion showing on her face in the flickering light. She straightened and when she spoke it was in a strong, determined tone. "You have carried a sword onto hallowed ground. You are required to fight a champion of the Keeper's choosing."

Kyrianna's head snapped up. "Keeper? Does Mount Veri have a Keeper once more?" She tried to keep her tone respectful as she asked the question.

The girl smiled at the question. "No, Mount Veri has not been so blessed, transgressor. Mount Veri has a single Kindling. I, unfortunately, am made to be your accuser, judge and its champion." She paused for a moment. "It speaks well of you that there is respect in your voice."

Kyrianna relaxed a little. The girl had called herself Kindling; she was a novice. *Why is my journey not simple?* She smiled and bowed to the girl then turned and walked closer to the fire. "Kindling, judge and champion, if I am to be judged, should it not be in his light?"

The girl gasped. "It is written that all actions should be performed in his light. To not do so is to show we are ashamed of those actions."

Her steps were quicker than Kyrianna could follow in the darkness. She entered the ring of the fire and Kyrianna took a sharp breath; the girl was a double for the woman she had seen in Brular's mind. "Rynalia?" She gasped out the name.

The girl frowned. "I don't understand. Rynalia was my great-grandmother. You confuse me for her?" She spread her feet apart and crouched slightly as she balanced her weight ready to fight. "Who are you and how do you know a face destroyed sixty years ago this night?"

This night? Kyrianna's mind reeled. She had arrived on the anniversary of those tragic events. *Chaos, can this get any worse?* She stood quietly letting her mind center itself again and watched as Cewyr and Shadow Seeker approached.

:Should we help? Cewyr asked in her mind.

:I have already committed one sacrilege this evening—that is quite enough. Wait, out of sight, but be ready—just in case.

"I am waiting, transgressor."

Kyrianna crossed her arms to show she had no intention of drawing her weapons. "You should know Brular Eglis showed more respect when he passed judgment; even when he did it on himself." She paused for a moment. "The transgressor has a name, Kindling. I am Kyrianna Dalynne, daughter of Lord Brygan and Lady Arielle of House Dalynne of Nydith. As I have stated, I have been traveling with Dywcia's blessing in this world. I came here tonight following a vision given me by Lord Hellavar. Honor this temple by showing respect to those whom you judge and wish to humble."

The girl's mouth dropped open as she stared at Kyrianna without saying anything.

Kyrianna kept the smile off her face as she continued speaking.

"Kindling of Mount Veri, I did not come here to commit sacrilege and I apologize if I violated temple edicts. However, you must admit, your walls are hardly closed nor are they marked to stop such inappropriate behavior."

"You are correct, but the policies are set. I must meet the code or my faith is forfeit."

"Chaos take it! What is the punishment?"

The girl stepped back, a frown on her face. "As I have said, you must fight me. If you win—you go free. If you lose—you are found guilty and must serve the temple for one year."

"Very well." She unclasped her cloak and started to remove her sword belts. "What other rules are there?" Her hand shot up to stop the girl's response.

"I don't want the entire litany of the church, just the rules of combat for this trial."

The girl smiled. "The rules are simple. Three contests; the winning of two decides the outcome. The fighters are not to touch the ground with any part of their body but their feet." She lifted her right foot straight out to demonstrate as her other stayed firmly planted. "Agreed?"

Kyrianna's mouth was dry as she spoke. "Agreed." The rules favored throwing styles but she had no intention of spending the next year pulling weeds and moving rubble. She forced her focus back on the fight as the girl's fist just cleared her nose and she turned to the side. "I didn't say I was ready." She was off balance and that wasn't good. Her left knee almost went to the ground as she ducked again.

It had been years since she had wrestled with her brother and she knew her skills in this type of fighting had never been very good to begin with. She found she was dodging too much and she ended up giving the girl one too many openings. She hit the ground hard as the girl's foot connected with her right knee. Through the blur of tears, she saw a flash of gold in the trees. :*Don't you dare. I will finish this.*

The girl reached for her knee. "I can help with that."

"You are a Flame Dancer and a cleric?" Kyrianna asked as the pain vanished.

"I am hardly either, but yes."

Kyrianna stood. "You never told me your name."

"Rynalana, after my great-grandmother, last Mistress of the

Flame of Mount Veri. How did you know her?"

Kyrianna smiled at the girl's eagerness but shook her head. "I think we both have questions, Rynalana. However, I know enough to know the order of things must be set right." She spoke as casually as if she were speaking to one of her friends or companions. "Ah, this will do." She knelt down to pick up a straight length of wood. "Not properly weighted, but sufficient to the task."

She walked back to the fire and looked at the girl. "Rynalana, you are a loyal servant to Hellavar, but I find your quick hands and feet to be far too much trouble. I don't have the time to spend a year in your service." She brought the quarterstaff up in a defensive position. "When you are ready, Kindling."

Rynalana smiled then exploded across the distance between them. Kyrianna brought the staff up and blocked the girl's approach and parried. The girl was fast but this was no game and the staff became a blur. Kyrianna caught the girl in the side then sidestepped and swept the staff behind the girl's right leg.

She rested the staff on the girl's chest as she lay on the ground.

She pulled the staff back and whistled. Cewyr stepped out of the trees.

Rynalana's face went white and she sat up to stare as the unicorn touched its horn to her leg. "You travel with a unicorn?"

"Her name is Cewyr; the wolf is Shadow Seeker."

"Ugh," Rynalana slapped at Shadow Seeker's muzzle as he licked her face.

Kyrianna swallowed a giggle at the silliness of the scene. Rynalana was obviously very earnest in her faith and determination to follow Hellavar, even without proper guidance. She didn't need to think she or her beliefs were being laughed at. She took a breath as Cewyr and Shadow Seeker backed off. "I don't have time for games right now, so let us finish this. Once the judgment has been determined, we can sit and talk." She raised the staff in salute as she waited for Rynalana to continue the match.

~ * ~

"Proving a point, were you?" Rynalana asked as she rubbed her head.

"You fight well, but you are still a novice," Kyrianna said. She didn't tell the girl she had had the benefit of training with the one of the finest arms masters to serve Nydith. "You're lucky I didn't want your head; others would not have been as kind."

Rynalana raised her head. "The temple edicts and traditions are all I have. I have no Keeper, Ember or priest to guide me," she said.

"Why do you stay here? Why not travel to Irrmar? There is a large temple there."

"I have no money. My parents are simple people. I would need a horse and supplies to travel those two weeks."

Kyrianna nodded. "Sorry, I forget you would need such things."

"What? Just how did you get here?"

She grinned at the confusion on Rynalana's face. "I'm sorry; my friend Cewyr is able to travel throughout these woods in a single moment."

Rynalana's eyes went wide. "You mean you could take me to Irrmar? That would be wonderful."

"Cewyr, can she come with us?" Kyrianna asked, looking from the girl to the unicorn.

"Is she still a maiden?" Cewyr looked from one to the other, her amethyst eyes glowing.

"Excuse me!" Rynalana stood up, her fists balled on her hips as she glared at the unicorn.

Kyrianna smiled at the scene. She knew Cewyr could sense whether or not Rynalana was still a maiden, but the mare apparently had decided to have some fun with the girl and Rynalana had obviously missed the humorous tone to the question.

:*I don't get it,* another voice whispered in Kyrianna's mind.

Kyrianna froze as Melissa continued speaking. :*She is obviously not married. Why would Cewyr question if she were a maiden?*

Kyrianna found herself gasping for air as she stood and walked away from the argument both Rynalana and Cewyr were having over the audacity of the question. At least the unicorn had managed to keep her thoughts on the edge of Kyrianna's mind so she could talk with Melissa. This would not be fun, and dealing with two conversations in her mind would make it even worse.

:*If you are not married, you are a maiden,* Melissa continued. :*If you are married, you are a woman. I know the definition. My mother told me about such things. Is there something more?*

Kyrianna closed her eyes and tried to will away the headache that was starting. She hadn't enjoyed this conversation with her mother and she definitely wasn't ready to speak from her mother's perspective.

:*Yes, Melissa, that is correct. Cewyr needn't have asked.* The last part was a mental shout directed toward the unicorn.

:*There's something you're not telling me,* Melissa said.

Kyrianna drew the silver sword from its scabbard and threw it point first into the ground. It wobbled a couple of times as she stood there. She had no doubt Melissa would try to bring the topic up again when she picked up the sword, but this way she would have time to try and think of something appropriate to say. "Sorry," she whispered.

:*That's okay,* Melissa said.

Kyrianna felt her stomach twist into a knot.

:*So, what is it you are not telling me?*

:*Melissa, how old are you?*

:*Older than you.*

The impatience in Melissa's voice gave Kyrianna the image of the child standing in front of her, hands on her hips and stamping her foot.

:*No. How old were you, when you…* She let the sentence trail off as she felt Melissa's attitude change. She drew her other sword and dropped it on the ground. This conversation was going from bad to worse and she had other things she needed to be doing other than explaining this to a ghost thirty years dead.

:*Kyri?* Melissa's voice was in her mind again.

:*You little minx, what are you doing?* She dropped her dagger on the ground and reached for her belt.

:*I can play hide and seek as well as anyone. Come on, Kyri, you're trying to hide something. What is it?*

Kyrianna continued to drop her gear on the ground, item by item only to hear Melissa laughing in her head. :*Nope, try again,* the girl said several times. She was finally left with only the long tunic and pants she wore under her armor and those were definitely not coming off. She paused and no longer heard Melissa in her head; either the girl couldn't move into the garments or she had gotten the idea.

"Does she do this often?" Rynalana asked.

Cewyr whinnied, a definite equestrian laugh. "It's the voices," she said as she bobbed her head in amusement.

Kyrianna spun around to glare at the girl and the unicorn. "One of those voices is usually yours, so I don't want to hear about it, horse," she said.

~ * ~

"This is the path back to the village," Rynalana said as they looked down at a trail overgrown with brush and crumbling.

"Cewyr, can you find another way down?" Kyrianna placed a hand on the mare's neck. "It would be too easy to break a leg on that path."

:*I'll meet you there.* She turned and vanished into the trees.

"Come on," Rynalana started down the trail with Shadow Seeker trotting ahead of her.

"Chaos," Kyrianna cursed as she slipped for the tenth or more time.

Rynalana grinned as she turned to assist. "It was said my great-grandmother could handle this trail faster than most can sprint."

Kyrianna nodded as she again felt her balance giving way. "She was a skilled Flame Dancer. However, at this point I will just be happy to not fall and slide the rest of the way."

The forest finally gave way to the village. A modest stone building greeted them as they left the trail. Kyrianna inhaled deeply at the scent of bread baking. "I doubt the gods understand the simple, lovely smell of fresh-baked bread," she whispered.

"Come in," Rynalana said as she opened the back door of the building.

Shadow Seeker darted past her and Kyrianna.

"Shadow! No!" Kyrianna made a grab for the wolf's tail, but missed.

Shouting came from inside the building and she and Rynalana ran in after him.

Kyrianna grinned. Shadow Seeker had not been in the house for more than a few seconds, but had already pounced on a fresh roll. A woman was screaming as the wolf ate his breakfast.

"It's okay, Mother," Rynalana said. "He's a friend, however ill-mannered." She placed her hands on her hips and frowned at the wolf.

Shadow Seeker lowered his head and took a step toward Kyrianna.

Before she could grab the collar he wore, he snatched another roll.

"Shadow!" Kyrianna slapped him as he escaped from the

room.

"I apologize for my friend's behavior," she said. "Please take it as a compliment to the skill of the baker." She reached for her coin purse. "I will pay for anything he has taken or ruined."

"No, you won't," Rynalana said.

The older woman stopped yelling and stared at her daughter.

"She has agreed to take me to Irrmar, and by all things—a unicorn. I will not let her pay for the food as I now owe her a debt I will never be able to repay."

"Lucas!" The woman leaned back against the wall.

A man of about forty seasons entered the room and looked around. His gaze lingered on Kyrianna for several moments before he turned to his wife.

"I think she is finally leaving us," the woman said. "She says she will go with this woman to Irrmar. I fear she has been bewitched. She says they travel by unicorn."

Kyrianna stepped in front of Rynalana. "Let's get something straight. If we talk about this to anyone else, she is a horse. Not a unicorn! I don't want some hunter or mage looking for my friend."

Rynalana looked at the floor. "I'm sorry. I did not realize the danger."

Kyrianna nodded then turned her attention to the girl's parents. "I am Kyrianna, a ranger of the goddess Frayrith, kindred of Dwycia. And I greet you in their and Hellavar's names.

"I assure you, Rynalana is not bewitched. She has met my friend, Cewyr. The three of us, Cewyr, Shadow Seeker and I, came to the ruins last night following a vision from Hellavar and there we met your daughter." Kyrianna paused. "She seeks a Keeper and I would consider it a partial repayment to another friend if you would allow me to see her safely to Irrmar."

Kyrianna waited as the couple stood there speechless. "No one from the clergy has returned here in ages," the woman finally said. "How can we trust you?"

"How dare you question her intentions?" Rynalana said.

Kyrianna, much to her own surprise, turned to glare at the girl. "And how dare you question your mother's concern?" She turned back to the couple and took a deep breath to calm her voice before speaking. "I do not follow Hellavar, but I owe a debt to one of his greatest servants. I would never lead your daughter away from him." Her voice trailed off for several heartbeats before she continued. "That one helped to lead me from a darkness deeper than you can image. To escort your daughter to a proper temple to continue her studies will be partial payment on what I owe to Brular Eglis." Her voice was only a harsh whisper as she stared at the floor.

"Our family owes a debt to the last Keeper of Mount Veri, also. Some of his last words placed my father in the care of a couple who lived next door to this very bakery. That act is seen as a blessing which brought my parents together. However, you are too young to have known the Keeper yourself. What debt do you speak of?"

Kyrianna looked up slowly as her vision blurred from the tears filling her eyes. "If only it were that simple. I can tell you I have met and traveled with him in these past few weeks. His faith is strong and his wish to guide his Kindling even greater. I journey soon to release him from the torment he has fallen into." Her voice grew harsher. "That is all I will say on this matter." Her voice choked and she swallowed hard before continuing. "It is too painful."

She closed her eyes as the image of Thynitic standing among the ruins of her throne came to her mind. Brular had smiled at her one last time just before his head rolled across the floor. She didn't fight the tears; instead letting them flow as she silently mourned.

"Ryna, gather your things and remember to take all of the texts with you," the man said, raising his hand to stop his wife's protest. He reached out and took his wife's hand in his. "I know it is sudden, but her tears show the truth of her words. Besides, if we stop Ryna now, she will only run down that road alone. Is that what we want?"

Rynalana's mother sighed then leaned her head against her husband's shoulder in a silent response.

The girl darted out of the room, as if afraid her parents would change their minds. "Ryna," her father called. "Do not leave without seeing your grandfather."

"Of course."

She came back into the room hunched over with a heavy pack. Kyrianna turned away, her chest tight as she watched Rynalana hug her parents. Her last memories of home were of heated words and being exiled by her father. Her throat tightened as the vision she had had in Torliana's chamber came back to her. A vision of her mother facing a group of Rynial elves, alone and unarmed. *It was one of her tricks*, she told herself. She felt Shadow Seeker bump her hand

and she glanced down to see him sitting next to her as he whined softly.

"I will be fine," Rynalana said. "Hellavar has provided and the path is well lit. All is to Order, as it should be."

Kyrianna leaned back against the wall. *It is like he is here.* She took a breath to settle her thoughts and stood straight as Rynalana approached her.

She stopped for a moment and sniffed. "Hmm, honey bread." She turned to her parents. "For the uni—ah, I mean horse." She gathered several rolls. "For Kyrianna and I also."

Kyrianna followed behind the girl leaving a few coins on a table as they entered the front room.

"Ryna, what was all that noise?" a man's voice called from a side room.

Rynalana walked into the room and bowed her head to the elderly man seated by the window. "I am sorry, Grandfather." Her voice was soft and soothing as she spoke. "I have found my light. It is time for me to go."

"You go with the woman?" He studied Kyrianna for several minutes, his bright and clear eyes giving a lie to his age. "You take care of her, you hear? She is the last Ember of Mount Veri."

Rynalana looked at the ground and blushed. "Grandfather, I am not an Ember, just a Kindling."

"It matters not," he said. "The clergy never deemed it important to restore the temple, yet this child herself stokes the fires of remembrance and studies the old texts. She has a light those in their high temples could never hope to have. You take care of her, you hear?"

Kyrianna found herself back in Brular's memories as she saw the years fade from the old man into the face of the boy. "There is no fear for the just," she said.

He looked at her and for a moment seemed lost in the memory as well. He smiled. "That is good."

Kyrianna bowed slightly. "Allow me to take this precious light to Irrmar. May its purity rekindle theirs."

~ * ~

Kyrianna checked Cewyr's legs as she waited for Rynalana to organize her pack. "Shadow, stop it," she called to the wolf who was nosing at the bundle of rolls.

"There," Rynalana straightened up, shouldered her pack and picked up the rolls. "Here, you greedy creature," she said, dropping a roll on the ground.

Shadow Seeker pounced on the roll.

"Here." Rynalana handed Kyrianna a honey roll.

Cewyr nipped at Kyrianna's hand as she broke off a piece and held it out to the unicorn.

Kyrianna let Cewyr have the roll, then turned back to face Rynalana. "I would suggest not eating very much at this time."

"What's the problem?"

"Teleportation is not very easy on the stomach," Cewyr said.

Kyrianna jumped onto Cewyr's back, then turned and offered a hand to Rynalana who ignored her. She jumped up behind Kyrianna on her own. Shadow Seeker positioned himself next to the unicorn.

Cewyr neighed as she lifted her head and the world began to swirl around them. The lush forest gave way to a riverside grove of trees.

Kyrianna fell forward against Cewyr's neck. She felt Rynalana roll off the unicorn's back then heard her start gagging. "This will take some getting used to," she said as she slid off Cewyr. She draped herself across the unicorn's back to keep her knees from giving out on her.

"Helped yourself at your parents before we left, did you?" Kyrianna asked as the girl continued to gag.

"You could have warned me," Rynalana said as she forced herself to her feet.

"I am not an expert at this." Kyrianna continued to cling to the mare as she waited for the world to settle back into place.

"Where are we?" Rynalana asked.

"Irrmar."

Rynalana stood next to her, leaning against Cewyr. "It is beautiful."

"It will be your new home, hopefully. We'll wait here for a while longer. I want my legs to stop wobbling. We will be walking in as I have no intention of parading Cewyr through the streets."

"The temple would ensure Order was maintained," Rynalana said. "How could we be in danger?"

Kyrianna turned to look at the girl. *I wish I were still that innocent,* she thought. "The temple does not rule here and there are many temples," she said. "Like many cities of this type, there are also several powerful Houses which hold power and have their own agendas and means of pursuing them. Be wary with your eyes and more so with your tongue."

Kyrianna removed the silver chain from Cewyr's neck. "Get some rest; we will be in short supply of that soon."

Cewyr brushed her muzzle against Kyrianna's cheek. :*Be careful,* she said before mist surrounded her and she vanished.

"She is a magical unicorn as well." Rynalana's jaw dropped as she stared at the figurine on the ground.

Kyrianna laughed as she put the figurine into her pocket. "Yes, she is more magical that most. However, I have another friend in the city with a horse that will take your breath away." She walked past the girl and toward the city.

They entered through one of the grand gates of the outer city. Kyrianna frowned at the high walled section that marked the homes of the nobility. *There are more nobles in this city than in Nydith, Bretinia and Calim combined; that cannot be a good thing. The more Houses there are, the more plots that follow.*

Kyrianna paused in front of a domed structure with several large towers. The dome glistened and reflected the light of the sun. The image created was of rays of sunlight streaming out from the center. Kyrianna shook her head as she realized the dome was covered with real gold. Her visions of Mount Veri before its fall showed no such flagrant exhibition of station or power. Brular had let his words and actions, not the temple's accoutrements, speak for his temple and faith. Words and actions closer to the truth than this extravagant display.

She started to step into the temple courtyard then froze as she felt an unseen presence examining her.

"Kyrianna, what's wrong?"

"I have a confession to make," she said as she pulled her cloak over her ears. "I am not a true human. Though my father's blood is strong in my spirit, it is my mother's elven blood that is most prominent physically."

"I have seen no signs of that heritage."

Kyrianna touched the ring and willed the magic to end. She pulled her cloak hood back to one side to show the girl her real face and ears. "I have been using magic to hide them. I have seen how half-elves are treated by some of the true elves of your world and even my own. I wanted to avoid problems."

"I understand. But you need not fear persecution in the light of the temple. Hellavar knows all beings shine brightly as they bask in his brilliance."

Kyrianna took a slow breath and nodded. *She speaks like him. How is that possible? They have never met.* She pulled the hood back. Trying to hide anything in the temple might be considered an insult. She would take the risk to prevent problems for Rynalana. "Let's go."

The carved doors that opened before them were easily thirty feet tall and inlayed with gold and jewels. Kyrianna felt her breath catch as she studied the mosaic inlaid in the marble floor. It was a sundial and a calendar. Various points along the path of the sun were marked with recessed gems. The light from the morning sun was shining just below a line of glittering rubies.

"The ruby marks High Summer; the Feast of the Summer Flame will be celebrated tomorrow."

Kyrianna's gaze moved into the great circular chamber. A huge altar sat in the middle on a raised platform. Flames danced on all sides of the platform with only a single narrow path between them.

The altar was as bright as the roof and Kyrianna swallowed hard. This was not Mount Veri. She suspected that not only was Hellavar worshipped here, but also some of the baser emotions of mankind.

"Rynalana, I have brought you here. However, it is not my temple and I am not versed in the proper traditions. I leave it in your hands. I am here if you need me."

Rynalana placed her pack on the floor and walked toward the altar.

Kyrianna placed a hand on the girl's shoulder. "I will return you home if you desire," she whispered. "Never feel you don't have a place to belong. It is an empty feeling."

Rynalana turned her head slightly and smiled. "Thank you."

She watched as the girl approached a priest and asked to speak to the Keeper. The priest disappeared for some time before an older man entered the room with another being. Tall and dark-skinned, Kyrianna was put into mind of the efreeti Brular had summoned.

The older man's robes were red, orange and yellow with the flame of Hellavar on one shoulder. Under the robes he wore a blue tunic. It was not the bright blue she remembered from Brular's vision, but instead it was pale, just enough color to prevent it from being white. The efreeti was wearing a black tunic and his robe was all the colors seen in a fire, except white. *An efreeti Flame Dancer. I don't care for this*, she thought.

She moved closer so she could hear what was being said.

"I come from the ruins of Mount Veri, Keeper," Rynalana said. "I seek a place in the light. I seek guidance. I seek to bear the light and be prepared as a true Kindling."

"It is not that simple, child," the Keeper said. "The temple has many students. The noble Houses see it as a worthy endeavor and have sought places for their children inside our walls. I have no place for a waif from outside the city."

Kyrianna felt her fists ball up. *This temple is nothing but a political sham. She comes for guidance and he turns her away without a moment's hesitation.*

The efreeti looked at her and she could see his eyes. She knew he could sense her anger. He approached her slowly and soundlessly. This was no novice as Rynalana was. There was purpose in his stride, there was power—he was a threat.

"You have brought she who would be Kindling?" he asked.

"Yes."

"Show your respect for the Keeper by not letting your anger radiate from you like this."

"He shows no respect to her. I find it difficult to show that for him."

"That is the way of things. I do not question. I act."

She lifted her head to look into his face and could feel the heat that radiated from his skin. Most definitely a native of the plane of fire.

She turned her attention back to Rynalana and the Keeper. The girl was on her knees and she felt her own heart breaking at seeing the girl's dream being destroyed by this pompous priest.

"Keeper, the light burns brightest for those who know not its radiance but its truth," Rynalana said. "The Order stands not for the many but for the one, the one who needs the structure to know their own self. I beg you, Keeper. I will stay in the forest and only come to the temple to study during the day. It is all I have desired to do for over four years."

"Child, you speak as if you quote texts to persuade me, but I know not these phrases, though the truth of them is strong." The Keeper looked down at her and frowned.

"I don't understand, Keeper. All the texts I call my faith are from Mount Veri's ruins."

"Do you challenge my recollection of the books of our faith?"

Rynalana turned ash gray as she bowed her head to the floor. "I don't understand; I have only tried to follow what was written."

"You teeter on heresy, child," the Keeper said. "In the temple, that is a high crime."

Rynalana was sobbing.

Kyrianna looked up at the efreeti.

"Questioning this Keeper is treated as sacrilege," his voice was a whisper. "It is a shame, for the girl speaks wisely. More so than I have heard in decades. She speaks almost as some of my efreeti brethren."

Kyrianna grinned. "Brular Eglis, Keeper of Mount Veri, has summoned some of your kin recently, has he not?"

His eyes went wide as he looked down at her. "You know that one! He had not shown his power in some fifty or more years until recently. Now he is silent once more."

"There are reasons for his silence." She looked away for a moment. "You said she spoke as some of your brethren." Her gazed moved to the heavy pack Rynalana had dropped. "Did Brular go there often many years ago?"

"Very often, he dealt with our priests and our rulers."

Kyrianna moved to Rynalana's pack and began rummaging through it. There were many worn books and then her hand touched something metallic. She pulled the box out to find a locked lid that had been pried from its hinges. She opened it as she looked at Rynalana still prostrate on the floor and the Keeper standing over her. The lid raised and she nodded as she touched the leather bound book.

"How many books of law have been written, Keeper?" she asked.

He blinked several times as he looked at her. "Three. Do not interfere lest the Brotherhood be forced to demonstrate their faith."

"Three? I don't understand," Rynalana said.

Kyrianna stood, the box in her hands, and turned toward the efreeti. "It appears your new Kindling has brought a gift. A gift from her first Keeper who still teaches, even though he is not of this plane any longer." She handed the box with the leather bound book to the efreeti. "She brings you the fourth book of law penned by Brular Eglis, Keeper of Mount Veri. She speaks no heresy. She speaks his words. The words of a Keeper strong in his faith and his place by the side of his god." She chose her next words carefully. "A Keeper willing to give anything to redeem a single lost Kindling."

The efreeti smiled. "The book is genuine."

"How can you be sure?" The Keeper turned to glare at Kyrianna.

"Every page has been enspelled. Only the heart's truth can be written on these pages. It is *his* book. The book his Speaker requested those many years ago." His tone turned harsh and accusing. "The book the clergy said could not be found."

"Keeper," Kyrianna fought to calm her emotions. "Has not Hellavar provided both the book and its first student? A student strong in her ideals because of the author, but lacking in the true understanding of the writings." Her voice was becoming forced. *She is a better priest than he. But she must enter the temple before she can rekindle it.*

The priest nodded and smiled; a smile not reflected in his eyes. "Yes." He looked down at Rynalana. "Kindling, you are accepted into this church. You shall carry the book to the library and I will have a priest see to finding you a room. I thank your companion for bringing us such a precious gift as your arrival with the fourth book." He paused as if considering his next words carefully. "We will celebrate the Feast of the Flame tonight," he said looking at Kyrianna. "I assume you will join us."

She was ready to refuse, but she saw the efreeti watching her from the corner of his eyes and Rynalana peering at her with pleading eyes. "I shall, but I do not know your customs."

"With you permission, Keeper, I will see to that myself."

"I leave it to you, Master of the Flames."

Kyrianna cocked her head to the side as she looked at the efreeti then bowed it slightly.

"Kindling and friend of Brular, let us see to the book," the Master of the Flames said, gesturing to a doorway.

Kyrianna saw the Keeper's eyes widen as he seemed to be studying her again. She nodded politely and smiled. *He and Lord Ravel are two of a kind*, she thought.

"While you are Kindling, you do not question the Keeper," the Master of the Flames said. "To question him is to question this church. Your thoughts are free, your mouth is not." He paused for a long moment letting his words sink in.

"He did not ask, so I will. Is it the clergy, the Brotherhood, the Order or the Walkers you wish to be Kindled to?"

"Walkers?" Kyrianna looked up at him. "I have not heard that title before."

"They are a druidic group devoted to the sun and the fire of Hellavar. They spurn his Order, but are accepted as they see to the balance of the forests and lands directly. This temple only houses the clergy."

"But…" Rynalana jerked her head up. "Mount Veri had all but Walkers beneath its roof."

"Only a strong Keeper can hope to have two of the following within one wall. Mount Veri was renowned for its devotion with both a Keeper and a Mistress. It is said Keeper Eglis was seeking a Sword to lead the Order when doom befell Mount Veri. But without a proper Sword, he had still made the paladins welcome, even among the Brotherhood."

Kyrianna looked at Rynalana. "The Order assisted in presiding over the rites of the Flame Dancers."

The Master of the Flames stopped. "Priests are not permitted by this Keeper to come to our rites." He shook his head and resumed walking. "Kindling, I await your answer."

Kyrianna knew what the girl's answer would be before she spoke. There could only be one for this Kindling.

"The Brotherhood calls me to the flames as it did my great-grandmother. I will find the path to its burning heart and then to Hellavar himself. I ask only that I be allowed to continue to learn from the fourth book."

The Master of the Flames smiled. "As I would have insisted."

This is the library of this wealthy church? Kyrianna looked around at the mostly empty and dusty shelves. Her father's study held more books than she saw here.

"Only books the clergy deem worthy are kept here," the Master of the Flames said.

Kyrianna took a deep breath and shook her head. "I care not for this temple. I had hoped to bring the Kindling to a place of learning. I have traveled with Brular Eglis and heard his words spoken from his heart. This is not what he would have wanted. Knowledge is power." She gestured toward the empty shelves. "So is the lack of it. It gives the power to control, manipulate and twist." She did nothing to hide the anger in her voice. "I leave her not in this Keeper's care but in yours. I place this trust in you because I hear more than just lip service to Hellavar's teachings in your words. However, I will have your word that you will guide her properly."

"That you have."

Kyrianna saw the half smile on his face and realized he approved both of her anger and her caution. Still the feel of this place did not sit well with her. "For your sake, I hope you do. If my friends and I are successful, it will not be me you will answer to, but the Keeper of Mount Veri himself. Believe me, his anger will be such that it will outshine the sun itself."

The Master of the Flames laughed. "Bring him; it will be glorious to see the Keepers meet."

~ * ~

The feast, as Kyrianna expected, was extravagant. The clothing of the female Flame Dancers was skimpy, almost nonexistent. Their normal robes were apparently not enough, or perhaps too much. Simple Order was not enough for this temple. The lurid movements of the Flame Dancers were suggestive of other activities to come and she had to restrain herself from drawing her dagger when one of the men gestured to her to join him. She couldn't believe she was seeing this. *This is not his world*, she thought. *This is a corruption of the ideals*.

She felt warmth behind her and Rynalana. They both turned to see the Master of the Flames standing there. He stepped forward and they made a space for him.

"The Kindling tells me you are a follower of Dwycia and another goddess she cannot recall hearing of before. From your dress and patrons, I believe you to be one who walks the paths of the forest and wilderness. Because of this, I sought out the Seer who leads the Walkers of the Great Grove. I explained our temple's good fortune and your quest." He opened his hand to show her a ruby ring with a band as red as the gem. "It is a ring of Hellavar's Favor. It can protect you indefinitely in most flames and even heal you for a time in the fires of the sun itself. It can transform your arms into wings of fire to soar the skies and will also allow you to hurl globes of fire at your enemies. More than this, you can command beings of fire. They will know your favor and will not approach."

Kyrianna took the ring from his hand and placed in on her finger. The ring was warm, but not uncomfortable. "Thank you. I appreciate the honor. May I never dishonor Hellavar's name in its use."

He nodded then stood and joined the other dancers.

Kyrianna let her thoughts wander. *It is time I returned home. I will ask Cewyr to take me to Kilenter. It feels like an eternity since I left and I should see them at least once before I take this journey.* For a brief moment, she saw her mother facing the Rynial elves again. *It was only one of her lies. One of her lies.* Still, no matter how much she tried to convince herself, she continued to wonder if she would ever see her mother again.

~ * ~

Cewyr's warm breath blew across the back of her neck as Kyrianna waited at the edge of the grove. She had stood there for several minutes waiting for the druid who was meditating to finish and acknowledge her before entering.

It was almost an hour before the woman stood and turned toward her. She lifted her eyebrows slightly, but did not betray any other sign of surprise on her face as she held out her hands in greeting. "Dwycia welcomes you, traveler," she said.

"I thank her for the welcome and for yours as well. My companions and I seek only to enter your grove as it will allow my mount to travel to my home."

The druid looked at the unicorn. "You have a unique gift. I gladly grant you access to this grove any time you have the need to travel between the worlds." She bowed her head and quickly stepped past them.

The air was still and quiet in the grove; no sounds from outside entered the area. "Are you ready?" Kyrianna asked as she placed a hand on Cewyr's neck.

The unicorn only bobbed her head.

She jumped onto the mare's back then motioned Shadow Seeker to do so also. She wrapped her arms around the wolf to steady him in front of her. Cewyr lifted her head high as she neighed and a flash of light surrounded them.

Kyrianna closed her eyes and dropped Shadow Seeker as the dizziness and nausea hit her. This was worse than walking the forest path. She fell forward against Cewyr's neck gasping. She didn't know how long she lay there with the unicorn frozen in place, waiting for the world to stop spinning. When her vision cleared, she sat up and looked around. This was the place her visions had shown her mother renouncing Thynitic. She winced as the goddess' name came to her thoughts. She knew she would never forget what she had suffered as a result of that one's interference in her life.

Her stomach settled, Kyrianna whistled for Shadow Seeker and pointed Cewyr at the road to Nydith.

~ * ~

Kyrianna sat up straighter as they approached the gates of Nydith. She doubted the banishment order her father had issued had ever been rescinded and there was a chance she would be recognized and turned away. However, she would not use the ring to sneak in. This was her home; she would ride Cewyr through the gates as if she belonged there.

:*No concern about anyone wanting to hunt me?* Cewyr asked.

:*No. The speaker of the Talidilith rides a unicorn when she comes to see the council. And I heard rumors one of the human druids of Neyalisi also rides a unicorn. It is unusual to see one, but not enough to cause alarm. Besides, there are no mages in Nydith.*

Before they were close enough for the guards to see her features clearly, she reached up and ruffled her hair, running her hand across her brow as if from the warmth of the day. In fact, she was trying to hide the most obvious feature of her elven heritage—her ears.

The guards only gave them a cursory glance as Cewyr and Shadow Seeker trotted past them and Kyrianna released the breath she hadn't realized she had been holding.

The streets were quiet as they approached the place where she had grown up. Had it really been less than six months since she had last ridden through these same streets? After everything she had been through, it felt more like decades had passed. The courtyard was empty and the area was unusually quiet for midday. There were no sounds of ringing metal coming from the training arena or of horses and riders in the pastures. She slid off Cewyr's back and hurried around the hedges to the main door.

"Chaos! No!"

There, next to the door was a black flag—the flag of mourning. She didn't even bother to knock as she burst into the entrance hall. The silver seal on the flag meant it was either the lord or the lady of the House who had recently died.

"How dare you intrude during this time?" a voice echoed in the darkness as she ran into the house.

"Father?" She stopped and turned in the direction he had called from. The great hall was cloaked in shadows, the curtains drawn and the lamps dimmed. "Father? What happened? Where's Mother?" She forced her feet to carry her into the room, her heart pounded as the vision came back to her.

"Kyrianna?" A figure rose in the shadows. "Why have you returned?"

She flinched at the anger in his voice. "I wanted to see my family again. I have been away for some time and hoped I would be allowed a brief visit. What has happened? Where are the others? Where is Mother?"

Lord Brygan stood in front of her, his eyes red as he stared at her. His once straight and proud stance was now stooped and she saw deeply etched lines in his face that not been there when she left. She reached out and took his right hand in both of hers. "Father, what happened?" Her voice broke and sounded small as she looked up at him. True, they had had many arguments over the years, but it hurt deeply for her to see him now. The fire that once burned so brightly in his eyes was gone.

"Five days ago, your mother was struck down in agony. No cause. During one of her more lucid moments, all she was able to say was your name and the name of that foul goddess she once served."

"Thynitic," Kyrianna whispered.

Her father jerked his hand away from her and with a speed she remembered from when she was younger, struck her hard across her cheek. "Do not speak that name in this house, ever!"

She bowed her head and took a half-step back. "My apologies. I meant no offense. I have had recent dealings with that one as well and know the pain she can inflict."

"Then it is no coincidence Arielle mentioned the two of you

together?"

Kyrianna kept her head bowed as she spoke. "No, it is not. The Chosen of that one was able to use her powers to trap me. She said she had linked Mother and I in such a way that Mother would suffer all of the torments she was dealing to me. It was only the courage of my friends that saved me." Kyrianna paused and swallowed hard, the tightness in her throat choking her. "They risked much in coming after me, but they would not abandon me. I owe them a great deal."

Her father reached out and raised her chin. There were fresh tears in his eyes and a slight smile on his face as he looked at her. "And, it would appear, so do I. Welcome home, my daughter." He shifted his hand to her shoulder and pulled her close and hugged her tightly for several minutes before releasing her and stepping back.

"What happened to Mother?"

"Two days ago, she came out of the enchantment or whatever it was that held her. All she would tell me was you were safe and she was being called to Kilenter. It was only after she left I realized she had not taken her weapons or any guards with her." His voice was rushed, as if he was afraid to stop speaking. "Several hours after she left, her horse returned without her. Your brother, uncle and a contingent of the guard went into Kilenter looking for her. A messenger brought me news of what I already knew—she was dead. They found her in the grove she had cared for all these years. The messenger said Erudus believed she was attacked by a group of the Rynial. He and the others are tracking them now."

"That is the same grove where she renounced Thyn—" She caught herself before she finished the name.

"It is."

"I was there before coming here. I saw no evidence of this."

"The messenger said your mother's body was covered by a golden mist then vanished. She was called by Frayrith."

"The Rynial are followers of that one. With Mother's original renunciation and my friends rescuing me from her, her anger had to find an outlet. Mother wasn't carrying her sword and the blessing laid on it by Frayrith was part of what protected Mother from her. The Lady of Chaos has much to answer for. She has taken another of my friends and those I travel with are preparing to enter her realm to find him. I cannot stay long and must return to them. I vow that if I am able, I will extract a blood price from the Lady of Chaos."

"No! I will not risk losing you as well. Go after your friend, yes. But do not seek that one out. When you are done, you will be welcomed back. This is your home—and it always will be." He smiled. "Wait here." He turned and left the room. Kyrianna walked to the large side windows and pulled the curtain open. The warmth of the sunlight flooded the room and she stood there letting it chase the shadows away. She reached to pull them closed as her father came back into the room.

"Leave them open. Your mother would have hated me hiding here in the dark. She was always quick to laugh and smile. I must remember her like that and not let this darkness fill me. She would never have wanted that. However, she would have wanted you to have these."

Kyrianna stared at the items her father was holding out for her to take. He held both the silver inlaid bow her mother had once carried as well as the unicorn horn sword. The simple gold hilt and pommel held the same rearing unicorn symbol that was on her wrist as well as three dark red gems. Frayrith's Tears, those gems were called, formed from the blood of a unicorn.

"May the sword help to protect you from the Lady of Chaos as it once protected her," her father said.

She took the weapons and nodded her thanks. She would carry and wield them proudly.

"Do you need a good mount? Smoke returned to us a few weeks after you left and he is still yours."

"Actually," she paused and grinned. "I have a mount. Come outside and meet her."

Her father followed her out to the courtyard. Her grin widened as he stopped and stared at the silver-gray unicorn chewing on a mouthful of grass. "Lord Brygan of House Dalynne of Nydith, this is Cewyr. Cewyr, this is my father."

The unicorn stepped over and touched Brygan's chest with her horn. "May your grief soon pass," she said softly. "The Lady of the Forests feels your sorrow as well. Know your lady is with her."

Brygan stepped back and bowed his head. "I thank you."

:Kyri, I will not be able to return to Shokar until tomorrow if you wish to pass the night with your family.

:If I stay, I may not want to leave. We should return to the grove so you

*can leave as early as possible. The others will be waiting and I didn't tell Myrith
I would be making this extra trip.*

Kyrianna looked up at her father. "Tell Erudus I was here and
give him my love. I will return as soon as I can."

"I'm glad you came back, Kyrianna. Please forgive my harsh
words; I was wrong."

"As was I. I'm sorry."

"Here, one more thing." He handed her a small ring with the
symbol of Ibacia on it.

She froze as she looked at the ring and back up at her father.
He had welcomed her back, and asked her to forgive him. Now he
was reminding her of the reason he had exiled her.

"That ring belonged to Lord Ravel. He and several other minor
lords were finally tied to the Thieves Guild and evidence was found
of their blackmail of different members of the council. I thought
you would appreciate the news."

"Thank you." She swallowed hard as she glanced back down
at the ring.

"Even though I want you to stay here, particularly at this time,
I understand you have a duty to your friends. You had best leave
now, before I find a way to keep you here. Frayrith and Oliaric go
with you, daughter."

"And with you." She climbed on Cewyr's back and tightened
her knees as the unicorn reared up then pivoted on her hind feet
and darted through the gate.

~ * ~

When they reached the grove, Kyrianna slid off Cewyr's back
and sat on the ground, her mother's sword held across lap, her tears
falling.

"Frayrith, Lady of the Forests," she whispered. "I know I no
longer have any right to call on you. My faith wavered and many
times I thought you and Dwycia had abandoned me to Thynitic. I
ask your forgiveness for my weakness."

A unicorn stepped into the area. As Kyrianna looked up, it
changed into an elven woman. "Kyrianna, daughter of Arielle, there
is no need to ask for forgiveness. The road we have asked you to
travel was difficult and it will continue to be so. I cannot explain
but this part of your trial was needed to hold Thynitic's power in
check and prepare the path you and others will walk later."

She knelt down and lifted Kyrianna's chin. "Do you know why the gods work through others? It is because we are governed by our natures. We are prisoners of what is expected of us, our follower's beliefs and the dominions of our faith and power. You, Kyrianna, have free will. You can choose. That gave you the ability to reject Thynitic's power. And that gives you the chance to rescue the Keeper of Mount Veri. You did something I cannot. You were able to doubt."

Kyrianna shook her head. "Doubt?"

"Yes. Doubt, the greatest weakness. But where there is doubt, there can be redemption, rededication and rebirth."

She slipped her quiver from her shoulder and handed it to Kyrianna. "A gift. The right side holds up to one hundred arrows and each will come immediately to your hand. The left holds a charm that creates a single arrow as needed." She smiled. "Your bow need never worry it will be lonely for an arrow. The sword and its magic are indeed strong against the powers of chaos. The bow is also empowered; any arrow fired from it is able to pierce even the best concealment. Use them well."

She stood and pulled Kyrianna up with her. "I know you will go after Brular, and you cannot pretend there is no need for urgency. He cannot withstand her renewed assault for long."

Kyrianna twisted the strap of the quiver in her hands as she stared at the ground. "But he endured for over a decade before. His will is the strongest I have seen. Why would he be vulner—?" her voice trailed off, then her head jerked up and she gasped out a single word. "Torliana!"

"Correct. What he did not realize about Torliana or his own heart protected him. He had a fortress of scripture and no emotions to betray him. Now, that crack has been found and it is being chipped at as we speak. He fights hard, Kyrianna, but he will lose. You and the others must save him before that happens." Frayrith paused, a slight smile on her lips. "Cewyr cannot return to Shokar until tomorrow, therefore it is time for you to rest and be restored."

Kyrianna felt her eyelids grow heavy then strong arms were holding her as blackness claimed her.

~ * ~

Kyrianna woke to hear a child laughing and Shadow Seeker barking. She was surrounded by the fragrance of flowers and found the area filled with their bright colors. "These weren't here before," she said as she sat up and turned toward the laughter. A ghostly child was chasing the wolf around the trees. She smiled as she watched them. *Melissa, how long since you last laughed like this? Some thirty years, I suppose.*

She heard a soft thud behind her and turned to see Cewyr off to the side; the unicorn's eyes watched the girl as well. *:Kyri, what is to become of her?*

:I don't know. Denied a life. Denied a family. I have a father and brother who will welcome me home. She has no one.

"What are you thinking about?" a soft voice whispered next to her.

Kyrianna turned at the whisper to see Melissa standing there. She studied the almost transparent girl for a moment. "Melissa, you followed me because we were both homesick and lost within our own darkness. You helped to bring me back to my friends and even my family. I go now to the Abyss itself where the wrath of the Lady of Chaos awaits us. You need not go."

Melissa frowned. "And where would I go?"

"I could take you to a temple of Mykaylene. They should have a way to send your soul to your mother and father's side."

"Then who would watch over you?"

Kyrianna smiled. "I thank you for that, little sister. But it is time for someone to watch over you for a while."

"It has been a long time since someone called me sister."

Kyrianna stared at the girl as an idea came to her. "Would you want to live with me and my family? I know Father would allow you to stay. Perhaps you could be the obedient daughter he never had."

Melissa's face glowed with an inner light. "You mean live." She stared at her ghostly hands. "I have been so long among the dead I doubt it is even possible."

Kyrianna shrugged then placed her hands in Melissa's just as she had done for the girl's mother. "If it is possible, I will find a way to make it happen."

:Kyri, there is someone coming, Cewyr said.

She stood as Melissa faded. A buckskin horse entered the clearing ridden by a person in half-plate armor, a full helm covering his face. The gold braid of a district commander was on his shoulder. "Erudus?" she asked.

Without a word, the man reached up and removed the helm.

"Kyrianna?"

He stared at her for a moment then dropped the helm and jumped off his horse. "Kyri!" He grabbed her arms and pulled her into a tight hug. "What are you doing here?" He released her and stepped back.

"I came back to see my family. Unfortunately, I must be leaving soon to rejoin my companions."

"You've already been home?"

"I have." She glanced around.

"The others are returning there. I told Uncle Dysiren I wanted to spend some time here alone." He stopped and looked at her. "However, I am glad you are here as well."

She nodded. "Did you find them?"

"We did. I also found this." He reached into his saddlebags and removed a nine-strand whip. He held the whip between his fingers and passed it to her.

"Are you sure?" Kyrianna asked as she took the whip.

"Yes. It is the same one that hung in the hall; the one that belonged to Mother."

Kyrianna stared at the braided leather in her hand. Everything Thynitic had shown her had been true. "Let me keep this. Father will not want it and I have a use for it."

"What use could you possibly have for *that?*"

"I intend to return it to the Lady of Chaos personally." She stuffed the whip into her pack then whistled for Shadow Seeker. She removed the long sword she had been carrying; the green metal glowed slightly. "Here, a souvenir from another world. Give it to Father for me."

"Kyri, what are you up to?" Erudus took the blade and slipped it into a loop on his saddle.

"I have a personal score to settle with Thynitic, as well as a friend to rescue. I intend to make her pay for what happened to Mother."

She moved to climb on Cewyr's back. The unicorn neighed and danced away from her. "What's wrong?" She reached out to place a hand on the mare's neck and again the unicorn moved away from her.

"Kyri?" Erudus approached her and Cewyr cautiously.

The unicorn neighed shrilly. "I will not carry that vile thing. Leave it behind," she said.

"What?"

"Mother's whip. She doesn't want you taking Mother's whip with you," Erudus said.

"I'm sorry, but it's going. As I said, I intend to give it back to Thynitic personally."

"Kyrianna, you're being rash. Remember the last time you let your rashness lead you somewhere it shouldn't have," Erudus said.

Kyrianna spun around and glared at her brother. "It led me straight to my brother. My brother, whose duty was more important to him than his family!"

"What are you doing?" Melissa appeared between Kyrianna and Erudus. "Why are you doing this? You just managed to reconcile with your father and now you're trying to put a barrier between you and your brother. You already know what it's like to lose your family once, don't lose them again." She faded away.

Kyrianna took a half-step back. "I'm sorry." She shook her head. "I am still taking the whip with me, though." She turned to look at the unicorn.

Cewyr turned and Kyrianna saw a star-shaped scar on the mare's right flank. :*Courtesy of that whip when it was in your mother's hands.*

Kyrianna continued to stare at the scar; her breath short and coming in quick gasps. "I didn't know." She caught her breath and tried to ignore the tightening in her chest. "I have no intentions of using it, except to throw it at Thynitic's feet." She paused as she moved her gaze away from the scar to Cewyr's eyes. "I need to do this, please."

The unicorn stared at her for several heartbeats, the amethyst eyes dark as they seemed to be studying her. Finally, the mare bobbed her head in agreement. "I don't like it, and I don't trust that thing. Look at the anger and pain it has already tried to bring to those here."

"You think our fight was due to the presence of the whip?" Erudus asked.

"I do. It has a vile aura surrounding it. As long as you do not use it and it remains secure, I will carry it."

Kyrianna nodded. "Thank you." She turned toward her brother. "I'm sorry."

"I understand." He grabbed her shoulders and hugged her again. "Be careful. I don't want to lose you again."

"I will." She grabbed her pack, jumped on Cewyr's back and wrapped her arms around the wolf that followed her.

"Tell Father I love him and hope to be back soon," she said as Cewyr lifted her head. "Take care of yourself." She raised her hand in salute as the world fell away.

Chapter Nine
Myrith

Myrith walked through the corridors of the coliseum. The place seemed lonely since the rest of the group left yesterday. Kyrianna had been the last of the group to go, waiting until all the others had left to seek the meaning of their visions. They had stood together at the gates to the Coliseum. Kyrianna had looked up at her, started to say something then turned and walked away in silence. The girl then stopped after a few steps and turned back. "Thank you," was all she said before she headed for the Great Grove.

Myrith had stood there for several minutes watching Kyrianna walk away before going to meet with Sarasnar. The Shield had said he wanted to talk to her about her position within the Order, but that conversation had instead taken the form of an interrogation. She didn't trust Sarasnar; he had hidden the extent of his abilities from them when they were at the Duvall Estate. Then the way he acted when they arrived here. He had demanded Vyroris be sent back to Rhysia. He claimed he was being generous as the normal policy was to destroy draconic creatures immediately to prevent the evil they brought with them from being released.

Then after Vyroris was gone, Sarasnar was willing to let everyone but Kyrianna enter, claiming she had been touched by the foulest of evil and could not be allowed within the temple. Andrinor had been ready to tear Sarasnar apart over the insults.

Myrith had convinced Sarasnar to allow Kyrianna into the temple and he had used powerful magics to heal her body and calm her spirit. It appeared he had agreed to her request because Myrith was favored of Mykaylene. And perhaps that was the reason. If he felt she held special favor, maybe he was hoping to gain some of it for himself. Now, after their conversation, she knew he would no longer be willing to go out of his way to help her. He had called her lowborn and pointed out the majority of the members of the Order were from noble Houses. The only thing he hadn't called her, and she knew he had thought it, was a whore.

His accusation she had forsaken Geladas still stung. True she had never truly served Geladas, being called by him as she was pulled into the portal. She had only found her way to his temple because others had sought to use her. She had not partaken in his religious training—seeking only to be trained as a warrior. She had not forsaken Geladas; instead Geladas had allowed Mykaylene to adopt her as he could not be with her in this world. She had no doubts Geladas was pleased she was serving the Battle Maiden in this place.

She had left that meeting upset and feeling even more alone. Except for the tutors who had been assigned to her, most of the clergy and knights avoided her. None of them were happy she and the others were here. The ranking clerics would stop talking when she came into rooms and watch her until she left. There was something more going on than just her being an outsider. Something linked to Kyrianna and Thynitic and she had the feeling it involved her as well. That sensation of a connection between her and Kyrianna, one deeper than the friendship they shared, came back. When the girl got back from her trip to Mount Veri, they would need to talk about this. For now, she had to get to her morning lessons, then after lunch she would be helping with training the recruits to the Order. Why she had agreed to that after the interview with Sarasnar, she wasn't sure.

~ * ~

Myrith looked up from her meal as the bells began announcing the afternoon sparring session. This morning's lessons had been much the same as yesterday evening's. Long dry lectures on the proper behavior and piety of one called by Mykaylene. So far none of the clerics who lectured her had spent any time trying to teach her about the religious precepts of the Battle Maiden, only ways in which her servants could earn glory and honor within the church.

"Lady Myrith?"

She looked up to see one of the pages for the temple standing in front of her table.

"Yes?"

"Sir Gwideon of the Grey has sent a message that he will be arriving at the Coliseum shortly and he wishes to speak with you."

"The Grey?"

"They are the Order who serve Resare," the boy said.

"I am not from here, and do not know much about the other churches. Will you walk with me to the gates and tell me what you have learned of Resare and the Grey?"

The boy beamed and seemed to bounce as they walked through the corridors and he was able to instruct her on what he knew of Resare's church.

The Grey were the sword arm of Resare the Lord of Death. As such, they held no allegiance to any other lord. Resare himself held no allegiances with any of the other deities and was looked on as a nature god, one who was charged with maintaining balance in the world. His knights and assassins were responsible for seeing to those who would cheat death and to the eradication of the abominations of the undead.

Myrith shook her head as the boy continued with his explanation. Some of the things he was telling her were confusing. On one hand they destroyed the undead, but on the other they punished the vile by making them serve the church as undead servants for a time.

"They do not normally take sides in times of war," the boy said. "The only time they take the field is during times of great carnage when the newly dead call for retribution en masse. It is said when his priests take the field, their enemies cower. To lose can be more costly than simple death. His knights serve his cause to death and beyond."

They stopped at the gate and Myrith patted the boy on the shoulder. "I thank you for taking the time to educate me," she said. "However, I would not want you to get into trouble for missing any of your duties." The boy bowed then hurried away.

She looked down from the top of the steps, over the crowd that had gathered. She gripped her sword as she caught her breath. There was no mistaking Riker being led toward the temple. A glowing silver rein was held by a man in full plate and riding a tiger that was as tall as the ghostly horse. She walked slowly down the stairs as the man dismounted and waited for her. He was tall, taller than her by a few inches. But it was not his height which caught her attention; it was the size of the sword on his back. *Impressive—if he can wield it effectively*, she thought.

Her gaze went to Riker. She had been told yesterday he had been summoned by the Gatekeeper of Resare, and it was this which had prevented her from calling the horse to her. As she took the time to study him, she did not see or feel any sign Riker was under any magical compulsion. She turned her attention back to the knight. He was kneeling at the base of the stairs, his head bowed slightly.

"Lady Myrith Lake, knight in service to Mykaylene, I have been told you seek to release the Keeper of Mount Veri from the Abyss."

She gritted her teeth. "That is correct, Sir Gwideon of the Grey." He bowed his head deeper and she frowned at the aura that radiated from the pommel of his sword. "I see your weapon speaks as well," she said. "It speaks ill."

Gwideon raised his head slightly, but not his eyes, as he spoke. "It is Drinker, the desiccator and eradicator of Resare's enemies. I know of what you speak. One of the enchantments bound to its blade is necromantic and allows it to drain strength from my opponents. I also must pay a price for this magic and Resare accepts this as a prayer from his servant. I assure you it has no fouler power than that." He reached back and drew the weapon from its sheath and held it in front of him. "I will present it to your clerics if you wish." He paused then continued. "There are far uglier weapons I could have brought. However, out of respect to the path you walk, they have remained behind."

"As well they should. You have brought my companion to me, who I understand was summoned by your Gatekeeper—explain this."

"The spirit was compelled to stand before the Gatekeeper, as is his right with any being of the realm of the dead within his domain. The Gatekeeper sought to understand why this spirit was still among the living. Riker told the Gatekeeper of your deeds at the Duvall Estate and how Mykaylene allowed him to remain behind to serve you. He then told the Gatekeeper you seek Brular Eglis. Resare has added his support to your quest and I have returned Riker to you with a magical rein that allows him to remain among the living without consequence. Resare and my Gatekeeper offer one other gift."

Gwideon bowed his head again as he raised Drinker and held the blade out to Myrith in both hands. "I swear my life and sword to you and your quest. The Keeper of Mount Veri has suffered much; it is time that ended."

Myrith glanced around and saw the respect in the eyes of the crowd that had gathered. *I must learn more about him*, she thought. *He has them in such awe that his offering his oath to me has caused them to have respect for me. These are the same people who looked down on me just yester-day—this makes no sense.*

"While I am honored by your words and actions, I cannot accept your oath."

She raised a hand to stop the mutterings she heard from the crowd. "An oath of this nature cannot simply be given, it must be earned." She turned and headed back into the Coliseum then stopped and looked back at the knight still kneeling on the step. "Come, Gwideon, let us test each other's strength and mettle. Let me earn what you have offered and then you can earn your place with my companions and I as we travel into the Abyss itself."

"As it should be," he said as he stood. "A sword should be measured by deeds—not words."

As she turned away, she heard him sheath the sword and mount the tiger. *This should be interesting.*

Myrith called Riker and he charged through the walls of the Coliseum drawing a gasp from the growing crowd of spectators. She mounted the horse and gestured to one of the squires to hand her a lance. The time she had spent away from her tutors yesterday had been used in training. The horse master for the Coliseum had even praised how quickly she had picked up the basics of the lance. Now that she was on Riker, she had no doubts in her abilities to face an opponent. She watched as Gwideon waved off the offer of a lance from one of the other squires and drew his sword. "Favored weapon for all situations?" she muttered.

She nodded again and tightened her knees to signal Riker. The horse charged toward their opponents. Her lance connected first, and while Gwideon's seat wavered, he remained on the tiger. She ground her teeth together to keep from crying out in pain as Gwideon swung his sword in a backwards arc to catch her as she passed. *That sword in the hands of someone more practiced in mounted combat could be devastating.*

Riker spun to face the tiger again and Myrith smiled as the great cat leapt forward before Gwideon was ready, setting the knight back in the saddle and off balance. Even with the solid blow her lance delivered, the knight kept his seat and was able to hit her again. Riker turned again and she checked his charge as Gwideon pulled the tiger up.

"Well fought, Lady Lake. This contest is yours. Shall we see how we fare on the ground?"

"Yes."

The tiger growled and shook as Gwideon dismounted causing the knight to stumble. As soon as he had stepped away, the tiger turned toward Myrith and roared a challenge as its right paw scraped the dirt.

"My apologies, Lady Lake," Gwideon said. "It appears my companion refuses to leave the field."

"The mount should heed its rider. Perhaps it needs a lesson in proper behavior."

Riker reared as the tiger stalked toward them. :*It is powerful.* She heard Riker's voice in her mind.

"It is a challenge I must accept," she whispered as she tightened her knees and leaned forward.

One quick charge and that should be it, she thought. She was wrong. The tiger shifted smoothly into a run, its pace that of a predator. She caught the tiger with her lance, but it leapt at her, teeth and claws bared, heedless of possible injury to itself. The claws dug into her armor, dragging her from Riker. Her hand went to her sword, but the tiger's teeth were already at her throat. She kept her gaze steady and refused to flinch at the sharpness of the tiger's teeth against her skin.

They remained like that for several heartbeats, then the tiger opened his jaws. She never took her gaze from it as it appeared to glow then its paw touched her shoulder, where the claws had torn her armor. The pain in her shoulder vanished and she watched as the tiger's shoulder was torn and blood flowed. It stepped back and roared then turned and walked away.

"Your mount is powerful," Myrith said as she turned to face Gwideon.

"I never called him my mount. I was told by the Gatekeeper that a companion would meet me at the gates of the catacombs." He nodded toward the tiger. "He was there this morning. I took that as a sign my horse was not required on this trip and I should accept the tiger as my transportation through the Abyss."

Myrith nodded. "He has earned his place, can you?" She raised her hand to summon the clerics. They were both still hurt, and this match needed to start out on an even footing for them. She raised her sword in salute as the clerics left and waited for Gwideon to draw his blade.

He stepped into her swing and ignored the blow she delivered to his side as he brought his blade down hard. The force of the blow rocked her and she staggered back a few steps.

Gwideon ignored her repeated hits against his armor as he waited for his opening. First one swing, then a second and a third; each one forcing her back and causing pain. The stabbing pain in her side was enough to tell her the force of the last hit had broken at least one rib. Another solid strike and her knee hit the ground as she fell back. "Well fought," she said.

Myrith was gasping as she looked up at Gwideon. He raised his visor, then held his hand out to her. "Are we done?"

She grabbed his wrist and pulled herself up as she tested his balance. He didn't move. "Not at all, Gwideon; not at all." Myrith waited as a cleric tended to each of them.

"You should be cautious, Lady Lake," the cleric said. "It is not uncommon for warriors to die on this field, even in practice. Do not let your pride be the cause of your death."

She stared at the cleric for a moment then glanced at Gwideon. *How can I lead, if I don't have respect?*

She focused her thoughts on Mykaylene. :*How do I fight one such as he?*

:*His strength is in his blade, not his feet. Control the situation and you control him,* the goddess' voice whispered in her mind.

Myrith smiled as she moved to take her position thirty feet away from Gwideon. She nodded and he moved toward her. She waited for his charge; then as he came in, she stepped to the side and let his momentum carry his swing into her previous position. Her blade slammed against his side as she darted away. She wasn't able to move quickly in her armor, but at least he was just an encumbered as she was.

This time his steps were measured as he approached. She waited, then cut to the right. He followed her, but she was able to stay out of reach of his sword. They played at the hunter and hunted for over an hour as she continued to judge his strengths. When she had tired of the game, she turned and waited for him. The force of his strike almost took her off her feet, but she saw her opening and refused to miss it. He had overextended himself in his strike and was off balance and unable to recover as her sword came in hard several times against his chest and midsection. Myrith stepped back as Gwideon's right knee hit the ground.

He looked up and raised his visor. "Shall we go again?"

She shook her head. "What would be the point? I need not know which sword is better, only that they serve the same cause." She extended her hand. They had shown themselves to be each other's equal; there was nothing left to prove.

"Besides the sun will have set long before we finish another round," she said as Gwideon stood.

"Very well." He sheathed his blade. "Should you not have a stronger blade?"

"This one is enchanted to battle demons and the undead," she said.

"I meant no insult. However, to be effective, the blade should have been forged of cold iron or silver, not common steel."

"That may be, however, the blade is as I found it. I do not have access to the magics that would transmute it."

"Come to the Catacombs tomorrow, Riker knows the way, and allow me to see to having the blade prepared properly for the task."

"Very well."

He bowed. "I leave you to your rest," he said. He mounted the tiger and left.

~ * ~

Her morning lessons completed, Myrith let Riker take her to the Catacombs. She felt a shudder go through her as she looked around the graveyard surrounding a large tomb that apparently was the temple. She knew the uneasy feeling she had was the normal reaction for all who came to this place. She slipped off Riker and paused at the sight of the two armored skeletons guarding the entrance.

She removed the magical reins and patted Riker on the neck. "Go, I will call you when I wish to leave," she said.

Riker faded as he galloped out of the graveyard.

The guards did not hinder her as she entered the temple. The hall was dark and her footfalls echoed in the silence. A gasp escaped her throat as the altar came into view. It was not made of stone—but of bones.

"The altar disturbs you?"

She turned to see Gwideon kneeling a few feet away. A shroud covered his head. "The use of bones in my home for the construction of anything is considered an act of evil," she said.

"Why? They are nothing more than the past. We build upon

the past. Nothing more, nothing less. Is this any different than any other endeavor pursued by intelligent creatures? The bones hold no souls." He stood and removed the shroud as he turned to face her. "The evil would be if it were used for the sole purpose of holding the souls from Resare." He paused. "You did not come here to discuss architecture; let us see to your weapon."

Myrith found it hard to stay calm as they walked through the catacombs. Armored skeletons acted as guards. Zombie servants shuffled past them on various errands. Doors and hallways were framed in bone. *None of it radiates evil*, she thought. *How can that be?*

Gwideon led her to a small room. She held her elbows close to her sides to prevent knocking over any of the bottles of unknown substances perched on the shelves covering the walls. A man in gray robes turned as the sounds of rattling bones announced their entrance.

"Gwideon, you have brought the mismatched sword?"

"Yes, and you need to take care of this quickly. The lady does not find the temple to her liking." He turned to Myrith. "However, we have one other task to accomplish before we can depart."

"Very well." The gray-robed man held out his hand.

Myrith drew the sword. Her movements were clumsy as she tried to avoid contact with any of the bottles or other objects surrounding them. She placed the sword in his hand.

He looked at it and nodded then held out his other hand.

Before Myrith could reach for her coin pouch, Gwideon slapped the outstretched hand down. "Your request is an insult to me, the one I serve and the quest Resare bade me join."

"The power to do this costs me much," the man said.

"It is service, as is mine. You toil in this lab and give a little of yourself to each creation. I sacrifice a bit of myself in battle against the monstrosities that would destroy the balance and the cycle." He pulled open a piece of his armor to show a horrid scar on his left shoulder where the flesh was shriveled. "Be done with the sword, lest I see the Gatekeeper and tell him of your lack of faith and abundance of greed."

"That was not necessary," Myrith whispered as the man stepped into another room.

"You think not?" Gwideon shook his head slowly. "It was absolutely necessary."

They stood there in silence as they waited for the mage to return the sword. Myrith's unease grew as she fought to keep from fidgeting. She didn't know what was in the bottles around her; any one of them could unleash a deadly poison or fouler substances. She remained frozen in place to keep from finding out.

The mage returned with the sword and held it out to Myrith. She took it and stared at the polished surface. It gleamed with the luster of Andrinor's scales in his dragon form. "The sword has been transmuted to its core," the mage said. "It cannot be dispelled."

Myrith nodded then turned. She waited until she was in the hallway to sheath the sword.

"Myrith, who is to be our planar guide?" Gwideon asked.

She stopped and looked up at him. "In truth, the one we go to rescue was the one with the knowledge you ask about." She frowned. "It has crossed my mind several times, that we do not truly know which path to take."

"We will see the Gatekeeper. He may be able provide a guide for this journey."

Myrith followed Gwideon through the hallways to a large set of iron-bound doors. Two ogre-sized bone constructs stood as sentries. As they approached, two figures appeared to push the door open. Myrith glanced at the spirits as she passed through the doorway. They were nothing more than children. *This is wrong. How can there not be evil in binding children to this plane and not letting them rest?*

"You cannot judge without knowing the truth of the matter," a voice said.

Myrith stepped from behind Gwideon to see another man shrouded in black, his face concealed from view. She started to move past Gwideon but stopped as he knelt before the man. She paused then also knelt.

"I am the Gatekeeper, master of this temple, servant of Resare. Gwideon, I take it this is Lady Lake, the Knight of Mykaylene."

"Yes, Gatekeeper."

"You seemed distressed, Lady Lake."

"The spirits are only children. Explain how the act of binding such to this plane is not evil." She stared at the Gatekeeper as she spoke.

"The innocent waifs you are so concerned about burned down a house. They did it not out of curiosity or through accident. It was done out of hate. Two halfling children died in that fire as did their father trying to save them. The boys had no remorse and were put to death for their crime. Their souls were forfeit to the darkness of the Abyss. Instead, they were brought here to serve penance. When their service is complete, they will be released, with their deeds paid for. They will be allowed to rest and not be doomed to endless torment. Would you prefer I release them now, to the punishment they have earned?" His tone never changed. It remained even and without emotion.

"No, Gatekeeper. You are correct. I should not judge without knowing all. I did not realize you offered redemption to those who had fallen. Forgive my rudeness and ignorance. My home is much different."

"Rudeness and ignorance are easy to forgive as they are simple to correct when they stem from the same cause. However, rash thought and action can be harder. See you learn to curb your own rashness even as you condemn it in others."

Even though she could not see his face, Myrith felt relief as his attention turned from her to Gwideon.

"Why have you come?"

"We need a planar guide. We will journey the layers and require one with great knowledge."

"Urric, you shall go with them. Upon your return, your service will be complete."

"As you direct, Gatekeeper," a voice said.

Myrith glanced in the direction the voice had come from and saw a wall of skulls; the eye sockets of one glowing.

Gwideon moved to the wall and removed a gold chain. He touched the chain to the skull and it shrank to the size of a large amulet. He looped the chain over his neck and the skull now rested on his chest.

"My thanks, Gatekeeper," he said. "We can now depart."

Myrith bowed her head to the Gatekeeper then stood and followed Gwideon out of the temple.

"I dislike this," Myrith said as Riker appeared. "A skull is to lead us into the land of demons and undead."

"You are a fine one to talk, Sword of Mykaylene," the skull said. "You ride a ghost."

Her hand went to her sword as she stared at the skull.

"How did you intend to navigate the layers? Were you going

to jump into every portal along the way? That would be an interesting, though short journey."

"If you are a planar expert, tell me, where does one find the demoness Drezmona?"

The skull remained silent and Myrith turned back to Riker. "Take it back. I will not have that foul, useless thing in my presence," she said.

"The question is not a fair one," Urric said. "Drezmona weaves too many plots and sides with too many individuals. She has served Thynitic, Ballan and Corrinna. She has been the consort of the First Lord of the Abyss. She is rumored to have tempted most of the deities, lords and princes of that realm to her bed. The only one I know for sure she has not tempted is Thynitic, which is unusual as Thynitic once counted passion as one of her domains." The skull paused for a moment then continued. "Drezmona's primary stronghold is on the edge of the sixty-third layer; it guards one of the only portals to that layer. She has one son, whose father was an elf."

Myrith froze but did not turn around. "If he leads us into a trap, I will crush him."

"Lady Lake, do you return to the Coliseum?" Gwideon asked.

"No, I need to see about a better sword for use against the demons. This one will serve well against the undead, but they are not our primary concern."

"We will come with you." He whistled and the ground shook as the tiger leapt down from the top of one of the mausoleums. His back was bare, but when Gwideon touched him, a saddled appeared.

"He dislikes the saddle, so the Gatekeeper saw to an adequate enchantment."

They rode through the streets of Irrmar as Myrith told of her poor reception within the Coliseum, though she held back the information of her former occupation. Both the Shield and the head of the Order had refused her access to the armory, saying it was reserved to those properly ordained by the temple.

"You seek to restore a Keeper of Hellavar," Gwideon said. "Perhaps we should see what assistance his temple might give."

"I was thinking the same," Myrith said as she spurred Riker ahead.

~ * ~

Myrith stared at the gilded roof of the temple of Hellavar and felt her hopes for assistance fade. She had seen Mount Veri through Brular's eyes and this was not the same simple, pristine order. The smell of alcohol was heavy as they entered the temple, several students and novices were there cleaning the remains of some festival. The golden altar stood as a testament to the greed of the temple, just as the bone altar in the catacombs stood for the souls who had passed to Resare.

"I wish to see the Keeper," she told one of the Kindling as they approached.

"The Keeper will see no one until this afternoon, my Lady. He was quite specific in this," he said.

"Who is currently in charge?"

"The Keeper does not delegate his power. There is no one who may assist you at this time." He stepped away and continued with his task.

She glanced again at the altar, the great fire pit surrounding it was only smoldering; another testament to the state of this temple. She walked over and glanced down to see a lone Kindling stoking the weak flames. "Should this not be blazing?"

"Yes, it should," Gwideon said. "The faith of this temple is weak." It was a simple pronouncement, as if he was completing a burial ritual.

"Weak flames can be reborn. They conserve their fuel; with the proper stoking, they will blossom with his true radiance."

The voice echoed in the chamber and Myrith was confused as to the source for a moment, then she looked down into the pit. "Rynalia?" A young woman dressed in the robes of a Kindling was looking up at her.

"Myrith Lake," she said.

Myrith's mouth dropped open. *How can she be here? She died at Mount Veri.*

She shook her head to clear the images as Gwideon took the girl's outstretched hand to assist her out of the pit.

"I am not Rynalia; I am her great-granddaughter, Rynalana." She smiled. "I received a similar reaction from Kyrianna."

"Kyrianna?"

"She brought me here on Cewyr and remained for the Feast of the Flame last night. She departed early this morning. You are exactly as she described, however I cannot place your companion."

"I am Gwideon of the Grey."

"My apologies, I am not familiar with many religions; I, unfortunately, am self-taught. Excuse me for a moment." She placed her hands together then fanned them out as fire shot from her body to ignite two of the pits. "It seems I am the only one here who sees the flames of greater importance than heeding the words of a Keeper who enjoyed too much drink during the Feast."

"He told them not to see to the flames?" Myrith stared at the girl.

"Not exactly. He told them the remains of the Feast were to be cleansed prior to anything else. His word is law here, but his words were slurred and not to the proper Order of things. I have been told I risk his wrath by disobeying. However, it is Hellavar I serve and not a drunken Keeper."

"Since Kyrianna has been here, I assume the temple's assistance has already been requested."

Rynalana closed her eyes and dropped her head. "Requested and denied."

Myrith looked around at the ornate chamber and heard Rynalana's words echo in her mind. 'His word is law here.' She understood the reason for the denial of assistance. If they were successful and returned Brular from the Abyss, there would be a Keeper in search of a temple to lead. This Keeper feared that.

"This was a waste of time," she said as she turned to leave.

"Wait," Rynalana said. "There is one who has helped. The Master of Flames would see you, of that I am certain."

Myrith shook her head. "I have little time left to waste."

"He helped Kyrianna and me. I know he would assist you." Myrith saw the desperation in the girl's face.

"Very well, I will meet with the Master of Flames."

Rynalana led them down several corridors to a room that held shelves with a few scattered books on them. Near the back a tall man appeared to be studying one of the books.

Myrith's hand went to her sword as she sensed the darkness in the man's aura. She also felt the heat radiating from his body and frowned. He was part efreeti.

"Master, friends of Kyrianna's."

He raised his head. "First Dwycia, now Mykaylene and Resare. How many go on this journey, yet none of Hellavar? It is a sad statement the servants of other gods place a higher importance on the Keeper of Mount Veri than Hellevar's own priests. Did Kyrianna send you here?"

"I have not seen Kyrianna since our group separated to follow the visions Hellavar gave us," Myrith said. *And just where did she go? She told us she had been guided to visit an area near Mount Veri. If she went there and brought Rynalana here, it would seem her trip should be done.*

"Then she did not tell you of the Fourth Book of Law."

"Fourth Book of Law," Gwideon said. "I have only heard of three."

"The fourth book was commissioned by the then Speaker of the Flames at the beginning of Brular's time at Mount Veri. When the temple fell, the priests made little effort to reclaim the site and recover items from the temple. This young woman sought so much to embrace her great-grandmother's past, she located many texts, including this copy penned by Keeper Eglis. I have only been studying it for one day but it speaks well to his faith and his interpretation of the Order." The Master of the Flames smiled at them.

"The manuscript is of little aid to you on your journey; however the last section lists many of Brular's allies by name. If you have clerics or mages traveling with you, those names may be of value to them." His smile broadened. "Some are of the lower planes, but others are of the higher ones. You might be surprised at his resources."

"Few things would surprise me about that one. He penned what you believe will be your fourth holy text; his faith and magic were strong—did he leave anything of that?"

The Master of the Flames nodded. "Also in the last section of the book are clerical spells. Powerful spells that will allow the caster to become one with the plane of fire or to directly channel the power of Order."

"Interesting, but of little help to myself. Does the Order of the Purifying Flame have residence here?"

"No, it is rare to have more than one of the branches under one roof. You assume Veri was like all—it was not. It takes the will of a strong Keeper to maintain both a Brotherhood and Order within a temple."

"Thank you for the information, but I must be going," Myrith said.

"May Hellavar warm you on your journey and scorch your enemies," the Master of Flames said.

~ * ~

"Pathetic," Myrith said as she mounted Riker.

"Excuse me?" Gwideon said.

"Not you, my friend. Myself. I am to lead this journey and I am not properly armed or trained to the task. Others seem to complete their tasks and do not bother to let me know and then vanish again. I should have gone with Jerietlan; I have no doubt Ferdinand could have provided proper equipment."

"Myrith, you said your vision bade you stay here. Why would Hellavar wish you to stay for no reason?"

Myrith flinched at the challenge in Gwideon's voice. *Why indeed? I have failed in this task, my Lady,* she thought. *I have let another god dictate my actions. I trusted he was true to this, but he has let him suffer for so long. Why? Did he lie to me to let him suffer even more?*

Riker stopped at the next intersection and Myrith looked up at the buildings around them. She was tired and the glow from the setting sun stung as her gaze searched for some sign of where to go. She was ready to turn back to the Coliseum when the glare from the sun faded and she could now see the emblem at the top of the gates across from them. "House Vernas." She nudged Riker forward through the gates.

"You are the one who has been concerned about wasted time," Gwideon said from behind her. "What business do we have here?"

"I don't know, but I am certain we do," She dismounted.

A squire ran up to take charge of the two mounts but kept his distance.

"Let them be, boy. The tiger has a foul temper and the horse goes where it wills."

She didn't bother to knock as she opened the doors to the house. "May I help you?" an elderly servant asked.

"I'm not sure," she said as she looked around the room at the portraits on the wall. Her gaze stopped on one. "Ferdinand and Marcus Vernas," she whispered.

She turned to the servant. "Ferdinand Vernas, priest of Mykaylene, comes from this House?"

"Yes, he was the king's brother."

"Was? When was the reign of this king?"

The servant looked up at her with wide eyes. "It lasted for twenty-five years and ended four years past."

"Who is king now?" There was something at the edge of her memory tugging at her.

"Through good negotiations and clever planning, his nephew, Petre Dracenhalts."

"I see. So King Dracenhalts' mother comes from the same line as Ferdinand and Marcus?"

"Yes," he said, pointing to another portrait. "The Lady Stephanie."

The memory that had been teasing her came back as she stared at the portrait. A woman in chains, the flash of a dagger, a promise made. "I wish to see Krella," she said.

"There is no one of the lineage of that name."

"She is not of the lineage of House Vernas. Krella Eglis, Knight of Hellavar and adopted mother to the one who brought Stephanie Vernas back all those years ago."

The servant stepped back. "You have no right to demand such a thing. You are neither of this House or hers no doubt. The master will return in several days. You may make your request of him. You will now leave this house."

"I do not have several days. That I find myself here, at this time, at the place where the tomb of my companion's mother is cannot be a coincidence."

"No!"

"I am Gwideon of the Grey," Gwideon said, stepping forward.

His voice resonated and echoed in the large room and Myrith felt a shiver go through her as she realized it was much the same echo she had heard when the Gatekeeper had first spoken in the Catacombs.

"By my church's sanction, I am allowed to inspect any tomb I wish. You will take me and the lady to the tomb now, or you will find yourself in one shortly." The servant hesitated for a moment, then hurried out of the room.

"That was not necessary," Myrith said.

"I stated nothing more than the law and the fact I am its sword in this matter." He stopped and looked at Myrith. "I am not a judge. He judges. I only see that those called stand before him for that judgment."

"You speak of his law, but remember, you are also sworn to follow me on this journey. You will not raise a sword against an unarmed foe unless I command it." She left Gwideon standing there in silence as she hurried to catch up to the servant.

The crypt lay in a well-tended graveyard. The interior, though not lavish, was carved with many of the same symbols Myrith had seen in the temple of Hellavar. The servant left after he opened the door.

Gwideon pushed the lid to the tomb back enough to reveal the corpse that lay within, then moved to the corner of the crypt and waited.

Myrith stepped to the tomb and looked in. The skeleton of a woman rested there, still clad in the plate mail armor she had been wearing and holding a rust covered sword to her chest. She had no idea what to do at this point. "Krella Eglis, I Myrith Lake, a paladin of Mykaylene, have come seeking assistance for my journey."

She waited for several minutes in the heavy silence of the crypt. "Can you help me?"

Again a long silence followed her question.

"What foolishness is this?" A male voice spoke from nowhere and yet everywhere. Myrith glanced at Gwideon who was still standing in the corner as if he had heard nothing.

"You come to a knight of another order to support your cause," the voice said again. "You speak to what remains of a true servant of her god. Her spirit is not here. However, I find it curious you are here. Did you even ask another of your own order? Or have they grown so weak you did not think to ask?"

Myrith felt tears stinging her eyes. The voice was mocking her. "I am an outsider to this land. They do not trust me, though Mykaylene has shown me her favor. My journey is directly related to Krella. It is for her son, Brular."

"The boy priest would have long since joined his mother."

"No!" she almost shouted the word. "Powerful magic binds his soul. He is held by the goddess Thynitic, the Lady of Chaos." She looked around for some sign of where the guardian speaking to her might be hidden. She could see no place to hide in the crypt. "I have fought alongside him in these past weeks. I seek to free him, but to do so is to go into the Abyss itself. My heart and will are strong, but my weapons lacking. I ask only assistance."

"You shall have it. I will go with you, Lady Lake. Let the demons know we come. Let them fear the power of Order and Righteousness."

"I do not see you."

"Remove me from her hands and break this insulting shell from my blade."

Myrith moved back to the tomb and reached in to grasp the blade Krella held. The fingers of the skeleton seemed to move on their own as she lifted the blade free from their grasp. Despite its size, she found the weapon easy to handle. She raised it up and brought it down hard against the floor. The rust fell away to reveal a blade forged of cold iron that ignited with a red flame.

"I am Conflagration, Order's sword, Hellavar's Flame," the blade said as flames surrounded them. "Together we will rescue the priest and be a beacon of doom to our enemies."

Myrith waited as Gwideon whispered a prayer before placing the cover back over the tomb.

The elderly servant stood at the door with his arms crossed over his chest and two guards standing behind him. "Your companion claimed his rights to inspect the tomb as is required by Resare and the law. However, that right does not allow you to remove that which does not belong you," he said.

Conflagration flamed briefly. "Your House has given Krella great honor and for that I am grateful. However, I wish to go with this person. Krella would have wanted it so. I thank you for your concern and vigilance."

The servant bowed his head and stepped to the side to allow them to leave the house.

~ * ~

Myrith decided she would not spend her last day wasting it with the clerics tutoring her. She had no idea when the others would be back today, and she knew she wouldn't be able to concentrate because of that. She had to be ready to face whatever they might encounter in the Abyss. She wanted Gwideon to be ready and she was still worried about the tiger. It was not a proper mount; it would not yield to its rider. It might be powerful, but Gwideon could not fight from the saddle. She had asked Mykaylene for guidance in finding a way to merge their strengths together and the goddess had told her that together, they were weaker; yet apart, they were stronger. Gwideon had been practicing quick dismounts, allowing the tiger to attack on its own while he also engaged an opponent. So far it was working.

She watched the pair face a group of students. Gwideon dismounted as the tiger leapt into the air. The Grey's stance did not falter; they had found their balance. She flinched as the tiger pulled one of the students from his horse and dragged him to the ground. "Cleric!" It was becoming second nature to call for them. Gwideon knew how to check his blows; the tiger did not.

"Who are those two?" a familiar voice said from behind her.

"Recruits," she said as she turned and clasped Jerietlan's arm. "They will be coming with us."

Jerietlan rested the tower shield he was carrying against the wall and reached back to loosen the one he wore on his back. "I believe you would be better served to carry this shield," he said as he handed it to her.

"Why? Has Ferdinand enchanted it?"

"No. But he saw something you and I missed. The shield is nothing more than a finely crafted piece of steel when held by anyone but a follower of Mykaylene. In one of her servants' hands, it can be empowered with higher levels of protection. Though the shield is not magical, I can enchant it daily and the power granted it by Mykaylene will work in harmony with that enchantment."

He reached for his shield. "I need a meal; send word to me when the others arrive as I have things to show you, but I don't want to explain myself over and over again."

Myrith nodded. "Before you go, please examine the tiger."

"The tiger?" Jerietlan raised an eyebrow then nodded. His hands moved slowly as he chanted softly. "It radiates very strong transmutation magic."

"Anything else?"

He focused on the tiger and Gwideon. "The warrior radiates with a strong sense of Order, similar to your own." His brow creased in concentration. "The tiger is not malevolent. Quite the opposite. It radiates strong ties to a god of light. Very strong indeed; stronger than even you do."

"I suspected power. But it does not answer the primary questions I still have. Why did it come and what god does it follow?"

"Clear the field," a voice called from above them. "This time is reserved for trials. Clear the field. This time is reserved for trials."

Myrith waited as the tiger trotted out of the arena and Gwideon joined him and Jerietlan. "So, what happened on your journey?" she asked as they walked back into the temple.

"Ferdinand is dying," Jerietlan whispered. "And I have pledged myself to another task when this one is completed."

"What would that be?" Myrith stopped and stared at the cleric.

"The destruction of the Hammer of Forging."

"That may turn out to be a more difficult task than the one we currently face," Myrith said.

"However, if we succeed, it may not be that difficult at all. Zanif told me it must be destroyed in the volcanic heart of the plane of fire. Do you think Brular could get me there?"

Myrith nodded. "I'm sure he could get us there."

Jerietlan smiled and nodded.

"Myrith," Nirev's voice called from behind them.

She turned to see the dwarf standing in the corridor, with a new war hammer in his hands. She concentrated for a moment on his aura and relaxed as she found no darkness there.

"I see I be beaten by at least one other," Nirev said. "Anyone else be back?"

"Yes." Falden stepped up behind Nirev.

Myrith could only stare at the mage. He had changed—dramatically. She wasn't sure she wanted to see Andrinor or Kyrianna's reactions when they saw him. Falden was covered in green scales and his eyes were green and had a reptilian look to them. She was relieved when she detected no darkness surrounding him.

"What happened?" Jerietlan asked.

"Cassandra Shindar of the Circle," Falden said. He took a deep breath as he told them about his visit to Gormanghast.

Before Falden was very far into the account, Andrinor staggered up. Again, Myrith found herself staring. He hadn't been transformed as Falden had; however, she had never seen him look so worn out. He was swaying on his feet, there were new scars and bruises on his arms and what she could see of his chest under his vest appeared to have been burned. Andrinor's gaze stopped on Falden and she saw his grip on his sword tighten as two blades appeared.

"Who has done this and why?" Andrinor's voice was harsh and low.

"Cassandra Shindar of the Circle," Falden said. "I believe you have also encountered her."

"I have."

"Your aim was too low."

Andrinor only nodded and Falden continued with his story. He told them what Cassandra had told him about the Faithless and that the Council wanted Brular returned. He also told them Cassandra was insistent Torliana remain among the living.

"You will have a hard time convincing Kyri of that," Andrinor said.

"Cassandra promised if Torliana was not among the living, she would drag Kyrianna back to Thynitic, no matter how many of us were left dead as a result."

"Let her try," Nirev said, slapping his hammer.

Myrith didn't say anything, but her mind was racing. *Is this Cassandra Shindar the reason Kyrianna isn't back yet? She apparently finished her task yesterday and had even been in Irrmar but did not return to the Coliseum. Where is she?* She glanced around at the others. The only other one missing was Hendandra.

"I met with one of the last dragons left in Shokar," Andrinor was saying.

"One of the last?" Jerietlan asked.

"Yes. The Faithless created a disease that killed the oldest and the youngest first when they came to Shokar. A disease they called dracoblight." He paused and caught his breath before continuing. "This disease even killed the avatar of the Great Mother here on Shokar."

"How can that be?" Myrith stared at Andrinor. "To kill the avatar of a god, you would have to be able to kill the god itself."

"There be an elf who calls himself Godfeller; he destroyed the temple of Mulog in Domar," Nirev said. "There always be those who think they can destroy the gods."

"If it were that easy, we wouldn't have to worry about Thynitic," Myrith said. "Is there anything else we need to know about your travels?" The three of them shook their heads.

"In that case, I still have something to show everyone," Jerietlan said.

"Who be this?" Nirev said, looking at Gwideon.

"My apologies," Myrith said. "This is Gwideon of the Grey; a knight of Resare who was directed by his god to join our group." She finished introducing the rest of the group and was relieved when none of the others objected to Gwideon's presence.

"Come with me," Jerietlan said, leading the group to a small room. He bolted the door behind them then raised his shield.

"I seek safe rest, my Lady, so I can carry my battle further in your name." Myrith stepped back as the shield grew into a set of large double doors.

"It is called the Shield of the Great Keep." Jerietlan led them through the keep explaining each of the rooms.

"We might as well eat since the food is here," Falden said as the group entered the dining hall.

No one had to tell Andrinor or Nirev again as they both reached for the large turkey in the middle of the table. Myrith shook her head as they both yanked one of the legs from the bird and sat down.

~ * ~

"A safe place for us to rest as we seek Brular," Myrith said when they exited the keep. "This will be very useful."

They stepped out of the room and Myrith caught one of the pages. "Have either of my other companions returned?"

"No, Lady Lake, they have not."

She took a deep breath. She had told Hendandra she would not wait if she were late. If it were only Hendandra and not also Kyrianna, she would keep that promise and not risk the threats Drezmona had made. She should leave them both behind; they both knew when they were to be back and they were both late. But, if she did that, she also knew Kyrianna would try to follow on her own. She had seen the determination in the girl's eyes when she had come out of the fog and depression that had engulfed her—Kyrianna felt she owed Brular a debt. And if she tried to follow them on her own, Myrith knew she would lose her friend to Thynitic, possibly forever this time. "Chaos! We waste a day waiting for those two." She turned and stalked down the corridor.

Chapter Ten
Hendandra

Hendandra smiled when the rod deposited her in a small room. The lantern, symbol of the Wayfinders Guild, on the wall showed this was the normal arrival point within the Coliseum. However, there was no guild representative there to charge her the expected fee. *Perhaps the temple pays a flat fee for all usage*, she thought.

Isdela had told her to get rid of all her metal and the best way to do that was to leave everything she didn't need with the others. She made her way through the corridors back to the rooms they had been assigned. It appeared no one else was back yet, and Myrith was already out of her room as Hendandra slipped in. She laid the two swords on the older woman's bed along with a few other items someone in the party might want or use. The rapier she had been given on the Duvall Estate was a different story. That was hers; she would do with it as she pleased.

She left the Coliseum and made her way to the merchant district. A few well placed questions about the reputation of various dealers as well as the occasional coin led her to a shop that dealt primarily with nobles. She reached up and touched the ebony circlet and smiled at the clerk as she entered the store.

He raised an eyebrow as she laid the rapier on the counter and waited. "I can give you a hundred gold for it. It appears to be in decent condition, so I'm sure I can sell it as a training blade."

"A training blade? You insult the history of this weapon," Hendandra said. "I recovered this blade from the ruins of the Duvall Estate. An adventure in and of itself." She paused and smiled again. "If you will look closely at the blade, just below the guard, who will see the mark of Lord Terissian. This blade belonged to the only son of that House, who was to marry the eldest daughter of House Duvall. The history of this blade alone makes it worth at least fifty thousand gold."

She reached into her pack and removed the armor she had borrowed from Kyrianna. "I will include this as well."

The clerk looked at the armor. "Another relic from the Duvall

Estate?"

"No, just something I picked up while traveling in a pocket plane created by the Chosen of the Lady of Chaos."

"I will give you twenty thousand for both."

She cocked her head to the side and frowned. He was good. Nothing on his face indicated he really wanted the items and it was a reasonable counteroffer that gave them room to negotiate. "Forty-five," she said.

They went back and forth a few times. "Thirty-two," the clerk said. "I can go no higher."

"Done. I prefer gems please."

He pulled several gems from under the counter and placed them next to the rapier. He then laid a handful of coins down as well.

"Just gems, please."

"I do not have anything valued at the appropriate amount to complete the sale. The smallest stone I have left would still be two thousand more than we agreed on."

"Easily solved." She removed the sack with the party's gold and laid several platinum coins on the counter.

She flipped her hair back as she left the shop and headed for the jeweler she had chosen as the place to exchange her coins.

She ignored the clerk who was talking to two customers at the counter and made her way to the back. "I need this converted to gems please," she said, smiling at the owner of the shop.

The man nodded, opened the bag and poured the contents into a tray. He shook the tray and the coins sorted themselves into different bags through different size holes.

"I will give you ten thousand in gems," he said, after weighing each of the bags.

Hendandra smiled and shook her head. "There is at least fifteen thousand there."

"That is correct, but how am I to make a profit if I give you the exact amount? I charge for the handling and conversion as well as possible fluctuations in the value of the gems I will be giving you."

"One-third is bit excessive. I will give you one percent of the value."

"And that does not even pay for my time. Twenty-five."

"Five."

The man smiled. "Twenty. You should also know there are magics in place nullifying the effects of that circlet you are wearing."

"I will pay the standard ten percent," Hendandra said. "No more."

He glanced toward the customers in the outer room. "Very well." He pulled six pouches from one of the drawers in the wall. After removing a few of the gems from one of them, he handed all six to Hendandra.

Hendandra paused as she exited the back room. The customer at the counter was negotiating over the sale of a jewelry set. One that featured wolves and unicorns. She had seen that set once before; it was the same one she had found and been planning to give to Kyrianna. It had been with the other jewelry and gems that vanished from her house.

She paused and glanced at a couple of the items on display as the nobleman cursed the clerk for his greed, pocketed the jewelry and headed for the door. Hendandra followed him and smiled as he held the door for her. She stumbled slightly bumping into the nobleman who placed a hand on her arm to steady her.

"My apologies, my Lord," she said as she slipped the jewelry set into her own pocket.

Leikor's luck, she thought. *Now, I can give this to Kyri as compensation for selling her old set of leathers.* She paused as another thought came to her. *What were the chances he would be selling there, today? What were the chances he would be leaving with me?* Her mind raced. *What are the chances this is a trap?*

She looked around. "Leikor's cursed luck," she muttered, seeing the guards on the street. She dropped the jewelry into a watering trough and turned down an alley. Without thinking she slipped her hand into her pocket and stopped, her feet frozen to the ground as she pulled the jewelry out. Her heart was racing faster than she would have thought possible as she stared at the sapphires and moonstones. She threw the items to the side, no longer caring if someone saw, then ran. There was something in her pocket, and her hand felt the familiar shape of the necklace when she reached in. She had heard of cursed items, which could not be removed. She had never thought of using one in a setup though. She turned the corner and ran into a group of guards being led by a priest.

"She has the items," the priest said. "She is your thief."

The guards grabbed her arms and pulled her with them toward

the Coliseum.

~ * ~

They kept her for over an hour under close guard in a small cell.

"Why all this attention?" she asked.

"The jewelry you stole was the property of a man who is a member of House Lors Underian, the second ranked House of Irrmar. They requested the guards."

Great, she thought.

She looked up as one of the guards opened the cell and gestured for her to come with him. He took her to a large chamber where a judge waited along with the nobleman from the shop.

"Do not dare to speak in this court using any kind of magic to sway me. If you do, I will have your head taken."

There went that plan, she thought as she removed the circlet and ring.

The judge nodded. "You are charged with thievery. How do you plead?"

"Innocent. The items were mine before he ever had possession of them. They were stolen from my house in Raspa. I returned four days ago to find my house had been burglarized and those items and several others missing."

"If I may, your Honor," the nobleman said. "My family bought those items through reputable merchants and their arrival is detailed in this manifest." He handed the documents to the judge.

"What proof of ownership can you provide, young lady?" the judge asked.

She glanced at her accuser and realized this had been well planned. She had no documents. The items had been found in one of the many rooms they had fought through. A chill went down her back as she realized the items technically weren't hers, but belonged to everyone in the group and these were to have been given to Kyrianna. She had told the judge they were hers.

"Young lady, I can cast a spell that will verify the truth of your statements if that will help your case," the judge said.

She glanced again at the nobleman who smiled at her.

That's what he wants. The truth is mixed up in half-truths already. He will make me look like a fool. I will not give him that. "No, your Honor," she whispered. "I must ask for mercy in your judgment."

"Then I have no choice but to find you guilty." He looked down at her and shook his head. "Unfortunately, the law is specific in cases such as this: Your right hand will be removed. As it appears you are a person of some means, I warn you using magic to undo your punishment will be considered contempt and you will be put to death."

Hendandra's heart stopped beating as she tried to draw breath. They were going to take her hand and she could not even ask her friends for help. She knew they would give it regardless of the risk. She turned toward the nobleman again. He had thought of everything. If the clerics provided their help, they would be outcast or worse from the city and possibly their church. She didn't fight the tears as she was pulled from the room.

"No!" She jerked away from one of the guards. "There has to be another way."

The judge nodded slowly. "You may request trail by champions, but I would not suggest that."

"Champions?" Her heart started beating again. "I have friends who are willing to face a god." She turned toward the nobleman. "Bring your best."

"Oh, I will," he said with a smile. "I will bring my House's champion. Who is yours?"

"House?" She turned toward the judge.

"You accepted the trial by champions. I cannot undo that. Your champion must be related to you by House or blood."

Her legs collapsed and one of the guards caught her. Andrinor, Kyrianna, Falden, Myrith, Nirev or Jerietlan could not help her. The nobleman dropped a wooden coin in her hand as he walked past. The shifting veil of Rhyra floated on the surface; she had played right into their hands.

"This way," the guard said.

~ * ~

Hendandra stood in the doorway and looked out into the arena. She stared at the warrior in full plate waiting for her. She was sure the spirit blade would have no problems with the armor, but she was concerned about the sword he was carrying: a great sword that dripped black ichor onto the sand.

"Marcus Underian," the nobleman said from behind her. "He is expected to earn one of the arms master positions here at the

Coliseum." He stepped past her. "Don't let the blade even nick you, as the ichor will eat through your skin." He stopped and turned back to face her. "One other thing, I saw that special blade of yours. Very nice, but Marcus does not wear his usual armor. I believe you will find it very resilient."

Her head dropped. Rhyra had sent a House and its resources to seek her revenge. Her eyes welled up again, but she would not cry. Not now. Not again. She would face this and at least it would be over.

She looked up as she heard laughter from the spectators. Even they knew this was only an exercise for her opponent. The laughter grew as a figure walked across the field.

"Who is he?" the judge asked.

Her mouth went dry. It was Feric. She closed her eyes as he approached.

"Wife?" She felt his hand touch the heart token.

She could only nod.

"I am here."

"This is what Rhyra wants. She wants me to watch you die."

His voice was cold. "You think this human is the one who controls life and death here?" His hand went to her face and his voice softened. "He does not. You do. Do you wish him to live?"

She wasn't sure how to respond as she looked at Feric. "Just don't lose," was all she said.

He smiled and turned to face Marcus Underian.

"Who is this?" the nobleman asked.

"He is my husband." She felt strength in those words as she repeated them. "He is my husband and my champion."

The nobleman shook his head. "This is absurd. He is unarmed."

"She may choose the champion of her House as she wishes," the judge said. "However, I would suggest a good sword."

Feric looked back at her and she smiled as she remembered telling him the same thing on the island before he had left to come here.

Feric turned back to face Marcus.

"Very well." The judge raised his hand.

"You and yours made her cry. You made her afraid. That ends now, prey."

The warrior laughed as he looked down at Feric. "You want

me to pray?"

Feric knelt and placed his hands to the ground. "No, you are prey." The judge dropped his hand.

Hendandra's breath caught in her throat as she watched Feric's body convulse. The change only took a moment, but the scene would be etched in her mind forever. His body grew, became huge and covered in scales. His head elongated and his teeth were as long as her forearm. He wasn't as tall as one of the thunder lizards, but his arms were clawed and his legs powerful. *Rega was right*, she thought. *He is their protector and their nightmares.*

He snapped out at Marcus as the warrior charged toward him. There was no blood and Hendandra knew the snap was only a warning as Feric took a step back and watched his opponent.

The crowd was silent as they watched. Hendandra waited as several of the guards raised their crossbows and others ran from the area. *Probably, to get more guards*, she thought.

Marcus didn't hesitate as he charged in again.

Hendandra watched in amazement at what happened. Feric lunged forward as Marcus came in; his teeth ripping into the armor as he lifted the warrior from the ground. The claws of his forearms ripped the sword from Marcus' grasp and it fell to the ground. She waited for Feric to tear the warrior apart, but instead he tossed his head up and swallowed him.

Feric roared and looked at the spectators.

"Shouldn't you end this?" Hendandra asked the judge.

"No, Marcus is not dead yet, but soon."

"Not dead. You mean he's…? Ugh, that's awful." She looked at Feric for a moment and his words echoed in her mind.

She raced out onto the field. "Feric, let him go."

He looked down at her.

"You heard me. Let him go."

He just stood there.

She kicked him in the leg. "Spit him out. Right now!"

He lowered his head to within inches of hers.

"I. Said. Now!"

He turned to the side and coughed up the warrior. He was a ragged mess, but still alive.

She patted Feric's nose. "Good. Who know where he's been?" She smiled and took a step toward Marcus. "Concede the trial, or do you want the entire tour of his stomach?"

He looked up and nodded.

The judge raised his hand toward Hendandra. "You have won the trial." Feric looked at the nobleman and roared.

"I agree," Hendandra said. "I won the trial. Can I challenge him on the grounds of false accusation?"

"Yes, you can."

Feric roared again.

"Wait." The judge's voice echoed in the arena. "Only the accused may fight the accuser in this trial."

Hendandra drew the spirit blade. "I'll take those odds."

Feric's head brushed against her shoulder before he roared again.

The nobleman took a step back and stumbled. Hendandra sprang across the distance, the tip of the spirit blade pressed through the armor.

"Stop, I can give you gold and jewelry."

Hendandra paused. "Speak quickly."

He produced a bag with several articles of jewelry; some she recognized as those she and the others had collected.

She paused then glanced back at Feric and the sword that still lay on the ground. "The tribe is right. I don't want your gold or these other items. You have nothing I want." She pressed the blade forward a bit.

"I have a house. My house, not that of Lors Underian."

Her blade retreated. *A house. A place to call home in this city.* She looked again at Feric. "I already have a home, but my friends might appreciate it." She stood and turned to the judge. "See to the exchange." She started to turn then stopped. "And I want the items that started this mess in the first place. Those were to be a gift for a friend and I still intend to see she gets them. However, whatever curse you laid on them—you will have removed."

"It has already been removed," he said as he held out the jewelry set.

"Good." She took the items and dropped them into her pocket then turned toward the judge. "The following names will be added to the house papers: Andrinor, Myrith, Kyrianna, Nirev, Falden and Jerietlan as well as myself."

She turned to see Feric had returned to his own form. He stood with his head down, not looking at her. Rega said the others had never truly accepted him. She broke one of the vines of the armor.

The moon ivy dried and flaked off in the time it took her to reach Feric.

He smiled when she lifted his chin so he would have to look at her. She saw both hope and fear in his eyes as he lowered them again. She knew he was waiting for her to give in to the same fear the villagers had for him. Instead, she wrapped her arms around his neck and pressed her lips to his. She could feel his surprise in his initial hesitation, then it was gone. Gone too was the Coliseum as everything melted back to that night in the jungle. She could taste something metallic and sweet in his mouth and paused when she realized it was Marcus' blood, however she didn't let go. He had come to her. She would not pull away. She would not break the embrace. He deserved that. Her body tingled and she knew she had found the way to receive the blessings Shyada had told her about.

She leaned in close to his ear. "We need to talk," she whispered. "You became the bird that night; is there something more wondrous you can be as we leave?"

He nodded as he took a step back.

Hendandra watched as he transformed into a winged horse. She smiled and leapt onto his back. "There is a great forest nearby. Take us there." She hugged the horse's neck as he took flight.

~ * ~

They landed deep in the forest. Hendandra didn't want to risk being interrupted by some hunter looking for the flying horse. She wasn't worried about Feric, but concerned she would have to save the hunter from him.

He landed in a clearing, his momentum carrying him into a gallop through the trees. When he stopped his ears flicked back and forth a couple of times before he turned and trotted off toward the west. Hendandra gasped as the trees opened up into another clearing, this one with a small pool to one side.

"Very nice, but we need to talk," she said as she slid off his back.

Feric changed back into a halfling and took a step toward her, but she stepped back and turned away. "Feric, the last few days have been very confusing," she said. "I never dreamed of many of the things that have happened and honestly I wasn't thinking during some of the things that did happen."

Feric held his head low and she could see he was worried about what she might say next. She reached out and placed her hand on his cheek. "There are many things I regret in my life, but being here is not one of them." She leaned in and brushed her lips against his. She felt him reach out to her, and she pulled back. "I did not kiss you that first time…" She hesitated. "I wanted you to help me. I didn't want you to fall in love with me."

Feric stepped away from her and sat by the edge of the pool.

"I didn't want it then," she continued. "I didn't know what I wanted at all."

She sat next to him. "You left the island and had Rega give me your heart token. Tell me, did you give me that just to help or do you love me?"

Feric placed his hand around her neck as he leaned into her. He found her lips and did not let her retreat as his arm held her tight. Her thoughts melted away into feelings and then into nothing. When he let her go, she knew she had the answer to her question. She removed the heart token and dropped it before him, even though he wouldn't understand the gesture. By the customs of his people the token could only be returned in front of the chief. He reached down and picked the token up.

She smiled as she shifted so her back was to him. She lifted her hair up and waited. It was only a moment before she felt his hands on her back as he placed the heart token around her neck.

She turned back to face him. "Feric, I have accepted your heart token and by your…our village's customs, we are married." She placed her forehead against his. "I can't deny that there is something between us, but I am not ready." She looked into his eyes and saw understanding. She smiled and kissed him.

She let the kiss linger, but not too long. She didn't want to boil his blood or hers. She leaned back. "You found me. How?"

"My goddess sent me to you," he said, placing a hand on her cheek.

She pressed her head against his hand. "Can you stay till morning?"

"Even the great spine could not drag me from you," he said.

As they settled to the ground and slept next to each other, Hendandra knew her heart wanted to love him, but she wasn't ready yet. She rolled over to face him and kissed him once more before rolling back. She licked her lips. Besides, the courtship was supposed to be all the fun; a couple of days was too short. She went to sleep thinking of moonlit Justula and her husband. *Yes*, she thought, *my husband.*

Chapter Eleven
Kyrianna

:Myrith is going to be mad about this, Cewyr's voice echoed in Kyrianna's mind. *:We were supposed to be back today.*

"Let her be mad. I said we were going to Raspa and we're going."

:And if she leaves without you?

"Then I'll find a way to follow them."

Cewyr stopped in the middle of the trail and turned her head back toward Kyrianna. *:By yourself, into the Abyss?*

"If necessary."

:Not a good idea. Shadow Seeker's voice joined the conversation.

Kyrianna glanced down at the wolf who had dropped to the ground, his tongue hanging out of his mouth as he panted. His voice in her mind had been hesitant and in pain. They had been running for almost five hours since they left the Johran Woods. The wolf would never have been able to keep up with Cewyr except for Frayrith restoring her magical abilities. Now he was exhausted and needed rest.

She slipped off Cewyr and poured some water for Shadow Seeker. "I'm sorry, Shadow." She ruffled his ears and his tail twitched. "Have a little more." She poured some more water into her hand. "When you're ready, we'll keep it to a walk from here."

:We should have at least sent a message to Myrith letting her know you would be delayed. She is not going to be happy when we get there—late, Cewyr said.

"So you don't think she'll leave without me."

:No. She knows you well enough to realize you would go after them if she did, as foolish as that may be.

"She'll get over it." Kyrianna offered the wolf some more water.

:Perhaps. But how much will your delay cost Brular? And how much of her power will the Lady of Chaos have recovered?

Kyrianna took a deep breath and refused to answer the unicorn. Shadow Seeker nuzzled her hand then climbed to his feet. His head and tail held low, he walked in front of Cewyr, turned and gave a short bark.

Kyrianna jumped on Cewyr's back. "Let's keep it slow," she said.

~ * ~

"Tristan said the city was renowned for its artisans," Kyrianna said as the towers began to come into view. "I see he spoke well of the architects. Irrmar has beautiful buildings, but no structures that show this level of skill."

:Maybe his city will be more to your liking, Cewyr said.

Kyrianna picked up some amusement from the unicorn in their bond, but no reason for it so she ignored it. "Possibly. As I recall this city is ruled by a senate, not a king; a system similar to the one in Nydith. If this city is indeed enlightened, as Tristan said, it would be the first."

:You are so quick to judge, Kyri, Melissa's voice said.

"Part of my nature, I'm afraid. If my judgment seems cynical of late, it is because I have learned to expect the worst." Her voice dropped to a whisper. "It allows for less disappointment." Her thoughts returned to the hope she had tried to foster and had shattered after her vision from Thynitic about her mother.

Cewyr stopped several yards from the gates and stepped off the road into a small group of trees. "Let's go see your nephew," Kyrianna said as she swung to the ground.

She placed a hand on Cewyr's neck and removed the chain. "I will call you first thing in the morning," she said. "Get some rest." Cewyr whinnied and vanished.

"Come on, Shadow; let's see if we can find House Duvall in this place." She concentrated for a moment on the magic of the ring she wore on her left hand then glanced down at the wolf.

:Your appearance has changed. The first time she had heard Shadow Seeker's voice in her head had been a shock, but now she could hear the echoing howls that wrapped around his words, even when he wasn't speaking directly to her. She found the wolf song to be pleasant and soothing when she relaxed enough to listen to it.

They wandered the streets of Raspa for over an hour trying to find House Duvall. Melissa's memories weren't much use as it had been several years prior to her death when she had last visited the manor house in Raspa, and the city had changed in the last thirty years. Many of the people Kyrianna attempted to ask for directions looked at her then at Shadow Seeker and walked away.

She paused at the entrance to a mercantile house and glanced up at the ornate carvings above the door. A man standing guard nodded to her and smiled. "May I be of assistance?"

"Perhaps." Kyrianna forced a smile. "I am looking for House Duvall."

"House Duvall?" The guard's eye went wide. "Lord Duvall has had numerous friends and relatives arrive in the city in the last month or so, since his House regained their position on the council. Many of whom were neither." His eyes went to the two swords she was wearing then the bow on her shoulder.

How can I convince him I am a friend? I carry no token from Tristan. If there have been problems as he hinted, then my word should not be enough.

:*The sword,* Melissa said. :*The silver sword was in our family for many years; I believe it is marked with the House seal.*

"I believe I can put your suspicions to rest. I carry a weapon given to me by Lord Duvall, which I believe bears his House seal." Kyrianna placed her hand on the hilt of the sword, but made no move to draw it.

The guard took a step back, just out of reach of the blade then nodded. She drew the blade slowly then turned it and presented it to him, hilt first. He took the sword and looked at the seal stamped into the metal. "This was the personal seal of Lord Rhinehart Duvall," he said. "How did you come by this sword? You are too young for him to have given it to you."

"My friends and I assisted his grandson, Tristan, in laying the spirits of his family to rest."

"That story has been told several times since his return to Raspa. Come, I will escort you to House Duvall."

Kyrianna followed the guard through the winding twisting streets. :*I hope you can get me back out of here in the morning,* she said to Shadow Seeker.

:*The path is convoluted only because he wants it to be.*

:*I suspected as much. He left his post unattended. Perhaps he is hoping for a reward for his kindness.*

Kyrianna nodded her thanks, but didn't offer the guard any coins as he pointed out the gate to House Duvall. He saluted, then turned and left.

The grounds had only a shoulder-high wall surrounding them,

not one of the high grand walls she had seen in other parts of the city or in Irrmar. She thought she understood Tristan enough to know appearances didn't bother him. The Duvall Estate near Duvshire had been turned into a place of misery because of the chaos and evil Mikyl had embraced. This place in no way resembled that one. Perhaps that was part of the reason for the more austere appearance. The house was made of stone, strong but modest. A proper house for a proud lineage looking to be reborn.

The sound of ringing metal caught her attention and Kyrianna paused as she remembered the Nydith guards training with her father and uncle. She and Shadow Seeker followed the sounds of combat and cheering around to the back of the house to find two armored men practicing with two-handed swords. She recognized the symbol of Mykaylene displayed on both suits and the symbol of House Duvall emblazoned in the center of the crest of one. To the sides stood two squires, each holding a mace and cheering.

She sat down to watch what was apparently a battle of endurance as well as skill. The two fought with two-handed swords then changed to maces, long swords and finally the humble quarterstaff. As she watched the whirling staffs, Kyrianna thought about the match she and Rynalana had had and smiled.

:*Did we have to leave her there?* Melissa's voice was a bit distant as she spoke in Kyrianna's mind. :*I don't like that Keeper. He reminds of Mikyl.*

Kyrianna felt a sudden chill at the mention of Melissa's older brother and she wasn't sure if it was her reaction or Melissa's. "First we see to rescuing Brular, then we let him see to Rynalana. Until then I will trust the Master of Flames to keep her in her faith," she said.

:*The boys are finished*, Melissa said before she giggled.

"Don't laugh," Kyrianna said as she stood up and dismissed the magic of the ring. She looked down at Shadow Seeker, who only twitched his tail. "I'm sure Myrith is training just as hard or even harder."

:*Yeah, but Hendandra is probably lying on a beach relaxing.*

"No doubt, but I don't begrudge her the moments she is able to steal." She glanced toward the two knights and raised her hand and her voice. "Lord Duvall, a word when you have your breath and a drink."

One of the men removed his helmet and stared at her. "Kyri-anna?" He grinned as he tossed the helmet to his squire. "You have returned. What happened? Laraf and I consulted with various mages and clerics after you vanished on the road; nothing could be learned. The only thing they were able to discern was you were not dead, of that the Temple of Resare was certain. We were finally able to learn the area you and the others were trapped in was a place surrounded by strong, chaotic power. After a time, Laraf decided to seek out Ferdinand Vernas to see if he might be able to locate you and get him there. Did he make it?"

Kyrianna looked at the ground. "I'm sorry. My journeys have been far more dire than you know," she said.

Tristan had an arm around her shoulder as he lifted her chin with his other hand. "Myrith, Laraf, Hendandra? One of the others? Come inside and tell me everything."

Kyrianna let him lead her into a small chapel and to one of the benches near the altar. "Kyri?" His voice was soft as he held her.

She let the tears come as she told him about what had happened, not leaving out any of the details. Her voice broke and she had to stop for breath several times as she talked about Thynitic and what the goddess had done to her and the others. She choked as she told him about Laraf's death when he had stepped in front of the chimera's attack meant for her. She had to stop for several minutes and finally stood and moved to the altar. Tristan came up beside her, placed a hand on her shoulder and didn't say anything as he waited for her to continue. She took a deep breath and told him of the actions she had taken as she had twice called on Thynitic's power. Sobs racked her body as she finally forced herself to tell Tristan about Brular and the sacrifice he had made.

Tristan's hand tightened on her shoulder and he pulled her into a gentle embrace as he helped her to the floor. He just held her as sobs wracked her body and she leaned against him. She wasn't sure how long they sat there before she finally pulled away and wiped her eyes.

"I had no idea," Tristan said, taking her hands. His voice was low and soft as he spoke and Kyrianna could hear the same sooth-ing, melodic tones she had heard in his grandmother's voice. "Is there anything I can do?"

"No. I'm sorry to have burdened you with my troubles. This was supposed to have been a pleasant visit before we left for the

Abyss."

"Do not ever worry about sharing your troubles with me, Kyri," Tristan said, squeezing her hand. "I will be there whenever you need me."

She shook her head, her emotions were racing. A part of her wanted to stay here and let him hold her and the rest of her was ready to leave for Irrmar. However, there was a reason why she had come here. She had taken the time to see her family and she wanted to give Melissa a chance to see hers before they left. She wiped again at her eyes then smiled. "As I said, this was not the reason for my visit. I wanted to let you know Melissa has been with me since we left the estate."

Tristan's eyes widened, but it was not surprise she saw in them, instead a slow burning anger smoldered. "I thought she rested." He spoke slowly, as if measuring his words. "I brought all of the bodies to Raspa and Irrmar. The bodies of my grandparents and aunt rest in the mausoleum there at the edge of the garden. Her sister lies with her betrothed in the Terissian plot in Irrmar."

Kyrianna felt his hand tighten on hers but she didn't pull away. "She is too curious to rest," she said. She took a breath and continued. "I have promised her a life."

Tristan leaned back and stared at her.

"I have promised that after we rescue Brular, I will find a way to return her to the land of the living."

"Is that possible? I am not a cleric, but it would seem quite difficult given the passage of time."

"If it is even remotely possible, I will see that it happens." Her voice softened. "My companions have seen and been part of many extraordinary events recently. I am positive there is magic powerful enough to meet the challenge. It is a matter of finding the proper one to wield it."

She stood and moved to the door of the chapel and looked out at the sun setting behind the trees of a wooded area.

:Kyri, can we stay here—among the trees? Melissa asked.

"Yes, but why?"

:I would like to speak to him. I can feel peace. It is strong here.

Kyrianna looked around. The knight Tristan had been sparring with and the two squires were still waiting nearby. "Tristan, can you please dismiss your comrade and the squires, I..." She paused. "No, we would like to talk further." He smiled as he waved off the others.

They walked together through the grounds as the sun set, painting the trees in a golden-red glow. As the last rays faded, Melissa appeared beside her, her hand resting in Kyrianna's.

"Greetings, nephew." Her voice was barely louder than a whisper.

Tristan knelt on the ground and held out his arms to the girl. She wrapped her arms around and in some places through him.

"Melissa, would you prefer to stay here, with your family?" Kyrianna asked.

"You can't get rid of me that easily, big sister," Melissa said.

Tristan looked up at Kyrianna and grinned.

"Nephew, I have a favor to ask," Melissa said.

"Whatever I can do."

"Kyri and her friends served you well."

Tristan leaned back from the ghost and nodded. "They did."

"Can you provide them with anything which might help them?"

"I still have the lance from the estate."

Kyrianna grinned. "Myrith was talking about training with the lance when I left Irrmar. The idea of mounted combat seems to have grabbed her attention. If you are willing to part with it, considering its history, I know she would be honored to carry it. However, its history is also your own." Her hand rested on the unicorn horn sword she now wore.

"Except for my grandfather's sword, much of the magic I have is relatively weak and of little value in the Abyss. Wait…" He pulled a ring off his finger and held it in front of Melissa. "This belonged to my father; it has the power to store magic."

"Falden could do much with that," Kyrianna said.

"True, but I have been studying the texts on ghosts and spirits…" He paused for a second, looked at Melissa and smiled. "Both of you stay here." He stood and walked to the mausoleum.

"Kyri, look." Melissa held up her hand to show a translucent ring had appeared on her finger.

"I see my research was not in vain," Tristan said as he walked back. "Can you sense the magic it contains?"

"Yes. It can enchant a sword and aid in healing." She smiled.

Tristan looked at Kyrianna. "Items that were worn by or have a strong connection to the departed can be placed on a body and the spirit can draw on their power. That ring was worn by my father for years and as such is connected at least in part to his sister. Because of the way the magic works, it will renew itself each night so there is no need for Falden or Jerietlan to cast the spells to be placed in it as they would if it were worn by any other."

"A truly marvelous gift, Lord Duvall; thank you." Kyrianna bowed her head.

"Melissa, I must ask your permission for something," Tristan said.

"What?" Melissa looked at him and then at Kyrianna.

"I would like your permission to summon you once a week, through the powers of the Resarian church. They can contact your spirit with stronger necromancy than others wield. That way I will know how you fare and if the ring's spells should be changed."

Melissa nodded then faded.

"We can stay but a little while longer; Myrith expected us back this day," Kyrianna said.

She turned as Shadow Seeker started barking. Melissa was playing a game of tag with him as she ducked in and out of the trees. "Actually, she won't mind too much if we stay the night." Kyrianna knew that would not be true, but the look on Melissa's face as she played with the wolf told her facing her friend's anger would be worth it for her to let the ghost have this time to be an eight-year-old girl again.

"I will bring drinks and have the servants prepare dinner on the porch. Let her play as long as she wants," Tristan said.

"Thank you Lord Duvall."

"Please, it will always be Tristan to you and the others."

~ * ~

Kyrianna awoke the next morning and rolled back over in the bed, pulling the down-filled comforter around her. Last night had passed much as a dinner in her father's house would have if he were entertaining a friend. She had requested time for a proper bath and had then dressed in the blue and silver gown for her dinner with Lord Duvall.

Despite her conflicted emotions, she and Tristan had played flirtatious games during dinner; it felt good to have someone paying attention to her in that manner. She knew he was interested, but so far he had been a gentleman and had not said or done anything to force her to make any decisions. For that she was grateful. She needed time to think. She had credited her initial reactions to his actions when the worg had almost killed her and now, with her emotions being so drained after telling him about what had happened with Thynitic and Torliana, she couldn't be sure her current feelings weren't just a reaction to his kindness and assistance.

Still the dinner and talk had been pleasant. She had been surprised to hear Laraf was not dead as everyone suspected. Tristan had told her Laraf had visited recently and warned him to be wary of strange magics. While he thought Laraf might be associating with the Thieves Guild in Raspa, he was certain the young man was working directly for the Church of Resare. It was comforting to know Laraf, whom they thought killed when he pushed her out of the way of the chimera's attack, was still alive. When his body vanished, Brular suggested he had been called by Resare; she was glad that assumption had been correct. It was one less thing she had to carry the guilt of.

She had wanted to try and contact Laraf, to know he didn't blame her for what happened, but Tristan did not know how and Laraf was carrying magic that shielded him from detection.

She was glad this trip would give her some pleasant memories to take with her when they left. She sat up and threw the comforter to the side. Had they left already? Myrith wanted everyone back yesterday.

"Kyrianna," Tristan's voice called through the closed door. "There is a brunch prepared if you're ready."

:And it is past time we were on our way, Cewyr's voice said in her mind.

:What are you doing here? She dressed and gathered her gear as quickly as she could. She touched the dress she had worn last night, then left it on the bed as she hurried out of the room.

Tristan met her on the porch and nodded toward the unicorn standing in the yard with Shadow Seeker. "A friend of yours?"

"Yes, but how did she get here? I didn't call her."

"Oh." Tristan's voice sounded distant as he took a step away from her.

Cewyr only stared at her, her gaze judging Kyrianna. Kyrianna shook her head and sighed. She wasn't going to get any answers from the unicorn at this time. *:We'll talk later*, she sent. *:Let me make my goodbyes here then we head back. For now, it would be best if you returned to your home.*

After the unicorn vanish Kyrianna picked up the unicorn figurine and slipped it into her pocket.

:*Melissa, did you call Cewyr?*

:*Yes. I asked Shadow to bring me the figurine so I could talk to her. Are you mad at me?*

:*Of course not. You can call her to talk to and play with anytime she is willing to come.*

"Okay, that mystery is solved. Melissa called her earlier." Kyrianna turned her attention back to Tristan who was staring at her. "I thank you for your hospitality this past day, but I really must be returning to Irrmar."

Tristan only nodded as he looked at her, his hand held out. Kyrianna took the offered hand and smiled as he gripped her forearm in the traditional handshake of fellow warriors.

"The Battle Maiden go with you, Kyrianna," he whispered.

~ * ~

Kyrianna slipped into a wooded area just off the road after she was out of Raspa. She pulled the unicorn figurine out of her pocket. "Cewyr," she said.

The unicorn appeared standing before her, the disapproving look still in her eyes.

"Okay, what's going on?" Kyrianna looked at the unicorn and dropped her hand flat against the silver sword that housed Melissa's spirit.

:*Melissa told me how you were acting with her nephew last night*, Cewyr said.

:*I only wanted to know if she thought you would be marrying Tristan.*

"What?" Kyrianna felt her knees buckle and she sat down hard on the ground as she stared up at the unicorn.

"You wanted to know what? If I would be marrying Tristan?" She took a deep breath and shook her head. Her emotions were racing again. "Melissa, Tristan is a nice man and a dear friend, but I have no intention of marrying him or anyone else at this time." She closed her eyes for a moment then opened them and drew the silver sword. :*Melissa, please do me a favor and stay with the sword. I need to speak with Cewyr alone.*

:*Okay.*

Kyrianna laid the sword against the nearest tree and walked over to the unicorn. She placed a hand on the mare's neck and led her several yards away from where the sword was. "You're worried about what Melissa told you."

The mare bobbed her head.

"Silly horse. Men and women who are friends can play those kinds of games and never have anything come from them, as long as they understand the rules. I have no intentions of doing anything that would separate us. I will stand by you, as long as you will let me."

:Kyri, I'm not worried about losing you to Tristan. I'm worried you are not interpreting the rules correctly yourself. It is not fair to play with someone's emotions—even if you only think it a game you are both playing.

"Even when it's your own emotions you are playing with?" Kyrianna whispered.

Cewyr nickered then pressed her muzzle against Kyrianna's neck. The unicorn's breath was warm on her skin and she pressed her head against Cewyr's cheek.

:We should be getting back.

Kyrianna looked up at the sky and frowned. "It is past midday; Myrith will want to kill me for being late."

:If she gives you too much trouble, tell her you will take the lance back where you got it from, Cewyr said.

Kyrianna laughed as she retrieved the sword. *:Thank you, Melissa.*

:You're welcome.

Kyrianna pulled the crystal rod from her pack and held it in one hand as she whistled for Shadow Seeker. "You had best go back to your home, Cewyr. I'll call you when we're ready."

The unicorn vanished and Kyrianna secured the figurine in the protected pocket of her pack. Taking a deep breath, she knelt down and took hold of Shadow Seeker's collar with one hand. With her knee resting on the lance Tristan had given her for Myrith, she broke the rod.

Chapter Twelve

Myrith looked up at the stands as Gwideon entered the Coliseum.

Everyone was here, except Kyrianna and Hendandra. As she glanced again at Gwideon, she realized another member of the group was missing. "Where's the tiger?"

"I do not know," Gwideon said. "He did not meet me this morning." He raised his sword in salute and gestured to the field.

"Great! Now he is missing." She blocked his swing and slapped him on the shoulder with Conflagration as she danced out of his way. "I believe Hendandra is in the city—somewhere, as the extra gear she was carrying was in my room when I returned last night. Kyrianna was here only a few days ago and has vanished. By the time we get this group together, Thynitic will have regained her strength and we will have no chance of rescuing Brular and will probably lose a few, if not all of us, in the process." She swung again, this time missing Gwideon as he backed away.

"Hold, Lady Lake," Gwideon said. "You are letting your anger affect you too much. There is no benefit in training like this." He sheathed his sword as an older man, wearing the robes of a clerk approached them.

"Are you Myrith Lake?" The man looked at her and Conflagration and took a slow step back.

"I am."

"Good." He took a step forward, a thick bundle of papers in his hand. "I need you to sign this." He pulled a sheet out of the bundle and placed it on top of the rest. "And could you direct me to…" he pulled a small piece of paper from his pocket, "Andrinor, Falden, Hendandra, Kyrianna, Jerietlan and Nirev?"

Myrith stared at him and frowned. "Four of those you named are sitting there in the stands." She pointed with her sword. "Hendandra and Kyrianna are not anywhere I am aware of at this time. What is this?"

"It is the deed to the house." He looked around as the others came out of the stands to stand around Myrith and Gwideon. "I will need signatures from each of you as well."

"Deed to the house? What house?" Myrith handed the papers to Jerietlan.

"All I know is yesterday Arkan of House Lors Underian was bested in a trial of champions and the title of this house was ordered transferred to Hendandra. It was also ordered that the others I have named are to be listed as members of her house. If each of you will sign the top paper, that will show your acknowledgement as a member of the House. While not completely necessary as Hendandra can formally name anyone she wishes as members of her House, it makes the paperwork easier." He held a quill out to Myrith.

She held her hand up refusing the quill. "I know nothing of this and will not sign these papers."

The clerk shook his head. "I assure you it is a perfectly legal transfer."

"Myrith!" Hendandra's voice called across the field.

"You have some explaining to do," Myrith said, stepping away from the clerk. "Where have you been?"

"Excuse me." The clerk stepped between them. "You match the description I was given for Hendandra. Is that correct?"

Hendandra looked up at Myrith then quickly turned her attention to the clerk. "It is."

"Good." He took the papers back from Falden who had just signed them. "I need you to sign here." He flipped through a couple of the pages and handed her the quill. "And here."

"What is this?"

"It is the paperwork to transfer title to property from Arkan of House Lors Underian to you as well as the formal declaration of those you've named as members of your House."

"That was quick." She signed the papers in the requested locations and handed the papers back to the clerk.

"I believe that's everyone," the clerk said, looking at the paper, "except one. Where can I locate Kyrianna?"

"That is a question I would like the answer to as well," Myrith said.

"She's not back yet?" Hendandra looked around. "I'm not the last one back? Guess that explains why you're still here after you promised to leave me behind if I was late."

"And why are you late?" Myrith asked.

"I was back on time, but ran into a little trouble with a man who accused me of pick pocketing these." She held up the wolf and unicorn necklace.

"Is that the same set we found?" Myrith asked. "I thought you were going to give it to Kyrianna."

"I was, but we got busy and I forgot. Thing is, this nobleman had it and was trying to sell it, so I reclaimed it and in the process ended up in a trial of champions. When that was settled, I accused the nobleman of making a false accusation and well, that's when I ended up with the house."

"Myrith!" Kyrianna's voice echoed in the arena.

Myrith looked up and frowned as her senses alerted her to some darkness on her friend. She concentrated for a moment; the feeling was the same as what she received from Gwideon's sword. She paused as she saw movement behind Kyrianna, Gwideon was standing there. She relaxed; it was only the aura from his sword she was picking up.

"Why are you late? Of everyone here, I would have expected you to be the first to get back. Particularly since I know you were back in Irrmar a few days ago."

Myrith watched as Kyrianna closed her eyes and her hand dropped to the sword she was wearing. "It's personal," she whispered.

"Personal?" Myrith couldn't believe what she had just heard. First, Hendandra insisting on taking the time to go home before traveling to Justula and now Kyrianna took the time for a personal trip as well. At least Hendandra told her what she was doing. "We do not have time for personal trips; you, of all people, should know that."

"You are Kyrianna?" The clerk held out the papers.

Myrith shook her head at the man's persistence to get what he needed done. If only other members of this group would learn something from him. Hendandra, she could almost forgive. It hadn't been completely the girl's fault; she had run into trouble after getting back, so technically had been in the city on time. Kyrianna had been here and left.

"What is this?" Kyrianna looked through the papers.

"As I was explaining when you arrived," Hendandra said. "Yesterday, I had some nobleman accuse me of picking his pocket and I ended up in a trial of champions here in the coliseum. A..." She hesitated. "A friend of mine fought for me and won. I then made a charge of false accusation against the nobleman and I won that contest and he agreed to give me the property as compensation."

"Who was this nobleman?" Gwideon asked.

Myrith turned to look at him. He was standing next to her, but she had not seen him walk up. She looked at Kyrianna again; there was nothing there she could sense. Still something was wrong. She was normally not this blind to things going on around her and this was twice in a short period of time Gwideon had managed to move around her and she had not noticed.

"I didn't get his name, but he is a member of House Lors Underian."

"Arkan," the clerk said.

"They are the second ranked House," Gwideon said. "You have made a powerful enemy."

"Then it is a good thing I have powerful friends to defend me." She smiled as she looked around at the group. "Has everyone signed the papers?"

"Everyone except Myrith Lake and Jerietlan," the clerk said.

"Very well. I still want them listed as members of my House. And, if you will, I would appreciate it if you would guide us to the property."

"Of course." The clerk gestured to the nearest exit and led the way through the streets of Irrmar.

Myrith followed at the back of group, watching the others and the area around them. She frowned as Kyrianna approached Falden. Andrinor's reaction had been far calmer than she expected it to be when he had seen the mage yesterday. Kyrianna was the other one she expected to go after Cassandra Shindar for what she had done to their friend.

"I'm sure you have already told the tale," she heard Kyrianna say, "but who did this to you?"

"Cassandra Shindar, a member of the Circle of Gormanghast. She was angry I did not tell her about Andrinor's draconic powers and he surprised her as she was harvesting the blood of a recently deceased dragon. She will pay for her actions. For this and what others have suffered as a result of her and the Circle's tampering with nature, they will pay."

"Let me know if you need any help," Kyrianna said.

Myrith was surprised Falden didn't say anything about Cassandra's threats toward Kyrianna. She knew the girl didn't need anything else to worry about, but Falden didn't know about the amulet so had no reason to hold back that information.

"This is your property," the clerk said, pointing to a walled area. "Good day to you."

Hendandra pushed open the gate and held it as the others walked through.

Myrith found herself staring at the large house. While not as grand as House Vernas, this was not what she would have expected to be the home of a minor nobleman either. The grounds were expansive and heavily wooded in one area; the house was almost as large as the one on the Duvall Estate.

"Come on, let's see the inside," Hendandra said, heading for the door.

The doors opened into a large hall with a staircase at the far end. An archway to the left led into the main room. Across the hall was the dining hall. It appeared everything had been left as it was. There was nothing disturbed as they checked the lower level. Most of the books were still in the library and the pantry was still stocked.

"Someone is probably expecting to find a way to reclaim the property," Falden said, "and didn't want to have to move things twice."

"In that case, he better show up soon to claim anything, other than the furniture," Hendandra said. "I have no intention of letting him have the property back." She headed up the stairs.

The stairs came out in a large room that had chairs and a small table set up. Along the sides were several smaller rooms. Hendandra headed for the largest of the rooms and dropped her pack on the bed. Myrith watched as the others claimed rooms for themselves as well.

"Which room are you taking?" Kyrianna asked.

"I'll be staying at the temple," Myrith said.

"As will I," Jerietlan said. "Something about this doesn't feel right."

"Paranoid," Hendandra said.

"Cautious," Myrith said. "We need to get ready and leave as soon as possible. All this is doing is wasting time."

"I would suggest taking inventory of our equipment and finding out what we need first," Andrinor said.

"Other than a few basic items, I am ready." Myrith looked around at the others.

"Let me get my pack." Kyrianna vanished into the room she and claimed and shut the door behind her.

Myrith dropped into a nearby chair as the others did the same.

"Some potions of healing, poison antidotes and maybe some enhancements to our magical protections," Jerietlan said after everyone had dumped their gear in the middle of the room.

"I need more arrows," Kyrianna said.

"If you get them enchanted, remember most demons are resistant to things like fire, acid and cold," Gwideon said.

"Thank you."

"Myrith, I have the tiger, and you have Riker," Gwideon said. "How will the rest be traveling once we reach the Abyss?"

"I have Cewyr," Kyrianna said.

"I can keep up," Andrinor said.

Falden held out his staff. "I can summon a mount from this. Both Hendandra and I are light enough that I believe we can ride together."

Jerietlan turned to Nirev. "We could, perhaps summon allies to assist us."

Nirev shook his head. "My powers be not at the same level as yours. Besides, I be happier with a well trained war pony."

"I might be able to help with that," Andrinor said, "if Falden is willing to transport Nirev and I to Tormasus. I earned the respect of the Fifth Sword; perhaps I can convince him to provide us with appropriate mounts."

Falden nodded. "I do not require anything before we leave; therefore I am ready when you are."

"Despite the time it will cost us, I believe this is a good idea," Myrith said. "Before you leave, do you need anything?"

Both Nirev and Andrinor shook their heads.

"Then the rest of us will get what we need. We will all meet at the Coliseum at first light."

Chapter Thirteen

Hendandra let her hand drag across the sheets on the bed. It had been a long day as the group had gone to various shops in Irrmar, selling old equipment and buying new. The ring and circlet given to her by Vesir had proven valuable as she handled the bartering. She had been surprised no one in the group had questioned her about the missing gems and jewelry. She had however, held only a reasonable portion of the gems she had received from the sale of the rapier back for herself and pooled the rest with the group funds. After all, if she wanted to make it back in one piece from this, she would need all of them to protect her.

She grinned as she snapped the moon ivy choker and the vines withered. She liked the feel of the soft carpet through her moccasins and didn't want to spoil it with the crackling of leaves. She stepped out on the balcony and stared up at the stars and the rising moon. The night was cool and she shivered; the island was much warmer than Irrmar.

She went back into the room and jumped into the bed. She was rewarded with her body sinking into the soft mattress. The sheets slid under her arms and legs creating a different kind of chill in her body. *Justula is warmer*, she thought. *But they do not have sheets, let alone cloth that makes your skin tingle.* She lay there as her thoughts turned to Feric. She caught her breath as she imagined she could feel his hand on her back.

She was startled out of her dream by the sound of barking. She slid from the bed and went back out on the balcony. Kyrianna was leaning against a tree and waved at her as Shadow Seeker pounced and barked at something in the hedges. Hendandra returned the wave, then took a step back toward her room.

Don't want her to see the tattoo, she thought as she blew out her lantern.

Her eyes adjusted quickly as the moonlight bathed the room. The pale light seemed to make all the colors blend together, but it was still beautiful. She leaned her head against the doorframe to the balcony. "How many weeks and months did we fight, Kyri?" she whispered as she pulled the silk of the curtain around her. The feel of the fabric was intoxicating. "All those awful places and now we have a chance to live. Why go to the Abyss? I could stay here or on Justula. I need not constantly strive for more. I have everything I ever wanted." She paused as she pictured Feric in her mind. "I have everything. A beautiful house in the noble district, riches that are not even considered such and a loving husband." She smiled as the fabric brushed across her face. "A husband who keeps me safe, even against the forces of an entire House."

She stepped back out onto the balcony; she didn't hear the wolf barking, but she thought she could see him playing in the bushes and trees. Kyrianna had stuck the silver sword from the Duvall Estate in the ground and was sitting against a nearby tree.

Good, she's not paying attention to the house. Hendandra climbed onto the stone railing then reached up to grab the roof. Her feet dangled for just a moment as she pulled herself up. Without thinking about her steps, she moved away from the edge into the shadows then to the top of the roof, where she would be able to look out over the other houses.

She frowned. There was a time when she would have found the view of the city from this angle to be beautiful, but now, after seeing Justula from above, it was just another city. There was too much smoke in the air from the chimneys and the natural beauty of the land was hidden by the human-built structures. Feric had shown her what true beauty was. "Where are you now?" she whispered into the wind.

She could picture the animals he had become. The reptile from the arena made her heart stop, but the eagle and winged horse were breathtaking. She remembered how she had lain with her back to his chest. It had given her a feeling of security she had never felt before. She knew he would not let anything harm her. However, she had a long road ahead of her, and he would not be traveling it with her.

I am still here, husband. I want to see you. Can you hear me? Can you see me? The night wind cut through her dress and she shivered again. *Can you smell me?*

~ * ~

Melissa laughed as Shadow Seeker tried to catch her. However, she could move through the hedges and he couldn't. He didn't have a chance. It was good to be out of the sword. She was also glad Kyrianna had a home for the moment. Her 'sister' needed a place to call home. Despite being welcomed back by her father and brother, Kyrianna still carried the memories of being banished as well as a deep guilt over her mother's death. She doubted Kyrianna would feel at home there again for a long time.

Melissa froze; she had felt something. It was almost as if the trees were speaking to her. Then a small figure stepped from one of them. She faded back into the bushes as he turned to look at her. He was a halfling, dressed only in a jerkin and pants—nothing more. He looked around and sniffed the air, then smiled as he looked toward the roof of the house.

She watched as he moved toward the house. His gaze seemed to move along the hedges then stop on her as he stepped past some trees. He never stepped out.

Where did he go? She glided around the trees and did not see him. She circled the spot where she had last seen him, but now there was nothing. *Did he step into another tree?* She turned to see a large snake hanging from the branch above her and staring into her eyes.

Her gaze met the snake's and it struck at her. She jumped back as its fangs found nothing but ethereal mist. *It attacked me. That has not happened before.* The snaked moved quickly toward her. *Something's wrong. It shouldn't able to follow me like this.*

The snake struck again and this time she felt the fangs. She jerked her hand back to see the two punctures in her hand. :*Kyri!*

She flew through the bushes, past Shadow Seeker and straight to Kyrianna, who was holding the silver sword. She let herself flow back into the metal.

"What's wrong?" Kyrianna was shaking as she asked the question.

:*A snake. A snake.*

Kyrianna laughed and Melissa could sense her relaxing. "A snake can't hurt a ghost."

:*This one can!* Melissa was shouting.

Kyrianna tensed again and Melissa could sense the mist that rolled through the bushes and lapped at her feet.

:*It is like the estate. Kyri, is it my brother—back for me?*

Kyrianna whistled and Shadow Seeker brushed against her leg, then touched his nose against the sword.

:*We will protect you*, the wolf said.

Everything went silent.

:Kyri, what is happening? Where is the sound of the wind?

"Melissa, let me concentrate." She transferred the silver sword to her left hand then drew the unicorn horn sword.

Kyrianna spun around as something warm breathed on her neck. Melissa felt a sharp stab of fear go through her sister. A large reptile stood there looking down at her. Kyrianna took a half-step back as she raised her swords, then stopped.

:Kyri! Melissa screamed. *:Run!*

:No! There are two more of them.

Kyrianna stood frozen as the one in front of her flicked its tongue in front of her nose. It sniffed at the silver sword then lifted its head and chirruped several times. The reptile then stepped back into the mist and vanished.

:Did they leave?

"Yes." Kyrianna turned slowly and scanned the area.

:Why were they here?

"Hendandra!" Kyrianna sprinted through the fog toward the house.

~ * ~

Hendandra knew she shouldn't have stayed in the wind. Her body was shaking and she felt the cold start to burn as she held the heart token in her hand. "He can't hear me," she whispered.

She turned at the sound of clicking on the roof. A small reddish-brown creature, about the size of a ferret, looked at her and cocked its head. "And what are you?"

It sprang forward and wrapped itself around her neck. The fur warm against her skin. Hendandra found herself stoking it under its chin as it raised its head to look at her. While it resembled a ferret in body shape, it had sharper teeth and a bushy tail.

"You are too tame to just be hanging about," she said. "Where is he?" The animal moved its head to the side and was looking behind her.

She felt something touch her ear and the cold vanished. "More magic," she said as she turned to see Feric smiling at her. "Our people need to have something more than these dresses, if I am going to wear them in my world."

Feric held up a piece of fabric, the same color as her dress. He opened it up to show it was several feet in width and length. Hendandra smiled as he folded it over and held it out for her. She guided his hand to her hip, then twirled around, letting the cloth wrap itself around her waist like a skirt. Her lips touched his as he tucked the end of the fabric into the rest.

Hendandra leaned her head against his shoulder as he held her. "You came to me. How did you find the house?"

He turned his face toward her neck as he sniffed and kissed it lightly. "My big friend was right."

She pulled back. "What friend?"

"The sloth you met when you first came to the island."

She looked into his eyes. "What did he say?"

He placed his cheek against hers as he inhaled. "That you smelled delicious."

Hendandra laughed as his lips again found hers.

She wasn't sure how long they held the embrace before she stepped back and shook her head to clear it. Feric looked at her, concern written on his face. "Feric, I stand by my acceptance of your token," she said, placing her hand over the heart token. "But this has happened so fast. I need time to think."

Feric nodded and smiled. "I understand."

She leaned forward and kissed him gently, then turned and slipped back down to the balcony. She stood there looking out over the grounds in the darkness. She didn't see Kyrianna or Shadow Seeker anywhere in the area and wondered where they had gone. It would have helped to have another woman to talk to about this, but she didn't want to talk to Myrith. The older woman was wrapped up in her own issues and in preparing to go after Brular. She was also a bit too judgmental.

She glanced back up at the roof. There was an attraction between her and Feric; she couldn't deny that. But did she really love him? Right now, she wasn't sure. She had no doubts that he loved her. His actions spoke for that: From not asking her to knowingly participate in a lie to his village, to not trying to take any kind of advantage, to fighting to defend her in the Coliseum.

The first time she had kissed him, her motivations had been to make him feel something for her, so he would get his father to help her. That had worked in a way she had never anticipated. He had decided he loved her and had tricked her into marrying him by not telling her about the token he had commissioned for her. She had been angry with him for his deception and then when she realized the village now considered her to be one of them, she had decided to use that also.

She glanced back down at the heart token she wore near her heart. Rega had told her the placement of the heart token was considered an indicator of the strength of the union. She had replied that Feric's actions spoke for the strength of their marriage. She had not said anything about her love for him being that strong.

Do I love him? she wondered. *Or are my feelings nothing more than a reaction to his rescuing me—not once but twice?*

She glanced up at the roof and smiled. It would take some time to sort out her feelings. She honestly felt the attraction was genuine and with the way Feric obviously felt about her, there was something they could build on. She held the heart token; it would remain where it was. What she wanted for now was for her and Feric to become friends so this marriage could be something other than one of convenience for her. She had everything she needed in her marriage to Feric. A husband who would protect her—no matter what, the security of a home and family and something else she had always wanted—respect. Now, it was time to slow down, catch her breath and make sure this was what she truly wanted.

She blew a silent kiss toward the roof and headed back into the house and the soft bed. She giggled as the little creature unwound himself from her neck and sprang onto a separate pillow, fluffed it up and went to sleep.

~ * ~

Kyrianna sat with her back against the wall of the grounds. She and Melissa had both been surprised to find Hendandra on the roof of the house with a male halfling. The embrace the two were sharing was enough to tell her to leave them alone. As long as Hendandra knew what she was doing, she didn't need anyone else interfering. Shadow Seeker lay next to her with his head in her lap and Melissa was sitting nearby playing with some flowers. Everything was peaceful for the moment.

"Kyri." Melissa turned toward her.

"Yes." Kyrianna failed to stifle a yawn.

"They don't treat Myrith very well at the temple."

"No."

"Why?"

Kyrianna yawned again. "She, like myself, is not from here. They do not accept her."

"My nephew belongs to that Order. Our family helped found that Order. I want to help her. He could help."

"It is possible, but I have a feeling it will take more than that. He has the lineage, but this is Irrmar not Raspa. She really needs the help of a noble House here." Kyrianna rubbed Shadow Seeker's ears as he whined in his sleep.

"The sword she carries appears to be the one Krella Eglis was carrying in the memories Brular showed us. If it is, she must have received it from House Vernas. Maybe Ferdinand and his house could help."

"An outcast priest? It is doubtful that would do much good." Kyrianna looked up at the sky.

Melissa sat there for several minutes. "Stephanie Vernas," she said.

"Who?" Kyrianna stared at the ghost.

"It was common knowledge at the time. Marcus Vernas, King of Irrmar, his older sister was married to House Dracenhalts. There was but one son in that House at that time. It was the talk of the court that House Dracenhalts would have no heir as it was believed the lady could not bear children. She finally had a child, late in life. His name is Petre."

Kyrianna shook her head. "I don't understand."

Melissa smiled. "Kyri, do you not read the proclamations on the streets? Petre Dracenhalts is the current king."

Kyrianna slammed her head against the wall. "You mean we have been running around this continent and a man who owes his very existence to Brular's actions is king of this realm?"

Melissa's smile widened and she seemed to glow. "Exactly. And Myrith now wields the sword of the other person who was responsible for his mother's rescue."

Kyrianna shook her head as she stared at Melissa. The girl was right. Who better to knight her friend than a king? The question now—how did she convince a king to do so?

Melissa glided over to stand next to Kyrianna. "Did my tutor teach me well?"

She reached out to the girl, who faded back into the sword. :*Very well, little sister, very well.*

Chapter Fourteen

Myrith and Gwideon were already on the field with Riker and the tiger. Kyrianna grinned at Hendandra as she pulled the unicorn figure from its pocket. "Think I should join them?"

"No!" Hendandra's face paled then she grinned back. "Let them have their fun. Besides, I don't want to see Cewyr or you get hurt."

Kyrianna raised an eyebrow then nodded. "Perhaps you're right. It would appear the tiger has little control and would be a very dangerous sparring partner."

"Care for another target, Myrith?" Andrinor's voice called across the field.

"What, in the name of Frayrith, is that abomination?" Kyrianna's hand went to her swords as she stared at the creature Nirev was mounted on. It was the size of a war pony, blood-red in color and its face seemed to be a cross between a dog and a horse. The teeth it showed as it growled were definitely those of a carnivore and predator.

"I know it's a bit unusual," Andrinor said. "But we have been assured it is a much better mount than a regular horse or pony would be in the Abyss."

Kyrianna drew her blades at a roar that came from across the field. The tiger reared up and tossed Gwideon off then charged Andrinor and Nirev.

"Chaos," Kyrianna said, starting toward the tiger. "Stay here," she said to Hendandra and Shadow Seeker.

"Hold!" Gwideon yelled as he and Myrith also sprinted toward the tiger.

The tiger hit Andrinor, knocking him to the side as he pounced at the pony. Nirev slid off the pony and brought his war hammer up. He hit the tiger in the shoulder. The great cat only shrugged as he turned toward the dwarf. His teeth sank into Nirev's armor and he dragged the dwarf beneath his hind claws. Nirev was struggling to wrestle himself free of the tiger, but was unable to move.

"Andrinor, get that thing out of here." Kyrianna pointed at the pony as she tried to draw the tiger's attention. She focused her senses and concentrated on calming the great cat so they could get it away from Nirev, but it was too intent on its prey.

Out of the corner of her eye, she saw Hendandra moving along the wall to a position where she was directly in front of the tiger. Kyrianna watched as the tiger paused and glanced at Hendandra. The smaller woman appeared to be praying as she watched the scene. Kyrianna took a few steps toward Hendandra. *This is interesting,* she thought. *She is calling on Shyada.*

She waited as Hendandra continued to call on the goddess of predators, cats and pleasure seekers and added her own silent plea to Dwycia to intercede with her sister as well.

Andrinor and the pony left the field and the tiger moved off Nirev. Kyrianna stared as his body glowed with a soft radiance and he touched Nirev with one paw. The wounds the dwarf had vanished and similar ones appeared on the tiger.

She watched as Myrith and Gwideon approached Nirev, their blades still drawn and ready. *Let them sort it out; I happen to agree with the tiger's attitude toward that thing.* She sheathed her own swords and walked over to Hendandra.

"You were calling on Shyada. I didn't think you followed any particular god?"

"True, but as the Lady of Cats and Predators it seemed appropriate to ask for her assistance," Kyrianna followed her gaze to the tiger who was still watching Hendandra, "...considering."

"Sounds like you had an interesting time on that island. I have yet to hear anyone else's tales, care to share yours?"

"Actually yes, I would. Just," she stopped and looked around, "not here."

"Let's find our rooms." Kyrianna looked at Shadow Seeker who trotted into the Coliseum. After several turns, they came to the quiet corridor where the priests had provided them with sleeping quarters that first night. Kyrianna opened the door to her room and motioned Shadow Seeker to remain outside.

"So what happened?" she asked as she closed the door.

Hendandra looked down at the floor then back up at her and smiled. "I got married."

"Married? What? Congratulations, I think." She stared at the smaller woman for a moment. "The friend who defended you?"

"His name is Feric." Hendandra went on to tell Kyrianna about the events on the island, and her relationship with the halflings.

"That was Feric who visited you last night I take it?" Kyrianna asked.

Hendandra jerked her head back. "You know about that?"

Kyrianna smiled and nodded. "As long as you know what you're doing and you're happy, it's really not my business to pry. However, I was concerned when I met three large lizards on the grounds and an unnatural fog rolled in. As Gwideon said, you have made an enemy of the second-ranked House in Irrmar. I went to check on you, found you on the roof with him and left."

"Kyri, I'm not sure I do know what I'm doing. My first reactions to Feric were to try and use him to get the help we needed to rescue Brular."

"And now?"

"And now?" Hendandra paused. "Now, I'm not so sure. His actions tell me he truly loves me. There is a definite attraction between us. I think, in my heart I do love him, but this has happened so fast."

"I know I've spoken very little about my past. Where I am from, my father is considered a noble. I have seen marriages that were made only for convenience, to seal alliances between Houses, that kind of thing. However, if you have the sense to step back and examine your feelings like this, there is hope your marriage will end up based on something more than convenience. Marriages of convenience need not remain only that. Follow your heart—few enough people in the world ever do." She paused. "Princess," she said, bowing her head.

Hendandra giggled then stopped. "Kyri, have you ever been in love?"

Kyrianna felt her breath catch as she thought about Tristan. "I played flirtatious games with the noble born boys my father would have had me marry, but I was never in love. Being a half-elf, in a place where elves are despised and hated, I had no illusions I would be able to truly find love."

"Was your parent's marriage for convenience?"

"No, it wasn't. My father was deeply in love with my mother, even with the problems it caused him—being married to an elf." She turned her head away to hide the tears she felt.

"Was?" Hendandra placed a hand over hers. "I'm sorry; I didn't mean to open a wound."

"You didn't know." She took a deep breath and turned back to face Hendandra.

"Enough of the bad news and back to you. You said you met Shyada and Isdela—what happened? If you don't mind sharing."

"I don't mind at all. You would have loved it. Rhyra showed up and was threatening me when Shyada and Isdela appeared and put her in her place. Shyada actually clawed Rhyra's face."

"Threatening you? Why would Rhyra be threatening you? I thought she had asked you to follow her?"

"Oh, that's right, you don't know."

"Don't know what?"

"Both Vesir and Rhyra ask me to follow them, saying if something happened to me in the last place we all were, Thynitic could trap my soul. Both gave me gifts to choose one over the other and I now call Vesir my patron. Apparently Rhyra wasn't pleased by this and has been tormenting me because of it. I even believe she was behind the accusation made by Arkan."

"So you have an even more dangerous enemy than the second House. Have you consulted with a temple of Vesir yet?"

Hendandra's eye went wide. "That was the same advice Brular gave me. How did you know?"

"I didn't. However, it seems the most reasonable course." She paused and drew the silver sword. "Since you're sharing secrets, let me share one also." She placed Hendandra's hand on the sword.

"Remember the little girl we found in the hedge maze on the Duvall Estate?"

Hendandra nodded.

"She has been traveling with me since we left that place. Melissa, meet Hendandra."

:Hello, Hendandra. Thank you for your help in freeing us from my brother's evil, Melissa said in Kyrianna's mind. From the dazed look on Hendandra's face, she knew her friend had heard the girl as well.

"Uh, you're welcome." Hendandra pulled her hands away from the sword and looked up at Kyrianna. "So you have gained a sister, while I gained a husband. We have had interesting travels." She stopped then stood and turned around. "There is one more thing you should see." She shifted her armor.

Kyrianna found herself staring at the beautiful tattoo of a tiger surrounded by jungle foliage. There was something familiar about the markings and she gasped as her mind imposed the image of

Gwideon's mount over the image of the tattoo. They were the same. "It's a beautiful likeness," she said.

"Likeness? What do you mean?"

"You don't know? That tattoo looks exactly like the tiger traveling with Gwideon."

Hendandra stared at her then frowned. "Feric. The tiger is Feric. Somehow, I knew there was something familiar about it." She shook her head and smiled.

Kyrianna grinned. "No wonder he likes you. Are you going to tell the others?"

"No! And you can't tell them either."

"It's not my place to tell them. However, be careful. Myrith will get suspicious if you are able to control the tiger when no one else can." Hendandra nodded.

"We need to get back out there. Come on."

"Wait." Hendandra grabbed her arm. "Kyri, I need to talk to Feric, but I don't want the others to know. Can you bring him here?"

Kyrianna stopped and looked down at her friend. "What if he doesn't want to come?"

Hendandra pulled a piece of cloth from her pack. "I wore it last night."

"That should help." She wrapped the cloth around her hand and headed down the hallway. *I hope he wants to come; Nirev's hammer just seemed to make him angry.*

~ * ~

Kyrianna paused as she entered the arena. The tiger was in the far corner watching Myrith and Gwideon where they stood together talking. There was no sign of any of the others. She took a deep breath and walked toward the tiger. His eyes—the eyes of a predator—focused on her. She refused to look away even as she heard her name called. She now knew the tiger was intelligent, not just an animal, but that knowledge only further disconcerted her. His attitude toward the group was dangerous.

"Kyrianna!" Myrith called again. "Get away from him and come over here. Now!"

She backed away from the tiger, still watching him just as he watched her.

"What?" She kept her voice low.

"We should have been gone already." Myrith glanced at the tiger. "It is a risk. We must be able to control it or it will be our undoing. Gwideon has been trying to convince me Resare saw the tiger as a needed ally. Jerietlan and Nirev have both told me it serves a deity of light. However, its actions are erratic and dangerous, and I cannot understand its motives. Andrinor and Nirev, though somewhat erratic in their methods, I do understand. I know where they stand in a fight, but not the tiger. We need three mounts—not two."

"I don't think you should leave him behind, but I will take my horse, if that is your decision," Gwideon said.

"And who tells the tiger?" Kyrianna glanced at them then turned her attention back to Feric. "Not only no, but by all the demons of Chaos—no." She paused then turned back to Myrith. "Let me talk to him—alone."

She waited as they both stared at her. "Kyrianna, he took the hammer hit and just tore into Nirev," Gwideon said. "If he had wanted to, it could have left him a ragged mess."

Myrith shook her head and sighed. "You think you can talk to it?"

"I do. However, I don't think he will talk with either of you present. He seems to have a particular dislike for those wearing steel. To tell the truth, I'm amazed he lets Gwideon ride him."

"And what of the steel you are wearing?"

"I carry fewer items that are made of metal than either of you." She started walking toward the tiger. "Enough of this, we have other things to deal with as well, but first the tiger."

The tiger growled as she approached and Kyrianna forced herself to keep her hands away from her weapons as it grew louder with each step she took. Behind her, she heard the sound of two blades being drawn and she knew they stood ready. She flipped her wrist, letting the cloth Hendandra had given her unroll a bit as she held her arm out to the tiger. He paused and stopped growling as he stood and sniffed the cloth.

"She wants to see you," she whispered. She turned and she heard the tiger following her.

~ * ~

"She waits," Kyrianna said as she opened the door and nodded toward Hendandra.

"Change," Hendandra said after the door closed and they were alone. She waited as the tiger melted into the halfling and he stood.

"So, you knew your goddess wanted you to follow me and did not tell me." She held her head high as she tried to still the wavering in her voice. He had lied to her and it hurt.

"No, my wife," Feric said. "I did not know until I entered the arena. I did not realize this Myrith was the one you spoke of." He kept his gaze on the ground.

"Why did you not tell me last night?"

"I was going to tell you," he said quickly.

Hendandra shook her head. As one practiced in the art of lies and deceit, she knew when someone else was lying to her. "That was the first time you have directly lied to me—why?"

He did not respond.

Her hands went to the heart token. "I want an answer or I don't deserve this." She undid the knot in the leather holding the amulet. "Maybe we don't deserve this after all," she whispered as she closed her eyes.

She felt his hand on hers as she held the heart token. "Shyada told me to tell no one. I played with you a bit hoping you would realize it was me without words."

She opened her eyes and looked into his. There was no deception she could read in their depths. "You would tempt your goddess' anger to let me know?"

"Yes. You are my wife. I should not hide from you, but her words must be heeded as well."

She smiled as she heard the reverence echoed in his voice at the mention of 'his wife' and 'Shyada'. He respected and loved them both with the same passion and spirit.

She tightened the knot. "I need to know about the pony."

He stood straighter as his eyes darkened. "It is an abomination. It reeks of the foul magic and putridness of humans who would attempt to twist the natural balance to suit their whims."

"Feric, I am human," Hendandra said. "I may have some halfling in my blood but far more is human. Is that how you see me?"

"No. You are different. You have embraced my home."

"Yes, Feric, I have. I did it for several reasons. One was to see the smile on your face, but I am the only one who has changed." She took a step back. "You are still in that jungle, ready to kill the first human who dares set foot on the island."

He started to turn away, but she grabbed his arm. "I know the slavers did terrible things. I know they still come. I also know if not for you, Rega's children would have been taken as well as many others." She released his arm and placed a hand on his cheek. "I don't judge you for your actions. I respect that you defend your home as fiercely as you do. But, because they are human, you don't see the others as worthy of your respect."

"No."

"You feel you could do this without them?"

"Yes." He placed his hand over hers and pressed his face into her palm.

"With you at my side, I would rip our way through the layers to her citadel."

She shook her head.

"You doubt my power."

She moved her other hand up and cupped his face. "Not your power—your wisdom. You do not know this enemy, Feric. We would not survive."

"I would never let anything happen to you."

She lowered her voice. "I know, but we need more than each other for this task, my husband. The others walk with their gods as well. Some stronger than others." She pulled her hands away. "But they are your enemy. They are the world that takes our people. They are the ones who took your grandmother." His answer came as a growl and Hendandra grabbed his arm again.

"They are all I have left in this world. They. Are. My. Family."

She could feel his muscles tense under her hand as he stared at her. "I respect your family and your home. Please respect mine." She released his arm and sat on the bed. All of her energy was drained as she waited.

He smiled and leaned close to her. "Even the mailed woman?"

She leaned forward and let her lips brush his. "Especially her." She kissed him then pulled back.

"We have another problem to deal with now. Jerietlan and Nirev still need mounts."

"What of you?"

She laughed. "Gwideon doesn't even slow you down and I am not letting you out of my sight. I will ride behind him and make sure you behave."

He nodded. "The dwarf mentioned stone horses. I have seen

them here, but they require your gold."

She looked down at the pearl ring she wore. "Gold is typical, but other things have value here. Much value." She smiled and cocked her head. "This city is hundreds of leagues from Justula. How did you get here so quickly?"

"I walk through the trees."

"How long does that take?" She stood up and grabbed her pack. "Could you get us to Justula and back within an hour?" He nodded.

"Good." She gave him a quick kiss on the cheek. "Kyri," she called as she moved to open the door.

Feric placed his foot against the door. "Shyada told me to tell no one."

Hendandra grinned. "I understand, however, she is the one who figured it out. You played with her last night as well. What she described was a sickle claw." She placed a hand on her chest and took a deep breath. "Playing with me wasn't enough?"

He stared at her, his mouth open. She leaned in and kissed him deeply as she guided him away from the door and reached past him to open it.

"Ahem," Kyrianna said.

"Shut the door." Hendandra released Feric and looked up.

Kyrianna extended her hand. "I am Kyrianna. Though the goddess I follow is not a part of your world, she is kindred to Dwycia who is sister to Shyada."

Feric nodded and grasped Kyrianna's hand. "I sensed as much last night when we met. Hendandra has told me much about you and your companions."

"I would be interested in learning more about your people; however, from the story we heard from Brular, I understand any distrust you have for others. At this time, though, we must resolve the issue Myrith has with the tiger." She paused then lowered herself to sit on the floor. "Myrith does not trust the tiger and sees him as a risk to the group as a whole. In a group like this, all members must trust each other or the distractions caused by not doing so will get us all killed."

Feric glared at her and started to say something, but Hendandra stopped him by placing a hand on his shoulder. "Shyada told him to tell no one. You found out without being told, but you cannot tell the others."

"I understand. In that case, Feric, you must remain in your tiger form throughout the journey and accept the role you have been given: that of Gwideon's mount."

He nodded then shifted back into the tiger form.

"Explain to Myrith the tiger understands his place, but it serves Shyada and abhors society," Hendandra said. "It accepts you and I because of our kinship to nature. Gwideon is accepted because of the dictates of Shyada. He is intelligent but still a creature of instinct."

"I will. However, Feric, you will answer to and heed Myrith's commands."

The tiger roared and Hendandra pulled hard on his ear. "Just do it for me," she said.

The tiger stopped and brushed his head against her face.

Kyrianna cleared her throat.

Hendandra looked up and felt her cheeks grow warm. "Sorry. His fur is so soft."

"There is one other thing we should do," Kyrianna said. "Give the tiger a name."

"His name is Feric," Hendandra said.

"True, but I doubt it's a good idea to use his true name—particularly for you. There is too much risk you will be thinking of him as Feric and not the tiger if you are talking to him and using his correct name. That could cause suspicion. I doubt you want that."

Hendandra looked at Feric then at Kyrianna. "Okay, that makes sense, but what are we going to call him? Everyone just seems to be calling him tiger."

"And that is why I want to give him a proper name. As long as Myrith calls him tiger, she will not see him as anything other than a tiger." She turned attention to Feric. "She must see and treat you as an intelligent creature for her to able to accept you as a part of the group instead of as just Gwideon's mount." She stopped and cocked her head to the side. "Shydaran—it means warrior in the language of the dawn elves of Rhysia and it is close enough to Shyada's name it should remind the others of your primary allegiance to her," she said as she stood up.

Feric nodded.

"Shydaran, I like it," Hendandra said. She slapped his side. "You go with her, be good and show Myrith you will listen to her. When you are done with that, disappear and meet me at the house.

I need something to trade and I think I know just the thing that will be perfect." "Trade?" Kyrianna asked.

"I think a short trip back to Justula would be profitable." She winked at Kyrianna. "For the clerics."

Hendandra saw Kyrianna's eyes light up, but her friend didn't say anything. "Would you like to come?" She grabbed Feric's ears as he started to growl.

"I would love to, but I'm worried about Myrith. She needs confidence. She is working so hard, but getting what seems like nothing in return. I have an idea, but we need to gain an audience. I may need to make a side trip as well."

"To where?"

"Back to Raspa, to see someone."

Hendandra pulled Feric's head against her cheek. "We would love to take you." He started to growl again, but she turned his head toward her and kissed his nose. He lowered his head.

~ * ~

Kyrianna walked back into the stadium, the tiger next to her. As she approached Myrith and Gwideon, she could see a smile on her friend's face.

"Well, you calmed him down at least," Myrith said.

She stopped a few feet from them, placed a hand on the tiger's head and stroked his fur. *Hendandra is right; his fur is soft.*

She nodded. "His name is Shydaran and he is a servant of Shyada; one of her most highly favored pets and she sent him here to go with us," she said. "He is intelligent and understands everything we say, however he cannot speak. He abhors society and the way society tries to twist and control nature. The pony was an abomination and abhorrent to him. Because of this, he was compelled to destroy it." She took a breath. "And if he had not, I would have."

"Kyri!"

She ignored the anger on Myrith's face. "One of the stories I have learned about Shyada, is that she was raised by a tigress, who was then twisted by Ballan into a werecreature."

Myrith stared at her, her brow now creased in confusion.

Kyrianna turned to Gwideon. "Do you know the story I am referring to?"

"Yes." He turned to Myrith. "Shyada is the adopted daughter of Kaleden, god of all nature and Dynissa, goddess of the earth. She is said to be half-elven, but in truth I believe that is just an allegory saying she is part of nature and a part of humanity."

Myrith's eyes went wide.

"As a child she was found by the true-born deity, Dwycia who is nature's protector. She took the child to her mother, Dynissa who sought to raise the child as her own. Kaleden told his wife it was not possible, so they gave the child to a great tigress to raise and watch over. She grew into a beautiful woman who learned to run with Dwycia and it is said her grace is without comparison. Her time with the great cats gave her a unique perspective on life. She likes to play and lounge in the sun and shadows, and she relishes the hunt. She became the patron of predators and pleasure seekers." Gwideon paused for a moment. "It is an odd combination, but her demeanor is often passive and pleasant until forced to action. When that happens, she is primal and deadly efficient as she relies on her teeth, claws and instinct."

Myrith's gaze went from Gwideon to Kyrianna and back. "Obviously, there is a long and involved history here, but do we need all of it to understand Shydaran is a follower of Shyada?"

Gwideon shook his head. "You carry the favor of your goddess, but you still need to understand the other gods of this world. When dealing with them there are no straightforward answers."

"It would make things a lot easier if there were."

Kyrianna nodded. "That it would."

Gwideon looked at her then back at Myrith. "To continue. Ballan, the dark goddess of magic, also seeks to pervert nature and mold it to her uses. She took the tigress and twisted her by giving her the parts of a human and a great hunger for blood. In this form she caused great destruction. Both Dwycia and Shyada pursued the creature for weeks until Dwycia was able to wound it badly enough to force it to stand its ground. The tigress was infused with Ballan's power and attacked Dwycia and her teeth tore into the goddess."

He turned toward Kyrianna. "Dwycia was only a toy in her grip. She could not bring her bow or swords into play. Her sister attacked the tigress while she was distracted by her prey and slashed open the creature's belly."

"This makes no sense," Myrith said, shaking her head. "Even Thynitic does not create creatures that kill gods."

"Lady Lake, it is through the use of such stories that priests teach about the relationships and motives of the gods. Did your teachers never explain this?"

"I have never had much patience for long stories," she said.

Kyrianna looked from Myrith to Gwideon. Her friend had never hidden her lack of knowledge regarding the gods in general and of Shokar in particular. She knew Myrith had been trying to learn more about Mykaylene, but doubted the priests of this temple had been very helpful. Myrith was getting angry with this conversation, but Kyrianna knew much of that anger was being directed internally because of Myrith's lack of knowledge and not truly at Gwideon. It was just very hard to read Myrith correctly in these matters, as she herself had had cause to learn.

"Only the short ones?" Gwideon said. "Will they make good epitaphs, Shield Maiden?" He snapped the question as he stared at Myrith.

Kyrianna heard the slight intake of breath from Myrith and the tightening of her back as she met Gwideon's gaze. *Chaos*, she thought. *Unless she told him about her past, Gwideon would have no way to know how much that last word would have hurt Myrith.* The sarcasm in his voice would have made that term, maiden, a painful reminder of her past, a past Kyrianna knew still haunted her friend.

She took a step forward, but froze at the forbidding sound of Myrith's voice. "How dare you suggest I would deliberately place my companions at risk?"

"Deliberately? No," Gwideon said. His voice was calm and smooth, almost as if he had expected a more violent outburst from Myrith and was now continuing with a practiced speech. "I know you would give your life for them. But there are more types of power than the strength of your arm and the temper of your steel, Lady Lake. You must be prepared to use all of them, as our lessons from this day forward will cost us blood, companions, and even our very souls if we do not pay attention and learn." Myrith nodded.

"The truth is rarely short and almost never as neat as a sword blow." He glanced at Kyrianna for a moment. "Though it can be as painful." He turned back to Myrith. "Shall I continue?"

Myrith took a deep breath. "Please."

"Shyada was forced to kill her adoptive mother in order to save her sister. It is said her anger is unbounded against those who bring ill to nature's order for their own purposes." He nodded toward the tiger. "He is not the one to be punished here; instead it is the creator who should be taken to task. You should note, he has not attacked

Falden. Possibly, because he knows what happened to the mage was not by his choice and Falden has vowed to settle the matter with the Circle as well."

Kyrianna placed her hand on the tiger's head.

"He seeks to preserve nature," Gwideon said. "The existence of such creatures can disturb the balance and order of things. Resare understands this as well. I respect why he did what he did, though not his methods."

"Very well." Myrith turned toward Kyrianna and the tiger. "Shydaran, I will not speak again of what happened today. You were acting as required by the one you follow. However, as you have been directed to join this group in our undertaking, I expect you to heed my orders. If you do not, while I cannot force you to remain behind, I will hold you and your goddess responsible if your actions or inactions cause the others to fall or be hurt."

Kyrianna felt the muscles in the tiger's head tighten for a moment, then he lowered his head slightly.

"Good." Myrith turned away. "We still need to see to transports for Jerietlan and Nirev," she said as she and Gwideon walked toward the temple entrance.

"You are a complete contradiction," Kyrianna heard Myrith say. "You are a warrior in service to a god of death and undeath. You have trained to battle the powers of darkness, but are surrounded by it in your very temple."

"How better to understand and fight something than to call it home?" Gwideon said.

Kyrianna felt a shudder go through her at Gwideon's words. She was walking a path that would have her fighting Thynitic's chaos and darkness, but she had no intention of ever calling it home; at least she would never do so willingly.

She waited a few more seconds as she watched the two of them disappear into the temple. "They're gone," she whispered.

The tiger took off, leaving her to find her own way back to the house.

Chapter Fifteen

"We're upstairs," Hendandra called when she heard the door to the house slam and Kyrianna coming in.

She looked up as Kyrianna came up the stairs. "Myrith is satisfied?"

"For now. Are we ready?"

"You are not going like that," Feric said.

"What?"

Hendandra smiled at the confused look on her friend's face. "Kyri, because of the things humans have done to them, the halflings of Justula have an intense dislike of metal and anything fashioned from it. Please change out of your armor and leave all of your weapons and anything else of metal you are wearing or carrying here."

"Give me a minute."

"Feric, not everyone has the same knowledge as you," Hendandra said.

"Try asking before making demands." She kissed him on the cheek and smiled.

"Hendandra, can you step in here a moment?" Kyrianna called from her room.

"Be right back." She kissed him again then darted away.

"What's wrong?"

Kyrianna was standing in her room holding the silver sword.

"Melissa wants to go, but I have nothing for her to possess."

"What about the unicorn pendant you are wearing?"

"There is something blocking her from being able to transfer into it."

"Oh." Her hand went to the heart token. "Perhaps..."

"No!" Feric's hand grasped hers.

Hendandra turned toward him and smiled. "It will be okay," she said placing a hand on his cheek. "It can be her home for just this little while." She turned back to Kyrianna and held the heart token in her hand.

"Are you sure?" Kyrianna's gaze moved from her to Feric and

back.

"Yes."

She shivered as Kyrianna touched the tip of the sword to the heart token and she felt it grow cold in her hand. Previously, she had always felt warmth in the token, to have it go cold like this was unsettling.

:*Thank you, Hendandra*, she heard Melissa's voice in her head.

"You're welcome," she whispered. She was no longer concerned about the chill. Melissa had spent thirty years trapped in the hedge maze on the Duvall Estate—alone. Yes, the heart token could be her home for a short period of time, if only to keep her from being left here and alone while they were gone.

"Okay, I'm ready." Kyrianna closed the lid to the chest by her bed.

"This house was owned by someone who would do me harm," Hendandra said, looking at the chest. "We have not changed anything—not even the locks."

Kyrianna frowned. "The bow and sword belonged to my mother. They go with me if we cannot be sure they will be safe," she said as she reached for the lid.

Feric placed a hand on Kyrianna's and muttered something Hendandra couldn't understand. "The lid will not open now," he said as a glow surrounded the chest. "Jhoro."

"Yes," the mongoose ran into the room and up onto the bed.

Hendandra giggled at Kyrianna who was staring at the creature. "His name is Jhoro," she said.

Feric laid several berries around the chest then looked at the mongoose. "If anyone approaches this chest, speak the halfling word for fire."

"Of course." Jhoro bobbed his head. "Please bring me a bit of food tonight; the hunting is poor here."

Kyrianna held her hand out for Jhoro to sniff. "Let me find something tasty for him," she said.

"I like her."

"Jhoro," Hendandra said. "Please tell anyone who enters this room Hendandra asked you to warn them off." She paused and looked up at Kyrianna.

"Would hate to blow up one of the others; might make them a little angry."

"We should hurry," Kyrianna said.

~ * ~

Hendandra watched as Kyrianna stared at the beach then turned to look around at the area where they stood. "It's beautiful," she said.

Hendandra smiled. "No, it's more than that." She took Feric's hand. "It's home."

She waved to two girls who disappeared into a nearby hut. Another halfling emerged from the hut and frowned. "Hendandra, Feric, I was not expecting to see either of you for weeks."

"Rega, I need a favor."

"Come inside." She gestured to the hut, her gaze locked on Kyrianna.

"This is my friend, Kyrianna," Hendandra said.

"More humans," Rega muttered as she shook her head.

"She is my friend," Hendandra said, slipping her pack off her shoulder. "Unfortunately, we don't have much time." She pulled the sheets she had taken from the house out of the pack and handed the material to Rega.

Hendandra sat on the floor and motioned Kyrianna to do the same. She watched as the youngest of Rega's daughters approached and stared at her friend's ears, her hand reaching out to touch the tip where it just poked through her hair.

"Stop that," Rega said.

Her daughter pulled her hand away from Kyrianna's ear and sat on the floor next to the half-elf.

"What is this called?" Rega held the cloth up to her face. "It is so soft."

Hendandra smiled. "Silk. I would like you to have dresses made for the women who accepted heart tokens during the celebration for Feric and myself," she said. "You may do whatever you wish with the rest of the material."

"Thank you. I have some new dresses ready for you as well." She went into the other room and came out with the dresses in her arms. "Feric said you were cold and asked for them."

Hendandra glanced out the window, looking for her husband. Feric stood in front of the hut with several of the men from the village facing him. They were all carrying weapons. Kyrianna had complied with their request that she carry nothing of metal, but there was no way to disguise her height. To them she was still a human and one of those who would enslave them. It had been easier for the halflings to accept her when she had come here; she was short, almost as short as they were. They could see her as being a halfling.

"Rega, I'm sorry to ask this, but could I take one of your sculptures back with me?" She pointed to several pieces of jade on a nearby shelf.

Rega smiled. "Of course. Which one would you like?"

Hendandra moved to examine the sculptures and her hand settled on one depicting the mountains to the west. "This one; its colors are exquisite." Her mind was racing as she appraised the value at several thousand gold. *It should be enough to get the stone horses we need for Nirev and Jerietlan.*

"What do you think?" She handed the piece to Kyrianna.

"It is beautiful," she said. "Rega, you don't trade here. Do you give these to the others?"

"Actually they are sometimes given as tribute to tribes from neighboring islands," Rega said.

"Hmm. Tribute?" Hendandra looked at Kyrianna and saw the slight smile on her face.

"We should go," Feric said, stepping into the hut. "Kyrianna, you are drawing too much attention."

"Raspa?" Hendandra took the jade sculpture from Kyrianna.

"Yes." Kyrianna stood and nodded.

"Feric," Hendandra said. He turned to face her and she placed the dresses Rega had given her in his arms. "Please carry them."

"You could just place them in your sack."

She laughed and shook her head. "And wrinkle them?" She kissed him then waited for him to lead the way out of the hut.

~ * ~

"Down there," Kyrianna said, pointing to a set of buildings.

Hendandra tapped the winged horse on the neck and pointed to the area.

The horse landed in the greenery of the yard and a man dressed in fine clothes and carrying a longsword stepped out of the house to greet them.

"Kyrianna!" he called. "Back so soon."

"I'm sorry, Tristan, but I need your assistance," Kyrianna said, hugging him.

"We can discuss it over something to drink. Hendandra, I will have someone stable the horse, please join us."

Kyrianna smiled as the horse neighed and pawed the ground at Tristan's suggestion. "It would be better to just let him be."

"I'll stay here," Hendandra said. She stroked the horse's muzzle.

"Please come inside and tell me what is going on." Tristan motioned to the door.

"We don't have much time. I need your help for Myrith."

"What is needed? I will do what I can."

"She is not being accepted by the church in Irrmar and it weighs heavily on her and is causing her to question her abilities."

"That is not good. With the road you are to travel, self-doubt can be deadly. However, there is little I can do in Irrmar. Here the Order only requires a single sponsor. Unfortunately, in Irrmar the politics of the city have infiltrated the churches. To become a member of one of the Orders requires at least a priest, a member of the Order and a representative from one of the Irrmarian Houses."

"Chaos, this is going to be more complicated than I expected," Kyrianna said. "However, I believe we can convince someone to stand for her, but I will need your help. Are the things I left here still in the guestroom?"

"Yes."

"Good."

"Where are we going?"

Kyrianna winked. "That would be telling." She gave him a coy smile. "Please dress for an audience, but also prepare something appropriate for your Order for travel."

She started up the steps. "Hendandra, bring your new clothes." She didn't wait for the girl as she hurried up the stairs to the guestroom.

~ * ~

Hendandra looked at Kyrianna as she sat in front of the mirror. Her movements with the makeup brushes were practiced and precise along her cheeks and around her eyes. "Kyri, I would never have pictured you in make-up, let alone putting it on with such practiced ease."

"I'm full of surprises. Now, hurry up, we need to go soon."

She picked up one of the brushes and started on her cheeks. It wasn't working; this was something she had never had the patience to learn to do. All she was doing was making a mess. She dropped the brush on the table and grabbed a wet towel to clean her face.

"What's wrong?"

Hendandra rubbed her face. "Kyri, I'm not a lady. I grew up on the streets. I don't know how to do this."

:*I don't think Feric believes you need make-up. By the way he acts, he likes you just the way you are.*

Hendandra smiled. :*Thank you, Melissa.*

Kyrianna finished with her own make-up and turned toward Hendandra. "Where we are going, appearances are very important. I want everyone to look his or her best. Let me help you."

"Melissa and I both agree. I don't need the make-up."

"Normally I would agree, but we are going to see royalty." She picked up the brush and turned Hendandra's face toward her. "Only a few strokes here and there will be needed."

Hendandra smiled, closed her eyes and let the brushes lightly touch her face.

:*Hendandra, can I ask you a question?* Melissa's voice whispered. :*Since you are married, that means you are not a maiden, correct?*

"What?"

"Chaos!" Kyrianna said. "Hendandra?"

She closed her eyes again, Melissa was still chattering.

:*My mother always told me married girls became women and were no longer maidens. But Cewyr asked Rynalana—she is the great-granddaughter of Rynalia of Mount Veri—if she was a maiden. I think there is some legend regarding only maidens being able to ride unicorns. So I asked Kyri about it and she got all defensive. It was quite funny but I never got an answer. You are being all defensive, so it is not just about marriage.*

"Hendandra, what was that for?" Kyrianna handed her the wet towel.

"You won't believe what she just asked me."

"Melissa, leave her alone!"

:*Well, it doesn't concern kissing a man. Kyri and I have seen that you are quite good at that.*

"That does it. Out, and I mean right now."

:*If it isn't kissing and marriage, what is it?*

The voice in Hendandra's head stopped. She looked in the mirror and her mouth dropped open. Kyrianna held the heart token in her hand.

Kyrianna froze as she stared at the pendant she held. "Chaos."

Hendandra snatched the heart token back. She glared at Kyrianna ignoring the pleading she saw in her friend's eyes. "Listen to me, Melissa. Get out of the heart token or I will tell Feric you have defiled our union by being in it."

"Hendandra, I'm sorry." Kyrianna's voice was barely a whisper as she picked up a sapphire necklace from the table and placed it in Hendandra's hand. "Melissa, come to me," she said.

Hendandra felt the chill of the girl's spirit moving from the heart token and into the necklace.

Kyrianna dropped her head as she cradled the necklace. "She was only eight when she was killed. She doesn't know any better."

Hendandra replaced the heart token around her neck and checked its positioning as she stepped to the window. Feric, as the winged horse, was pacing in the yard, but seemed otherwise undisturbed. "Never take it from me again."

Kyrianna kept her head bowed. "I'm sorry I took it. I was only trying to help. It was not my intention to take it; only to separate Melissa from you. I didn't realize it would hurt you like this."

"It is mine." Hendandra glanced back down at Feric. "He gave it to me." She cradled the heart token as Kyrianna had the sapphire necklace. "You know I was never really given anything. I always had to take it. I wouldn't beg. That was beneath me. I took what I needed to survive and usually nothing more. This was the first thing ever given to me." She let her finger trace the design. "And every time I look at it, I question whether I stole it."

"Oh, Hendandra. Never ask that question. I have seen you with him. He gave it to you. The question you should be asking is whether you can return his gift with your own." Kyrianna placed a hand on her shoulder. "I will not take it from you again and I truly doubt anyone could take him from you."

Hendandra turned, looked up at her friend and smiled. "I guess we should get finished."

They sat in silence as Kyrianna completed Hendandra's make-up.

~ * ~

Kyrianna walked slowly around Tristan before they descended the stairs.

"Adequate, Lord Tristan," she said as she let her gaze take in his appearance. He had dressed in a dark blue tunic and pants with tall boots, all of the finest materials. Everything he wore spoke to his position as the lord of a noble House and a member of the Raspa Council. She felt her breath catch as she looked at him and he also seemed to be studying her. "Quite adequate."

He smiled as he copied her movements and moved around her. "More than adequate, Lady Dalynne," said from behind her. "Actually, quite nice." He was back in front of her and caught her gaze with his own as he took her hand and kissed it. "Absolutely ravishing."

Kyrianna felt her cheeks grow hot and she closed her eyes as she tried to calm her racing heart. She opened her eyes then lowered them. "Correction, my Lord. It is Lady Kyrianna. The custom in my home is to use the title and given name. In full formal address it would be Lady Kyrianna of House Dalynne of Nydith."

He bowed. "Lady Kyrianna it is then."

"Ahem."

Kyrianna turned to see Hendandra smiling at them.

"I see I am to escort two beautiful ladies," Tristan said, offering Hendandra a bow.

"I'll be in the yard," Hendandra said as she descended the stairs.

"Did we offend her?" Tristan stared down the stairs.

"No, she has other things on her mind," Kyrianna said. "We do need to leave soon, but I want to give her a few minutes to herself."

"Then I can think of no one better to spend my time with while we wait." His hand went to the necklace she was wearing. "Is this from the guestroom?"

"I hope you don't mind."

"Not at all, though I would have preferred to be able to give it to you myself as I had planned."

"My Lord?" Kyrianna's hand went to the necklace and she gasped at the tingle that went through her as she touched Tristan's.

"Kyri…"

"Hey," Hendandra called from the doorway. "Are we leaving or not? I thought we were in a hurry."

Kyrianna didn't say anything as she lifted the hem of her dress and hurried down the stairs.

"He can't come like that," Hendandra said when Tristan exited the house.

Kyrianna winked at her friend and pulled a length of black cloth from around her waist. "Certainly not," she said. "Tristan, please turn around."

Tristan looked at her then at the cloth in her hand. "I take it I am being kidnapped then," he said.

Hendandra giggled and the horse snorted.

Kyrianna placed the cloth over his eyes. "Kidnapped by two beautiful women on a winged horse; that sounds like the start to a very interesting dream." She tied the knot tight, then leaned close to his ear, her voice low as she made sure to breathe across his neck. "Let your mind have that thought for just a few minutes as we travel to Irrmar." She exhaled across his ear and paused.

"However, I assure you it will be nothing more than just that."

She stepped back and took a more serious tone. "All women have secrets, Tristan. Ours is the magic we used to get here. Indulge us, please."

He nodded and let her lead him to the horse. Feric knelt down so he could mount and then Kyrianna and Hendandra joined him on the horse.

"Back to the house," Hendandra said.

The horse whinnied, then stepped into a tree.

~ * ~

"Are you okay, Tristan?" Kyrianna asked as they slid from the horse's back. "You look a bit pale."

"Not on the horse," Hendandra said.

Tristan leaned against the horse as he regained his balance. "I think the blindfold helped," he said after a few minutes.

Kyrianna and Hendandra both laughed. "You can remove the blindfold," Kyrianna said.

"We are in the city itself?" Tristan dropped the cloth as he looked around. "Do you know the laws regarding this?"

Hendandra felt a sudden chill; Falden had warned them about the seriousness of teleporting within cities. But she had not thought about it herself. Her hand went to Feric's neck.

Kyrianna looked at her and then Feric. "What would happen?" she asked.

"In Raspa several members of the guard, supported by wizards, would be dispatched. That would happen within minutes of the incident."

An image of her previous house flashed in Hendandra's mind and of the destruction that had occurred to it after she had been taken back to the group by Ferdinand. She watched as Kyrianna moved slowly around the area of the tree, examining the ground.

"I assume the reaction is the same both for arriving and leaving—correct?" Kyrianna asked.

"It is," Tristan said.

"We left from this spot some two hours ago, but I see no trace of such a party and our tracks are very distinct here."

"That should not be. I will have to ask about this while I am here."

"Maybe it was the way we traveled?" Hendandra asked.

"That might be. I—" Tristan was cut off by Kyrianna.

"No! We cannot tell you. Ask your questions as you will of others, but not that of us!" She smiled at him. "Never ask a lady her secrets."

Tristan smiled and nodded.

Hendandra looked at them, then at Feric, This was what she had missed with her marriage to Feric. The time of becoming friends and actually finding out she was falling in love with the other person. The time of flirting and courtship. Maybe they would be able to recapture that after this journey was over—if they both survived.

"Is it permitted to know where we are going from here?" Tristan asked.

"We will be seeking an audience with King Dracenhalts," Kyrianna said as she helped Hendandra back on the horse and mounted behind her.

"I doubt having the three of us on the horse will be a good idea," Hendandra said.

"Agreed," Tristan said. "I can walk next to you."

~ * ~

The group received a number of curious looks as they walked through the streets of Irrmar. Kyrianna watched for the man who had offered to buy Cewyr from her, but fortunately no similar offers were made for Feric, She doubted they would be able to control him if there had been.

Hendandra laughed and tossed her head as they rode. "Usually the only attention I get in a city is followed by—stop her," she said.

Kyrianna smiled at the comment. *She seems to like being the center of a different type of attention.* She patted the horse's side as she watched Hendandra wave to the onlookers. *I think you're good for her. Give her time, Feric. Don't push her. I honestly think she wants to love you. She just brings too much with her.* She looked up at the gates to House Dracenhalts, still some distance away, but very recognizable. *For now, let's see if we can help Myrith through some of hers.*

"Hendandra, I had hoped you would have told me by now. I know about the incident," Tristan said.

Kyrianna leaned forward. "What is he talking about?"

Hendandra shook her head. "Ah, Tristan, I don't know how to tell you this…" she paused. "You will have to be a bit more specific; 'the incident' could describe any number of events I have been involved in."

Kyrianna stifled her laugh.

Tristan stopped the horse and turned to look at Hendandra. "I think you know very well what I am talking about."

Hendandra only stared at him then held up her hand and counted off on her fingers. "The Duvall Estate, the edge of the Abyss, the demi-plane, the Isle of Ju—" She stopped. "Ah, more recent events. Help me out here."

Kyrianna felt Feric's muscles tense.

"Your house," Tristan said.

"My house?" She looked at Kyrianna who only shook her head.

"My…my house in Raspa," she said. "Oh yes, you're on the Council, of course you heard about its destruction." There was an edge to her voice. "I had nothing to do with that very nasty affair. I had been there not quite a full day and that rampaging cleric of Mykaylene." She looked at Tristan. "I'm sorry, but that is what Ferdinand is. He dragged me back to Torliana's realm of all places and even threatened my life."

The horse snorted and stamped his feet.

Why did you have to mention that? Kyrianna thought. She watched Hendandra pat the horse's neck and hoped her friend could calm him quickly.

"Nearest I could tell," Hendandra continued, "given some things said by Falden, is he triggered the response you told us of earlier. Your guards showed up and then something really nasty showed up afterwards. I cannot explain it. Take it up with Jerietlan; he just visited Ferdinand. Me, I came home for a day, got kidnapped and had my house destroyed by uninvited guests."

Tristan nodded. "Very well, I will speak to him." He patted the horse's neck then gestured down the street as he resuming walking.

When they reached the gates of House Dracenhalts, Kyrianna slid off the horse and approached with Tristan.

"Please inform the majordomo that Lady Kyrianna of House Dalynne of Nydith and Lord Tristan Duvall of Raspa seek an audience with Lord Dracenhalts, King of Irrmar," Tristan said.

The guard bowed to both of them. "My apologies, my Lord and Lady. However, while your request will be forwarded, we must inform you Lord Dracenhalts' duties this day prevent him from seeing anyone. It will be tomorrow before he will be able to see you. As captain of the guard, I can see your names are added to the audience list. Please return tomorrow at this same time."

Kyrianna nodded and walked back to where Feric and Hendandra were waiting.

"So how long?" Hendandra was lying across the horse's back with her hands behind her head. "I hope it isn't longer than an hour. Kyri and I already have a reputation as being the latest in the group."

"So Myrith wasn't happy with you for staying that night at my house," Tristan said.

Hendandra sat up and looked at Kyrianna. "Excuse me? You spent the night with Tristan before returning to the Coliseum? No wonder you said it was personal."

Kyrianna glared at Hendandra. "It won't be an hour," she said in an attempt to change the subject. "It will be tomorrow before we can see the king."

Hendandra jumped off the horse, reached up to straighten her hair then started toward the gate. "Bring the horse," she said.

"Afraid someone will make off with him?" Tristan asked.

"No, I'm afraid he will get hungry." Hendandra flashed them a smile.

Kyrianna smiled at the look Tristan gave her. "Let's just say he has a unique diet. And believe me, he can get real nasty if he doesn't get his meals regularly."

"As I told your master, Lord Duvall, an audience with the king cannot happen until tomorrow."

"My good man," Hendandra said, "I believe there has been a misunderstanding. I do not travel with them. They travel with me. I am Princess Hendandra of the Isle of Justula."

Kyrianna grabbed a handful of the horse's mane and held tight as he pawed at the ground. She turned and stuck an arm around Tristan's as he took a step forward. "Trust her," she said. It was meant more to calm Feric, but she hoped Tristan would also take the advice.

"I have come to meet with the king of these realms. I must consult with him a bit." She paused and looked around. "I wish to be able to return home as quickly as possible as I truly miss the sea. Now, please be good enough to inform him that I am here."

The guard only stared at her. "We have no idea where you are talking about."

:*Repeat what I tell you*, Melissa said to Kyrianna.

"Justula is a large island located in a series of islands southwest of Jahli. Johanus Farshreiber first documented it some sixty years ago."

"Do you have any paperwork to state your title?" the guard asked.

"Paperwork? We of Justula do not use paper." She reached up and scratched at her temple for a moment. "Please tell your ruler that I bring a gift." She stuck her hand into her pack and withdrew the jade sculpture.

The guard's mouth dropped open as did Tristan's.

Kyrianna released Feric's mane as he quieted and rubbed the area where she had pulled out several hairs. "I told you to trust her."

~ * ~

After stabling Feric, something Kyrianna had not thought Hendandra would succeed in doing, they were escorted to a pleasant room to wait. Hendandra claimed a seat on the largest couch and sat there looking every bit the smug princess she had pretended to be.

"I do not believe it is appropriate for a commoner to sit by one of lineage," she said when Kyrianna started to sit next to her.

Kyrianna smiled. "And even less appropriate for one to sit on one of lineage." She laughed as Hendandra scrambled to the side of the couch.

"My Lord," Tristan said as an older man entered the room.

"May I present Princess Hendandra of the Isle of Justula and her companion Lady Kyrianna of the House of Dalynne of Nydith." He paused as they both stood to face the king.

"Ladies, King Dracenhalts, Lord of the Dh'Mark Realms."

Kyrianna and Hendandra both curtsied; Kyrianna made sure hers was deeper than her friend's. She was surprised when the king offered his own bow to Hendandra.

"Princess Hendandra," King Dracenhalts said. "Your visit is nothing if not unexpected. It is rare a royal visitor comes from so far away. I was told you brought a gift. However, I was unaware our lands had formal relations." The king did nothing to hide his confusion.

"Justula has been isolated…" She stopped and exhaled. "I am a princess of Justula. However, I have not come to speak for them. My people have retreated from the world, a world that would treat them as cattle and property. I have not come to establish relations as they would not want me to do so, nor would they allow it and I will not attempt to force them. I apologize for any misperceptions I may have caused, however I have come to ask your assistance Petre Dracenhalts, son of Stephanie Vernas. I do offer this jade sculpture as a gift from Justula to you for your kindness in assisting."

The king looked down at Hendandra, a frown on his lips and in his eyes as he took the offered sculpture. "What is it I am supposed to help you with? Justula is hundreds of leagues from our borders."

"My female companion and I are members of a group which leaves shortly from Irrmar to enter the Abyss. We seek to free the man known as Justula's Lawgiver from the citadel of the Lady of Chaos." Hendandra's words were precise and forceful as she spoke.

The king looked at the sculpture then handed it back to Hendandra. "I cannot get involved with a matter that has nothing to do with Dh'Mark." He turned to leave the room.

"So you would leave the son of Krella Eglis to suffer at the hands of the Chaos Demons who serve the Lady of Chaos?" Kyrianna took a step forward.

"Krella Eglis?" The king stopped and turned back. "She died more than sixty years ago. Her son was already past his prime though strong in his faith. He fought for Dh'Mark in the Arena of Tormasus. He could not be alive after all this time and in of all places the Abyss. What madness is this you speak?"

Hendandra took a step back and Kyrianna nodded. "It is not madness, My Lord. By some foul twist of fate he was betrayed and cast down. Not only that; but the most vile of goddesses, Thynitic, sought to make him her eternal toy. He cannot even die to escape her." Her voice broke. *And I may end up trapped in the same way.* "Will you help us to save him?" Her voice was barely above a whisper.

"Irrmar is full of turmoil. Every House is trying to usurp or stave off a usurping of its power. I cannot. It would put too much at risk," the king said.

Kyrianna's head snapped up. "Is that what he would have said when he lost his own mother to save yours?" She felt her anger building, not at the king but as she thought about having lost her own mother. "Having traveled with him recently, I wondered why he left this city after so many years of service as a judge to the provinces of Dh'Mark. I now know why. You are without the strength to do what you know must be done. You bow to your own avarice in your political motives. He left so he could create Order in Mount Veri, away from the temples of the cities that seem to have completely succumbed to the very sins they should defend their faithful from. He left so he could teach the next generation the true path of his god. I was wrong. He was not betrayed once; he was betrayed every step of the way. Even by your mother who produced a son unworthy of Krella's sacrifice."

She grabbed Hendandra by the arm and started for the door. "I have had enough of the political games of this city. We should leave."

Before she reached the doorway, blocked by Tristan, she heard the king clear his throat. She turned to see him staring at the floor.

"I knew of his plight before you came here," he said, looking up, but not at her. "The current Keeper of the Temple of Hellavar made it known to me that if I helped in this endeavor he would see to it the Houses would shift against me."

"A Keeper of Hellavar dictates covertly how Houses are to act?" Tristan asked. "What twisted version of that god's order does this man serve?"

She turned to face Tristan. "He serves nothing but his own greed. His temple praises the world of material things. Their feasts even seem to praise the sins of lust more than the purity of Order and the flames." She turned back to the king.

"If he returns with us, I can assure you the current Keeper will be too busy defending himself to the Keeper of Veri. Manipulating the Houses will be the least of his concerns." She stepped forward and knelt before the king. "Please, help us."

"And if you don't return?" He offered her his hand and helped her up.

"Then at least Krella's sacrifice for your mother will be paid."

He nodded. "What is it you wish?"

Kyrianna quickly explained what was happening with Myrith as well as their need for the stone horses.

"I can provide the horses and some other equipment, but I will not guarantee I will stand as sponsor for your friend." He raised his hand to prevent her protest. "What I will do is go with you to the Coliseum and hear your friend speak for herself. Then I will decide. That is the best I can do."

Kyrianna nodded.

"I think it looks good there," Hendandra said.

Kyrianna smiled at the girl who had climbed on one of the chairs to place the jade sculpture on the mantel.

"Yes, it does look good there," she said. "Thank you." She bowed her head to the king.

Chapter Sixteen

Myrith jerked her shield around and winced as it caught Gwideon's blade. "You seem distracted," Gwideon said.

"Distracted?" Myrith jerked the shield around again. "Hendandra and Kyri run off without telling me; I am not distracted." She swung Conflagration and frowned as it glanced off his armor. "I. Am. Incensed. We should have left hours ago." She raised her shield again in time to catch his blade. "Falden and Andrinor returned in less than two hours." This time she missed getting her shield up and stumbled back to avoid Gwideon's blade. "How can I lead without the respect of the person I thought was my closest..." Her sword again glanced off Gwideon's armor. "...friend?" She lowered her sword and shield and stood there waiting.

"Lady Lake!" one of the clerics called from the doorway. "You are summoned to the chapel by Shield Sarasnar and Lord Balthas of the Order."

Myrith sheathed Conflagration. "We will be there," she said.

~ * ~

The doors to the temple were closed as she approached and Myrith frowned as she glanced at Gwideon. He only shrugged. She took a deep breath and pushed the doors open.

The temple was full. All of the clergy and members of the Order were there and she stopped on the threshold as she looked around. Tristan Duvall stood at the altar flanked by Shield Sarasnar and Lord Balthas.

"Lady Myrith Lake," Tristan called. "I call you to the Order."

She felt herself tense. "I was not told of this," she whispered.

Gwideon stood next to her. "Nor was I. However, I see the most likely conspirator on your behalf in the group to the left of the altar."

Myrith let her gaze move from the three standing at the altar in the area to the left. All of those she would be traveling with stood together in a group, including the tiger. Kyrianna gave her a slight nod.

"I don't like ceremonies," she whispered. "Especially those in my honor and most especially ones which are a complete surprise."

"It is your decision; do we flee or advance?"

"I prefer to walk up to Kyrianna and throttle her," she said.

"I do not believe that is really an option at the moment, but noted for later reference."

Myrith looked at him and gave him a slight smile. "Let's go."

He shook his head. "It is not *we*. This is your temple. I will stay here and bear witness." He nodded toward Tristan. "He has called you to the Order of Mykaylene's knights; it is time you answered him as you answered Her."

She took another deep breath and nodded. He was correct. She moved down the aisle toward the altar. Behind her she heard Gwideon's boots shift and she could picture him standing in the middle of the doors, holding them for her.

As she stood in front of the altar she felt very alone. *No, I am not alone*, she thought. *Mykaylene is here with me.* "I answer your call, Lord Duvall." Tristan gave her a nod.

"I am Lord Balthas of House Wailing, the Battle Lord of the Order," Balthas said, taking a step forward past Tristan. He was a dark-haired, bearded man whose dark eyes were locked on her in something resembling hatred. The lines of his face were set and she felt an involuntary shudder go through her.

Myrith felt her brow crease as Sarasnar also stepped forward. The two of them now effectively blocked Tristan so she would face only them.

"Why do you not kneel before the altar?" Sarasnar asked.

Chaos. Myrith dropped to one knee. This was not going to be a proper ordination ceremony, she realized. Instead these two were going to use this opportunity to humiliate her. She glanced again at Kyrianna who was glaring at Balthas. *This was not what she was expecting either.*

"I see you have won the favor of House Duvall of Raspa. However, this is not Raspa. Where is the Irrmarian House that would represent you here?" The room went silent.

Balthas raised his head and scanned the assemblage behind her. "If there is no one from the Irrmarian houses who will stand with this woman, this proceeding is dis—"

"I would hear her speak," a voice called from the doorway.

Myrith turned her head to see a man step past Gwideon. He

was tall, with black hair starting to silver a bit with age.

"House Dracenhalts would hear the lady."

She tried to hide the smile that came to her lips at the looks on both Sarasnar and Balthas' faces. *They were not expecting this.*

He stopped and stood next to her. "I, King Petre Dracenhalts have heard of your deeds from your friends. I have heard of how you led them through many trials and battles, keeping always to your faith and protecting them as She would ask you to do. I have heard how you brought not one but two of them back from darkness and utter damnation. I have been told how Rhinehart Duvall has already acknowledged you and would have gifted you with his sword except it needed to go to another. And I have been told how your actions returned one who would have renounced Mykaylene to Her service." He paused.

"Yes, I have heard of all these deeds and they shine as the deeds of one who is a true knight in Her service. However, they are tainted by the prejudice of your friends. I would prefer to hear now from one whom I know is unbiased in their assessment. Your sword." He held out his hand.

Myrith drew Conflagration and placed it in his hand.

"You are the sword wielded by an Irrmarian knight of the Purifying Flame of Hellavar. What say you of this one? Is she the equal of Krella Eglis?"

"She is not." The sword spoke in a booming voice that echoed in the temple.

Myrith saw Balthas and Sarasnar exchange smiles and she felt her heart stop. The sword had never said anything to her; what had she done or not done that it would judge her so harshly now?

"She is young yet," the sword continued. "Her flame has yet to find the heart of its wood, but she burns long and steady. She will find the true spark that will make her the inferno. She knows her duty and her cause. Let her have her honor, lest this temple belittle the goddess who called her to service."

"House Dracenhalts will stand with Lady Lake," the king said, handing her the sword.

Myrith saw Balthas flush, then nod as Sarasnar leaned close to him.

"Where is the cleric who will speak to your virtues?" Again the room was silent.

She knew the clerics of this temple would not stand with her.

The ones who had been assigned to tutor her had made a point of reminding her again and again that Mykaylene was known as the Battle Maiden. Sarasnar had all but called her a whore at the end of their interview. *This is worthless,* she thought. She glanced back at the doors. Gwideon still stood there. He had not moved, not even for the king. *I should leave.* She started to rise then stopped as Balthas smiled at her. *No! Mykaylene would not want me to leave like this. They have made the rules of this game, but I will not surrender to them.* She looked at the group of her companions as she placed her knee back on the floor. "Jerietlan."

"I am here." His voice was shaking.

"Will you stand with me?"

"I will, but I feel I am unworthy."

She locked her gaze with Sarasnar. "You are the only cleric here I find worthy. You have tempted Mykaylene's wrath and paid the price. You have proven yourself to Her and earned the right to wield Her power once again. You have been tested. Have they?"

Balthas shook his head as he looked down at her. "Those who have come to support this woman, take your place with her."

Tristan nodded and winked as he moved to kneel behind her. The king and Jerietlan knelt on either side of her.

"So the church, the Order and the nobility have found this one worthy. But I have not heard witness of her deeds. Who here has witnessed her deeds?"

"I would bear witness," Kyrianna called.

"No." Myrith heard Tristan whisper behind her.

She looked at her friend, who had taken a step toward them then glanced back up at the altar. Sarasnar was grinning as he leaned over and whispered in Balthas' ear.

"Who are you?" Balthas asked.

"Kyrianna Dalynne—"

"Are you a person worthy of speaking here as a witness? What Order do you belong to? What noble House? Who has honored you?" Balthas snapped the questions off in quick succession. "You must show us your words are worthy."

"I am Lady Kyrianna of House Dalynne of Nydith."

Myrith closed her eyes; this would not go well. She had seen how Sarasnar had twisted her own words during her interview. Balthas seemed be cut from the same cloth and was perhaps a bit more practiced at this game.

"Neither the House nor the land is known to me. Is it known to anyone here?" Balthas gestured toward the assemblage, but it remained quiet.

Myrith watched as Kyrianna forced herself to stand straighter and raised her arms, letting the sleeves of her dress fall to reveal the two marks. Once again, the marks of Frayrith and Dwycia were visible on her friend's wrist. Despite her suspicions of how this would end, she was proud of Kyrianna for what she was doing.

"I bear the mark of Frayrith, who is kindred to Dwycia as well as the mark of Dwycia who has served as my patron in his land."

"You say you have served them with complete devotion and faithfulness? Never wavering or doubting?" Balthas asked.

Myrith knew there was no way Kyrianna could truthfully answer the question as he had phrased it. Her faith had wavered and she had even called on the power of Thynitic, not just once, but twice as she had fought against the chaos and darkness.

"I…" Kyrianna's voice cracked and she looked at Myrith and shook her head.

Myrith shook her head. *Don't do this to yourself,* she thought.

"I am waiting, Lady Kyrianna of House Dalynne of Nydith." The smile on Balthas' face reminded Myrith of the one Thynitic had given Kyrianna when she had appeared to them. "How did you serve with complete and utter faith?"

Kyrianna dropped her head and stepped back.

"I did not say I was finished, *your* Ladyship."

Kyrianna looked around and Myrith saw her go pale as several members of the Order took a step toward her. The threat was obvious. She would be forced to answer Balthas' question. Behind her Myrith heard the faint sound of metal sliding on cloth.

"Answer the question." Balthas' gaze turned from Kyrianna to Myrith and she knew she could not do anything to defend her friend.

"I did falter and fall. I accepted the darkness and chaos of the Lady of Chaos when I could see no light. I did it not for myself but to save my friends." She paused and pointed toward Myrith. "It was Myrith who drew me back from that darkness, restored my faith and returned me to the Lady of the Forests who has forgiven me my actions and even asked my forgiveness for what had to happen. If you wish the truth, that is it—both its tarnish and glory."

Myrith did not hide the smile that came to her lips as she

watched Balthas. Kyrianna had spoken truthfully, but had ensured what she said had still reflected what she wanted it to.

"You cannot stand as witness. You are tainted by the evil you admit you willingly accepted," Balthas said.

"Her words are more worthy than yours," Myrith heard Tristan whisper.

"Anyone else?"

"I am Andrinor and I have fought many a vile creature and even faced an evil goddess with the one you would seek to humiliate." His voice echoed in the room.

"What proof of your words and deeds do you bring?"

Please don't change form. Please don't change form. Myrith found herself repeating the plea over and over in her mind. With the attitude toward dragons this world held, if Andrinor changed into a silver dragon, he would be attacked by every cleric and knight in this room.

He turned showing the brands on his arms that marked him as an arena slave and as being freed.

"Hardly impressive. The Arena is notorious for marking their fighters. You carry the common markings of one used for sport. What crime did you perpetrate? Pickpocketing?"

Balthas turned away as the crowd laughed.

Myrith flinched as Andrinor threw his chain vest to the ground and the sound echoed in the room. The crowd grew silent as Andrinor turned and they could see the brand that covered his back. He turned back and the crossed swords that had been burned into his chest were now visible along with the brightly colored mark of Ghainaess. A mark that had not been damaged in any way by the branding.

"My crime was wounding Cassandra Shindar of the Circle and wife of Orlundru Shindar, the Fifth Sword of Tormasus. I forfeited my life to him some five days ago." He paused as he held out the pommel of his weapon and the silver and bone blades appeared. "I earned it back from him in three. If there is further proof required, let us go to the Arena; your Coliseum bores me."

Myrith grinned at the shock evident on Balthas' face.

"Take your place behind Lord Duvall, Andrinor—he who took his life back from the Arena."

"I have heard one, but three witnesses are required."

"This be utter nonsense!"

There was a collective gasp from the assemblage.

"I find this temple to be wanting while the most worthy of yer members kneel before ye in judgment."

"Who dares?" Sarasnar's voice was shrill.

"I, Nirev, First Hammer of Mulog."

"You call yourself First Hammer. What is your proof?"

"Proof? Ye ask for proof? What be faith if it must be proven?" He stepped forward and slapped his hand against his hammer. "I will show ye my proof when ye show me yers."

Balthas pointed to the back wall. A ten-foot tall statue stood there. "In recognition of my deeds for the church."

Nirev looked at the statue then hurled his hammer. The stone cracked, scorched and shattered from the lightning and thunder that struck it. Nirev smiled as the hammer returned to his hands. "In recognition of yer deeds for this church on this day." He walked over and sat behind the king.

"If ye need more proof," Nirev said, "I will do to this temple what I did after seeing the sorry state of mine in Domar. I called down Mulog's might and collapsed the temple. I know not if he will answer me in yers, but I be willing to see if ye be as well."

Balthas ignored Nirev's challenge as he looked down at Myrith. "I need your final witness."

"Then you shall have it," Falden stepped forward.

"Who are you and what are your deeds?"

"I see no point to a statement of the inconsequential. You have asked for a witness. I shall provide him for you."

"I demand your name."

"I am Falden."

He pushed the cowl of his cloak back and his revealed himself to the assemblage. Myrith heard several gasps in the crowd as well as muttered prayers to Mykaylene for protection.

"I am Falden the Damned. Now, if you are through with your questions for me, I will bring your witness. If you have more make them quick. Be warned, I agree with the First Hammer and I am quite capable of seeing the task done if Mulog is not."

Myrith flinched as Nirev's hammer slammed against the floor and a crack appeared in front of the altar.

Balthas, despite his impassive face, gave away his impatience as his hand gripped his sword.

Falden snapped his fingers and a dog-headed human appeared

in front of the altar. He stood ready for combat, his two-handed sword held high and his sentryl shirt chiming with his movements.

"Tarnarius, celestial servant of Mykaylene, I summon you to bear witness to the deeds of the woman kneeling before the altar."

He lowered his sword and turned to look at Myrith. "I have watched this one through many trials and I do not understand why I am to be questioned. Her sword has served Mykaylene well every time she has had need to draw it." He turned to Balthas. "How does this serve the Order?"

"We wish only the strongest, bravest and holiest among the Order."

"And how are they to be known? Many times have the greatest of Thedrin's court been the only ones to stand in the face of the fiercest enemies. Would you deny them a place of honor here in Irrmar just because another could not speak to their actions? I find this most disturbing. I shall inform Mykaylene and Thedrin of this abomination to his court."

He turned back to Myrith. "You make a court to try one of your own; this is a most foul injustice." He raised his sword and laid it on her shoulder. "Mykaylene has given you her highest blessing and has called you to serve as her Sword." He bowed then vanished.

Myrith bowed her head. This ceremony no longer meant anything to her. She appreciated what her friends had wanted to do here, but acceptance by the temple was nothing compared to what Tarnarius had just said. *Mykaylene has called me to serve as her Sword. There is no honor this church could give that will compare to that.*

Balthas' voice was harsh as his hand tightened on his sword. "As the servant of Mykaylene cannot stay to take his place, Falden, you will take it for him."

Falden moved slowly as he passed the altar and went to kneel behind Jerietlan.

"It is obvious you have your allies, Myrith Lake, but as the Battle Lord, I still find you unworthy. Your deeds these past few months may have earned you the respect of those you traveled with, but it is the deeds and nobility of the whole life we must concern ourselves with. And because of your past, *whore*, I will not allow you to disgrace this church by being named as a member of this Order."

"And yet, Mykaylene's servant said Myrith had been called as the goddess' sword," Kyrianna called.

Myrith glanced at her friend. *What is she doing? He has already humiliated her by twisting her words around to his purpose. Why would she risk him attacking her again?*

Balthas ignored Kyrianna's comment as he looked down at her. "Myrith Lake, I bar you from our doors unless someone from one of the Orders will champion you against myself in the Coliseum."

Behind her, she heard Tristan stand and her breath caught. He was more noble than warrior and he knew as much.

"I will champion her," Tristan said.

"No!" Myrith heard Kyrianna's harsh whisper and her head snapped toward her. She had gone pale, her eyes wide and ringed with fear as she clutched at the necklace she wore.

"Are you sure, Lord Duvall? I have heard of you. You know the court and its Houses well, but your sword has seen little use. I take my guardianship of the Order with deadly seriousness. You could die." His gaze darted to Kyrianna for a moment and he smiled. "Why would you risk your life for an outsider?"

He heard her as well. Myrith felt her breath catch again.

"I do it because your words show her to be more worthy than many of the nobles you would allow into the Order simply because of the manner of their birth. I do it because she would do it for me. I accept your terms."

"No!" Myrith stood. "I find your Order to be insufficient. I will not risk the life of another simply to further my own name. That would be a sin before Mykaylene."

"You renounce your claim then?" Balthas asked.

"She does not. That Lord Duvall, a servant of the goddess of this temple, would risk his life against your sword should be enough to attest to her worthiness," Gwideon said, stepping forward. "She is correct; it is a sin against Mykaylene to even ask such a thing." He drew his sword. "I am Gwideon of the Grey, properly ordained by the Gatekeeper of this city. You have asked for a champion from one of the Orders; you have one. I will champion her."

He continued to approach the altar and stood in front of her like a shield as he continued to speak. "Why does this temple hold such high regard for ceremony? Did Mykaylene herself? No! You do it so you can hold power. So the nobility can lord over even the churches. I held high regard for this temple once. I even sought to be a member, but what were your words, Sir Balthas? 'There is no room in this church for the Houseless son of a beggar and a whore.'"

Myrith looked at him as his words sank into her heart.

"I thank you for that day," Gwideon continued. "You showed me what darkness could hide even in those who serve on the side of light. You showed me my path—the path of ultimate equality. We are all equal in death." He nodded and the tiger joined him. "I accept your request for a champion and as is the custom, I set the style—mounted combat."

The tiger roared and dug its claws into the ground and Myrith smiled when she saw the furrows cut into the stone.

Gwideon mounted the tiger and pointed his sword at Balthas. "Come, Sir Balthas, let our steel decide this matter. Resare is the god of death; every drop of my blood spilled is praise to his name. I promise you, I will be victorious. By Resare's word I shall not see you leave that field among the living."

"That will not be necessary, Sir Gwideon." Balthas' voice was not as harsh nor did it seem to carry the same level of power it had earlier. "Your actions speak louder than even the tiger's roar. I withdraw my challenge. Kneel behind Andrinor." He turned, walked back two steps and the tiger lunged.

"Hold!" Myrith called.

The tiger's teeth grazed Balthas' armor as he stumbled back from the beast.

The tiger moved forward again.

"Shydaran, hold," Myrith said again.

The tiger had his teeth bared and ready, but turned instead to face her. His head turned slightly and Myrith followed his gaze to where Hendandra and Kyrianna stood. Color had returned to Kyrianna's face though she was still watching Tristan. Hendandra was clutching the pendant she wore and staring at the tiger.

"The animal…" Balthas interrupted her thoughts.

"Stays!" Myrith said.

Balthas glared at her, but she only stared back as she again knelt before the altar.

"Very well." Balthas drew his sword.

Myrith heard those behind her shifting their position. If Balthas tried something, they would be ready.

Balthas kept his gaze locked on her as he raised the sword and then laid it first on her left shoulder and then her right. "Lady Myrith Lake, servant of Mykaylene, you have been found worthy by her servants and your friends to carry her name. I christen you Lady

Myrith Lake, the Battle Mai—"

"No," Gwideon interrupted. "Sword. She is the Sword of Mykaylene."

Balthas glared.

"Maiden is a term for someone yet to know the whole. She has fought more battles than many. She has faced the vilest of evil and came to the temple today with her friends. She drew her dearest friend back from the brink of utter damnation. She need not know more as she already is tempered like a blade. She is Mykaylene's Sword."

"And did not Tarnarius, Mykaylene's servant, already name her so?" the king said.

"He did. Lady Myrith Lake, the Sword of Mykaylene it shall be from this day forth."

Myrith heard the words, but she no longer cared. She had found things of more value this day than an empty title within a temple lacking in true faith. The companions she had sometimes feared would hardly meet a challenge on the field had instead stood by her here. Nirev, though he would never yield entirely to her authority had openly insulted the man who would humiliate and bar her. Andrinor had challenged the entire temple to join him in the Arena, while at the same time defending her. Falden had summoned one of the holy servants of Mykaylene who had spoken words that had touched her heart and soul the deepest. Tristan had been ready to give his life for her honor and Conflagration, though admitting her lacking, had said she would be a beacon in time. Jerietlan knelt next to her though he feared he was not worthy to the task. The tiger had even yielded to her authority. The first time it had shown any deference. The first time it had shown it would yield to anything. Then there was Gwideon. He was the same as her in many ways. Today was not a victory just for her, but for all of them.

She turned toward Kyrianna as she stood and offered a nod and brief smile. Then she balled her fist and raised it slightly. Kyrianna grinned. She owed the girl a great deal for doing this to her, both good and ill. Still, she figured the balances did sit more with the good. Kyrianna had let herself be humiliated by Balthas as he reopened wounds Myrith knew had barely started to heal and then had stepped forward again challenging him and risking another such attack. She nodded; she would eventually settle with Kyrianna for setting up this ceremony, but it wouldn't be today.

Chapter Seventeen

Kyrianna watched as Myrith stood in front of the mirror and smoothed the dark burgundy dress. It had taken her over an hour to talk the woman into wearing it and then another hour to do her hair, nails and make-up. Still it would be worth it to see the others' faces when Myrith entered the dining hall this night.

"Myrith, I knew it wouldn't be easy today, but I never realized how much the leaders of this church were opposed to you," Kyrianna said. "If I had, I wouldn't have put you through that."

"Then why did you do it? Do you really think I crave the recognition and glory?"

"Chaos, no!" Kyrianna reached out and took Myrith's hands. Despite the work that had been done, her hands were still rough and covered in calluses. "I did it, because I saw the way the temple was treating you was undermining your confidence. And, that, Myrith, is something that could get all of us killed in the days to come."

"The way the temple was treating me?" Myrith jerked her hands away. "What about the way you have been treating me?"

"What?" Kyrianna took a step back at the anger she saw in Myrith's face. "The way I have been treating you?"

"You're late getting back and when I ask why all you'll tell me is it's personal. Then when we think we have almost everything ready, you vanish for hours without saying anything and I end up before an inquisition as a result. An inquisition where not only am I humiliated, but I have to watch as my friends are also. And I cannot do anything to protect them. I do not like being helpless, Rangerette."

"I'm sorry. However, your tone when you demanded why I was late was also inquisitional." She turned away from Myrith. "And I couldn't deal with that at the time."

"Kyri, I haven't told you this, but ever since I first met you, I have felt like there was a connection between us. I've told you enough about my past for you to understand I don't trust very easily, but something told me to trust you. That's why it bothered me so much when you wouldn't trust me enough to tell me what was going on with Thynitic."

Kyrianna lowered her head though she refused to turn around. "The reason I was late was I went home for a day."

Myrith grabbed her shoulders and forced her to turn around. "How did you manage that?"

"Cewyr has been gifted with the ability to travel between Shokar and Rhysia. She took me home."

"And you came back. All we wanted when we first met was to get home and you found a way to get there."

"I can go home whenever I want to, but I will not leave Brular in Thynitic's hands. Myrith, while Torliana was holding me, he found a way to switch our minds so I was in his body and away from her, able to rest, for several hours. He knew what she would be doing and he willingly took my place for that time."

"I am not surprised that he would do so."

"When the magic ended and I was returned to my body, Thynitic sent a vision of my mother facing a group of midnight elves. A vision of her death."

"Kyri, I'm sorry."

Kyrianna nodded and pulled away to look out the window at the darkening sky. "I kept telling myself it was only another of her lies, but I knew the only way to be sure was to go home. It was true." She turned back around. "That's why I said it was personal. I wasn't ready to share that with everyone."

"Then I will say nothing further about it."

Kyrianna nodded then smiled. "We have a celebration to get to and I can't play the hostess looking like this," she said.

"Indeed you can't. I was wondering something; did Tristan provide your dress as well as mine?"

"No. I brought this one from home. Although," her hand went to the sapphire necklace." "This came from him."

"Well at least he chose a different tailor for mine than the one Hendandra seems to be using lately."

"Hey, I like the new dresses I got from Rega." Hendandra slammed the door behind her as she entered the room. "It is very similar to what the women on my island wear. It is comfortable and they, meaning the women and the men, find it quite appropriate as well. I could say things regarding your constant dressing in heavy plate armor and what that could mean, but I won't."

"Wait a minute. What do you mean by your island?" Myrith

looked down at Hendandra. "You didn't win the island in some game of chance—did you?"

Kyrianna glanced at both women. Hendandra hadn't told anyone other than her about her marriage. She stepped back so she was out of Myrith's line of sight to hide the concern she knew was on her face.

"You and Kyri are not the only ones in this group to have rank or title, Lady Myrith Lake, Sword of Mykaylene," she said. "I also have a new title."

Myrith cocked her head and crossed her arms over her chest. "And what would that title be?"

"Princess Hendandra of Justula."

"Princess?" Myrith turned to look at Kyrianna. "You knew about this?" Kyrianna nodded, but didn't say anything.

"Princess? How?"

"I fought a large sea creature, by myself, rescuing a couple who had been attacked. The chief of the island, in recognition of my actions, named me his daughter. I am a princess." She placed her hands on her hips and glared up at Myrith.

"Sounds like you had a very interesting time on that island, Princess Hendandra," Myrith said, giving Hendandra a mock bow. "I was only joking. On you, the dress looks very nice, but it is not something I would care to wear. To tell the truth, it is amazing you were able to get me into this dress." She turned to the mirror. "It is lovely. How much was it?"

"Tristan paid. I have no idea and will never ask. He doesn't want the latest knight of his order wanting for proper attire," Kyrianna said with a smile. "Come on, let's not disappoint him."

"It goes nice with your hair," Hendandra said. "But it still needs something."

"You're right." Kyrianna looked around for a moment then picked up a small box that had been delivered with the dress. "Tristan thinks of everything," she said. "Myrith we have..." She stopped and turned as Hendandra began laughing.

Myrith was adjusting Conflagration's scabbard on her back.

"Much better," Myrith said.

"Myrith." Kyrianna crossed her arms across her chest and tapped her foot. "That is hardly appropriate. We are going to the dining hall, not the layers."

"Exactly." Myrith straightened her dress. "I would never wear this to the Abyss." She winked at Hendandra. "Black would be far more appropriate."

Hendandra dropped to her knees laughing and Kyrianna found she could no longer suppress her own laughter.

"Okay, the joke's over," Kyrianna said once she was able to catch her breath. "Take off the sword." She pointed to the large chest where the rest of Myrith's gear was stored.

"You want it, take it," Myrith said.

Kyrianna sighed and frowned. "Myrith, please. Tonight you are to be the guest of honor at the table of a nobleman. Please try to act like a lady."

"I am not a highborn lady," Myrith said. "Why should I act like one?"

"Wait here." Kyrianna gathered her skirt and darted out of the room to her own. She picked up a dagger from her dresser and returned to Myrith's room. "If you feel the need to wear steel tonight, take this." She held the dagger with the unicorn symbol on it. "The dagger was touched by an avatar of Frayrith before I met you. While I know this is not the goddess you follow, I also know Frayrith would take no offense, nor would Mykaylene I am sure."

"I am honored you would offer it, but no. That is my last word on the subject. Besides, if I left him behind, it would be an insult to Conflagration. Remember he spoke for me at the inquisition also."

Kyrianna bowed her head. "I concede this battle." She picked up the small box and removed a pair of dark red garnet earrings. "I will ask that you at least wear these."

"My ears have never been pierced."

"Not a problem." Kyrianna pushed Myrith back onto the bench. "This won't hurt—much." She forced the post of the first earring through the lobe of Myrith's ear, then moved to the other. A quickly whispered healing spell stopped the bleeding.

"Myrith, I know you don't care for ceremony, but please indulge Tristan as he wishes to present you when everyone is ready," Kyrianna said.

"Make sure he makes it quick," Myrith said.

"Thank you. Come on, Hendandra, we need to make sure everything is ready." She grabbed the girl's hand and pulled her out of the room.

~ * ~

They came down the stairs to find Tristan waiting for them. "Is the Sword of Mykaylene ready for her introduction?"

"Don't you dare call it that," Kyrianna said. "She will tear that dress apart and both of us with it."

"Hey, who locked the doors to the dining hall?" Hendandra asked.

"I did," Tristan said as he tossed her a key. "How else did you expect me to keep Andrinor and Nirev from starting without us?"

Hendandra grinned as she opened the door then dropped the key on a small table.

Kyrianna followed her into the room. The table was loaded with food in many different varieties. She looked at Shadow Seeker sitting near the table, his gaze on the large turkey and a pool of saliva on the floor in front of him.

"Drooling on the floor! Kyrianna, get that fleabag out of here." Hendandra picked up a small chunk of meat and tossed it to the wolf.

"Out you go, Shadow." Kyrianna opened the glass doors to the garden and shooed him out of the room.

"Well at least he waited until he was given something. That's more than I expect from Andrinor or Nirev," Hendandra said.

Kyrianna laughed and stepped back into the hallway. "Tristan, could you check on the others, please?"

Tristan nodded and headed up the stairs.

"You did offer him a room to stay the evening I assume," Hendandra asked.

"The middle one on the left."

"The one next to yours," Hendandra said with a grin.

"It's not like that," Kyrianna said. "He is a good friend and nothing more."

"Nothing more? I saw your face at that farce of an ordination when he was willing to face Balthas. And I saw his face when Balthas was verbally attacking you. Neither of you may have admitted it yet, not even to yourselves, but it is definitely more than that."

Kyrianna couldn't think of anything to say and breathed a sigh of relief when a knock came at the front door.

"Sir Gwideon, this house is honored by your presence this evening," she said, giving him the appropriate half-bow as he stepped through the door.

He wore no helm or armor and Kyrianna was surprised to see

his soft gray eyes. His clothes were as fine as Tristan's though in varying shades of gray. In the center of his chest hung a large pendant of quartz that pulsed with shadows.

"May I?" She stared at the pendant.

"Of course, Lady Kyrianna." He removed the pendant from his neck and handed it to her.

"Resare's?" There was a slight chill to the stone as her fingers caressed it.

"Given to me by the Gatekeeper at my own ordination."

"It is beautiful." She held it out and he bowed his head so she could slip it around his neck. "Thank you again for coming."

Kyrianna shook her head at the sword he carried across his back. *He and Myrith are two of a kind,* she thought. *Whore, Balthas called her. And what was it Gwideon said Balthas had told him? There was no place for the Houseless son of a beggar and whore. They are more alike than many would realize.*

Gwideon stopped and she followed his gaze to the top of the stairs where the other members of their group stood. Nirev was still in his armor, but at least it was clean. His war hammer hung on a loop at his side and he carried a small hand ax. Andrinor was dressed in a pair of silver-gray pants and tunic with his chainmail vest. The pommel of his sword was also visible on his belt.

Her hand went to the dagger she had decided to wear as well. At least she wouldn't be unarmed at this dinner. She knew Hendandra was wearing her own dagger in a sheath on her leg. Tristan she wasn't sure about.

Andrinor and Nirev walked straight into the dining hall, ignoring her. She smiled as Jerietlan and Falden came down. Both were dressed in the finest ceremonial robes they had. She almost missed the dagger Jerietlan carried, but it was there. Falden had his staff and at least one wand was visible in his belt.

"Wait for Myrith," Hendandra's voice called from the dining hall. "She should be down in a minute."

Kyrianna saw Nirev and Andrinor both look at each other then the turkey. They each grabbed a leg and tore it free then moved back to the doorway. She covered her mouth with her hand as she couldn't decide whether to laugh or cry.

"I think it would be best to hurry before they find the ale," Tristan said as he came down the stairs.

"Ale?" Nirev started back toward the dining hall.

Hendandra stood in the doorway, her hands on her hips and glared at the dwarf. Nirev only smiled and took a step forward, but stopped as he hit something invisible.

"Dragon mage comes between a dwarf and his drink. Not a very wise thing." Nirev waved his turkey leg at Falden.

Tristan cleared his throat and everyone turned to face the stairs. "Lady Myrith Lake, Sword of Mykaylene," he said.

Kyrianna smiled as Myrith appeared at the top of the stairs and Nirev and Andrinor almost dropped their turkey legs.

"My friends, I thank you for the honor you have paid me. And understand the honors I received today came from you—not the leaders of the Coliseum. It is you who have shown your faith in me and I hope I will always prove worthy of it.

"Tristan and Kyrianna have offered this feast as a way of wishing us luck before we journey to the heart of the Abyss and the darkness and chaos Thynitic commands. It is a custom in Kyrianna's home and while I despair at the additional delay this will cost us, I understand and appreciate the reasons and the sentiment. May the level of generosity Tristan has shown us this night be reflected in the amount of luck we carry with us tomorrow. Let us enjoy ourselves tonight, but do so in moderation for tomorrow, we will need all of our senses alert and ready." She gestured to the dining hall.

"Come on, you two, the food is getting cold." Kyrianna looked at Nirev and Andrinor who were both still staring at Myrith. "Awestruck by her beauty?" she asked.

Andrinor stepped back and shook his head. "No."

Myrith's jaw dropped open as she spun around to face them.

He smiled. "I just never thought anyone would get her to wear anything less than banded mail."

"Nor did I," Nirev said as he tossed a gem to Hendandra.

Myrith shook her head. "You bet on whether I would come down in this?"

Hendandra held the stone up to the light and nodded. "We did, and I won. I knew Kyri would be able to convince you; I just didn't know it would take that long."

Andrinor picked Hendandra up and stood her on the sideboard as he and Nirev headed for the table. She never stopped examining the stone.

Tristan placed his hand on Kyrianna's arm. "I feel overdressed," she said.

"I am more concerned that we are underarmed," he said.

Kyrianna smiled and gestured to the table. "I will wait for the others," she said.

He nodded and stepped into the room.

Kyrianna watched as Myrith paused in front of the polished mirror on the wall. "Sword of Mykaylene," she heard her whisper.

Gwideon handed Myrith a glass of wine. "Nice sword," he said. "The rubies in the hilt go marvelously with the dress and your hair."

Myrith laughed. "I hadn't noticed."

He smiled again and raised his glass. "So you brought the sword because ones such as us may be called to duty by our patrons at any time." Myrith smiled and sipped her wine.

He glanced at Kyrianna watching them from the doorway and grinned. "The fact it seems to vex Kyrianna never even crossed your mind?" He took a sip of his wine. "It was just a happy coincidence, I take it?"

Myrith turned toward the door and winked at Kyrianna as she and Gwideon walked past her. "It was a marvelous happenstance," she said.

Kyrianna laughed and shook her head as she joined the group at the table.

Chapter Eighteen

Once everyone was finished, except Nirev and Andrinor, Hendandra picked up her violin from where it rested on a piano in the corner of the room and began playing.

Kyrianna felt herself drawn to the piano and she sat down and relaxed as her fingers began playing an accompaniment to Hendandra's violin.

"I didn't know she could play," she heard Myrith say.

"I believe she has had a tutor of late," Tristan replied.

A late tutor, Kyrianna thought. She heard Melissa giggle at the comment.

She grinned at Hendandra as they finished and the group applauded.

"That was my grandmother's, wasn't it?" Tristan asked as Hendandra placed the violin back on the piano.

Kyrianna snapped her head to look at Tristan and also saw the flash of panic in Hendandra's eyes as she placed a hand on the instrument.

"I do not wish to take it. I said you could have it when we left the estate; it is yours. I only wish to play it."

"Oh. I'm sorry. Of course, you can play it." Hendandra handed him the instrument then took a seat near the table of pastries.

Kyrianna found herself staring at Tristan as the bow flowed with the music. She knew he had talent from when he recreated the song his grandmother's ghost had played on the piano at the estate, but this was amazing.

:*Of course he can play*, Melissa said. :*My brother was very good with the violin, while I prefer the piano.*

Kyrianna rested her fingers on the keys, but could not find the pattern to accompany him.

:*You would not know this music, Kyri; it is my mother's composition. Christian and I played it many nights.* She paused. :*May I?*

She let herself relax and felt the spirit of the girl almost merging with her own as her fingers began to move over the keys. She lost herself in the music as Melissa guided her hands and the piano and violin began to weave a tapestry of sound. When they finished, everyone in the room seemed to be holding their breath for a moment then they applauded.

Hendandra crossed her arms across her chest and looked at her. *Showoff,* she mouthed and Kyrianna grinned.

Tristan laid the violin back on the piano. "Thank you." He bowed to Hendandra.

He turned and offered Kyrianna his arm. "Please thank Melissa for me," he whispered as she stood up. "My father always said he missed playing with his little sister."

Kyrianna smiled as they walked out into the gardens. "She misses him also. I believe she felt he was here for that brief time."

"Tell me about him," Kyrianna said, arranging her skirts as she sat on one of the stone pedestals in the garden.

Tristan began telling her about his father and Kyrianna smiled as she felt Melissa's attention focused on listening to everything he had to say about her only sibling who had survived that night.

As he finished speaking, she found her own thoughts turning to her family and her mother. That memory had been brought back by her conversation with Myrith earlier and now Melissa's feelings about her brother caused her own sorrow to rush forward. She looked up at the moon and closed her eyes. "Tristan, can I ask you to give me some time out here—alone?"

"Of course, my Lady." He placed a hand against her cheek for a moment then reached down, lifted her hand and kissed it. "Enjoy the night air." He went back into the house. Kyrianna's gaze followed him and she saw Hendandra with another glass of wine as he closed the glass doors.

She stood and looked into the darkness of the garden. Shadow Seeker materialized next to her as she lifted her skirts and darted away from the house.

"Kyri, are you okay?" Melissa asked when she stopped and sat on a large rock in a small grove.

She looked down to see the ghostly girl standing next to her. "Just a few memories, little sister. That's all."

"Torliana and Thynitic? Balthas?"

"That's only a small part of it." She looked back at the house again.

Melissa followed her gaze. "You miss her."

"I do." She looked up at the stars and began singing softly in elven. She sang of her mother and called on Frayrith to welcome and protect her spirit. It was the first chance she had taken to offer the song and she was upset she hadn't done it sooner.

She sat there for a few more minutes calming her emotions before she stood. "We should be getting back, before Myrith notices I've vanished again," she said. "It's a wonder she didn't throttle me for arranging that farce of a ceremony."

Melissa laughed then faded back into the necklace.

Kyrianna took a step toward the house then stopped when she saw Tristan standing at the window looking into the garden. Her heart raced for a moment and her emotions swirled. She had told Hendandra only a few hours ago, he was only a friend and Hendandra had all but called her a liar for it. She had been right about her reaction to Tristan's acceptance of Balthas' challenge, even if she wasn't ready to admit it to herself. There was something there, something she knew she was fighting and she wasn't sure why. He had been nothing but a true gentleman with her even though they had played flirtatious games that one evening as well as some verbal back and forth this past day. What was it Cewyr had told her? 'It is not fair to play with someone's emotions—even if you only think it a game you are both playing.'

Her thoughts at that time had been, even when it's your own emotions you are playing with? Had Cewyr been warning her that Tristan had similar feelings toward her? "Chaos," she whispered harshly.

She watched as he turned away from the window. "There is nothing there," she said. "It's only the games we've been playing. There can't be anything there."

She took a deep breath and headed back to the house. "Going to see someone?" she asked as Hendandra came out of the house.

Hendandra gave her a broad smile as she stumbled a bit.

Kyrianna frowned as she watched her friend continue to stagger as she walked away. She reached for the door as the laughter inside continued and paused. Perhaps all Hendandra needed was some air. She entered the dining hall as Andrinor began telling of his battles in the Arena and she cheered with the rest of them as he finished.

"I bet he whimpered like an elf when they branded him," Nirev said.

Kyrianna laughed for a moment then caught her breath as Andrinor slammed his mug down and headed for the dwarf. Her hand went to her dagger as Myrith and Gwideon both reached for their swords.

"Definitely underarmed for this affair," Tristan muttered next to her.

"Listen, Warrior of the Arena, Dragon Warrior of the Great Mother," Nirev said as he placed a small barrel on the table, "I decide the combat. Death by dwarven spirits."

"I do not care for the drink, only the insult," Andrinor said.

Nirev looked up at Andrinor. "Ye think that an insult? I know yer weakness, Silver Dragon Warrior. Ye faced one of the things ye fear the most. Laugh at the jest as it be intended. Tomorrow there will be no laughter. If we be lucky we will not have to bury one of our own during this journey. Would ye rather sit here politely like a bunch of stuffy nobles who insult each other behind curtains or would ye trade joking insults with one who has yer back?"

Nirev brought his hammer's haft down on the table with a loud thud. "Mulog sees everything as a contest. I have not shared a barrel with someone worthy in many months."

He nodded toward Myrith and Tristan. "They will have none of it with their purely holy attitudes and Gwideon—well he is dead to such things. The little thief, we can see the wine handles her better than she it. These two," he jerked his thumb behind him at Falden and Jerietlan, "I could give them but a spoonful and they would fold under the table."

He pushed a mug toward Andrinor. "I would be honored to have yer strength and fortitude at my table to share my drink. I seek another to battle this keg. A challenge and contest for Mulog to laugh with and at this night."

Andrinor nodded and sat down. "This one time, my friend."

Nirev filled their mugs and Kyrianna coughed at the stench that filled the air. "So be it," Nirev said. "And may we both live to see the day when I ask again and ye refuse."

Kyrianna shook her head as Myrith and Gwideon left the room. She wasn't sure whether to be insulted or relieved Nirev hadn't said something about her not being able to compete.

Andrinor picked up the mug and winced. "What demon did you stick in a vat to make this?"

Nirev laughed. "We do not talk of the ingredients, but demons be not foul enough."

Andrinor looked at Nirev, raised his mug then downed the drink.

Nirev laughed. "Tastes better than it smells."

"No." Andrinor frowned. "And I don't want to know what the chunks were." He pushed the mug back and smiled at Nirev.

~ * ~

Falden watched Andrinor and Nirev as they both downed another mug of the foul-smelling liquid. He glanced around and realized he and Jerietlan were the only ones left in the room to witness this contest.

"The deviled eggs are wonderful," a voice said next to him.

Jerietlan leaned forward and looked around him while Falden only shifted his head. There on the table was something that reminded Falden of a ferret with a bushy tail.

"They really are quite delicious," it said, looking at them with bright eyes and forward-pricked ears.

"Did a rodent just speak to us?" Jerietlan asked as he settled back in his chair.

Falden just nodded. "Nothing should surprise you anymore," he said.

Nirev and Andrinor slammed their mugs down on the table.

"There are spells that remove the effects of drink, correct?" Falden said.

Jerietlan nodded.

"Is that magic that can be cast through the links clerics use to heal and help others?"

"Yes, but I have never seen a creature make a person drunk before, so I cannot see its usefulness." Jerietlan turned to look at Falden.

Falden grinned. "I can." He nodded toward Nirev and Andrinor. "Wouldn't it be something to see me outdrink them?"

Jerietlan's face lit up as he grinned and nodded. "Actually the look on Myrith's face would be even better." He whispered the spell and placed his hand on Falden's shoulder. "There, the link is established."

Falden stood up and moved to join the others. He took a seat where he still faced Jerietlan and slid a mug toward Nirev.

Andrinor picked up a spoon and gave it to the dwarf. "For

him," he said as he motioned to Falden. Both he and Nirev began laughing hysterically.

Falden reached across the table, took Nirev's mug and downed the contents. The mug hit the table and both Nirev and Andrinor stared at him.

Finally Nirev nodded and poured three full mugs, passing one to Falden.

Falden glanced at Jerietlan who smiled and nodded.

~ * ~

Myrith walked through the great hall of the house to the library, which also served as a sitting room. Gwideon was with her, but she ignored him as she stared out one of the large windows.

"Please sit," Gwideon said behind her.

"I prefer to stand." She didn't turn.

"Why is that? You should enjoy the comfort that is available before we enter the Abyss."

"I will stand." She didn't take her gaze from her reflection in the window.

"To be ready for the demons that come through the door or those which come from within your own mind?"

She turned at the challenge she heard in his voice. "Don't you dare judge me! I have had enough of that this day." She turned back to the window.

"You cannot fight everything with a sword," he whispered.

Her gaze went to his reflection in the window.

"If all you do is fight every moment of every day, when do you have time to remember what you are fighting for? That is the primary purpose of the tradition behind this feast we are having tonight. To remember what we are fighting for. To celebrate with friends and family and give us the memories we will carry with us so we fight to return. We have this night to remember Hendandra playing her violin, not having to worry about disarming a trap. You saw Andrinor and Nirev celebrating their strength in a contest of drinking, not fighting against demons. And Kyrianna was laughing instead of trapped by the demons following her. You are the only one who cannot let go of their demons and live in the moment this night. Why is that?"

Myrith spun around and swung Conflagration's scabbard from her shoulder. She sat in a chair as he seated himself across from her and raised his glass in salute. "Satisfied?" she asked.

Gwideon smiled. "It is not a question of if I am satisfied. Are you comfortable?"

She leaned back so the wing-back of the chair would obscure her face from him. "Yes, but bored. At least when I am standing, I have something to occupy my time."

"Would you like to hear a story?" He leaned back in his chair, but she noticed that his gaze never left her.

"A story or a drinking contest." She sighed and sipped from her glass. "Very well, I would like to hear your story."

"As you may have gathered from my words today, I was not born to means. I was the fatherless child of a woman who was the mistress to one of the nobles of this city. My mother's name was Rheathea. When she was found to be with child she was cast out into the streets without so much as a few coppers. She was alone and with no means to sustain herself." He paused for a moment as shadows moved across his face. "The city can be a cruel place to those without a House or a family.

"She found shelter with a beggar. The man's name was Panarian. He was an old man, who said he saw a bit of his daughter in my mother. He helped her as best he could, but his body was damaged from years of hard work and the accident that left him with a ruined hand. Begging was his only means of income. He pleaded with my mother to give me to one of the churches of the Court of Thedrin; that it would be better for both her and me. She told him she would not have me at the mercy of any church; she had seen the cruelness behind the façade.

"She took to the streets to support me. That type of life is hard on a woman. She survived that way for some seven years until someone didn't like the way she looked at him or the way she talked or maybe he just had too much to drink. I found her in an alleyway. We didn't even have enough coins to pay a cleric to see to her soul. She was laid to rest in the Catacombs. I know now she had paid enough in this life and Resare would ask nothing more of her. However, it was a time of great sorrow for me; my only parent was dead and my caretaker could scarcely take care of himself."

Myrith could see her own mother's face in her mind. The woman had worked in the Silver Dragon to take care of both of them, but had left her there when she was old enough to take up the same work herself. It had been her choice to abandon her child, while Gwideon's mother had been taken from him.

"I decided I could not stay with Panarian. I felt I had to make my own way in the world, but I had no trade.

"It was fate that brought me to the square in front of the Coliseum that day. A Tormasian had come to challenge any and all. His name was Sulbarus. It was said he earned his life back in the Tormasian Arena much as Andrinor did." He cocked his head slightly as his gaze searched for her. "He was a paragon of focused brutality. Balthas, though just a squire at the time, attempted to best him with five other young warriors. The results were humorous—except for one." He paused for a breath. "That one had struck a cowardly blow and Sulbarus snapped him like a twig.

"The display had me in awe. I found his horse and waited. As he prepared to leave, I barreled into him, purposely spooking the horse. He was absolutely beside himself with rage. He slapped me and almost sent me against a wall, but I stood up quickly. He told me my stupidity had cost him and his horse time and me my freedom. From that day I became his servant. I watched and learned from him as he made his way through the world. We journeyed to Domar and even the Malavian Dominion. All my waking hours I was learning from him and practicing. I chose the great sword, not for its physical effects, but instead for the way it infuses dread in others. It is amazing sometimes how the sheer size of a weapon speaks louder than words in a room.

"When we returned to Domar some eight years after my servitude began, he released me. He found me worthy of my life and gave me a sword to punish all those who would stand in the way of that life. I know not where his journeys took him, but I'm sure that somewhere his voice still rallies to the cry of battle.

"I'm sorry, my Lady, have I put you to sleep?"

She raised her glass for him to see. "Just listening. How does the temple of Mykaylene fit into the story?"

"I worked my way back to Irrmar. I had learned more than just swordsmanship from the Tormasian. He taught me his people believed every day was a battle and they could be called from this world at any time. He made his peace with all of the gods he felt watched him—both good and evil. Mykaylene and Nalath of course were the strongest. Resare who waits on the other side was close behind. Mulog as the God of Strength was honored as well.

"As I made my way back to Irrmar, I took time everyday to

reconcile what I had done and what I would do and how the Battle Maiden would view me in her eyes. I kept my sword clean of unnecessary blood and gave mercy where I could. I helped those I could and I prayed for those I could not."

Myrith took another sip of the wine. Her mind going to the trials she had faced. It seemed he sought the path almost as blindly as she had.

"When I entered that very same temple, my hopes of finding acceptance were dashed. Sir Balthas, now an ordained knight, stood in opposition to me, barring me from entrance. I had no House or clergyman to stand by me. I had reentered the void of my childhood. I left that temple vowing never to return. It took a request from my Gatekeeper for me to go back." He leaned forward and smiled. "I am glad he asked me to return. I have found there is at least one rose of enlightenment left in that shallow garden."

Myrith leaned back in the seat to hide the blush she felt on her cheeks.

"I left the temple dejected until I heard a woman call for help. I unsheathed my sword and sprinted to the yelling. Two men had her on the ground. One was holding her arms while another fought with her legs. I called to them to stop and they turned to look at me: a young man with an oversized, unwieldy weapon, and laughed.

"Myrith, there is a time when it seems fate lays open its hand and that day the shroud of the Great Watcher from the Shadows rested on that alleyway. On the other side of the alley, I saw a gray-robed man; a Greymancer of Resare, I would learn. They saw him and froze. Many men do not fear for their lives, but they do fear for their souls and Resare's followers are known for their punishments into the next life.

"The Greymancer spoke softly and calmly. 'Only he can judge your actions this day.' I looked in the darkness of his robes as he whispered his next words. 'I send you now to his judgment.' A burning light sprang from his hand and seared through one as the other tried to charge past me. He fell in two pieces. I never took my eyes from the Greymancer.

"The Greymancer looked at me. 'You seem lost; do you seek the light?'

"As I helped the woman to her feet and she ran off, I answered, 'No, I seek a place where the light has no meaning. I have seen those who bask in it and it holds no glory. I have seen the darkness and it only hides those who would twist and deceive.'

"'You seek not the light or the darkness. Do you seek both or neither?' the Greymancer asked.

"'I do not know that answer,' I told him.

"'Good, because I cannot answer that for myself, even now.' He turned away and started to walk back along the alleyway. 'Walk the path between the two long enough and you will see they are both the same. One just uses prettier words than the other.' I started after him and never looked back. I had found a place where no House had influence and no one judged anyone except by their deeds."

Myrith stood as she heard Hendandra shouting Kyrianna's name. "I have one question, you may refuse to answer if it is too personal," she said. "Who was your father?"

"Victor Wailing. Sir Balthas' father."

Myrith gasped and her glass shattered as it hit the floor.

Chapter Nineteen

Kyrianna watched Tristan go up the stairs and glancing back at the others still in the dining hall, she could think of no better company. As she went up the stairs, she again found herself debating what she was doing. She had been through this once already this evening, but the emotions she was feeling were not going to be denied that easily.

I shouldn't be doing this, she thought. *I should stay with the others. Why—just so I can try to stop the brawl that will eventually be coming? If I go up there, I will be tempted by something I don't want,* she thought. *But, if I don't want it, how can I be tempted?* She didn't try to answer the question as she paused only briefly by his door then moved past to her own room.

"Chaos," she whispered as she entered the room. She had left the balcony door open to air out the room and she could see Tristan leaning against the frame.

"Turning in already?" He smiled as he looked at her.

"Lord Duvall, you should know better than to enter a lady's room without her permission."

He stood straight and looked at the doorway. "I have not entered. Nor would I think of entering. That would not be proper."

She smiled and moved past him to the stone railing of the balcony. He stayed by the door a moment then moved to stand at the railing, a respectful distance from her. She jerked her head up as her ears caught a sound. She wasn't sure at first, but it came again; a faint giggle. She looked down and just below her, in a dark corner of the garden, she saw Hendandra and Feric.

Hendandra had her head turned toward the sky with her eyes closed and her husband's lips on her neck. She was smiling, but not with the rapture the moment would normally call for, but with a dull expression more in line with a drunken stupor.

"Chaos take it." She turned and looked around. She barely even saw Tristan who was standing only feet from her. He had not heard and could not see the two of them. She stormed back into her room and her gaze stopped on the water pitcher on the dresser.

She picked it up and walked back out onto the balcony. "Sorry," she whispered as she dumped the water over the railing and heard both male and female voices give muffled yells of surprise.

"Tristan, would you be so kind as to get me some fresh water?"

He looked at her for a moment, his brows creased with concern, then he took the pitcher from her. He walked back to his room to go down the stairs.

"Don't hurry back and make sure no one comes up here until I call for you," she said. After his door closed, she turned back to the garden. She could see only Feric; his face was almost feral as he looked up at her.

"Kyrianna!" Hendandra's voice followed the slamming of the garden doors and laughter from those in the dining hall.

She took a deep breath and nodded. *Good, she's on her way up.* She glanced back down at Feric and she took an involuntary step back from the railing. He was the reptile she had met the first night at the house. He looked at her intently and took several steps back.

She took another step back from the railing and turned toward her door. The balcony was nearly eleven feet from the ground, half again the height of the reptile and it was not built for climbing. A scraping noise behind her caused her to catch her breath as she turned back around. The reptile was perched on the railing, which it gripped with very long claws. The middle claw on each foot tapped against the stone several times. He stretched out his neck and gave a low hiss.

Her gaze went to her weapons; they were within reach if she dove, but she wasn't wearing any armor. She had seen the cat attack Nirev. She knew Feric could be as efficient as any predator, probably more so. He was the favored of Shyada.

Her heart stopped as his gaze caught and held hers. "Chaos," she whispered. Shyada was the goddess of cats, predators and pleasure seekers. She had just interrupted him and his mate and Shyada would mandate a punishment for such an affront to her pursuits.

When she had first seen him in this form, he had been impassive; now she saw his animalistic power merged with an intelligent host. Hendandra was right; he was Shyada's perfect pet and he was here for her.

"Get out!" Kyrianna heard Hendandra yell as she came into the room.

Feric turned his head slightly.

"You heard me. Get out!"

Feric nodded his head, evidently deciding she had as much right in this matter as he did. Something Kyrianna was grateful for as he jumped off the railing and back into the garden.

She let herself relax as she turned toward Hendandra. She stumbled back into the wall as Hendandra's fist connected with her abdomen. "How could you! I confided in you!" Hendandra hit her again. "I trusted you. Just when I found the courage for this, you ruin it for him."

Kyrianna gasped as the wall helped hold her up. "Listen to yourself. For what you were about to do, you needed courage? You talk about him, but not about the two of you."

Hendandra took a step back and Kyrianna staggered to the chest in front of the bed and sat down.

"Is that what you want? How do you think he will feel to know his wife needed to be drunk before she could be with him? How do you think you will feel when you think back on that moment and realize you had to numb your senses to be there?"

Hendandra started crying and Kyrianna only watched her.

"I can't believe this," Hendandra said. "This is hopeless. I just make things worse. I should never have kept it. I could have given it back today at the island, but I didn't." She looked at Kyrianna. "How pathetic am I to do this to him?"

Kyrianna reached out, pulled Hendandra into a hug and held her for a minute, letting the other woman cry on her shoulder. "You are not pathetic. Most women go through many decisions regarding their suitors. Yours is complicated by the fact you are already married." She pushed Hendandra back, slid off the chest and knelt down so they were eye to eye. She brushed the long blonde hair back from her friend's face and wiped the tears. "You think certain things are expected of you, even required," she said as she shook her head. "Did he try to stop you from coming in when I dropped the water?"

"No," Hendandra said with a whimper.

Kyrianna smiled. "Then he is willing to let you make your own decisions. He might have been anxious for his wife, but I doubt he wants you to regret that first night."

Hendandra turned toward the balcony. "I need to talk to him."

"It is late; Gwideon will be leaving soon to return to his temple. He will be looking for Shydaran."

"Can you stall them, Kyri?"

Kyrianna shook her head at the sad look Hendandra gave her. "You've been practicing that look," she said.

"Please."

"I will, but only on one condition. There is something you must do first."

~ * ~

Tristan sat in the dining hall and waited for whatever was happening upstairs to be settled.

"Custard?" Jerietlan gestured to the table next to him.

Tristan took the pastry from the mongoose who held it out to him. "Thank you."

"Where did he come from?" he asked Jerietlan.

"I stopped asking that question after a unicorn showed up. Now, when something new shows up with fur, I just assume someone summoned or befriended it."

"Unicorn?" Tristan whispered.

"Yes, Brular gave Kyrianna a magical figurine that summons a unicorn for her."

He slumped back in his chair. "I forgot about the unicorn."

"Huh?"

"Would you like another?" a voice said.

"Yes, that w—" He stopped and stared at the mongoose.

"By the way, I forgot to mention—he talks also."

Tristan took the custard and nodded his thanks as he turned back to the table and three mugs were slammed back down.

Falden looked at them and Tristan saw Jerietlan make several discreet motions with his hands and whisper a short chant. He shook his head. "I don't think Mykaylene will punish you for the joke, but I bet those two will," he whispered.

"If they find out," Jerietlan said. He smiled and nodded to the pitcher Tristan had placed on the floor. "So, is the water for Kyrianna, Hendandra or both?"

"In all honestly, I do not know. Nor do I think I want to know."

Tristan looked up as both Kyrianna and Hendandra entered the room. The smaller woman was dry and wearing a different dress.

"Jerietlan, my head won't stop spinning," Hendandra said.

"Can you remove my dizzied state?"

"Of course." He muttered a short spell and placed his hands on her shoulders.

"Thank you." She headed for the garden doors.

"Remember what I said," Kyrianna said.

Hendandra only nodded as she stepped through the doors.

Kyrianna turned and headed for the main doors.

Tristan stood and started to follow her; they needed to talk. He stopped as he heard the chairs at the table slam against the floor. Andrinor was standing in front of Jerietlan and Nirev had grabbed Falden.

Andrinor reached out, took Jerietlan's collar and guided him to the table. "Sit."

Tristan sighed and cleared his throat. "You won't hurt them?"

"No," Andrinor said.

Nirev pushed Falden back into his seat. "No, we be finishing the game and he be joining us." Nirev's gaze went from Falden to Jerietlan and back as Andrinor set a fourth mug on the table. "And there will no more cheating this time, my friends."

"Very well. Enjoy the rest of your evening." He picked up the pitcher and then held up the key to the main door. He closed the doors and locked them.

Tristan saw Kyrianna walking into the great room with Gwideon and Myrith and set the pitcher and key down on the table next to the door as he followed.

~ * ~

"Before you go, I have a question I hope you can help me with," Kyrianna said as the doors closed behind her. She glanced back and saw Tristan standing there then turned her attention back to Gwideon. "With the dangers we will be facing in the Abyss— how does one return the undead to the living?"

"The question is not a simple one, Kyrianna. There are many factors to take into account."

Kyrianna ignored the look Myrith shot her. She was not sure if her friend was annoyed by the idea of a forthcoming lecture on the undead or if she was unhappy about being disturbed as she was seeing Gwideon to the door.

~ * ~

Hendandra entered the garden and moved to one of the unlit corners. She stopped and listened for a moment, but heard nothing. *You are here, but where?* She jumped when she felt a hand on her arm. She relaxed as his arms folded around hers. She let him pull her into him as he sat back against a tree.

She felt his hand along her neck and ear and sighed.

"Kyrianna was right," she said. "I wasn't ready and it was not fair to either of us." Her breath caught as he continued to play with her neck.

"It seems I disappoint you at every turn." She leaned forward and away from him. "Maybe it would have been better for you to have had me squished by your large furry friend." She felt his hand on her shoulder. "Honestly, give me one good reason why you saved me."

She felt him lean forward, place his hand on her face and turn it toward him. She kept her eyes closed as she felt his other hand on her cheek and his lips touch hers. It was a gentle caress. He didn't need to speak for her to understand. She felt his fingers moving behind her neck. She realized it was an unspoken request and she pressed into him for a moment. As he withdrew, she pressed forward slightly for one last draw of his lips. She settled against his chest when he leaned back, and laughed. "Okay, that is a good reason not to squish me."

His fingers returned to the slow stroking of her neck.

"You threatened Kyri," she whispered.

He did not respond in either words or how he moved his hands.

"I saw the look in your eyes," she said. "Don't do that again, husband. She did not mean to harm us or to shame you. Don't ever force me to make such a choice." Her voice broke. "It would be too difficult and painful."

In response he kissed her neck then whispered in her ear, "You did not seem to mind that I drew blood from the dwarf?"

She adjusted her position as his fingers worked her shoulder and neck. "He attacked you. He shouldn't have done that. You pushed Andrinor, but did not use your teeth or claws. You made your point without hurting him." Her hand came up to his and squeezed lightly. "You will obey Myrith?"

His fingers moved over her ear and she turned into his shoulder. "I will—to a point."

She tensed.

"I could not bear to see you hurt. If you are in trouble, I will act and damn her wants to your needs." His voice was low and forbidding.

She moved her hand to his and drew it to her lips. "I would have it no other way." She kissed the hand of Justula's great protector—her great protector.

~ * ~

Kyrianna took a breath then began to sum up the over-twenty-minute detailed explanation of the realms of the dead. "So the longer someone has been dead, the greater the magic needed to bring them back. A priest of some power can raise someone who has been dead for a few days, but the taint of the negative or even positive plane interferes with weaker magics. To raise those dead for years, you need someone of higher power, and if they have been among the walking dead, they may still require the greatest magic a god can give."

Gwideon nodded. "Be advised, if one dies of old age he cannot return to the land of the living."

Kyrianna nodded.

"Thank you," Tristan said. "I believe we have taken enough of your time and should allow you to go to your rest."

"It is indeed late. However, I also have a request. Lady Kyrianna, may I see your necklace?" Gwideon held out his hand.

Kyrianna felt her body go numb and she turned toward Tristan whose eyes went wide.

"I will not harm it," Gwideon said.

Kyrianna placed her hand over the necklace, guarding it.

"Kyri," Myrith said. "He said he will not harm it."

Kyrianna stood frozen as Tristan removed the necklace and handed it to the Knight of Resare, the God of Death. "It is from my house," he said.

Gwideon held the necklace and caressed it for several minutes before handing it back. "It is said many objects have their own spirit. This one has a very lovely soul about it."

Kyrianna could only stare at Gwideon and Myrith as they left the room.

~ * ~

"Cat!" Gwideon called as the door closed behind him and Myrith. "Cat!"

Myrith leaned against one of the columns. "You really need to work on keeping control of him. Try calling him by his name."

"As Kyrianna said, he is an intelligent creature and therefore will not be easily controlled." He took a breath. "Shydaran!"

The tiger came bounding up and lowered his head as if he were apologizing. Gwideon touched the tiger's back and the saddle appeared. "I will return to the Coliseum in the morning as you have directed." He turned and took her hand.

Myrith hesitated and she thought to pull away, but she didn't as he kissed it.

"I enjoyed your company as much as your victory this day," Gwideon said and he mounted the tiger. He turned toward her and smiled again. "May the darkness not call you for yet one more day, my Lady."

"Mykaylene give you strength," she said.

He touched the tiger with his heels and they headed for the gates.

Myrith released a sigh of relief as Gwideon and the tiger trotted through the gates. It had been a pleasant but awkward evening. His life spoke so much to her, but she would not speak of hers as he did. She had told Kyrianna a little of her past, but even that had been hard to do. Most of them knew she had worked in a bar and they would understand what that implied. Balthas would have confirmed their suspicions today when he called her a whore in front of the assemblage in the temple. And still they stood by her.

She grabbed the wall to hold herself steady as she felt a wave of emotion hit her. Emotions she had thought long buried behind the steel she wore in her mind as much as on her body. She knew Gwideon was attracted to her, but while she also felt an attraction, her heart and soul belonged to Mykaylene. There were no specific prohibitions on personal relationships. Tristan even came from a House with a lineage of holy warriors, so Mykaylene allowed marriage. However, she knew she wasn't ready for anything like that at this time. She had too much in her past and she wouldn't risk dividing her loyalties.

She took a breath and glanced again in the direction Gwideon had taken. She knew he wouldn't press the issue; he had too much respect for her and she for him, but he would be there for her when she needed him.

"Enough of this," she said. "Time to see to the foolishness in the dining hall."

~ * ~

Tristan took the necklace and replaced it around her neck.

:*Melissa?* Kyrianna whispered in her mind.

:*He knew I was here and in the sword the entire time. He said he has a sense for those who have not passed over,* the girl said.

:*You spoke with him?*

:*No, he spoke to me. He said Riker informed his Gatekeeper of another spirit in the party. He said I will have to choose between this world and the next, but that choice will not be forced at this time.* She paused for a moment. :*I trust his word.*

Kyrianna waited as Myrith and Gwideon left the room. She felt Tristan's hand on her neck and then slight pressure on the chain of the necklace.

:*Yes, Tristan, I am fine.* She heard Melissa's voice answer the question she couldn't hear. :*He means me no harm. At least, not at this time.*

Kyrianna felt his grip tighten a little as if to give assurance to both of them.

She placed her hand over his and returned the pressure.

"Are you okay?" he asked.

"I'm sorry," she said. "I didn't know he was aware of Melissa's presence. This could have gone very bad." She turned to face Tristan and smiled softly. "I have a tendency to be a bit rash in my actions sometimes." She reached out and placed her hands on either side of his face, leaned in and raised up on her toes as she kissed him. "Like now."

"Kyri?" Tristan looked at her, smiled and reached out to brush her hair back behind her ears.

She closed her eyes as she let her lips brush his again.

:*Kyri? Does this mean you're not going to be a maiden anymore?*

"What!" Kyrianna pulled away from Tristan. Her hand went to the necklace and she yanked it from around her neck. "You explain it to her." She turned and ran out of the room.

~ * ~

Myrith opened the doors to the dining hall and frowned at the sight that greeted her. Nirev was on the floor, using his mug as a pillow. Andrinor was in a corner, snoring away. Falden and Jerietlan looked up at her. "We won," they said together.

She could only stare at them.

"You were right," Falden said. "The look on her face is priceless." They both started laughing and fell off their chairs.

"Kyri?" Myrith called as the girl pushed her way past her and ran out into the garden.

"Chaos take it," she said as she turned to head up the stairs. She glanced at Tristan who was standing there holding the sapphire necklace and staring past her toward the garden.

"I don't want to know," Myrith said as she headed up the stairs to her room.

Chapter Twenty

Tristan watched as Kyrianna ran out of the house and into the gardens.

Holding the necklace he heard Melissa's voice in his mind.

:Kyri, I'm sorry. I didn't mean it.

Caught up in trying to understand what had happened, he barely noticed when Myrith passed him headed upstairs. He looked down at the necklace and back up the way Kyrianna had gone and shook his head. He wasn't going to follow her, at least not yet. There was something more going on that he needed to know about first.

He focused his thoughts on the necklace. "Melissa, what did you say to her?"

No response came. "Melissa, I know you care about her. I think you know I do as well. How can I help her if I don't know what's wrong?" He entered his room and started to close the door.

:I just asked her, when you two were kissing, if this meant she didn't want to be a maiden anymore. Melissa's voice was scared as it came into his mind. Full of emotion like a small child who thought a game she had been playing had been fun and had now seen it hurt someone she didn't want to hurt.

The door slammed and he fell against it. "Melissa, what do you know of such things?" His thoughts were a jumble of surprise and dread. She had only been eight when she was killed; why would she even be asking the question?

:Up until a few days ago, I thought I knew exactly what it meant. But everyone is acting so strangely when I use it. Mother told me a lady is a maiden before she marries and then she is a woman. It was all very clear. Melissa's voice paused. *:Does that make sense?*

"Perfect," he said. "It is a simplification though. You asking the question of Kyrianna is legitimate since you think of each other as sisters, though it is still not proper. It is not polite to question any woman about the subject of maidenhood." He thought of Myrith and her title for a moment, then remembered she had been a server in a bar for some time. He smiled when he remembered the title she had been given. Gwideon's insistence had spared her from being given one that could be used as a joke against her.

:*Tristan, what does a bar have to do with being a maiden?*

He shook his head as he forced his thoughts away from the subject. He leaned on the railing and looked out over the garden. He thought he could make out whispering in the darkness, but it was too low to hear.

:*Cewyr asked Rynalana if she was a maiden.*

"Who asked whom?" Tristan shook his head trying to make sense of Melissa's rambling.

:*Cewyr is the unicorn that travels with Kyri and Rynalana is a monk or priest or something of Hellavar. Cewyr said only maidens could ride her. Rynalana's reaction was shock and anger at the question.*

"As it should have been. But it is different in that context and in that company." His thoughts were fleeting, but he understood now why Kyrianna's feelings appeared to be tearing her apart.

"I don't think I want to ask, but has this question come up more than once?"

:*Several times. I asked Hendandra at your house.*

"Why would you ask someone else that?" His tone was sharp as he tried to picture Melissa standing there. "I can see you and Kyri are close and sisters say things to each other that otherwise should never be asked, but why Hendandra?"

:*It seemed okay to ask her, She just got marrie*—She stopped abruptly as if she had just placed her hands over her mouth.

"When did this happen? She never said anything at the estate."

:*It was far more recently.* Her voice was hesitant.

Tristan nodded. "That explains a few things." He thought about Kyrianna pouring the water over the balcony railing. "Is he here?"

:*Yes, but in hiding.* Melissa's words seemed more measured now as she spoke.

"Okay. I understand why you asked. However, as I said, it is not proper to ask such questions. You are not to ask them again. You are to leave that subject be with Kyrianna and talk to her about it only if she brings it up."

Her voice was becoming little more than a whisper. :*I'm sorry. It's just that I have been alone for so long.*

He softened his tone as he remembered the little girl's body trapped in the hedge maze. "You will come stay with me when this is over," he said.

:I want to stay with Kyri.

"She travels the road. As you are now, you are safe from most threats. As flesh and blood, you would be a distraction and hindrance. You will stay with me once you return in body to this world. You are a Duvall. Your place is in my House, where eventually, when you are ready, you can take your leave."

:I want to be with Kyri. He could hear her crying.

"She came to see me to find out if you wanted to stay with me. I believe it is for the best." He tried to maintain a calm and soothing tone in his voice. "She will not fight me on this issue, I assure you."

All he heard was the sound of a little girl sobbing and he let his thoughts merge with hers. "I want to be with her also," he whispered.

~ * ~

Kyrianna stopped in the small grove she had found earlier and dropped to the ground, crying. "What am I doing? I can't be feeling this. I can't."

Shadow Seeker whined softly as he pressed his nose into her hand.

Kyrianna rubbed the wolf's muzzle as the tears continued. *The Reishalli, Mother called it: the Soul Weaving. How can this be happening? He is not from my world. How can we be destined for each other? How can we be two halves of one whole? This cannot be happening.* But it was happening. Now that she had acknowledged her feelings, she could feel her and Tristan becoming a part of each other, as if their souls were being woven together. Humans called it soul mates: two people who were considered perfect counterparts to each other. But the Reishalli was something much deeper and more sacred. It was the true blending together of two to make one.

"Frayrith, guide me," she whispered.

"Kyri," Hendandra's voice came from nearby.

She looked up at Hendandra leaning against a nearby tree. "I'm sorry, but I was worried something was wrong when I saw you running from the house, then I heard you crying. Did Tristan say something that made you weep?"

Kyrianna wiped her face. "No. I wish it were that simple. Why do you ask?"

"Look." Hendandra glanced back up at the house.

Tristan stood looking out over the gardens from the balcony.

She looked at him then turned away. "I should...I can't stay here tonight. I can't even go back inside." She turned to her friend and she knew she was doing a poor job of hiding her feelings. "Can you bring me my clothes and equipment?"

Hendandra looked up at her then up at the man on the balcony. "If that's what you want. You don't even want to say goodbye?"

She turned her head and shook it as more tears fell.

"I'll help you, but I need you to help me tomorrow with Feric."

"Did something happen? I saw him leave with Gwideon." She was glad the subject had shifted, but worried.

"He..." Hendandra paused.

"He what?"

Hendandra smiled. "He told me he loved me as he was leaving."

Kyrianna waited a moment. "And?"

"And I thought about it the entire time I watched him leave."

Kyrianna dropped her face into her hands. "You thought about it? Thought about it? You did not tell him anything?"

Hendandra went pale. "I know it was stupid and then he was gone," she said. "I finally stopped trying to analyze and weigh everything and I realized I was a fool." She looked at her. "I do love him and I couldn't even tell him."

Kyrianna pulled her into a hug. "We are both fools as I can't tell him either." She glanced back up at Tristan.

"Kyri, please help me tomorrow. What if..." Her voice broke. "I have to tell him before we go. I have to."

Kyrianna again looked up at the balcony. "You're right. I will get Shydaran alone near one of the doorways." She smiled as she looked at Hendandra. "He can easily hide you as you talk to him."

"Thank you. I'll be back in a few minutes."

~ * ~

"Tristan."

He turned to see Hendandra in Kyrianna's room. She moved around gathering Kyrianna's belongings.

"She is leaving." It was a statement, not a question.

"Yes," Hendandra said, not turning around as she laid Kyrianna's bow and swords next to the pack.

He turned back to study the garden, searching the darkness.

:*I'm sorry. I didn't mean for this to happen.*

"I know. It is difficult for her. She is close to the unicorn." His hands gripped the railing. "I have forced her to make a choice."

:*You did not ask her.*

"There are many ways to ask something. I knew about the unicorn from your visit, but chose to forget. I should not have stayed so close to her this evening. She does not need the turmoil of this right now."

"Talking to Melissa?" Hendandra held Kyrianna's pack and weapons.

It took him a moment to remember she knew about the wraith. "Yes."

"Here, take them to her." She held out the pack.

He stared at her. "She wants me to bring her things to her?"

"Yes, she told me to ask Lord Duvall to deliver her things to her."

Hendandra continued to hold the pack and weapons. "Go on," she said.

He took the pack, walked into Kyrianna's room and let his senses scan the area. There, slipped under the mattress was the aura he was looking for. He removed the cloth-wrapped item from its hiding place and headed for the stairs.

~ * ~

Kyrianna leaned back against the rock and looked up at the stars. Hendandra had finally come to grips with her feelings; now she had to do the same. However, she knew it wouldn't be that simple. This was something more than desire; it was the Reishalli, the Soul Weaving. She had no way of knowing if Tristan was even aware of what was happening. She thought she had read him well enough to know he cared about her. But did he truly love her?

Hendandra wanted to tell Feric she did love him because they were leaving for the Abyss tomorrow. She wanted him to know in case something happened to one of them. For those same reasons and others, Kyrianna didn't want Tristan to know how she felt.

If I tell him about this, he will want to go with us tomorrow. That could get one or both of us killed. And if Thynitic realizes how we feel, she will try to use him to hurt me. Like she had my mother killed. And then there is Cewyr. I made her a promise. I will not do anything to separate us and I will not ask her to release me from that promise. I can't tell him. She felt the tears falling again.

It was taking longer than a few minutes. She looked back at the balcony and saw Tristan's room was now closed with only a single light on. She heard movement behind her, stood and turned. "Thank you, Hendan—" She stopped and stared at Tristan standing there holding her equipment.

"I see you were expecting someone else. I thought Hendandra was playing a game of some sort."

He glanced up at the balcony and she followed his gaze to see Hendandra wave as she stepped back into Tristan's room and close the door.

"I'm sorry. I see now the idea was for you to escape into the night without seeing me again." He placed her pack and equipment on the rock and turned back toward the house.

"My actions were rash and selfish," she said. "I shouldn't have."

Tristan stopped and turned around to face her. She lowered her head.

"You only did what I would have done far more awkwardly later this evening," he said.

Her heart leapt and she started crying once more. She couldn't tell if it was from joy or dread.

She heard him moving behind her. "Your changing room awaits." There was a pause, almost as if he was holding his breath. "That is, if you still wish to leave." His voice was soft and without judgment.

"Tristan, I can't do this right now. Not with…"

"Not with where you will be going tomorrow," he said. "I'm sorry to have done this to you."

She turned without looking at him. She couldn't right now. She knew what she would want if she did and that was not going to happen. A small "room" had been formed by a group of hedges. *Melissa's work*, she thought. "I have to talk to someone," she said.

"Cewyr?"

She froze before she stepped behind the hedges. "How did you know?"

She stopped him before he answered. "Melissa."

"She tried to explain to me what was going on. She sees you as her sister. She wanted to help. I know you said you couldn't do this right now, but there are things that need saying between us before you take to the road tomorrow."

"Tristan, I'm not ready for this," she said as she stepped behind the hedges.

"I'm sorry, but this must be said anyway, Lady Kyrianna." Tristan's voice was stern. She had never heard him speak like this.

"You go again into the darkness. Does it hold that much excitement for you?"

His words hung in the air as she sorted through her clothes and equipment. "I go not for myself, but for a friend." She refused to answer the challenge in his voice as she started to unlace her dress and looked again at the equipment laid out on the ground. Everything was there except…She reached for her pack.

"Does Myrith know about the whip?" His voice was soft.

She turned slowly as she heard him tapping the leather against his leg. Her breath caught. It was almost as if she were back in Nydith on that last night. She could hear her father's words echoing in her mind. 'Where did you get this?' She closed her eyes and saw him once again slamming the dagger with the emblem of the thieves' guild on the table. Like her father, she suspected Tristan already knew the answer to the question he had just asked.

She stepped out from behind the hedges holding her dress on her shoulders. She stared at him and the whip.

"She is a great fighter, but her powers of observation are not as good as one who listens to every word and notices every detail of the court and nobility."

She nodded then swallowed hard and turned away from his gaze. There was still no judgment in his voice or on his face, only fear and disappointment. She still couldn't believe he had found out about the whip. "When did you find out?"

"I sensed it when you came to visit. You were careless in putting it in your pack; one tail hung out. It wasn't in the things Hendandra gave me, so I checked your room and found it under the mattress. Again you were careless, letting part of it protrude so it could be detected. Its magic is faint, similar to Gwideon's sword, I believe, but it is a whip." He paused. "Is it Thynitic's whip?" He tossed it on the ground at her feet.

She looked at the whip where it lay in the grass for several minutes. "It was my mother's," she finally said. Her hands tightened into fists, crumpling the material of the dress where she held it. "She took my mother from me! To punish me!" she all but shouted in the quiet garden then turned away again.

"So you go not for him, but for retribution?" Tristan reached out and placed a hand on her shoulder, turning her back toward him.

"N—" She looked up at him. "In truth, for both." She stepped back, her back against the hedges. "Don't you dare judge me! Look at what Mikyl did to your family. You wanted retribution also."

"No," he whispered. "I wanted it to end. For Melissa. For my grandparents and the others. It had to stop, Kyri." He took a step toward her, reached up and touched her ears with his fingertips. "I don't want you on the path to the Abyss and utter damnation as well." He slid his hands back down to her shoulders. "I can do nothing to stop you, but Myrith will know eventually."

She jerked her head up. "You will not tell her?"

"No, but you should. If you trust her with your life, you must also trust her with this. However, it is your decision." He leaned forward and kissed her forehead. "Don't do something that not only you, but others will regret."

She looked up at him and she felt the pain in her heart. She wanted to be here—with him, but she couldn't. She stepped to the side and turned away again. "You're right, Tristan. It is my decision, not yours. I will not burden Myrith with more than she needs." She reached down and picked up the whip, letting the dress slide partially off her right shoulder. She turned back to face him just beyond his reach. "And, if I try to take a pound of flesh from the chaos-spawned bitch for what she has done, that is my decision as well."

He frowned.

"What now?" She dreaded the answer that could come with the look on his face.

The frown faded back into a soft smile. "I would still like the pleasure of your company, here under the stars, for a little while longer, my Lady."

"You are not angry with me?"

"Perhaps a little, but that does not change how I feel. Besides, how can I remain angry when you are true to your heart? I would not attempt to hold back the fury of a person who has been wronged, particularly not one who has been wronged as you have. I only pray the darkness doesn't consume you."

She nodded. "As do I."

"Don't face it alone, Kyri. You faced my darkness with me. I would walk this path with you, or even for you," he said.

She heard the pleading in his voice. "It's not that simple," she said. She searched for the right words. This is what she feared would happen. She needed to convince him without actually telling him no. "I would not have Thynitic attack me through you," she finally said.

He looked at her. "So, you would stop living and let her win."

There was a truth in his words she had not realized before and she could only stand there in silence as his words echoed in her heart. She finally shook her head and stepped back behind the hedges.

He turned away from her as she quickly changed out of the gown and back into her travel clothes. She repacked everything, except the dress, which she folded neatly and placed on the rock. Her pack, weapons and armor rested next to it.

She turned and looked at him, still standing with his back to her, waiting for her to tell him he could turn around. It was hard to keep distance from him. She reached for her equipment then stopped; she couldn't walk away, not now. She stepped up next to him and he turned to face her. He placed his arms around her and she rested her head on his shoulder.

"This is nice," Melissa's voice said and Kyrianna looked down to see the ghostly girl standing next to them.

"Is she always like this?" Tristan whispered.

"Always," she whispered back.

"Aunt." Tristan stopped and looked down at the girl. "No, that just doesn't fit. You are more like an annoying little sister. Do you mind if I refer to you as my sister, Melissa?"

"No. Actually that is what Kyri calls me," she said as she vanished.

Kyrianna removed her head from his shoulder. "If she is your sister, what does that make me?"

He smiled. "Beautiful."

They both leaned in and their lips met. Neither tried to hold the other longer as they pulled back.

Tristan's voice was a whisper as he removed the necklace from under his shirt and placed it around Kyrianna's neck. "You two take care of each other."

"We will," they said together.

Kyrianna gathered her gear, leaving the dress on the rock, and headed out of the garden. She glanced back to see him pick up the dress and hold it. He was holding a life for her to return to, if she was willing to accept it.

~ * ~

Hendandra had watched the two of them in the garden for only a few seconds, waving at them when they turned to look back toward the house. She knew Kyrianna might be upset with her, but she had to try and help her friend sort out her feelings after all Kyrianna had done for her and Feric. She left Tristan's room and went downstairs.

"My rug!" she screamed as she opened the doors to the dining hall.

Andrinor and the dwarf were asleep and snoring loudly, but Falden and Jerietlan were acting as if they were having nightmares. The mage lay near what appeared to be his attempt at keeping up with the two warriors. She saw his hawk entertaining himself with something behind one of the couches and went to investigate.

"Listen, you overgrown feather duster, I have a friend with really sharp teeth," she heard Jhoro say.

She shooed the hawk away. "Leave him be. You eat him and I guarantee something will do the same to you."

She looked down at the mongoose. "Stop playing. You have been all over this house. I need a bucket and cleaning supplies."

He sprang up to the couch then back down to the floor. "This way."

He took her to a storage area under the stairs where it appeared the household cleaning supplies were kept. She found what she needed and returned to the mess in the dining hall and set to work trying to clean the rug. The smell was so sickening she thought she would be adding to the mess herself.

"I am forbidding any of that dwarven rug stripper from ever being served in this house again," she said after several minutes of working on the rug. It didn't seem to be helping—only getting worse.

She stopped when she felt a hand on her shoulder. She looked up to see Tristan holding Kyrianna's dress. He placed it on a chair and motioned for her to follow him. He went out to the stairs and sat on the lowest riser.

"Thank you, Hendandra," he said.

"Are things good between you and Kyri?" She crossed her fingers.

"That is yet to be seen. She will be talking to Cewyr tonight."

"I hadn't thought about that." She silently cursed herself for making things worse for her friend.

"Don't concern yourself with this." He gestured to the dining hall. "I can have servants clean or even replace the rug." He paused and grinned at her. "Is there not someone you should see this evening?"

"Did Kyri…?"

"No, Melissa let it slip. Where is your husband?"

"He has already left."

Tristan nodded. "If you cannot spend the time with your husband, at least don't spend it with that smelly mess. Go to bed and dream some good dreams."

She smiled and gave him a peck on the cheek, before walking up the stairs.

"Hendandra," he called. "I can hire servants but is there someone you can trust with the management of the house?"

"Jhoro," she called as she turned back around.

The mongoose darted up the handrail and looked from her to Tristan and back.

"Can you handle managing the house and a few servants?" Hendandra asked.

"Does that include those four?" He nodded toward the dining hall.

"No."

"Good. As long as the overgrown pigeon leaves me alone, it should be no problem."

"There you go." She left Tristan and Jhoro to work out the details and returned to her room for the evening.

~ * ~

Kyrianna leaned back against the tree dreading the conversation to come. After paying her respects at the shrine dedicated to Dwycia, she had found a secluded spot in the Great Grove to call Cewyr. Shadow Seeker placed his head in her lap and she stoked his ears as she removed the figurine from her pocket and called the unicorn.

Cewyr appeared and lowered herself to the ground and

brushed Kyrianna's cheek with her muzzle.

"I-I-I'm…" Kyrianna's voice broke as she placed a hand on Cewyr's neck.

"I'm sorry."

The unicorn placed her cheek against hers. :*Why should you be sorry?*

Kyrianna took a deep breath and closed her eyes, enjoying the soft hair and warmth of Cewyr's cheek. "I gave you a promise," she finally said. "I would not do anything to break it. I did not want this." She wrapped her arm around the unicorn's neck. "It is the Reishalli and I cannot reject it."

:*That explains much, including her words.* She didn't fight Kyrianna's hold and only rested her head on her shoulder.

"Whose words?" Kyrianna sniffed back tears.

:*Frayrith said to me, 'Stay with her, Cewyr. I give the one who is to travel this difficult road a most precious gift. You may stay with her and the one she finds, even though all others must remain untouched. They have my special blessing in this.'*

Kyrianna pulled away and looked into the bright amethyst eyes.

Cewyr's voice in her head was like the notes of the song she and Tristan had played together. :*The gift obviously is love.*

She threw both arms around the mare's neck and hugged her tightly. She knew now her tears were of joy. She had been given a wonderful gift that was free of the despair of being forced to make a choice.

:*Kyri*, Melissa's voice whispered. :*What is the Reishalli? I have never heard that term.*

Kyrianna smiled. :*The Reishalli is simply the weaving together of two souls into one.*

:*It sounds like it is something very special.*

:*It is. The elves of my world almost never marry, unless they experience the Reishalli. It is one of the reasons their numbers are dwindling in some areas. Because of the nature of the Reishalli, I would not have expected this to happen. How can we be two halves of one soul when we are not from the same world? It makes no sense.*

:*It may not make any sense, but I think it's wonderful,* Melissa's voice was light and bubbly in her mind.

"So do I." Her whisper turned into a simple prayer. "Thank you, Frayrith."

She looked up at the sky. "We need to get some rest. Dawn

will be here soon and I want to get back to the house as quickly as we can in the morning. Maybe I can make it through one day without upsetting Myrith," Kyrianna said, patting the wolf and unicorn.

:Don't kid yourself; you're starting to enjoy upsetting Myrith, Melissa said.

Kyrianna laughed and she heard Melissa's echoing giggle in her mind.

As she lay against Cewyr, Kyrianna let her mind drift to the kiss she and Tristan had shared before she left and her soul sang. "If this is to be my last night above the darkness," she said, "at least it has shown brightly."

She let herself drift off to sleep with Melissa humming the tune they had played with Tristan.

About the Author

A native Texan, Carol found her way to her current home in Colorado by way of a five-year detour in The Nederlands - courtesy of her husband Tim and the US Air Force.

An avid reader at a young age, her strong desire to write came from her love of (her husband calls it her obsession with) Star Trek. It was this early love of Star Trek that led her to the Science Fiction and Fantasy genres.

In addition to her writing she has worked as a receptionist/office manager for two veterinary clinics, a deputy sheriff in El Paso County Colorado and for the Professional Bull Riders.

She has been published in various anthologies and magazines including "Creature Fantastic", PanGaia Magazine, "Stories of Strength", Baen's Universe, Tales of the Talisman and Kepler's Dozen. Her books include: *Call of Chaos*, *Chaos Embraced*, *The Road into Chaos*, and *Chaos Challenged*.

Carol has also edited several anthologies for Sky Warrior Books including: "Zombiefied", "These Vampires Don't Sparkle", and "The Dragon's Hoard".

In addition to her own writing, she is the editor and publisher of the online e-zines: The Lorelei Signal and Sorcerous Signals as well as running her own micro-press - WolfSinger Publications.

Answer the Call

Call of Chaos - Book One: The Chaos Reigns Saga

The exiled daughter of a minor noble, Kyrianna Dalynne, finds herself trapped in a temple dedicated to Thynitic, The Lady of Chaos. She and her companions, are charged with finding an ancient artifact before the ones guarding the portals out will allow them to leave. As their search continues, Kyrianna begins to question if there was a specific reason she and the others were brought to this place.

After the guardians claim the artifact has been secured, they offer to open the portals to allow the group to return to their homes. Instead of the familiar forest of Kilenter, Kyrianna finds herself in another world. Her companions from the temple arrive several days after her.

When one of the members is accused of murder, they are tasked with assisting Tristan Duvall, who must face the demons and ghosts of his family's past in order to claim his birthright as a nobleman of the city of Raspa. Kyrianna finds herself attracted to the young man and facing the difficult decision of accepting his invitation to remain with him or return to her own home.

Now Available from WolfSinger Publications

Chaos Embraced – Book Two: The Chaos Reigns Saga

Nowhere in all the worlds or planes is there no pain, torment or chaos. All we can do is accept those strikes which cannot be avoided and give back chaos and pain to those who offend. Kindness should be the only companion to pain and will increase the intensity of suffering and the chaos surrounding us. Do not ignore the sudden whim of compassion; let it always come, but only seldom as to give those who suffer a sense of hope. Hope is consort to chaos and torment is their offspring. Unending torment destroys pain and this in turn destroys the chaos that nurtures us. Act alluring to trap those who would never seek the Lady on their own. Confuse those that think they know the ways of the world around them. Bring pain and torment not only to those who enjoy it, or to those who deserve it, but also to the innocent and those who do not antici- pate it. The lash, fire and cold are the three physical pains that never fail the devout. Love, jealousy and hatred are the three pains that should follow in the footsteps of her devout. Spread Thynitic's theology whenever pain is meted out and chaos swirls. Wherever pain is, there is Thynitic. Wherever chaos is, there is Thynitic. Embrace the pain and chaos. Embrace Thynitic.

Trapped in a place where they are constantly faced with new opponents and challenges, Kyrianna and her friends, will also have to face the Goddess Thynitic and her Chosen Torliana.

Kyrianna finds Thynitic whispering in her mind, calling her deeper into the chaos. In order to save her friends from the evil goddess, will she finally Embrace the Chaos and accept her place as a Daughter of Chaos or will she succeed innrenouncing Thynitic forever? And if she does, what will the cost be?

Now Available from WolfSinger Publications

Chaos Challenged – Book Four: The Chaos Reigns Saga

FOR A FRIEND

Those were Hendandra's words when the group was asked to go to the Abyss to rescue Brular from Thynitic.

Now they find themselves facing the horrors of that cursed place, along with nightmares from their own past as they struggle to reach the Lady of Chaos' citadel.

The closer they get to their goal the more dangerous their jour- ney becomes and another deity enters the game—one who says she opposes Thynitic, but whose actions indicate she also wants to stop Kyrianna and her friends from facing the Lady of Chaos.

Even as she tries to fight her destiny as a Daughter of Chaos, Kyrianna finds herself being drawn deeper into Thynitic's plans.

Will she finally be able to separate herself from her destiny when she faces Thynitic or will the Lady of Chaos finally be able to claim her soul?

Coming Soon from WolfSinger Publications

www.ingramcontent.com/pod-product-compliance
Lightning Source LLC
Chambersburg PA
CBHW061544170626
46811CB00001B/84